THE
WELTALL
FILE

THE WELTALL FILE

A GORDIAN DIVISION NOVEL

DAVID WEBER & JACOB HOLO

THE WELTALL FILE

A Baen Books Original

Baen Publishing Enterprises
P.O. Box 1403
Riverdale, NY 10471
www.baen.com

ISBN: 978-1-9821-9265-5

Cover art by Kurt Miller

First printing, June 2023

Distributed by Simon & Schuster
1230 Avenue of the Americas
New York, NY 10020

Library of Congress Cataloging-in-Publication Data

Names: Weber, David, 1952– author. | Holo, Jacob, author.
Title: The Weltall file : a Gordian Division novel / David Weber & Jacob Holo.
Identifiers: LCCN 2023002644 (print) | LCCN 2023002645 (ebook) | ISBN 9781982192655 (hardcover) | ISBN 9781625799166 (ebook)
Subjects: LCGFT: Science fiction. | Novels.
Classification: LCC PS3573.E217 W45 2023 (print) | LCC PS3573.E217 (ebook) | DDC 813/.54—dc23/eng/20230203
LC record available at https://lccn.loc.gov/2023002644
LC ebook record available at https://lccn.loc.gov/2023002645

Printed in the United States of America

10 9 8 7 6 5 4 3 2 1

This one is for Jim Baen (1943–2006), the friend, editor, and mentor who founded Baen Books forty years ago this year. He was one of the best editors, publishers, and innovators our field has ever known, and all of those who knew him—including one of the authors of this novel—are the richer for the acquaintance and the sadder for the loss we suffered far too soon. No one in the publishing field was more farsighted than he when it came to electronic publishing and social media, as his early embrace of eARCs, not to mention Baen's Bar and the Baen Free Library, which endure to this day, attest. As Spider Robinson once said of Jim, he was one of the very few publishers of science fiction who truly wanted to live in the 21st century. Even more importantly, though, no one in the publishing field has ever been better than Jim was at identifying new talent, encouraging it, helping it to improve, and making it grow.

That process, which continues at Baen Books to this day, is perhaps his most enduring legacy. It was our great loss that he got to see so little of the century to which he so eagerly looked forward, but he left big footprints. Jacob and I like to think he would've approved of this one.

Wind to your wings, Jim.

—David Weber
January 2023

ENTER THE WELTALL TOURNAMENT AND BECOME A PART OF HISTORY!

DID YOU KNOW?

▶ The Weltall Tournament is a part of Chief Executor Christopher First's drive toward more open relations between the Admin and SysGov through his ambitious Million Handshake Initiative. There may be a great deal of transdimensional distance between us and SysGov, but that's no excuse not to engage in some good-natured competition! Think you have what it takes to go toe-to-toe with SysGov's finest players? Then sign up for the regional qualifiers today!

DID YOU KNOW?

▶ *Weltall* is truly the first of its kind. As a carefully scrutinized and approved piece of foreign software, it will soon become the first game created by a SysGov company but made available throughout the Admin! The game was developed by ActionStream and will be brought to market by the combined efforts of the Department of Software and the Department of Temporal Investigation.

DID YOU KNOW?

▶ There will be three stages of qualifiers: regional, planetary, and universal. While players will be responsible for their own travel plans and accommodations at the regional and planetary levels, the Admin will handle all expenses for qualifying players, who will be flown out to Byrgius University on Luna! Since *Weltall* has not yet been released, regional and planetary qualifiers will utilize the extremely popular *Legions of Patriots*, while the universal qualifier will feature the first competitive use of *Weltall* in the Admin! And if that isn't enough, all players who make it to the universal qualifier will receive free copies of *Weltall* one week prior to the competition!

DID YOU KNOW?

> Despite the fact that many SysGov citizens are of a purely artificial nature, government officials on both sides have agreed that only organic citizens—even those who have transitioned into synthetic bodies—will be eligible for the competition. That way, there's no need to fear losing to some SysGov AI with nanosecond reflexes! We've ensured a level playing field for what will undoubtedly be a spirited competition!

DID YOU KNOW?

> While our own universal qualifier will be held on Luna, as part of Chief Executor Christopher First's continuing outreach to the Lunar people, the finals will be held on Luna in *SysGov*! Not only will finalists enjoy the rare opportunity to travel to a whole other universe in one of the DTI's chronoports, but they'll also be one of the first citizens of the Admin to see the completely terraformed wonder of the SysGov moon!

SO WHAT ARE YOU WAITING FOR?
CLICK THE LINK BELOW TO APPLY NOW!
WEALTH, FAME, AND GLORY AWAIT YOU!

This message has been approved by:
System Cooperative Administration
Department of Public Relations

PROLOGUE

"YOU DUMPED ME FOR A FUCKING TIN MAN?!" GRAFTON LACAN spat from just outside the open hotel suite door.

Elly Sako crossed her arms underneath her breasts, shook her head at him like a disapproving parent, then sighed wearily and even gave the idiot a roll of her eyes for good measure. She stood at the threshold, weight centered over her back leg, dressed in a pair of sweatpants and a baggy T-shirt while water dripped from her short, black hair. She tried to avoid public appearances while looking this frumpy, but the hotel hallway was private enough, and Lacan had arrived—*uninvited*—at her door moments after she'd finished her shower, so it wasn't like she had much of a choice.

Except for ignoring him. Which, in hindsight, might have been the better option.

A glistening lock fell over her eyes, and she combed it back with her fingers.

Lacan stared at her with his reddened, teary, uncomposed, and utterly *unattractive* eyes. Moist trails rain down his cheeks, and his lower lip quivered. He seemed like a different person now, no longer the cocky young man with the gorgeous blonde braid, the mischievous baby blues, and those wonderfully adventurous hands of his. Those physical traits remained, of course, but they no longer added up to the same total anymore. Somewhere along the way, the vibrant young man she'd bedded during the Admin's universal qualifier had been replaced with this sniveling, emotional wreck standing before her, a wreck that *insisted* on having a pointless heart-to-heart when all she wanted to do was go to take a nap!

Uhh!

Lacan sniffled. Not in a subtle way either, but loud enough for her to hear suction moving viscous snot further back up his nasal cavity.

"Seriously?" Sako raised an eyebrow at him. "Of all the things you could say to me, *that's* what you picked?"

"He's not even flesh and blood!" Lacan whined.

"Oh, please," she scolded, her patience growing thin. "His mommy carried him in her womb, same as our moms did. He just transitioned into a synthoid, is all, and not that long ago either. Besides, I didn't 'dump' you. That's what I've been trying to drill through your thick skull! There was never anything to dump. It was a harmless diversion. Nothing more."

"A *diversion*?" He sucked in some more snot. "Is that all I mean to you?"

"Well, yeah." She shrugged her shoulders. "That's what I've been trying to tell you."

"But I love you!"

She sighed, put a delicate hand to her forehead, and rubbed her brow.

Fuck. Me.

He'd used the L-word. Why in Yanluo's burning hells did he have to toss *that* loaded word into the conversation?

You really should have seen this coming, she thought to herself.

She'd known Lacan wouldn't take this news well, and to a certain degree, the blame for that fell on her. After all, he'd used the L-word once or twice or . . . five times before? She wasn't sure, but she also had failed to make her own feelings clear at the time. In her defense, she'd been too busy saying things like *"Yes! Harder! Like that!"* to really concentrate on the long-term consequence of her nonexistent reply.

And so here we are. Fuck.

She'd known he'd take the news poorly—it was one of the reasons why she wanted to be done with him—but she never suspected he'd handle it *this* poorly, good grief! Honestly, she would have preferred not to say anything, instead letting him shuffle around blindly until he stumbled into the truth on his own. But he could be so *dense*, and then he'd wanted to try out sex in zero gravity on the way over, and so she'd made the nature of their relationship—or, more specifically, their *lack* of a relationship—crystal clear to him.

But now we're having this blasted heart-to-heart, or whatever he wants to call it.

"Do you actually love him?" he blubbered.

"Oh, grow up." Sako sighed heavily, frustration welling up within her. "How much clearer do you want me to make this?" She cupped her mouth and leaned toward him. "It's none of your business!"

"It is my business! I love you!"

"Well, I don't love you!" She shrugged her arms. "Sorry, but not sorry. What the hell do you want me to do about it?"

"Is this all I mean to you?"

"Oh, please!" she scoffed. "You're acting like we were married or something. You were a quick fling, Lacan, nothing more! It was fun while it lasted, but you know what? It's over now! Move on, already! I certainly have!"

"He's behind this, isn't he!" He pointed an unsteady finger at her. "He's trying to drive a wedge between us!"

"No, he's not!" she snapped, her frustration boiling over into anger.

"And how would you know that?"

"Because I'd choose him over you any day of the week, you fucking idiot!" she snapped, and immediately regretted her words. She'd wanted to end this stupid and pointless shouting match, but instead the sniveling wreck he'd become morphed before her eyes into a font of indignant rage. His back straightened, eyes ablaze with an inner fire, and he took a step toward her and poked her collar bone with a finger.

"Then why don't you do him already!" he bellowed in her face.

"No fucking need!" She flashed a condescending smirk.

"And why's that?" he shouted.

"Because I already did!" She glared at him with fierce, unflinching eyes.

"Fuck you!"

"Been there, done that," she countered. "And you know what? He's a better lover than you'll ever be!"

"Then you'd better enjoy it while it lasts! Because next time

I see him, I'm going to rip off his metal dick! And *then*, I'm going to find you and use it to beat the living shit out of y—"

"Excuse me."

The newcomer's voice was not particularly loud or forceful. Quite the opposite, in fact. It was almost a whisper, though it had the immediate effect of silencing both Lacan and Sako. Not because of his soft voice or simple words, but because of the body those words originated from.

Neither of them had noticed Agent Miguel Pérez's quiet arrival. The hotel hallway bent in a gentle curve, and Pérez stood just far enough around it that Lacan had to back up and turn to face him while Sako had to peek her head out past the threshold. Pérez's synthoid body was tall and broad shouldered with gray skin and yellow eyes, harkening from a time when closed-minded fools like Lacan were far more common throughout the Admin and the public had demanded these artificial supersoldiers be distinct from flesh-and-blood humans. He wore the blue uniform of an Admin Peacekeeper, peaked cap fitted neatly on his head, and a heavy sidearm at his hip.

"Is something wrong?" Pérez asked, as if he were unaware of their hormone-fueled shouting match. "If so, may I be of assistance?"

Sako hadn't heard him approach. Granted, she'd been preoccupied, but Pérez moved *quietly* for such a big man, synthetic or not.

"Umm. I, uhh..." Lacan sputtered, backing off, the fury gone from his eyes.

"Yes," Sako answered.

Pérez nodded to her. "What seems to be the problem, Miss Sako?"

"Lacan and I were engaged in what you might call a..." She smiled suddenly. "A scholarly debate."

"A debate, is it?"

"Yes. Perhaps you could help us sort it all out."

"Well, I'll certainly try. What's the subject?"

She flashed a toothy grin. "Synthoid genitalia."

"I see," he replied in a tone more appropriate to discussing the weather than his own synthetic anatomy. "I suppose, of the three of us, I can rightfully claim to be the expert on that front."

"Wonderful!" She clapped her hands together. "You see, Lacan seems to believe male synthoids in SysGov have metal dicks."

"Ah. Well, that's a bit different, then. I can't claim any direct experience with *SysGov* synthoids, though I can certainly share what I've heard."

"Oh, do tell," she said brightly. "I'd *love* to hear your take on this."

Lacan glared at her use of the word "love."

"Perhaps we could have that discussion some other time," Pérez said. "Agent Arlot?"

"Sir!" A second gray-skinned synthoid stepped forward. She hadn't heard *this one* either. She stuck her head out further and glanced down the hallway, wondering if Pérez had a whole squad of synthoids waiting nearby, but the rest of the hallway was empty as far back as she could see.

"I believe Mister Lacan would like an escort back to his suite." Pérez faced the young man. "Isn't that right, sir?"

"I . . ." Lacan's face twisted in a snarl, as if he were about to lash out at her again, but instead he let out a sharp exhale and looked away. "Fine. I'm done here."

"Very good, sir," Pérez said. "Arlot?"

"This way, sir."

Arlot stepped up behind Lacan and gestured down the hall with an open palm.

Lacan glanced over to Sako one last time, grief and rage swirling in his eyes like a tempest. His lips cracked open, as if he wanted to get in one last word, but then he shook his head and stomped off with Arlot close behind.

Sako waited for him to disappear beyond the hallway's curve, and then she let out a long, tired sigh.

"Thanks, Pérez."

"My pleasure. Now, before I head out—"

"Oh no!" Her eyes twinkled at him. "You're not getting off that easily!"

"Excuse me?"

"You still owe me an answer." She leaned her shoulder against the doorjamb. "What exactly *have* you heard about SysGov synthoids?"

"Seriously?"

"Come on. This is important cultural information." She spread her arms. "Lay the truth on me, baby!"

"It's more along the lines of secondhand testimony than truth."

"Yeah, yeah." She made a shooing gesture. "Just get to the good stuff."

"Well," he said with a brief, resigned exhale. "If you must know, it's my understanding that the cosmetics on SysGov synthoids, genitals included, are comparable to our own newer models. I doubt most people could tell the difference between a synthoid and an organic body, even under"—he smiled ever so slightly—"close, personal inspection."

"Yeah, that sounds about right." She nodded, but then tilted her head. "Wait a second. You said 'most.'"

"Just something I've heard while working with the people over here," Pérez continued.

"Anything juicy?" she pressed.

"I suppose a little. Truth be told, I haven't witnessed one myself, but I hear the people from this universe's Oort cloud are quite...adventurous in the kinds of bodies they inhabit."

"Adventurous how?"

"I'm afraid that's the limit of my knowledge. You'll have to ask someone else if you're still curious."

"I just might do that." She stepped away from the door and was about to palm it shut when Pérez placed his hand in the way.

"Actually, that's not what I was about to say." His eyes flicked past her. "I need to check your room."

"What? *Again?*"

"Yes."

"What the hell for? One of your minions checked it like, I don't know, half an hour ago."

"True, but the perimeter has been compromised."

"Come again?"

"You opened the door."

"Oh, good grief!" She rubbed her forehead.

"I'm sorry, but these are the rules. You opened the door, so now I need to sweep your room again."

"But I was standing at the door the whole time!"

"There are plenty of miniaturized drones that could have escaped your notice, just to name one possibility."

"Do you really think our hosts would be that nefarious?"

"Doesn't matter what I think. These are the rules. I just follow them."

"Can't this wait?" She yawned into her fist.

"Isn't it a little early in the day to be yawning?"

"Yeah, well, I was up partying all night before the flight over to Luna." She paused, and then grimaced. "I mean the flight over to *this* Luna. Which was a flight from *our* Luna." She crossed her arms. "You know what I mean?"

"Yes, I know exactly what you mean."

She nodded at the remark. The Admin's Department of Temporal Investigation was handling all their transportation and security needs, which meant Pérez and his minions were all veterans of the DTI's counterterrorism ops. Never mind that the "temporal" part of their name was something of a misnomer nowadays, since the DTI had expanded its role to regulate both temporal and *transdimensional* travel to and from the Admin's True Present, as well as taken the lead on foreign relations with SysGov.

"Okay, fine." She stepped back and waved him in. "Just hurry up and secure my perimeter again, or whatever you want to call it."

"Thank you. This won't take long."

Pérez took a device off his belt shaped like a stubby baton then walked past her and closed the door. He began a slow circuit of the room, holding the baton in front of him, occasionally raising or lowering it. It took longer than she'd have liked because this wasn't the only room in her suite, which sprawled over *three* floors and included four bedrooms, its own *gravity lift* to get between floors, a three-story waterfall along the back, and a private pool shaped like a giant leaf on top! She wasn't sure what their hosts thought she needed so much space and luxury for, but she wasn't about to complain.

She rested her back against the wall and yawned again, her thoughts wandering as she waited for Pérez to finish his sweep.

Am I doing the right thing? she asked herself, and not for the first time, though her thoughts always led her back to the same answer, the same firm resolve to see where it all would lead. She didn't know what the future held, but Opportunity or Fate or Good Fortune or Whatever-You-Wanted-To-Call-It had knocked at her door, and she'd answered.

The risks, though. And the reactions people would have . . .

What would my parents say? she wondered. *Hell, what would everyone in both universes think of what I'm about to do?*

She wasn't on an Admin planet or moon, where even the strange possessed a certain comfortable familiarity. She was in a different *universe*, with laws and culture all its own! The scope and wonder and alienness of this place boggled her mind. This Luna had open air *beaches*, for crying out loud!

Beaches!

On Earth's moon!

And that was hardly the most amazing spectacle over here. For one, her first experience with something as fantastical as artificial gravity had been when the grav tube had whisked her away to her *hotel suite!* What other marvels lurked around the corners of this society? And, more importantly, what treacherous pitfalls lay ahead, ready to snare her?

Because, after all, she was in a realm of powers and authority she had no true concept of.

And yet she was about to—

"All done," Pérez said, walking over. "Thank you for your patience."

She looked up at him wordlessly, and the two stood in silence for long seconds.

"Miss Sako?" he asked at last.

"Sorry." She blinked and shook her head. "Lost in my own head."

"Perhaps a nap might help refresh you. You don't want to be drowsy for the finals tomorrow."

"Well, I was about to take a nap, but Lacan showed up and then *you* had to secure the perimeter, and well..."

"Yes, yes. I'll be going now." Pérez opened the door, stepped through, then gave her a curt nod. "Have a pleasant day."

"You, too."

The door closed, and her exaggerated fatigue melted away. She walked purposefully over to the kitchen.

That was another thing about this place. The suite had a *kitchen*, of all things, but the hotel had also installed a high-end food printer, so why would anyone bother *manually* preparing their meals?

She picked her infosystem wearable off the counter and slipped the band around her wrist. Secure protocols in the wearable interfaced with her Personal Implant Network and translated the surrounding SysGov infostructure for her virtual senses. Artwork appeared over blank white walls, showing picturesque views from across the terraformed Luna, and a menu materialized beside the food printer.

She loaded the prepared order on her wearable, confirmed it, then leaned against the island counter in the middle of the kitchen. The timer ticked down, and she connected to the surrounding infostructure while she waited, sending a query for any news on the Weltall Tournament.

A segment from a news stream called the *Nectaris Daily* pulsed at the top of her search list, and she selected it and let the virtual presentation unfold around her. She smiled thinly as she watched an abstraction of herself taking her first steps in SysGov.

The DTI chronoport filled her virtual vision like a giant, looming manta ray with weapon pods slung under its delta wing and a ramp extending down from its armored belly. The virtual image of herself led the party down the ramp, waving and smiling at the press and tournament officials assembled in the hangar. The other five players formed a loose gaggle behind her with Pérez and another synthoid pulling up the rear.

Wong Fei and the other two SysGov finalists were returning from a two-week sight-seeing tour around Earth in the Admin, which she and the Admin players had accompanied them on.

He was a tall, handsome man with a dignified but not arrogant air about him and a pleasant, barely-there smile. His cool, dark eyes swept his surroundings studiously. He kept his dark hair short, which made him stand out from Admin men with their long braids or ponytails or hair spilling over their shoulders, but she kind of liked it. That and all the other ways he was different.

It was ... refreshing.

Especially after Lacan's blithering lack of self-control.

The thought drew her eyes to Lacan near the back of the players. Everyone else was waving and smiling, even the normally dour Shingo Masuda from the Admin's Earth. But not Lacan. Instead, he glared at his perceived rival's back. If his eyes had been lasers, they would have burned a hole through the back of Wong Fei's head.

"Love," she scoffed. "Ha!"

Her time together with Wong Fei had been short—barely a month since she first saw him at the universal qualifier—but it had also been *dense*, and once again a nervous flutter within her chest made her question if she was doing the right thing.

She pushed her doubts down, locking them away in her heart.

The food printer beeped, and she closed the news abstraction and pushed off the counter to walk over. Mechanisms built into the wall shifted her order up to the delivery port, the circular panel irised open, and a tray extended out—

But instead of food, the tray held a severed head atop a white plate. The head was her own, down to the very last detail, even though it couldn't be. Her own eyes were rolled back into their sockets, and her own tongue lolled out of a loose, lifeless jaw. Words written in blood formed an arch before the severed head, and it took her wearable a moment to translate the SysGov version of English into her own.

The gory message read: LEAVE OR DIE.

TEN DAYS EARLIER

CHAPTER ONE

DETECTIVE ISAAC CHO OF THE CONSOLIDATED SYSTEM POLICE SAT at his desk on Kronos Station, orbiting Saturn. He was a slender man with short, black hair and sharp eyes. Not tiny or scrawny, but certainly of a slighter build than most. He wore the dark blue of SysPol with the golden eye and magnifying glass of Themis Division on his shoulder, which distinguished him from his deputy, who sat at the desk opposite his.

Special Agent Susan Cantrell of the Department of Temporal Investigation possessed a lithe, predatory gracefulness, even seated with an elbow on her desk and her cheek propped up on her fist. She wore her shock of red hair in a neat pixie cut, and the lighter blue of her Peacekeeper uniform hugged the artificial curves of her synthoid body. Her peaked cap rested on her desk, and a silver shield with the letters DTI hung from her left breast.

Over a hundred desks formed a grid in the spacious room, but the majority were unoccupied. As was often the case, almost all of the department's detectives and specialists were out in the field.

Arrays of virtual screens filled the space between Isaac and Susan, and they both worked to organize and attach the various forensic files and testimonies to their respective reports. Both of their desks showed little use. Besides the virtual screens, the surfaces were almost totally devoid of personal effects.

A small, sealed terrarium sat on Isaac's desk, the flower inside growing so fast it was visible to the naked eye. It bloomed into a brilliant sunburst of oranges and reds this time, then began to wilt almost instantly. The terrarium sat precariously close to one of the corners of the desk furthest from Susan, and she seemed to subconsciously lean away from the self-replicating piece of art.

The ever-cycling flower had been a gift from a kidnapping victim they'd rescued, and the memento on Susan's desk had been collected from the same case.

It was a rock.

Just...a rock. And not a very interesting one at that.

It was, as Susan was prone to say about such things, "a long story."

In some ways, the two partners couldn't have been more different. Isaac had spent the last ten of his thirty years training to become a SysPol detective whereas Susan had joined the Peacekeepers in her early twenties and quickly transitioned from her frail flesh-and-blood to a military-grade body.

Isaac's approach to problem-solving was to sift through the evidence.

Carefully. Thoroughly. Picking the problem relentlessly apart one thread at a time.

Susan preferred more...explosive means of resolving issues.

Their backgrounds diverged in many other ways, even down to the histories of their respective universes, for the Admin timeline had split off from SysGov's all the way back in 1940 with the assassination of Adolf Hitler, leading to two wholly different 2980s.

But despite their differences, and despite whatever misgivings both had held at the start of the new SysPol–DTI officer exchange program, they'd worked well together for the last three months and were even now in the process of wrapping up another successful case.

"Susan?" Isaac asked.

"Yeah?" she replied without looking up.

"What's another good word for 'mulched'?"

She raised her gaze to meet his. "Why do you ask?"

"Because I think I'm overusing it in my report."

"It *is* an accurate description of what happened to his victims."

"I know, but I feel like the repetition is making my report sound less professional."

"How about... 'recycled' or 'reclaimed'?"

"Too sterile. That's for processing trash."

"Umm. What about 'blended'?"

"Too culinary. Sounds like he was making people-smoothies."

"'Pureed,' perhaps?"

"That's even worse."

"I don't know then."

"Hmm." Isaac glared at his unfinished report.

"Honestly, I think you're asking the wrong person." Susan passed a finger through her virtual screen. "I'm still using a translation program for all this. Why don't you use a thesaurus? That's what I do when I get stuck trying to figure out the correct word."

"Hmm," he murmured noncommittally.

The two resumed working on their reports in silence for several minutes before Susan looked up suddenly.

"You know something, Isaac?"

"Hmm?"

"This is kind of a weird change of pace."

"What do you mean?"

"The two of us in the office for more than a few hours straight."

"Well, Raviv wants us to clear out our documentation backlog, so here we are."

"I know that. I just, I don't know, would prefer to be out in the field. That's all."

Isaac raised an eyebrow. "Setting things on fire again?"

"Oh, come on!" she said, her eyes laughing. "A girl uses a flamethrower *one time*, and suddenly that's all people remember."

"At least it made it easier to follow your trail."

"You think Raviv will have another case for us soon?"

"Absolutely." He glowered down at his screens. "Once we've written all of our overdue reports."

"Yeah, I get it," she said with a sigh then hunkered down again.

The two continued their work. Isaac attached the last file in his case folder to the report, but then he frowned, noting a missing set of references.

"Cephalie?" he asked his integrated companion.

"You rang?"

The image of a miniature woman appeared on Isaac's desk. Today, Encephalon wore a dark green long coat with matching gloves and a white hat with a green flower stuck in it. A pair of circular wireframe glasses with opaque lenses finished the ensemble. She brought a wooden cane around, clicked the metal tip against his desktop, and leaned forward over it.

"Do you have the forensics file on victim four?" Isaac asked. "I seem to be missing that one."

"The one the state police processed for us?" A miniature blackboard materialized next to her, and text appeared. She stood up and knocked her cane against the blackboard. "Sure do. Got it right here."

"Thanks." He pulled the file into the case folder and then attached it to the report.

"Anytime."

"What would I do without you?"

"You looking for an honest answer?"

"I—" Isaac paused and clapped his mouth shut, then glanced down at the small woman grinning up at him. "Perhaps not this time."

"Suit yourself." She gave him a quick wave and vanished.

"Doesn't make any sense to me," Susan muttered.

"What doesn't?"

"The murderer." She put both elbows on her desk and leaned toward him. "Did the idiot really think feeding those people down the reclamation chute wouldn't leave evidence?"

"'Never underestimate the stupidity of the criminal mind.'"

"Is that a Raviv quote?" she asked, referring to the period when Isaac had mentored under the current chief inspector, back when Raviv was a senior detective.

"It is," Chief Inspector Omar Raviv said loudly, his voice echoing in the office as he walked over.

"Hey, boss." Isaac twisted around in his chair.

"Sir," Susan greeted curtly.

"You two busy?" Raviv asked.

"Just working on another report," Isaac said.

"Which one?"

"The Titan murders down in the Fridge."

"You mean that guy who mulched his coworkers?"

"That would be the one."

"See?" Susan reached over and nudged Isaac in the shoulder. "'Mulched' *is* the right word. You were worrying over nothing."

"Did I miss something?" Raviv asked.

"Not really," Isaac assured him. "What can we do for you?"

"What else? More work."

"Finally!" Susan said with a smile.

"Don't get too excited," Raviv cautioned. "This one's a little different."

"As long as it gets us away from our desks," Susan said.

"Well, it'll definitely do that. A request came in from an 'Under-Director Jonas Shigeki.' That name sound familiar to you?"

"Sure does," Susan said. "He's the DTI Director of Foreign Affairs. He selected me for the exchange program."

"Oh good. I like him already." Raviv raised his palm, and a virtual document appeared in their shared virtual vision.

Isaac glanced over at Susan and gave her a quick thumbs-up while Raviv was engrossed in the document. She winked back at him.

"Anyway, either of you two hear about the ongoing Weltall Tournament?"

"Vaguely," Isaac said.

Susan shook her head.

"I caught one of the qualifier streams," Raviv continued. "The Lagrange Republic one. Wong Fei was in it, obliterating the competition as usual. Interesting game mechanics, too. I might try it out when it finally gets published. Anyway, the director asked if the two of you can attend the finals on Luna. A bit last minute, but you can make it if you leave within the next day or so."

"What for?" Isaac asked dubiously, not liking the idea of being away from Saturn for the next three or more weeks. It would take them eight and a half days just to *reach* Earth's moon, given Earth's position relative to Saturn this time of year.

"Says here the tournament's a part of the Admin's ongoing series of cultural and economic exchanges. The 'Million Handshake Initiative.' Both SysGov and Admin players will be competing in the finals."

"And since the two of us are an example of cooperation between our governments..." Susan filled in.

"They'd like us to join them," Isaac finished glumly.

"Exactly," Raviv said. "See any problems with the request?"

"Will we have to give any speeches?" Isaac asked.

"It doesn't say anything here about speeches." Raviv skimmed over the document. "You'll have to attend the tournament as well as a few social dinners. Plus"—he smiled wryly—"you'll have the truly burdensome task of staying at the Crimson Flower."

"Oh?" Both of Isaac's eyebrows rose.

"Which," Raviv continued, "to fill you in, Susan, is a well-known resort. Probably *the* most famous on Luna."

"That works out perfectly, then," she said. "I've wanted to visit Luna since I got here, but I didn't think I'd get the opportunity."

"Wonderful!" Raviv minimized the file. "Then now's the perfect time for you to check that item off your list."

"Why Luna?" Isaac asked.

"Because it's so different from the one back home," Susan replied. "For one, it has an atmosphere, unlike the lifeless rock I went to college on. And two, it's not a haven for terrorist scum." She glanced up at Raviv. "Does Luna have any beaches?"

"You better believe it. Some gorgeous ones, too." Raviv smiled slyly. "I was actually thinking about taking the missus there for our next vacation. Elise loves low-gravity resorts."

"We have beaches here, too, you know," Isaac said to Susan, his tone perhaps a touch too defensive. As a native to Saturn, he took a great deal of pride in his home state. "There's at least one on Janus I know of."

"You mean *in* Janus," Susan corrected. "A beach in an enclosed megastructure floating through Saturn's atmosphere isn't the same as the open-air experience. Doesn't count."

"Well, *I* think it counts," Isaac replied, that defensive edge to his voice growing stronger.

"Where would you even put a beach in Janus, anyway?" Susan asked.

"It's situated near the top of the megastructure, about a kilometer below Ballast Heights. Nice little area called Tankville."

"Tankville?" Susan repeated dubiously. "Let me guess. It's built along the lip of Janus' main water reservoir?"

"One of them, yes."

"I'm sorry, but I still say that doesn't count."

Isaac frowned, not sure how to better explain the exceptionalism of Saturnite resorts to her.

"So, can I put the two of you down as attending?" Raviv asked.

"Sure," Isaac said with a shrug. "Why not? Though I'm not thrilled about being stuffed into one of our corvettes for over a week."

"Actually, the director has arranged civilian flights for you. You'll be taking a Polaris Traveler saucer back into the inner system."

"Even better," Susan said brightly.

"Seems like he's thought of everything," Isaac added.

"Also, Susan"—Raviv opened a second file—"your extension was approved. Looks like we'll have you for another three months. After you get back from Luna, of course."

"Yes!" She thumped the air victoriously.

"I don't think that was ever in doubt," Isaac commented.

"Still, it's good to know for certain I'm sticking around."

"You're not thinking about heading home anytime soon, are you?" Raviv asked.

"Nope!"

"Not getting homesick or anything?"

"Not even a little."

"She gets shot at less over here," Isaac explained.

"That's a big plus, certainly," Susan clarified, "but it's not the only reason."

"Are you sure about that?" Raviv said. "Because the superintendent brought you up during my quarterly review. Apparently, you suffered more injuries than any other detective last quarter."

"Sorry?" Susan shrugged, not looking repentant at all.

"And didn't that Fridge murderer shoot you in the face?"

"Yeah, but it's not like he did any real damage. Not with *that* peashooter!" She tapped her cheek. "Just knocked off some of my cosmetic layer. I was good as new in no time."

"Well, try to keep your head down more in the future."

"Yes, sir. I'll do my best."

"That's what I like to hear." Raviv made a few selections in his virtual mail and hit send. "All right, then. I've confirmed both of you for the event. Here are your itineraries."

Isaac eyed the new documents populating his inbox.

"Got 'em."

"Finish up whatever reports you're in the middle of then feel free to call it quits early. Your flight leaves tomorrow morning."

✧   ✧   ✧

Isaac was halfway through proofreading the latest section of his report when he felt a familiar presence approach him from behind. He let out a tired sigh but kept working.

The presence came closer until it loomed over him, casting a pale shadow over his desk.

He continued working, determined to ignore her for as long as possible.

"Ah-*hem*!"

Isaac finished the paragraph he was on then turned—slowly but deliberately—in his chair. He looked up at a slender woman slightly shorter than himself with hair and skin tone that closely matched his own, which wasn't surprising, since they were fraternal twins. The main difference was in her eyes, which, though they shared his dark coloration, were filled with zest and enthusiasm. In contrast, Isaac's eyes were focused and intense, always ready to tear through a problem piece by piece. His twin sister's eyes laughed at the world with every glance.

"Yes, Nina?" Isaac said, not unpleasantly, but still with a tone that declared *I have work to do. Can this wait until later?*

"Hey. How's my little brother doing?"

"Fine, but busy. Trying to finish up this Fridge murder report before I head home. Is there something I can help you with?"

"Heard you're shipping out."

"You heard right." He paused as a means to invite her to expound on her intrusion, but when she failed to fill the silence, he added, "Why do you ask?"

"Heard you're flying off to Luna."

"Correct again. It's almost like our schedules are posted in a central database any detective"—he gestured to her with an open palm—"or forensics specialist can access."

Susan snorted out a laugh but didn't look up from her work.

"Smartass," Nina said, but she smiled when she did. "It's the Weltall Tournament, isn't it? You two have been invited to attend?"

"We have. And?"

"Can I come along?"

"Uhh . . ." Isaac blinked in surprise. "I don't see how that's possible."

"*Please!*"

"It's not really my decision to make." He turned back to his desk. "Cephalie?"

The miniaturized avatar of his integrated companion appeared on the desk.

"Did we receive any spare tickets?" Isaac asked her.

"Nope. Just the two, plus I'm allowed to tag along since I'm your IC."

"Okay, thanks."

Cephalie vanished as Isaac turned back to his sister.

"Sorry." He shrugged an apology. "Can't help you, sis."

"But this is going to be the first time Admin and SysGov players compete together! It's a once-in-a-lifetime opportunity to see history in the making! Once it's gone, it's *gone!*"

"Nina, our society has time machines. The past is never truly out of reach."

"It might as well be, what with Gordian Division keeping a lid on time travel nowadays. When's the last time you saw them approve a temporal search warrant?"

"Can't seem to recall."

"Exactly! Besides, you know what I mean."

"Yes, I suppose I do."

"This would also be a perfect opportunity for me to meet some other people from the Admin." She clasped her hands together as if praying or begging. Or both. *"Please!"*

"I don't know what to say. We only have the two tickets."

"Then ask Raviv for another. Can't hurt to try."

"The tickets didn't come from Raviv," Isaac pointed out.

"Then who gave them to you?"

"DTI Director Jonas Shigeki," Susan filled in, looking up from her work. "He supplied the tickets."

"Can you ask him for another?"

"Uhh, no," Susan said with finality. "I don't think that's a good idea."

"Why not?"

"Because he's an *under-director* and I'm, well ... I'm just another agent."

"I think you're a little more than that, Susan," Isaac countered.

"The point is he's way higher up in the food chain than me. It's best if I don't bug him."

"Wait a second," Isaac began, a thought occurring to him. "Isn't he the director you send your status reports to? The ones on how the exchange program is working out?"

"Yeah, he's the one."

"Then don't you already have an open dialogue with him?"

"A one-way dialogue," Susan stressed. "Sent in the form of reports."

"Is it typical for a DTI agent to file reports straight to directors?"

"Well, no." Susan grimaced. "Actually, it's almost unheard of."

"I *see*," Isaac said, the gears of his mind turning.

"But that doesn't mean anything in this case. The whole exchange program is something of a new thing."

"Which Jonas Shigeki personally picked you for."

"*Ye-e-es*," Susan admitted guardedly.

"Which suggests if you were to ask him for something, he'd probably listen."

"I can't just ask him for a handout."

"But you wouldn't be," Isaac corrected, then patted Nina on the arm. "You'd be doing your part to promote...I don't know." He swirled his free hand through the air as he thought up a phrase. "You'd be promoting positive transdimensional relations."

"Ooh!" Nina's face lit up with hope. "I like that one. That could work!"

"I don't know..." Susan replied, clearly not enthusiastic about this.

"Have you ever asked him for something before?"

"No, of course not."

"Then he already knows you don't make frivolous requests."

"But this would *be* a frivolous request!" Susan stressed.

"Come on, Susan." Nina rounded their desks and came alongside the Admin agent. "Help me out here."

"I don't think you two fully realize what you're asking," Susan explained. "My superiors are *strict*. A request like this is going to be scrutinized in more ways than you can possibly imagine. Even if I do send it, there's no way it's getting approved." She shook her head. "No point in even trying."

"Susan." Nina put her arm around the other woman's shoulders. "Do you consider me a friend?"

"Umm...well, yeah. Of course, I do."

"And who was it, when you first started working in Themis Division, who invited you over for fun and games?"

"That would be the two of you."

"And who let you join in on our *Solar Descent* sessions? Who helped you set up your first character and gave you tips for making your build extra tanky?"

"Are you really going to guilt me into sending this message?" Susan asked, her brow creased with worry.

"Please!"

"Might as well give it a shot, Susan," Isaac said. "At the very least it'll stop her from whining about it."

"I . . ." Susan glanced to Nina, then to Isaac, then back to his sister. "Okay, I'll see what I can do."

"Thank you!" Nina gave Susan a tight hug.

"Though, I'm telling you, it's going to get rejected."

"Still worth a shot," Isaac said. "And besides, what's the harm in trying?"

Susan frowned at him.

CHAPTER TWO

FOUR HOURS LATER, ISAAC SENT HIS FINISHED REPORT OFF TO Raviv, then closed the virtual screens over his desk and stood up.

"I'm heading home," he said to Susan. "Don't work too late, okay?"

"I'll try not to," Susan replied, staring intently at her screen.

"Also, Nina's been bugging me for updates. You hear anything back from the director yet?"

"We won't be hearing back for a while."

"Why not? It's been long enough for his reply to come back."

"No, because I haven't sent the request yet."

"Excuse me?" Isaac asked. "You haven't *sent* it?"

"I'm still writing it."

"But didn't you start working on that four *hours* ago?"

"I want to make sure it's good enough," she defended.

"Don't you think you're cutting it a little close? Our flight leaves tomorrow morning, so if Nina's going to be on it . . ."

"I know." Susan checked a virtual clock on her desk. "I still have time."

"What seems to be the holdup?"

"It's . . . here. Would you mind taking a look? I could use a second opinion."

"Sure, no problem." Isaac rounded the desk and took a knee beside Susan. The privacy filter lifted, and the text of her message crystalized.

Except he couldn't read it. She'd written the message in the Admin's version of Modern English, which was a combination of what people nowadays referred to as Old English and Old Spanish. He could make out about half the words, but the sum of it was still gibberish to him.

He activated a translation program through his wetware, and the text reappeared as the SysGov version of Modern English, which incorporated pieces of Old English and Old Chinese, though the tonal inflections from Old Chinese were now used to convey a subtext of meaning to the words. However, since Admin English lacked any equivalent, the translated text read a bit flat to him.

Though that wasn't the only problem.

Not by a long shot.

"Oh dear." Isaac began scrolling through the message. It took a while to find the bottom.

"You see what I'm dealing with, don't you?"

"It's a tad on the long side, I'd say."

"I know, but all of it's important. Trust me on this. I need to make a solid case if we're to have any hope of getting Nina her ticket."

"Hmm." Isaac picked a passage at random. "'Allotment of additional resources will lead to multitudinous beneficial factors. See bullet point list below.'"

"What do you think?"

"Your bullet points have bullet points."

"That's because I have a lot of points to make."

"Maybe so, but..." He picked another passage. "'Incontrovertible positive influence on cross-transdimensional political and social landscape.'"

"You don't like it?" Susan asked, sounding worried.

"I think you're leaning too heavily on your thesaurus."

"Maybe, but I don't want to come across as an idiot."

"Don't you think you're overdoing it a bit?"

"Of course not. Trust me, Isaac. You have no idea how much scrutiny a request like this is going to receive. Never mind the fact that I'm"—she leaned toward him and whispered conspiratorially—"basically asking for a freebie so a friend can see the tournament live. Let's be honest, everything I've written here is complete crap."

"Yes, I think we can agree on that."

"But it's *necessary* crap. I'm trying my best to mask the true intent behind the request."

"Susan, I think you're getting more worked up over this than it warrants."

She leaned back from him. "You think so?"

"I do. Part of your job is to be a representative for your people. Doesn't this request fit in with all that?"

"You mean, by using my influence to help the sister of a coworker attend a first-of-its-kind event live?"

"Well, when you put it *that* way, it does sound a little dubious."

Susan let out a weary sigh and turned back to her letter.

"You think it's good enough to send like this?"

"Sure, why not?" He stood up. "*Zhǔ hǎo yún*," he added, inflecting the versatile SysGov phrase with a tonal subtext that transformed the Old Chinese words for "good luck" into something close to "nothing ventured, nothing gained" or "we make our own luck."

"Point taken," Susan said. "All right, I'm going to send it."

"That's the spirit." He patted her on the shoulder. "After all, what's the worst that could happen?"

"Ahh!" Susan covered her face. "Please stop saying things like that!"

✧   ✧   ✧

Over 1.3 billion kilometers away in Argus Station over Earth, Jonas Shigeki had a problem, and unlike most of the difficulties he faced in his position as head of DTI Foreign Affairs, the current problem was almost entirely his fault.

This is why I hate after-lunch meetings, he thought to himself as the mind-numbing presentation continued.

"And now here you can see a surprising breakdown from the survey results of grid nine-dash-three-dash-twelve," Doctor Andover-Chen continued to drone on, the mathematical equations under his synthoid's black, glassy skin glowing brighter with enthusiasm. "Surprisingly, chronometric field intensity in this transverse grid is three percent stronger than surrounding grids, indicating the presence of an as-yet-undiscovered anomaly. Please reference exhibit nine-dash-three-dash-twelve-alpha in your supplemental material for more details."

The room's four dozen occupants stirred from their lethargy, each person swiping to the next slide in their abstract handouts.

Researchers, agents, and analysts from both the Admin's DTI and SysPol's Gordian Division filled the conference room deep in Argus Station, all assembled for a soporific series of presentations put on by the Gordian Division's chief scientist, Doctor Andover-Chen, and his counterpart in the DTI, Doctor Katja Hinnerkopf.

The Gordian Division was the newest addition to SysPol, born out of the destruction caused by the Gordian Knot, a chaotic anomaly of knotted timelines centered around 1940 that nearly destroyed sixteen universes. The organization had grown in leaps and bounds since its inception, and its relationship with the DTI—while contentious and suspicious at first—had improved drastically after both groups joined forces to resolve a second existential calamity, now called the Dynasty Crisis.

The meeting Jonas now found himself in was part of a series of workshops and seminars put on by and for various members of both organizations, which would then culminate late next week in high-level discussions between DTI Director-General Csaba Shigeki, his father, and Commissioner Klaus-Wilhelm von Schröder of the Gordian Division, along with their respective senior staffs.

Jonas prided himself on sensing the flow of events hidden beneath the surface, of gauging where those eddies and currents might lead, extrapolating what dangers might lie ahead and then—with the utmost care—nudging the flow in the most beneficial direction.

But he couldn't do that if he had no idea what was coming down the chute!

Jonas glanced over at Hinnerkopf. The stern, compact woman with her severe buzz cut stood beside Andover-Chen at the head of the room, patiently attentive as her counterpart drudged through yet another banal exhibit.

Yes, surveying the transverse—the binding fabric that connected individual universes and held the greater multiverse together—was important. Yes, the TTVs of Gordian Division and chronoports of the DTI had discovered some unusual phenomena out there, but what he really wanted to know was what Andover-Chen and Hinnerkopf were up to, and so he'd signed up for *every single workshop* the two were putting on this week.

God help me, he thought sullenly.

Jonas had pressed Hinnerkopf repeatedly over the past few days, but she'd been tight-lipped, only hinting at a "proposal of monumental proportions," a description which did not put him at ease. He was the Director of Foreign Affairs, damn it! Any collaborative projects fell under his jurisdiction! But Hinnerkopf had insisted *this* unannounced project would fit under her authority as Under-Director of Technology.

Jonas knew his father had received a preview of Hinnerkopf's mystery proposal, and he assumed Commissioner Schröder had as well from Andover-Chen, which implied they'd given their consent for the upcoming negotiations to proceed. He'd tried hitting up his father for the details, but all that had gotten him was some vague reference to a "large, collaborative project" and instructions to wait for Hinnerkopf's formal presentation.

What *sort* of "large, collaborative project"? How was he supposed to ensure their two sides worked well together if he had no idea which cliff they were about to leap off?

But that wasn't the worst of it. Oh no!

The worst part—the *absolute* worst—was the fact that he could barely keep his eyes open!

"Moving on, please open exhibit nine-dash-three-dash-twelve-beta. Here you can see..."

The room stirred as everyone swiped.

It's my own damn fault, Jonas thought morosely.

As a rule, he ate light lunches because he knew of his tendency to become sleepy after a heavy meal. But today the chefs in the Argus executive café had served this absolutely *amazing* macaroni and cheese side with bacon bits, tomatoes, and mushrooms mixed in a creamy five-cheese blend and topped with seasoned bread crumbles. It tasted so good Jonas had ordered a second helping.

And then a third.

And then he boxed up a fourth to go.

Now all those carbs sat in his stomach like a leaden lump, dragging down his mental acuity and alertness with all the inevitability of a black hole consuming a neighboring star.

It didn't help that the room was dark and warm. He propped his cheek up on a fist and stared at the presentation through drooping eyelids.

"Chronoton movement in this region also bears investigation," Andover-Chen continued. "As you can tell from exhibit nine-dash-three-dash-twelve-gamma, the survey showed a statistical anomaly in the distribution of chronoton particles, with forty-seven percent moving forward in time and a surprisingly high fifty-three percent traveling into the past. This discrepancy in the distribution from the typical fifty-fifty split indicates..."

Jonas' brain waded through the thick, mental sludge. He had a strong desire to get up, walk over to the nearest wall, and beat his head into it until he felt better. The suffocating deluge of technical jargon oozed over him, threatening to drag him under—

An alert appeared in his virtual vision, and he perked up, thankful for the interruption. He saw it was from Special Agent Susan Cantrell, and he opened the message with privacy filters engaged.

He began reading, and soon a different kind of deluge assaulted his senses. He scrolled down through the message, skimming its contents.

What the hell is she after? he wondered, picking through the word salad in front of him. *"Further germinate positive foreign relations with enhanced social outreach." Germinate? Someone needs to confiscate this woman's thesaurus.*

He glanced up at Andover-Chen, and saw he was still talking about chronotons acting weird, so he returned to Cantrell's message and read on.

Why do her bullet points have bullet points? he asked himself. *"Showcase Admin generosity with unsolicited magnanimity." Come on, Agent, get to the frickin' point already!*

He started skipping more and more of the letter, searching without success for the purpose behind it all.

What the hell is she asking me for? An assault cruiser?

And then he found it, tucked neatly into the last paragraph of Cantrell's magnum opus of word mush.

All this for an extra ticket and a third hotel room? Oh, good grief!

Jonas swiped the APPROVE toggle and hit SEND without giving the request another thought.

✧   ✧   ✧

Isaac stood in the middle of his modest apartment on Kronos Station, hands on hips as he surveyed the room, trying to think if he'd forgotten anything. As a Themis Division detective, he spent most nights in hotel rooms, and the apartment reflected his frequent absence. The pale, cream-colored walls were almost completely devoid of decoration, except near his gaming recliner and its dual infosystem towers, where virtual character sheets from *Solar Descent* floated in the air.

"You think I should buy a swim trunk pattern? Susan mentioned she wanted to go to the beach."

"If you want," Cephalie said, her avatar seated atop the back of the recliner, legs dangling over the edge. "But there's no need to do that tonight. There'll be stores on the saucer, and plenty more at the resort."

"Yeah, you're right."

Isaac walked over to the bed and stared down at the modest travel case. It contained two spare uniforms, his pajamas (which were well-worn and super comfy, so he preferred not to reprint them at each hotel), as well as a collection of pattern permits for any formal- or casualwear he thought he'd need later.

"What's wrong?" Cephalie asked.

"I know I'm forgetting something."

"You've been living out of that case for five years. You'll be fine."

"Normally, I'd agree with you. But I don't travel for fun very much." He glanced over at his IC. "And yes, I know this isn't a vacation, but we're going to have some free time on Luna before we head back. Plus, I'm sure Susan will want to see the sights."

"Even if you do forget something, just buy it there and print it out when you need it."

"You're right, of course." He gave the travel case one last look then closed the lid. The programmable-steel exterior morphed to form a seamless outer shell.

An incoming message blinked in his abstract vision. He opened the comm window, and a smiling Susan appeared.

"Hey, Susan. What's up?"

"Isaac!" she began excitedly. "I received a reply from the director!"

"Oh, good. And?"

"He approved a third ticket! I've also got her flight pass for tomorrow, and she'll have her own hotel room in the Crimson Flower."

"That's wonderful. I'll let Nina know. Unless you already have."

"No, I called you first. You can tell her if you like."

"Okay. I'll take care of that."

"I'm actually surprised how quickly his response came. And

even then, I thought it'd be a message saying how my request has been forwarded to such-and-such group for further review. I didn't expect a positive response so soon!"

"See? I told you nothing bad would happen."

"I bet all those bullet points really helped sell my case."

"Something clearly caught his eye, though I'm not sure it was that."

"Or maybe it was all the fancy language I used." Susan rubbed her chin. "You know, I should keep that message handy for future reference. Next time I need something, I can pull it up as a template."

"If it isn't broke, don't fix it?"

"Exactly."

"Well, thanks again for helping out my sister. I'm going to give her a call and share the good news."

"Just glad I could help. Any time, Isaac."

"See you tomorrow."

"Later."

Susan disconnected from her side. Isaac opened a new window and selected Nina's connection string.

"Hey," she said after a few rings.

"Hey, sis."

"You got something good for me?"

"You bet. Susan has your ticket."

"Nice!"

"You're flying over with us, so make sure you don't miss the saucer. I'm sure Raviv has left for the day, but you know how he is. Just send him a priority message, and he'll process your PTO request, even when it's this late."

"What, are you kidding?" Nina gave him a sneaky smile. "He approved my vacation time *hours* ago. I knew Susan would pull through."

CHAPTER THREE

"I'M GOING TO . . ." SUSAN HESITATED AND TOOK THE MOMENT TO survey her precarious position once more. She sat at a small table across from Isaac within the *Betelgeuse*'s spacious Deck One Observation Dome. The dome was sparsely populated in the hours between breakfast and lunch with most of the other passengers seated in recliners, gazing up at a magnified view of the ship's next destination. Graviton thrusters accelerated the *Betelgeuse* at a pleasant one gravity, and its supplemental artificial gravity remained off.

"Yes?" Isaac asked after her delay dragged on.

"Hold on. I'm thinking." She looked down at the MechMaster board state between them. Abstract models of giant bipedal machines squared off on either side of the table with stats and special rules floating next to each game piece. Isaac's last turn had damaged the defenses around her base, but she was close—*so* close—to beating him this time, and she took a moment to carefully consider her next moves.

She reviewed the abstract cards in her "hand," then glanced over Isaac's own cards, the graphics on his obscured by a privacy filter. He had fewer cards in hand than she did and fewer cards left in his defense stack, which formed a player's "hit points" in this game.

If I can only weather his next attack, she thought, *I should be able to deploy enough mechs next turn for a fatal counterattack. I just need to survive that long, so . . .*

"Okay, here goes." She selected a card and placed it on the board. It transformed into a game piece. "I'll deploy one TemplarMech, paying three Power to do so, and then I'll deploy an IroncladMech for four Power."

"I see, I see," Isaac said, nodding. "Any attacks to declare?"

"Nope. I'm setting all my mechs to Overwatch, and that'll end my turn."

"Okay then." He sat up in his chair and cracked his knuckles, which made her nervous. "I'm going to start by upgrading my RifleerMech with a Heavy Cannon for one Power, transforming it into a Dual-RifleerMech." He placed the upgrade card next to the game piece, and a second cannon materialized on it.

She waited to see what he did next. This was just the start of whatever combo he was about to pull.

"Next, I'll spend two Power and use Guns, Guns, and More Guns"—he added the card to his battle area—"which allows any two mechs with Rifleer in their names to perform a free Combine Action. I'll apply the action to both Dual-Rifleers, and they'll form a TetraCannonMech."

The two game pieces leapt at each other, transforming and combining into a single, far larger bipedal machine with massive cannons on its shoulders.

There's the bastard, Susan thought. *But you're not beating me with it this time. I've got too many defenses up.*

"I will defend with—" she began.

"Hold on." He held up a hand. "I'm not attacking yet."

"You're not?" she asked, confused and concerned. This was normally the point where their games ended. Had she done something wrong?

"No." He selected a game piece in his base. "Next, I'll deploy one of my Death Bringer bombers and move it over to the TetraCannonMech. Then, I'll activate Excrucion, the Dark Master and use his Mastery Ability to perform a free Combine Action."

"What for?"

"So that the bomber and mech can combine—"

The bomber landed on top of the mech, and overly-complicated mechanisms interlocked between the two of them so that the delta wing of the bomber draped over the mech like a dramatic cape loaded with ordnance.

"—into Ultimate Form TetraArsenalMech Death."

"*What?!*" Susan blurted.

"And now I'll attack your base."

"I'll defend with the IronClad."

"That won't work."

"Why not?"

"TetraArsenal is attacking with missiles."

"When the hell did it get missiles?"

"After it combined into its ultimate form. Do any of your mechs have anti-air?"

"Uhh." Susan looked over her board pieces. "Shit."

"TetraArsenal will attack your base four times."

Susan let out a frustrated exhale and flipped over the last four of her defense cards.

"Do any of these stop it?"

"No."

"Didn't think so." She discarded the defense cards and surveyed the board state. "Well, at least I survived your turn."

"Next, I'll play—"

"There's *more*?" Susan exclaimed.

"Yes. I'll play There's No Such Thing as Too Many Missiles for zero Power, which will dismantle my second Death Bringer to allow any missile-equipped mech to attack again. I pick the TetraArsenal."

"Oh no," Susan uttered mournfully.

"And now TetraArsenal will attack your base directly."

"And that's game." Susan tossed her hand into the discard pile. "Damn. I thought I had you."

"I got lucky there at the end. If I hadn't drawn the last piece of my combo, you probably would have won."

The board state reset. Game figures morphed back into their original cards and returned to each player's respective deck.

"That deck of yours is *fierce*," Susan said.

"Well, I've been collecting MechMaster since I was twelve, so yeah." He smiled guiltily. "My main deck *should* be tough to beat by now."

"You ever participate in official tournaments?"

"Not often. That crowd can get really competitive."

"Says the guy who just comboed me into oblivion with his optimized TetraCannon deck."

"Sorry." Isaac tapped the top of his deck and it auto-shuffled.

"I can use a different deck if you're sick of facing this one. You've only been collecting for a few months, after all."

"No, it's all right." Susan shuffled her own deck and leaned back. "I don't want you to go easy on me. Adversity is a great teacher."

"That it is."

"Though," she began hesitantly, "I was thinking about buying a key card or three to help out my deck, but then it occurred to me how bad that would look on my expense report and thought otherwise."

"Any cards you have your eye on?"

"Anazaya, the Wandering Master."

"Oh, that's a good idea. She'll synergize well with your HeavyTemplarMechs. Her Reinforced Aegis will make them very hard to kill."

"That's what I was thinking."

"Would you like some?" Isaac opened his collection's main menu. "I think I have more copies of her than I'll ever need."

"Really?" Susan's eyes lit up.

"Sure. Why not? I'm not using them." Isaac pulled out four copies of Anazaya's card and transferred their ownership to Susan's collection. "There you go. A full play set, free of charge."

"Thanks!" Susan expanded her deck into sets of identical cards. "Now I just need to figure out which cards to swap out." She zoomed in on her new Anazaya card art and smiled at it. The armored woman struck a heroic pose, helmet slung under one arm, hand on her hip as she gazed into the distance. Her armor was light blue shot with a white lightning bolt down the front. "I think one of the reasons I was drawn to this card is the art." She held it up for him to see. "Don't you think her armor looks like my combat frame?"

"Somewhat." Isaac sighed and shook his head. "I still can't believe you brought it along."

"It's a part of my official kit. I'm supposed to take it wherever I go."

"I know."

"But?" she added for him.

"We're not even working a case."

"What if we need it and it's halfway across the solar system? Better safe than sorry."

"True, but what are the odds we're going to need an Admin death machine at a *gaming tournament*?"

"It's come in handy before."

"I..." Isaac sighed again. "Yes, it has," he admitted begrudgingly.

"More than once, too."

"I'm not saying it hasn't."

"Besides, if we don't need it, it stays in the cargo container."

"Yes, you've made your point." He tapped his deck, and it shuffled again. "Another round?"

"Give me a few minutes. I'm still debating which cards to pull out."

"Sure thing. No rush." He glanced up at the magnified view of Earth and Luna. They were still a week away. "We've got plenty of time."

"You think we'll have enough time to hit the beach when we get there?"

"We should. There's nothing on our schedule until late the first day. And even if something were to come up, we can fit in a beach trip before we leave for Saturn."

Susan smiled as she sorted through her cards.

"Though I'm still not sure what the big deal is," he confessed. "Tankville really is a lovely little town."

"It's just not the same, Isaac."

"If you say so."

"I hardly believe it!" said a vaguely familiar voice. "Detectives Cho and Cantrell?"

The two detectives turned to see a couple approaching their table. The man's bald synthoid possessed powder white skin and completely black eyes, while the young woman on his arm was either still organic or in a very lifelike synthoid with a sweet, round face and pulsing blue streaks through her dark hair. Both wore black formal attire with scarves depicting gentle snowfall.

"Who are they again, Doug?" the young woman asked.

"Why, these are the detectives who helped pull me out from underneath the Trinh Syndicate's boot."

"Hello, Mister Chowder," Isaac said. "Or should I say Neon Caravaggio?"

"Ah, you remember me!" Doug Chowder grinned at them. "For you, either identity will do. The secret's loose, I'm afraid. Everyone who might care now knows the aloof Lunarian artiste

Neon Caravaggio is actually some nobody named"—he grimaced as he spoke his real name—"Doug Chowder."

"How's that working out for you?" Susan asked. "I know you were worried about your alias becoming public."

"Surprisingly well, I must say." Chowder tapped his chest. "Turns out no one believes the truth! The art community is rife with speculation, but most people think Caravaggio is making a deep, allegorical statement about the fragility of the human condition." He swirled a hand through the air aimlessly. "Or some other bull-[BLEEP] like that."

Isaac frowned at the odd sound of Chowder's synthoid censoring his own speech.

"*Doug*," the young woman said.

"Sorry, dear." Chowder patted her forearm, then turned to the detectives. "Also, please let me introduce my fiancée, Ito Tomoe."

"Fiancée?" Isaac noted. "Congratulations. Last time we crossed paths, you two were just dating, if I'm not mistaken."

"No, you're quite right," Chowder said. "After the Trinh Syndicate landed in hot water over that time machine they were trying to construct, just about every government ministry you can name descended upon them, and their internal ranks got shaken up. I was able to use all that drama and confusion to my advantage. Even managed to negotiate an early end to my contract." He puffed out his chest. "I'm now a completely independent artiste. No corporate ties to speak of!"

"That's great to hear," Susan said. "You seem happier now."

"Because I am." He smiled at Tomoe and rubbed the top of her hand. "For more than one reason."

"What's bringing you to the inner system?" Isaac asked.

"The same business as you, I imagine, over at the Crimson Flower. I saw your names on the guest list, but I didn't realize until now we were on the same flight."

"You're involved in the tournament?" Susan asked.

"Indeed I am." Chowder flashed a toothy grin. "Or rather, Neon Caravaggio is. ActionStream commissioned me to design the uniforms for the SysGov finalists, and I'm quite pleased with how they turned out."

"I'll have to check them out during the finals," Isaac said.

"Also, have you two heard the news about this flight's entertainment?"

Susan and Isaac shook their heads.

"Then brace yourselves, because Markie Flavor-Sparkle is on this flight!" Chowder said excitedly. "I can hardly believe our luck! Ito and I missed his concerts during his Saturn tour, but it turns out we're in for a treat, because he's performing live tonight in the Deck Seven Theater!"

"That's . . . nice," Isaac said, noncommittally.

"Who's he again?" Susan asked, the name sounding vaguely familiar to her.

"A Lunarian actor and singer," Isaac replied, then mouthed the word, "Overrated."

"He's also scheduled to perform during the tournament pre-show," Chowder added, "but why wait when we're on the same flight as him?"

"You think I can get him to sign my scarf?" Tomoe asked.

"We'll certainly try," Chowder assured her with a wink. "I'll see if I can schmooze our way in for a chat. You know, one artist to another."

"You're the best, Doug!" Tomoe rested her head on his shoulder and gave him a hug.

"What do you think, Isaac?" Susan asked. "Shall we go?"

"Uhh . . ." Isaac had the look of a cornered animal. "Why?"

"Well, for one, I've never been to a live concert before," Susan said. "Even back in the Admin. And it's not like we have anything else to do while we wait. Besides, this sounds like a good opportunity to experience some live SysGov entertainment. You know, as part of the whole ongoing cultural exchange thing."

Isaac's face twisted up as if he'd swallowed something intensely sour. She wasn't sure why. She thought he'd throw out an objection, but when he opened his mouth he spoke in a soft voice that was almost a whisper and said:

"Okay."

✧　　✧　　✧

"Hey, you two," Nina said as she dragged a chair over to their table.

"Hey, sis," Isaac replied.

"Hello," Susan said, cards in hand, still debating which play to make next. Isaac was kicking her butt again, but she was determined to find a way out of this latest mess.

"You check your mail recently?" Nina asked.

"No," Isaac said. "Why?"

"Probably should check it." Nina swung her legs back and forth under her chair like a pendulum. "Might be something good in there."

"Doubt it," Isaac breathed, releasing his cards. They fell to the table and arranged themselves in a neat pile. "With my luck it'll be Raviv asking us to turn back to Saturn first chance we get."

"Nope!" Nina corrected. "Try again."

Isaac opened a window over his palm, navigated to his inbox, and began to read the headers.

"What is it?" Susan asked, lowering her cards.

"A message from ActionStream. There are some details here about the tournament schedule and what's expected of us. Nothing we didn't already know, but there's also an attachment. A big one, too. Hmm. Weltall dot U-A-M."

"UAM?" Susan asked, glancing up from her cards.

"Universal Abstraction Matrix," Nina explained. "That's your trial copy of *Weltall*. All three of us received the UAM along with an activation keycode."

"All four of us, actually," Cephalie said, materializing among the MechMaster game pieces. "I got a key, too."

"Oh, good." Isaac closed the message. "We can try it out later."

"*O-o-or*," Nina began, "we could all check it out right now."

"We're sort of in the middle of a game here," Isaac protested.

"Yeah, I see that." Nina turned to Susan. "You beat him yet?"

"Not. Yet," Susan said, still deliberating on her next move.

"Yeah, me neither. I gave up years ago."

"You barely dipped your toe in the game," Isaac protested.

"I had over five thousand cards!"

"Which were almost all commons and uncommons."

"Cephalie, back me up here," Nina said. "You want to play *Weltall*, too, right?"

"It would be a nice way to pass the time." Cephalie tapped her cane on a RifleerMech's chassis.

"I suppose so." Isaac placed his cards on the table. "What do you say, Susan?"

"Sure. I was going to lose, anyway. Let's all try something new."

"Fantastic!" Nina cleared the game state with a swipe of her hand and scooched her chair up to the table.

"What sort of game is it?" Isaac asked.

"You two don't even know *that*?"

"We were busy with work," Susan said.

"Me too," Nina said, "but I still found time to watch a few of the qualifiers."

"It's a real-time strategy game on a stellar scale," Cephalie explained. "It's based on plausible science, so you can build just about any sort of megastructure modern physics will allow, but the passage of time is greatly accelerated."

"Otherwise, the games would take *millennia* to finish," Nina said. "Each player starts in a random star system, and you set out from there, harvesting resources and building up your industrial and military might. Each player has an avatar core, which is both your point of view and where you issue orders from."

"The light-speed limit still applies," Cephalie added. "No magical FTL communication with your fleets or anything like that, and the restrictions affect both your perception of nearby events and your ability to send out orders. So if you spread out your forces, your orders will take effect with a significant delay. The game supports team matches, but the tournament will follow a six-way free-for-all format. There are also partial and full abstraction modes of play."

"Sounds fun," Susan said. "How about we dive into a partial-mode free-for-all to help acquaint us with the basics?"

"Works for me!" Nina opened her game file, and the loading abstraction unfolded around them.

Susan found herself floating within a starry void. The table, floor, and the rest of the ship's observation dome remained as a ghostly imprint upon an otherwise unblemished view of space.

"*Weltall* doesn't sound too unusual," Isaac said. "I've played similar strategy games before. I wonder why this one's garnered so much attention."

"Distribution," Nina said. "It's going to be the first SysGov game released in the Admin."

"Ah. Yes, that would do it."

"I see an option here to unlock the whole tech tree from the beginning for a tutorial match. That should help us all get up to speed. Creating the lobby now."

A menu opened near Susan, and she searched for and selected the local game lobby Nina had just created. She bypassed the various tutorial popups vying for her attention and dove into the game proper.

She found herself above a planet whose entire surface was encased in industry. Its molten core had been tapped, and not a blade of grass or puddle of water remained exposed on the surface. Even the atmosphere had been harvested into a massive bank of compressed resources.

"We start with a fully industrialized home planet?" Susan asked.

"Oh, don't worry," Nina said. "That's nothing. Things get *way* bigger than that."

Susan nodded and began to add ships and megastructures to her construction queue. She'd played similar games before, at least on a conceptual level. At one point, she'd almost considered a career as a professional gamer. Her varsity performance had been so high, she'd received scholarship offers from multiple colleges, but she'd turned them all down. Her heart had never been in it.

She liked games. Hell, she *loved* games, but as a diversion. As a source of stress relief, and as a way to connect with other people with similar interests. Not as a job. Not in a way that blurred the line between work and recreation, perverting something she loved and twisting it into an obligation.

This is much better, she thought as she sent her fastest ships to scout nearby star systems. She had no idea where Nina, Isaac, or Cephalie might have started, and if one of them was nearby, she needed to know as soon as possible.

The game's physics engine cranked along at over two million times normal speed. That sounded fast on the surface, but they were dealing with interstellar distances, and the nearest star was four light-years away. It took light from that system a whole in-game minute to reach her.

She focused on expanding her industrial infrastructure while she waited for the scouts to report back, systematically colonizing every rock in the system while also draining the gas giants of their fusible material. Her resource bank reached what seemed to be ludicrous levels, and she perused the menus to see what else she could build.

She selected the megastructure submenu and opened it.

"Oh," she uttered. "Wow."

She could barely afford a tenth of the projects on display.

Yes, the game escalated quite a bit from the humble beginnings on a single planet.

The schematic for an interstellar mass driver drew her eye,

one that could accelerate impressive kinetic payloads to near light speed. She noted how those payloads could hit planets in another solar system with enough kinetic energy to wipe out the dinosaurs all over again, and she began to hatch a plan. Once her scouts located the other players' worlds...

She began construction of the mass driver's megastructure frame while simultaneously expanding her resource gathering. She'd need a more substantial flow of resources if she were to finish the superweapon in a reasonable timeframe, and so she also began constructing a cluster of star-lifting satellites to harvest the matter of her sun.

"Isaac?" Nina said.

"Hmm?"

"Is that you?"

"Why do you ask?"

"Because I can see one of the stars moving."

"Might be me. Might be."

"What *are* you doing?"

"Just trying out this thing called a 'stellar engine.' Pay me no mind."

Susan noticed the far-flung star accelerating on a new heading, though later than Nina had. Isaac's star must have been closer to Nina's than her own. She wasn't sure how he was moving the star, but she could also see how that would benefit him. The star was by far the largest resource in any system, both in terms of energy and matter. And, if she understood her gravitational mechanics correctly, all the planets would come along for the ride as the star was moved.

So, she thought, *instead of sending ships to another star system and ordering them around at a distance, just pick up and move. Nice one, Isaac.*

Except for one fatal flaw.

She now knew precisely which star Isaac had started on, and her scouts hadn't even reached it yet.

That means building megastructures is a double-edged sword, she thought. *They can provide massive boosts to my forces, but they also alert nearby players of where I am. Interesting. I wonder if a stealthier approach is viable. Maybe I'll try that next game, but for now...*

She diverted her closest scouts toward Isaac's system and took measures to accelerate construction of her superweapon.

"Oh, crap," Nina groaned.

"What?" Isaac asked.

"I made a whoopsie."

"What sort of 'whoopsie'?"

"The kind where I just destroyed myself. Can we begin a new game?"

"Nina, we've barely started."

"I know, but I think this game is going to end really fast."

"What makes you think— What in the worlds? Oh, no! What *are* those things?!"

"Sorry. I made them by accident!"

"Oh, my goodness! They're eating my fleet!"

"Yeah. They did that to me too."

"What the hell are you two yacking about?" Cephalie asked. "I swear, you meat brains and your—hmm? What is . . . oh no, oh no, oh no, *oh no!*"

"Sorry!" Nina said, cringing.

"Nina?" Isaac drummed his fingers on the table.

"Yeah?"

"What did you do?"

"I built an All-Predator."

"And what, precisely, is an All-Predator?"

"It's a self-replicating, hegemonizing swarm. A nasty one, too. Normally, you can only access it in the late game, given how deep in the tech tree it resides. Basically, it eats everything and makes more of itself."

"Including the player who unleashes it?"

"Apparently so." Nina shrunk back into her seat. "Sorry! I know better now."

"What kind of idiot would put this in the game?" Cephalie asked.

"I know, right?" Nina agreed.

"Congratulations, Susan," Isaac sighed. "Well played."

"But I didn't even finish building my mass driver," she said mournfully.

"Shall we have another go at it?" Nina asked.

Isaac checked the time. "Maybe one more. Then how about we grab a bite to eat before the concert?"

"Sounds good to me," Susan said.

❖   ❖   ❖

Susan wasn't sure what she'd expected out of the concert, but it wasn't this. She'd imagined a SysGov celebrity prominent enough to be booked for entertainment at a cross-universal event to be a bit more...classy.

At least the performance by itself was visually stimulating. Even enjoyable, if she'd enjoyed rainbows vomiting their colors directly into her eye sockets. Markie Flavor-Sparkle danced and sang up on stage, resplendent in a white suit with long streamers undulating in his wake, quivering with each head bob and pelvic thrust. His glistening hair changed hues with the beat of the music, and those changing colors chased their way down the streamers.

A sleet of brilliant abstract shapes blew past her like debris kicked up by a wind tunnel, while his backup dancers—both abstract and physical—performed behind and around him with the same manic, sweating intensity.

The performance had started with one of his earliest songs, "Pants on the Ceiling Fan (I'm Late for Work)," then moved on to "Tired of Love (Now I Want Cake)" before shifting to a crowd favorite—if she judged by all the cheers at the opening notes—titled "Love Hurts (And I'm a Masochist)."

His latest hit, "A Song About Kitties (And I Don't Mean Cats)," followed that number, and the concert rolled on from there.

It was energetic, colorful, raunchy.

And loud.

Definitely loud.

Not the controlled loud of abstract sound experienced through shared virtual senses, but a real, visceral, feel-the-beat-in-your-chest loud.

"Are you enjoying yourself?" Susan shouted to Isaac.

"*What?*" Isaac shouted back.

"I said, are you enjoying yourself?"

"*What?*"

"Are *you*! Enjo*ying*! Your*self*!"

"That's great!"

"What's great?"

"*What?*"

"I *said*, 'what's *great?*'"

"'What's great?'"

"Yes!" Susan shouted, becoming exasperated with the exchange. "What's great?"

"It's great that you're enjoying yourself!"

Susan put a hand to her forehead and sighed.

The music died down, and Markie Flavor-Sparkle grabbed a glass of water from a counter-grav tray and chugged it as his backup dancers took their positions for the next number.

"This next one, ladies and gentlemen and abstracts," Markie Flavor-Sparkle began as he paced across the front of the stage, "is a very personal song." He tossed the glass away then patted his chest. "It comes from the heart. Even thinking about it takes a lot out of me. I don't know if I'll manage to get through it all tonight."

The crowd resonated with *oh-no*'s and *please try*'s and other vocalizations of worry and encouragement.

"But the show must go on. Am I right, everyone?"

The crowd chorused its approval.

"So, I'm going to need your support. I'm going to need your energy to get through this."

The crowd cheered its readiness.

"But I'm also going to need one of you to take on an extra burden. To be the rock I lean on as I struggle through this song. Do I have any volunteers?"

Hands shot up throughout the crowd, and those nearest the stage pressed forward, but he gazed over them into the middle of the crowd. A woman in a skimpy red dress tried to climb up onto the stage, but one of the black-clad security synthoids pulled her back down.

"You!" Markie pointed into the crowd, and the spotlight shone on a young woman in a tasteful baby blue dress with a scarf that scintillated with lightning. "Miss, I can feel your energy from up here on this stage. If you're willing, please join me."

The security synthoids made a path for her, and Markie extended a hand, helping her up onto the stage.

"Please give this young lady a warm welcome!" Markie cried out, and the crowd cheered obediently.

"Is that your sister?" Susan asked.

"I believe it is," Isaac replied dryly.

The song opened in a soft, subdued manner as Markie serenaded Nina with the opening lines.

"What's this one called?" Susan asked quietly.

"'I Hate People but I Love You (Mostly).'"

"Uh huh."

Markie trailed off with a lingering, falling note, and then the music crescendoed. Lights exploded around them, and the backup dancers launched into gyrating pelvic motion. Markie ripped his shirt off, threw it into the crowd, and then took a turn around Nina, now singing each word with escalating intensity.

"I hate people!" Markie sang. "But I love you!"

Nina extended her hand and Markie took it, pulling her close. He dipped her forward, almost lowering her all the way down to the stage. He then snapped her upright, and their bodies pressed together, faces close, lips almost touching.

"Mostly," he breathed in a whisper that was soft yet intense. A seductive exhale that wanted to caress its consonants and vowels across a woman's body, undressing her one syllable at a time until its phonemes could slip into more intimate regions.

Nina made a kissy face at him, and Markie smiled at her, then swung her out until they were separated by their combined arms' lengths.

"Wanna get out of here?" Susan asked.

"I think my brain already left ten minutes ago."

CHAPTER FOUR

"WHAT DO YOU MEAN THEY'RE NOT LETTING YOU IN?" FUMED Lieutenant Cameron Lotz of the Lunar State Police.

He was a tall, well-muscled man who filled out the dark grays of his trooper uniform well. He held one hand on his hip and leaned in that direction, giving onlookers the impression he was perpetually about to either tip over or sprint into action. He reached up with his free hand, took off his dark gray cap, and smoothed out his reddish buzz.

He and a half dozen other troopers had assembled in a wide, circular room lined with public grav tubes that could whisk visitors to most parts of the Crimson Flower within minutes. Gray, stony walls gave way to lush, green carpeting, while a crystal fountain burbled in the center. Water trickled down some of the stone walls, catching in a sedate stream around part of the room's edge, and a fine, fragrant mist cooled the air.

"That's just it, sir," Trooper O'Leary said. "We tried going into Miss Sako's room to scope out her printer, just like you ordered, but then the head of her security detail—a big synthoid named Pérez—came over and told us to leave."

"So what?" Lotz asked, fitting his cap back on.

"Sir?"

"You just let him have his way?"

"Not at first, but then he forced us out."

"*Forced* you out?"

"Yes, sir."

"How, exactly?"

"One of their big dog drones came over. You know the type. The ones with guns for faces."

"Did the drone attack you?"

"Well...no," O'Leary confessed. "But it started counting down."

"Counting!"

"In a threatening manner." O'Leary looked to his fellow troopers, who nodded in agreement.

"You afraid of math?"

"No, sir."

"Then why did you turn tail when a brainless drone started *counting* at you?"

"In a threatening manner."

"*Fine,*" Lotz growled. "You found its numbers threatening. And then what?"

"We decided to head back here and inform you." O'Leary glanced to the other troopers, who again backed him up with head nods.

"This is just *great.*"

Lotz blew out an exasperated breath, then reached up and rubbed his temples.

This was all he needed right now. Day-to-day crimes didn't stop just because a bunch of foreigners decided to visit. If anything, it'd grown worse, what with all the protesters outside causing a ruckus and other unsavory sorts mixing in with them. Never mind that he was *supposed* to be on vacation right now! His wife Sara had always wanted to visit Venus, and he'd spent the last year hoarding his time off so they could take a romantic tour through the planet's most decadent aerial cities. He'd locked in the trip months in advance, too, but then this tournament came up, and suddenly everyone found their personal plans put on hold by the captain.

Lotz was *really* looking forward to the Admin going home so the Crimson Flower—and his own life!—could return to their normal rhythms.

But now *this.*

Where the hell is SysPol when you actually need them? he thought bitterly. *No one bloody trained me on cross-dimensional law enforcement!*

He didn't understand what made this Pérez think he could keep state troopers away from a crime scene. The resort fell under the jurisdiction of the Crimson Flower Police Department first precinct—*his* precinct, and he'd be damned if he'd let some foreigner tell him where his team could or could not go.

"Henschel! Knudson!" Lotz called out, picking out the two members of his team with synthoid bodies. He didn't think this Admin numbskull would be stupid enough to resort to force, but then again, stupid came in many shapes and flavors.

"Sir?"

"All three of you, on me." He started down the corridor. "We're going to sort this out. Right *now!*"

The three state troopers hustled to catch up, falling into a rough formation behind their lieutenant. Together, they headed down the rounded hallway until they came face-to-face with one of those four-legged Admin drones.

"You have entered an exclusionary zone," warned the dog-drone. "Move back or I will be forced to subdue you."

"Subdue this, you tin can." Lotz extended a finger.

"You have ten seconds to comply. Ten. Nine."

Lotz crossed his arms and stood his ground. Behind him, the other troopers put their hands on their sidearms, but they took no other aggressive action.

"Three. Two. One. Zero."

An uncomfortable silence followed where nothing happened. Lotz raised an eyebrow at the machine.

"You have entered an exclusionary zone," the drone repeated. "Move back or I will be forced to subdue you."

"Thought so." Lotz pushed past the drone, and his team followed. "Good to see this Pérez isn't a complete moron. Where's the girl's room?"

"We're almost to it, sir. Just up ahead."

The room was on the inner curve, so he saw the two security synthoids in Admin Peacekeeper blues before he saw the door. The bigger of the two scowled at him and moved to intercept.

"Stop," the Peacekeeper barked.

"You Pérez?" Lotz transmitted his police badge.

"I am."

Lotz came face-to-face with the big Admin synthoid. Or rather, face to neck.

"Then how about you explain to me why you're obstructing my people," he demanded, looking up at the man.

"You seem to misunderstand what's going on," Pérez replied.

"Then make me understand." Lotz put a hand on one hip and leaned into it. "Because it certainly looks like obstruction to me."

"I'm protecting the crime scene. Nothing more."

"From what?"

"From outside interference and contamination." Pérez indicated the troopers behind Lotz.

"Just to be clear, that's *our* job."

"I'm well aware of who you are and what you think your job is. Nevertheless, I will not let you pass."

"You see this?" Lotz pointed to the badge on his uniform. "It says CFPD. That's Crimson Flower Police Department. You know where you are, right?"

"Of course."

"Then you should realize we have jurisdiction here."

"Again, you're mistaken," Pérez countered. "A threat has been made against a citizen of the System Cooperative Administration, which means *my* team has jurisdiction, not yours."

"The hell it does!"

"And, in accordance with that jurisdiction, we'll conduct an investigation into the threat made against Miss Sako. You're welcome to our findings, but I must insist you *not* interfere with our work."

"What about questioning the witness?" Lotz asked. "You have problems with us doing that, too?"

"It's not so much a matter of having a problem as lacking a need. We'll interview Miss Sako ourselves. Your services are not required."

A pair of gray-skinned synthoids took up position behind Pérez, and Lotz felt his jaw muscles tighten. Pushing past a lone synthoid was one thing, but now there was a fucking wall of gray-skinned belligerence in his way. He thought he saw Pérez crack the smallest of smiles, as if to say "Go ahead and try it, sucker."

Now all Pérez and his men had to do was stand in the way. The Peacekeeper already had what *he* wanted, which forced Lotz and his team to be the initiators if they were to gain access to the crime scene. And, oh boy! *That* wouldn't look good. Not for the CFPD and not for him, especially if some sort of... scuffle ensued. In fact, an altercation like that could land him in front of a SysPol detective.

Or worse.

Perhaps even end his career.

Maybe even get someone hurt. Even killed in the absolute worst-case scenario.

"And now, Lieutenant Lotz, would you kindly explain to the judge your rationale for what happened next? At which point did you feel assaulting our guests from the Admin was the wisest course of action?"

Lotz gritted his teeth and glowered at Pérez. The synthoid's face remained almost passive.

Almost. There was still that infuriating hint of a smile.

Because he knows he's won, Lotz thought. *I really don't know if I have authority here or not, and I'm not about to take it by force from the well-armed representatives of a scary foreign power.*

"I expect to see a copy of your report."

"Of course." Pérez dipped his head ever so slightly.

Lotz let out a noncommittal grunt, then spun around and headed back up the hallway.

"Is that it?" O'Leary asked once they were out of earshot.

"Hell, no," Lotz grunted. "We still need to get this situation under control."

"Then what do we do, sir?"

"What else?" Lotz cracked a savage smile. "Escalate the *shit* out of this!"

✧   ✧   ✧

Panoptes Station in orbit around Luna was one of the oldest SysPol bases in existence, having its original frame completed back in 2459—shortly after the founding of SysGov itself—before expanding outward from there in concentric, spherical layers as it grew over time.

Panoptes wasn't the largest station in the solar system by any stretch of the imagination, but it was perhaps the most famous.

Or infamous, depending on one's point of view.

Luna was on the smaller side when it came to SysGov member states, and Panoptes' 1.2 million officers represented the highest per capita deployment anywhere in the solar system. Additionally, if backup was ever needed, Earth's Argus Station, L4's Arestor Station, and L5's Mycene Station were all in close proximity with a grand total of 9.9 million officers available for support.

All of which meant Luna enjoyed a comfortable status under

SysPol's protective umbrella. Panoptes was overstaffed for the area and population it covered, and extra aid was nearby if a special need ever arose. However, the reason Panoptes was so heavily staffed was because of the Panopticon—SysPol's one and only maximum-security prison.

The prison existed as a compact nodule deep within the station's isolated core, but this was but one aspect of the full range of services the station provided to the member state under its protection. Certainly, the guards, wardens, counselors, and correctional officers of the Panoptics Division formed the bulk of Panoptes' officer count, but all the other divisions were represented within its halls.

Including Themis Division.

"Yes, Detective," Dispatcher Sara Lotz said over the secure channel from her desk on Panoptes Station. "I have an LSP hazmat team routed to your location."

"Good," Detective Joseph Tonetti replied. He sounded shaken. "Yeah, that's ... that's good."

"Would you like me to remain on the line in case you need further assistance?"

"Uhh, no. I don't think that'll be necessary. The victim isn't going anywhere. At least, not without me using a mop."

"On that note, I've routed a forensics team to your position as well. They should be there in about half an hour."

"Uh oh."

"Detective?"

"The floor here must be angled. The victim is ... I mean the puddle is starting to ooze toward a storm drain. Oh, I think I'm going to be sick. Oh dear. Oh no ... *huck! Huck! Huuurrrck!*"

"Please don't contaminate—"

The detective dropped the call.

"—the crime scene," Sara finished with a frown, then leaned back in her chair.

"New guy?" Marlee asked from the seat next to her.

"New guy." She nodded. "Fresh from the academy."

"Why was he on the line and not the senior detective?"

"I think his mentor wanted this to be a 'character building' experience for him."

"Oh. One of *those* deals." Marlee shook her head, then answered her next call. "Themis Dispatch. How may I be of service, Detective?"

Sara saved the call log and attached it to Tonetti's case file. She wasn't sure what kind of person he was, but if a liquefied body freaked him out, then perhaps he was in the wrong line of work.

Sara knew. She'd once been a Themis detective herself, but she'd grown tired of the never-ending slog of one case after another, of one heartrending interview after another. It wasn't that she'd hated her job or anything along those lines. She'd been a solid detective who could honestly say she'd made Luna a slightly better place for her efforts.

It was more a matter of fatigue. Of doing the same job for thirty years and needing a change of pace, though she was hesitant to quit SysPol entirely. Cut her open, and SysPol blue would pour out instead of blood (not literally, of course, even though she'd transitioned to a synthoid after being injured in the line of duty and didn't, technically, have blood anymore).

That was when her boss recommended a transfer to Dispatch.

The career shift had worked out better than she could have dreamed. It was the perfect compromise. It offered her a level of detachment from the grind in the field while still allowing her to make a difference, small though it might be. Plus, she certainly had the skill set and experience to make the life of a detective just that little bit easier!

She may have been a small cog in the vast apparatus of Themis Division, but she was an *important* cog, and that mattered to her.

Another message came in, and Sara gave this one a disapproving eye, since it was to her personal connection string and not through the dispatch center. It was from Cameron Lotz, her husband, and bore the title: "NEED YOUR HELP!!"

She gave the message a little shake of her head, but then opened it anyway. How bad could it be?

The first part read: *I need this case escalated to your commissioner. Can you take care of that for me, honey? Thanks! XOXOX—Love ya!*

Sara buried her face in her hands and let out a muffled scream. What was he *thinking*?!

"You okay?" Marlee asked.

Sara shook her head in her hands.

"Anything I can help with?"

She shook her head again.

"Suit yourself." Marlee opened another call. "Themis Dispatch. How can I be of service?"

Sara raked her fingers down, temporarily lengthening her face. She stared at the header once more, a million thoughts racing through her mind.

Her family had warned her when she'd started dating Cameron. He was too young for her, they'd said, too wild, too untempered by life and experience. She was half a century his senior, for goodness' sake! But that's what had drawn her to him. She'd fallen in love with his energy, his passion, his zeal for life. She'd been in a rut, and he'd help drag her out of it.

But it wasn't all positives. As with many relationships, the thing that had made her fall in love with him was also the thing that drove her up the wall.

"Sometimes, you just don't get it, do you?" she muttered to herself.

But then, because she was his wife and she loved him deeply (even if he drove her nutty sometimes) she began reading the case log, and, to her surprise, her opinion changed.

Normally, she would never even *consider* sending a message straight to a *commissioner*, but the problem Cameron faced was anything but normal. She could have forwarded it to the Panoptes superintendent who oversaw Luna's Themis Division. That would have, at the very least, followed a standard and acceptable escalation path.

But this case involved the *Admin*. What was a mere superintendent supposed to do? Besides forward it to the station commander, who'd then reach out to one of Tyrel's vice-commissioners, who would then—*finally*—go speak to the commissioner directly.

This case was going to end up on Tyrel's desk one way or another.

Plus, an Admin case could be a ticking time bomb, politically at least. Sure, she *could* follow standard procedures and forward it to the super, but was that really what the situation called for? Why not cut through all that bureaucracy and send the message straight to where it needed to go?

Sara opened the directory and searched for Vesna Tyrel, but nothing came up.

"Marlee?"

"Yeah?"

"Do you have Tyrel's direct string? It's not listed."

"Of course, it's not listed. We're not supposed to send cases to her directly. That's a serious breach of protocol."

"I know, but this one's different."

"You're going to get into *trou-ble*," Marlee warned in a sing-song manner.

"Do you have her string or not?" Sara pressed.

"Of course, I do." Marlee held out her hand, and a small file appeared over it. "I still have it saved from when I worked with *Detective* Tyrel. Hell, you should have seen her in action back then. Why, there was this one time—"

"Thanks." Sara grabbed the file and turned back to her virtual screens before Marlee could begin regaling her with another story from her "glorious" past.

"Hmph!" Marlee shook her head. "Don't blame me if this lands you in hot water."

"Don't worry. I won't."

Sara spent the next ten minutes drafting the letter. She read it, reread it, then reviewed it a third time, growing more nervous with each pass.

This really is going to land me in a heap of trouble, she thought.

But she took a deep breath and hit SEND anyway.

"Dauntless?" Vesna Tyrel called out. "Hey, Dauntless?"

She twisted around in her chair, searching her office with piercing gray eyes. Her silken white hair, bound in a long braid, fell down one uniformed shoulder as she placed a delicate hand on the artificial sapphire desktop and turned in the opposite direction.

A long, glass-fronted curio cabinet took up an entire wall of her office, its glass shelves filled with mementos from her days as both a detective and a chief inspector in charge of a whole department of detectives. They ranged from replicas of murder weapons to her many service awards to everyday items—including a bright pink pillow, an old-fashioned windup clock, a fork bent into a triangle, and a flame-animated scarf—objects that held no clear significance until one read the hovering abstract plaques explaining their background.

The disembodied eye from the cat synthoid was her favorite out of all the mementos. She liked how it followed visitors around her office. Quite literally. She'd set up the stand so it would do that. It amused her to see who noticed and who didn't. Also, it served as a reminder that no matter where a criminal hid, there was always an evidence trail to lead her to them.

The other walls of her office were physically bare, yet filled with abstract reports, charts, schedules, and many other reminders of her duties as a commissioner.

Which was what she wanted to talk about.

"Dauntless?" she tried again. "Where the hell is he?"

"Sorry! Sorry!" Her IC materialized in front of her desk, his avatar cloaked in a brown duster. He wore a wide-brimmed hat, a silver star on his chest, boots with shiny spurs, and a revolver at his hip. "Commissioner Peng was chatting my ears off, and I didn't realize you were calling. Need something?"

"Yes!" Tyrel said brightly, sitting up in her seat. "A momentous event has occurred, and I feel compelled to share."

"Oh?" A wooden rocking chair appeared before her desk, and Dauntless dropped into it, playing with the waxed end of his mustache. "And what might that be?"

"Behold!" She spun one of her screens around with a gesture and removed the privacy filter.

Dauntless frowned at the screen. "You called me over to show me your inbox?"

"It's not the inbox." She spread her hands grandly. "It's what's *in* the inbox!"

"But there's nothing in it."

"Precisely!" Tyrel stood up. "It took me two solid weeks of staying late to chip my way through it, but I have finally—*finally*—worked through my *entire* backlog!" She struck a pose with a hand on her hip, closed her eyes, and lifted her head. "This is the part where you shower me with praise."

Dauntless began to slow clap.

Her inbox dinged.

"You've got mail," he said.

"Oh, for crying out loud!"

"I'll leave you to it," Dauntless sniggered, and vanished.

"Uhh!" Tyrel dropped back into her seat and spun the screen around. "This had better be good."

She opened the message and read it. Then read it again.

By itself, this was a serious breach of protocol by the dispatcher.

She had no authority to circumvent her direct superior on Panoptes, to say nothing of the station commander or Tyrel's own vice-commissioners!

Normally, Tyrel would forward a message like this back to Oscar Ackermann, the Themis superintendent on Panoptes, with a stern note to make sure his dispatchers followed the chain of command. The chain was there for a reason, damn it!

But the nature of the incident...yes, she needed to know about this one as soon as possible, and the dispatcher had alerted her in a most expeditious way.

I'm not sure if I should discipline this Sara Lotz or congratulate her on her initiative. She pondered the problem for a moment. *Maybe a little of both, but I'll deal with that later.*

She opened a comm window and called Jonas Shigeki.

CHAPTER FIVE

JONAS THOUGHT HE POSSESSED A MORE FLEXIBLE MIND THAN most. He prided himself on his talent for spotting opportunities where others only saw insurmountable problems, but even so, Hinnerkopf and Andover-Chen's proposal had caught him completely by surprise!

It was, in a word, audacious. They had proposed nothing less than a permanent research base in the transverse, situated at the midpoint between the Admin and SysGov universes. A *joint* research base called Providence, to be designed, built, and crewed by a mixed team from both superpowers.

It was incredible. Inspirational! He would have never come up with it on his own, and admitting that blind spot made him a touch jealous. The Providence Project had his full, enthusiastic support.

Unfortunately, it was at risk of suffering a slow death in the womb.

"I understand your enthusiasm, Doctor Hinnerkopf," said Commissioner Klaus-Wilhelm von Schröder from the Gordian Division side of the conference table, sitting amidst his senior staff. Across from him sat Csaba Shigeki and *his* senior staff, including Jonas. It was an impressive, almost terrifying concentration of power and authority. These were people who commanded enough time ships and chronometric weapons to rend whole universes apart—and who *had* on one occasion.

"I can see the merits in such a collaborative work," Schröder continued, "but we must also root our decisions in reality. Neither of our organizations has fully recovered from the losses suffered during the Dynasty Crisis. Rebuilding our force strength remains a high priority for both of us. Furthermore, a joint design team strikes me as impractical. There are fundamental technical differences—as well as carefully guarded technological secrets—that would prevent experts from collaborating successfully."

"I would agree with you, Commissioner, under normal circumstances," Katja Hinnerkopf replied carefully, standing at the head of the room with an abstract slide from the presentation hovering behind her. "Which is why Doctor Andover-Chen and I believe a technological exchange is a necessary core component of the Providence Project."

"Which techs, specifically?"

"Sir," Andover-Chen spoke up. "That would be Admin impeller tech in exchange for SysGov artificial gravity."

The room fell silent as the magnitude of this proposal sank in.

Jonas leaned back in his seat, his face carefully passive, but on the inside he wanted to cheer on the two scientists. This was brilliant! Both sides lusted after what they didn't have, what the other side did better. Admin time drives were faster and quieter than SysGov models despite SysGov's superior exotic matter production methods, and the Admin was still decades away from their first functional counter-grav units. If a price was to be paid to enlist both sides in the Providence Project, *these* were the coins to use!

This was a bargain where both SysGov and the Admin could obtain what they wanted most, where *everyone* would step away from the table a winner. He loved where this was going! It was so beautiful, it almost brought a tear to his jaded eyes.

Bravo, Katja! Bravo! I'd clap, but I don't want to make a spectacle of myself.

"I'd like to point out," Csaba Shigeki said after the lengthy silence, "that any agreement we come to here will require ratification by higher levels of our governments."

"Undoubtedly, sir," Hinnerkopf agreed. "That said, I'm sure our recommendations will carry a certain amount of...weight, shall we say?"

An alert blinked in Jonas' virtual sight, and he expanded the message. It was a conference call request from Vesna Tyrel, which meant he would normally drop everything and answer it, but...

I'm in a meeting, he texted back. *Can I call you later?*

If you must, but I'd prefer we deal with this now, Vesna texted. *It's potentially time sensitive and involves one of your citizens.*

All right. Let me see what I can do.

He reached over and placed a hand on his father's shoulder. Their PINs interfaced, and they entered a closed-circuit chat.

"Yes?" Shigeki asked. His lips didn't move and no words came from his mouth, but Jonas' senses saw and heard both happen through their linked PINs.

"I've got an important call I need to answer. Mind proposing a break so I can take it?"

"Fine by me. I could use a breather."

Jonas removed his hand, and the senior Shigeki leaned forward.

"Everyone, we've been at this for a while. Before we dig any further into the particulars of the proposal, how about we take a fifteen-minute refresher? Any objections?"

"None here," Schröder said. "I was about to suggest the same."

"Good. Then I'll see everyone back here in fifteen."

Chairs shuffled, and staff members rose from both sides of the table. Jonas engaged a privacy filter and opened the call request. An abstraction of Tyrel's office materialized around him, with him seated in front of her desk.

"Ah, Jonas." Tyrel smiled at him. "That was quick. Hope I'm not interrupting anything too important."

"Oh, it's nothing." Jonas returned the smile. "We were just discussing whether or not we should build a joint DTI–Gordian base in the transverse."

Tyrel blinked as the words sank in. "Really?"

"Yeah."

"Wow."

"Yeah. Took me by surprise, too."

"You think we'll do it?"

"Hard to say," Jonas replied honestly.

Despite the heavier overlap between Gordian Division and the DTI, Jonas found himself working with Tyrel quite often as part of his efforts to improve relations between the two superpowers. And while their working relationship had started out on the icy side, it'd warmed considerably over the past three months.

He'd been a frequent visitor to her office, both physically and in the abstract, though he really wished she'd take down that damned eyeball on her curio shelf. The creepy thing followed him around the room! He'd mentioned the ghastly organ to her once, but for some reason, his revulsion to the eyeball had pleased her.

"There are a lot of issues to sort out between here and there," Jonas continued. "Anyway, you've got me for the next fifteen minutes."

"Right." Tyrel copied a case file over to him, and he opened it. "There's been an incident at the Weltall Tournament. One of your citizens received a threatening message of unknown origin."

"Elena Sako..." Jonas skimmed the documentation. "What sort of message?"

"It was a printed copy of her own severed head along with the phrase 'leave or die' written in blood."

"Damn!" Jonas cringed. "What a way to welcome a guest."

"My thoughts exactly. I think we can both agree an Admin citizen receiving threats while in SysGov is a situation that must be handled with care, given the potential for missteps of a... diplomatic nature."

"Yes, thank you for bringing this to me. I assume your division will look into this."

"Actually, that's what I need to talk to you about," Tyrel said. "State troopers are already on site, but they're being denied access to the victim and her room."

"Denied? By whom?"

"Her DTI security detail."

"Oh."

Shit, Jonas thought.

In hindsight, he should have seen this coming. DTI agents were, on average, a self-reliant sort because few in the Admin had the necessary skill set to work in such a specialized environment. They were used to getting the job done themselves, and so when foreign cops of an unknown quality came up and said *they* would handle a threat against someone under the agents' protection, Jonas could understand if those same agents got a little... touchy.

"I was hoping you could help me out with this," Tyrel added.

"Yes, certainly." Jonas sat up a little straighter. "I can talk to the security detail's team leader and stress the need for cooperation.

However, any investigation will need a point of command. Someone to take the lead. Otherwise, our people will be stepping all over each other, and we won't get *anything* done." He looked up at her. "Any thoughts on how you'd like us to proceed?"

"A few." Tyrel summoned a personnel profile. "May I present Senior Detective Matthew Graves. You're familiar with Sherlock Holmes, I take it?"

"Of course. Those stories were written before our timelines diverged."

"Then let me be blunt. Graves is better."

"Indeed?"

"It's safe to say you'll find no better detective in the entire solar system. Perhaps even in *both* our solar systems."

"That's quite a claim." Jonas flashed a half-smile at her. "We have some very talented investigators ourselves, you know."

"Perhaps, but I can have Graves on Luna in less than two hours."

"Hmm." Jonas stroked his chin.

"Thoughts?"

"I don't know. I'm sure he's quite capable, but I'm not sold on the idea."

"You would prefer someone from the DTI to take the lead instead?"

"That's right," Jonas confessed, "though perhaps not for the reasons you're thinking. If your man Graves failed and Sako was murdered, SysPol would be blamed for the failure, whether fairly or not, which could have repercussions for the Million Handshake Initiative and beyond."

"Unlikely."

"But not impossible." He held up a finger. "However, if the investigation is headed by the DTI, and we fail to protect our own citizen, well"—he shrugged—"that's our own fault. SysPol would be blameless."

"You're looking for ways to keep political fallout to a minimum, should the worst happen."

"Always."

"I appreciate the thought, but I have doubts about handing the reins over to a DTI agent. My detectives are far better equipped to lead an investigation on SysGov soil. Your agents would need too much time to get up to speed."

"True, but..." Jonas trailed off, and his brow creased as a thought occurred to him. Was the perfect compromise already on its way?

"Something on your mind?" Tyrel asked.

"One moment." He opened his mail archive, then performed a quick search until he found the RSVPs. He checked the dates and nodded. Yes, sure enough, *both* of them were about to arrive at the Crimson Flower.

"What if," Jonas began delicately, "we could each have what we want?"

He presented the RSVPs to her.

"Detective Cho and Agent Cantrell?" Tyrel asked doubtfully. "But they're all the way out at Saturn."

"Actually, they're not. They're about to land on Luna. I arranged their flights myself."

"They *are*?" Tyrel shook her head in bewilderment. "You arranged this? Don't tell me you somehow *predicted* the need for joint law enforcement at this event!"

"Vesna, please!" Jonas chuckled. "As much as I appreciate it when you assume I'm playing seven-dimensional chess and thinking twelve moves ahead of everyone else"—he gestured to the RSVPs—"this is nothing more than a happy coincidence. I invited them to the tournament because I thought it'd be good PR." He leaned back. "So, what do you think?"

"I don't know. I can see how Cantrell's position in the DTI would help, but that still leaves Cho out of the loop."

"A problem with an obvious solution," Jonas said. "We can give the detective temporary authority as a DTI investigator, much the same way your division granted Cantrell junior detective status."

"That...could work," Tyrel said guardedly.

"What do you think?"

"Well, I'm somewhat hesitant to assign a case this high profile to a detective with Cho's level of experience, but I'll admit this feels like a workable solution. Plus, he's the only detective I have with experience working with Admin personnel." She nodded after a thoughtful pause. "All right. I'm on board with this. We'll do it your way."

"Excellent. I'll make sure Cho is granted the necessary authority. And, if you don't mind, I'll also dispatch *Pathfinder-Prime* to Luna as well."

"What for?"

"To bolster the size of the security detail at the tournament. I want to make it clear SysPol is allowing us to do everything we can to protect our own citizens, and this is an obvious, visible way to show that cooperation. Also, with most of our senior staff over here for meetings this week, the one chronoport under my command is redundant. At least for the short term. Might as well put it to work."

"Good idea."

"Well, if you'll excuse me, I'm going to see if I can take care of this before the meeting starts up again."

"Go ahead. And Jonas? Thanks."

"Any time."

He closed out the call. The abstraction of Tyrel's office vanished, and the reality of the executive conference room reappeared to his senses. Most of the seats around the table were still empty, but the one person he needed to speak with had returned.

"Hey, Kloss," Jonas called out with a wry smile.

Under-Director of Espionage Dahvid Kloss turned to face him. His unruly dark hair and wrinkled clothes gave the impression of someone who'd overslept in his uniform and had to rush into work the next morning without so much as combing his hair, but the intense concentration in his dark eyes told a very different story.

"Yes?" Kloss asked.

"I need a favor."

"No."

"Oh, come on! You don't even know what I'm after!"

"I don't need to. There's this thing called 'past experience' I can rely on."

"This time might be different."

"I seriously doubt that."

"Come on, Kloss. It's important."

"Fine." Kloss rose with a huff, walked over, and dropped into the seat next to Jonas. "What do you need?"

Jonas put a hand on his shoulder, and their PINs integrated.

"I need you to make a SysPol detective one of your investigators."

"Oh, is that all?" Kloss shook his head. "No."

"Come on. I'm being serious here."

"So am I. I can't make a foreign citizen an investigator! Why would you even suggest such a thing?"

"Because there's a situation brewing over on Luna, and I'm confident this will defuse it."

Jonas did his best to rapidly summarize the problem. It took less than a minute.

"Okay, I can see why you want this," Kloss admitted, "but I can't make just anyone an investigator. Those posts come with strict requirements, and even if he wasn't a foreigner, this Cho person doesn't have enough experience at the DTI. Any experience even!"

"Then make up a new rank." Jonas swirled his hand through the air. "Name it, I don't know, a 'probationary junior investigator' or something. Doesn't matter what it's called. Just so long as it grants him the legal authority to question Admin citizens and the like."

"It's not that simple."

"It is, and you know it."

"Do you have any idea how many rules I need to bend to pull this off?"

"Not really, and I honestly don't care. What I do need is for you to suck it up and make us a new rank so I can give it to Cho. Someone is threatening to kill one of our citizens over here, and we need to make sure the situation is handled properly. You got that?"

Kloss disconnected from the closed-circuit chat and ran rough fingers back through his hair.

"Well?" Jonas pressed.

Kloss let out a long, frustrated sigh.

"I'm going to regret this, aren't I?"

CHAPTER SIX

"ATTENTION ALL GUESTS. THE *BETELGEUSE* HAS FINISHED DOCKING procedures with the New Nectaris City spaceport, Polaris Traveler branch. Local time is nine hundred fifty-one. Skies are clear and wind velocity is negligible. The external temperature is a balmy twenty-nine degrees Celsius with a high today of thirty-three. Please dress appropriately if venturing outdoors."

"Already got that covered." Isaac grinned at the others. He walked over in a pair of flip-flops and adjusted his wide-brimmed hat. He wore a cloud gray shirt over a pair of black swim trunks with purple glowing runes down one side.

"Oh no," Susan gasped.

"What's wrong?" Nina asked.

Isaac stopped next to the two women near the midpoint of the three-level boarding tunnel. Other passengers hurried past them, though some stole glances at his companions. The two had chosen bikinis for their beach excursion, with Nina in a red-and-white polka dot number and Susan wearing black with a sarong covered in animated wisps of smoke.

"I just realized something," Susan answered. "Don't we need to be careful when going outdoors? And by we, I mean the two of you. The extreme temperatures won't bother me."

"I'd hardly call thirty-three extreme," Isaac said. "Maybe a little toasty for my liking, but we *are* going to the beach."

"Yeah, but what about later in the day? Won't it get unbearably hot?"

"Not unless the forecast is way off."

"No. Not later today, Earth time. I mean later today, Luna time."

"What?"

Nina and Isaac exchanged confused looks.

"I'm sorry," Isaac said to Susan. "You've completely lost me."

"What I mean is Luna has month-long days. So that beach is going to get fried or frozen depending on where the sun is. Are we sure we're visiting it during the right window?"

"What are you talking about? A day is a day, not a month."

"Not on Luna it's not."

"Where did you get that idea?"

Cephalie popped into existence on Susan's shoulder, dressed in an old-fashioned, striped bathing suit. She held up a sign that read REMEMBER YOUR HISTORY CLASSES!

"My history..." Isaac snapped his fingers. "Oh! I remember now. Luna used to have longer days."

"It...used to?" Susan asked, her eyes growing wider.

"That's right. But now Luna and Earth share the same day and night cycle."

"What? Are you saying you people...changed the angular momentum of Earth's moon?"

"Of course we did," Isaac said matter-of-factly. "As you noted, who wants to get cooked during extra-long days? Kind of defeats the point of terraforming the place."

"When did this happen?" Nina asked.

"During the whole terraforming process, I believe."

"Ah. Makes sense."

"*How?*" Susan asked, clearly struggling with this latest revelation of SysGov technical mastery.

"Oh, let me think." Isaac crossed his arms and bowed his head. "Weren't there these big mirrors involved?"

"You're asking me?" Nina replied.

"Ah yes. Graviton reflectors. That's the ticket. Massive graviton reflectors. They work on a principle similar to graviton thrusters, but since they're reflecting gravitons shed off a stellar body, they don't require much in the way of a power source."

"And that sped up Luna's rotation?" Susan asked.

"Eventually. The whole process took decades."

"A century and a half," Cephalie corrected.

"Right. What she said."

"Huh." Susan shook her head.

"All I'm hearing is our beach trip is still a go." Nina thrust her arm forward. "Come on! No dawdling!"

The trio headed down the boarding tunnel toward the counter-grav tubes at the far end. Virtual arrows highlighted the path to their car rental.

Cephalie appeared on Isaac's shoulder and jabbed him in the neck with her cane. Even though she was an abstraction, his virtual sense of touch communicated the poke to his brain.

He took a weary breath, then glanced over at her.

<What am I doing wrong this time?> he asked privately.

<Just so you know, Susan stressed over what to wear today.>

<I suppose that makes sense. Honestly, I'm surprised she didn't want to go swimming in her Peacekeeper blues. She seems to wear her uniform everywhere.>

<Well, not to the beach, she won't. She even asked Nina for advice on picking out her swimsuit.>

<That would explain the bikini, then,> Isaac replied with a frown. <I was wondering about that. Couldn't see Susan picking something that revealing all on her own.>

<Don't you think she looks nice in it?>

<Of course. And your point is...what exactly?>

<That you should give her a compliment, you big dummy!> Cephalie thwacked his earlobe with her cane.

<Fine.>

Isaac's pace had slowed while he spoke to Cephalie, placing him a few strides behind the two women, and granting him a view of the abstract art on Susan's back—a depiction of a woman in flowing white robes with a crowned skull for a head.

He quickened his pace and came alongside her, then cleared his throat.

"Susan?"

"Yes?"

"You look nice. That swimsuit...suits you."

Good grief! he thought. *I'm so bad at this.*

"Oh." She paused for a moment, as if unsure how to respond, then flashed a friendly smile. "Thank you. Yours suits you, too."

The two nodded to each other, perhaps waiting for the other

to say something else. But then, each sensing the conversation had reached its terminus, they both turned away at the same time.

Isaac glanced over at Cephalie, who rose from his shoulder and started clapping, the sound only audible to Isaac. The clapping grew louder, multiplying into what resembled an entire theater rising to its feet in a thunderous standing ovation.

Isaac rolled his eyes.

He appreciated what he thought his IC was trying to do, but the truth was he was already in a relationship with Susan. A *professional* relationship, and it was abundantly clear to him that's all it would amount to, regardless of any inclination he might (or might not) have in other directions.

Certainly, Susan was an attractive young woman, and not just physically, though there was that. It was hard not to notice how the low Lunar gravity made parts of her more...buoyant, especially in that bikini.

But beyond basic physical attraction, she'd earned his respect for both her work ethic and her knack for presenting out-of-the-box approaches to problems, even if her solutions leaned a bit deeper into the use-of-force category than he would have preferred. On top of that, she was almost completely unflappable under pressure and never hesitated when decisive action was necessary, a trait which had already saved his life.

But it was clear to him she was laser-focused on her career, to the exclusion of all else. That was a personal choice of hers he both understood and appreciated since it resembled his own path to becoming a SysPol detective, and as her colleague, he had no desire to complicate both their lives. He respected her too much to do otherwise.

It wouldn't work out, anyway, he told himself.

They took a grav tube down to the car rentals where automated vehicles sat in neat rows along the wide underground street, waiting for their passengers with open gull wing doors. They followed virtual markers to their rental and had almost reached it when a high-priority alert appeared in his virtual senses.

He and Susan stopped walking at the same time while Nina continued on for a few paces before turning back.

"What's wrong?" she asked.

"Work." Isaac opened the alert. He read through it, his face growing dark. "Cephalie?"

"Yes?" she asked, appearing on his shoulder once more.

"Where's our luggage?"

"Somewhere in the spaceport's logistical center. Why?"

"Can we get to it?"

"I don't think so. Not easily, anyway. I set it up so everyone's luggage would be delivered to the hotel while you were at the beach, remember?"

"Yes," he said with a frown. "I remember."

"What's going on?" Nina asked again.

"Here." Susan removed the privacy filter from her copy. "Take a look for yourself."

"Direct orders from *Commissioner Tyrel!*" Nina exclaimed.

"So it would seem." Isaac cleared his throat. "Susan and I are to head directly and with all possible haste to the Crimson Flower where we will take charge of the unfolding situation. One of the Admin players, Miss Elena Sako, has received a death threat, and DTI security and LSP are butting heads on how to deal with it."

"Sounds like this could get worse any number of ways," Susan remarked.

"Yes, which is why we're taking the rental and heading straight over," Isaac said.

"What?" Susan gestured to her bikini and sarong. "Like this?"

"I'd prefer not to, but we have our orders direct from the commissioner."

"Do you honestly intend to head there in a pair of flip-flops?" Nina asked.

"My dignity will survive." Isaac frowned again. "Somehow. Cephalie?"

"Yeah?"

"Do what you can to expedite our luggage. If it takes too long, head for the nearest LSP station and print out uniforms for us. Also, a sidearm for Susan and a LENS for yourself," he added, referring to a SysPol detective's standard issue Lawful Enforcement and Neutralization System. "Go now."

"Got it." She gave him a quick wave then vanished.

"Nina, I know you're technically on vacation, but—"

"Say no more." She held up both hands. "I'll grab a taxi and pay LSP a visit on the way to the Crimson Flower. Once I'm uniformed and droned up, I'll join you at the crime scene. Raviv can refund my vacation days later."

"Thanks. I appreciate it."

Nina headed over to a different lane of waiting cars and found an empty taxi to board.

"You see the part where they temporarily made you a DTI investigator?" Susan asked.

"Yes, but I'm not sure what that means."

"It means when you tell our agents to jump, they say *ribbit* and leap into the air. Also, it should cut through any legal red tape on the Admin side when it comes to pursuing this case."

"Sounds useful." He gestured into the rental car. "After you."

The automated rental car pulled up to the Crimson Flower, which rose from the forested slopes that had once been a crater wall. The elaborate structure resembled a cross between a sprawling fantasy castle and a brilliantly red flower. A narrow cylindrical base rose upward before blooming into seven massive, angled structures shaped like flower petals, each attached "precariously" to the base by thin joins, made possible via a combination of advanced material sciences and Luna's low gravity, which gave the entire complex a delicate beauty. A narrow tower rose from where the petals met, and a translucent, domed stadium at its apex formed the Crimson Flower's pistil.

"Wow," Susan breathed, craning her neck as she gazed out the window. "It's bigger than I thought it'd be. How many people are staying here right now?"

"About a hundred thousand, give or take, but that's just for the hotels. The Crimson Flower also includes office space for numerous companies as well as a variety of entertainment venues, including the stadium at the top, and it's large enough to rate its own LSP precinct, located at the base of the pistil."

"Which part are we headed for?" Susan asked.

"The Gentle Rain Hotel in Petal Four. That one." Isaac pointed out the window. "A whole floor plus that petal's hangar have been set aside for Admin use."

The rental car followed a high-speed boulevard toward the base of the Crimson Flower, then veered away from the main flow of traffic and took an off-ramp, leading them to a circular street around the base.

"What's that?" Susan asked. "See the commotion up ahead?"

"Yeah, I see it," Isaac said, noting the mass of hundreds of people standing in the street, blocking easy access to the Crimson Flower's main ground entrance. "Vehicle, let us off here."

"Stopping," said the car's nonsentient program.

The rental car slowed down and pulled onto the curb. The door opened, and Isaac and Susan climbed out.

"Vehicle, find a parking space and shut down."

"Destination set. Departing."

The rental car dropped its gull wing doors and drove away, turning down a ramp that Isaac presumed led to the underground garage complex. The two detectives took a sidewalk over toward the entrance, and Isaac used their approach to scope out the crowd.

A few hundred people in black chanted and shouted at a line of state troopers while within the confines of a designated protest zone, delineated with virtual dashed lines on the ground. The protesters didn't seem to be engaged in anything beyond a few petty crimes, judging by the smart graffiti on the nearby sidewalks, barriers, and walls, and LSP drones were already cleaning up the most obscene examples of the crowd's "artistic expression."

Virtual signs floated over the crowd with phrases like REMEMBER THE DYNASTY! and TRADE YOUR HUBRIS FOR HUMILITY! Almost everyone in the crowd wore funeral black. Even their scarves, normally a vibrant way to express one's personal sense of SysGov fashion, were uniformly a static black. Others had eschewed scarves entirely, opting for headbands, hoods, and masks. The crowd trended toward the young and organic, if lack of synthoid skin variety was any indication.

A tall silhouette stood on a counter-grav platform at the head of the crowd, and his voice boomed over Isaac's shared virtual senses.

"What do we want?" shouted the leader.

"THE ADMIN TO LEAVE!" replied the crowd.

"When do we want it?"

"NOW!"

Isaac took them along a wide, arcing route around the crowd.

"Who are they?" Susan asked him after switching to SysPol security chat. His wetware translated her words via a shared key, but anyone else would only hear gibberish.

"LAST," he answered in security chat. "The League Against Stupid Time and Transdimensional Travel."

"That's quite a name."

"They changed it recently, after transdimensional flight was discovered. Used to be the League Against Stupid Time Travel. They're not exactly fans of the Admin."

"Yeah, I'm getting that." Susan snapped one of her bikini straps. "Guess we lucked out not being in uniform."

"I suppose so."

"Think one of these idiots is behind the death threat?"

"Let's not be hasty. We need to speak with LSP and DTI security first."

"Of course."

Isaac stepped up to one of several doorways leading into the Crimson Flower. Abstract signs alerted him that only hotel and event guests or local employees were permitted to enter. Isaac transmitted a copy of his tournament event pass, and the prog-steel doors split open.

✧　　✧　　✧

The grav tube dropped Isaac and Susan off in a circular transfer station with lush green carpeting and a crystalline fountain in the center. Half a dozen Lunar state troopers stood around the place, some with arms crossed and unhappy expressions on their faces. One of the troopers saw them arrive. He held up a hand and hurried over.

"I'm sorry, but this area is off-limits. You'll need to head back to the main concourse."

"This should clear up matters." Isaac transmitted his SysPol badge.

"You—" The trooper paused and summoned the badge over his hand. He frowned at it, then looked up at Isaac, then glanced to Susan, then studied the badge again, then back to Susan, then the badge once more before he turned over a shoulder. "Uhh, sir?"

A senior trooper with a reddish buzz under his cap and lieutenant bars on his shoulders walked over.

"What's going on?" he demanded. "Trooper, get these civilians out of here!"

"That's just it, sir. They're not civilians."

"What do you mean they're—" The lieutenant paused, his eye drawn to the SysPol badge hovering over the trooper's hand and all the power that symbol conveyed. He then took in their barely dressed status, his eyes lingering slightly longer on Susan. "The two of you are our support from SysPol?"

"That's correct," Isaac said.

"The *hell*?"

"We were diverted on short notice," Isaac explained. "Our uniforms and equipment should catch up with us shortly."

"I should hope so!"

"In the meantime, I need to speak with Lieutenant Cameron Lotz. Would you kindly direct us to him?"

"Easy. You're looking at him."

"Good." He placed a hand to his chest. "I'm Detective Isaac Cho, and this is my deputy, Agent Susan Cantrell."

"Agent?" Lotz asked.

"Of the Department of Temporal Investigation."

Lotz pointed. "She's with the *Admin*?"

"I am," Susan replied evenly.

"She's also a part of the officer exchange program and holds the rank of deputy detective within SysPol. Do you have a problem with this, Lieutenant?"

"What?" Lotz shook his head. "Uhh, no, of course not. Just surprised. I didn't expect SysPol to respond so quickly." He let out a soft chuckle. "Or to show up in swimwear and flip-flops."

"A situation which will be remedied shortly," Isaac assured him. "Now, Lieutenant, I've read your report, but I'd appreciate hearing your take on the current situation."

"That'll be easy, because it hasn't changed. DTI security still won't let us anywhere near the victim's room or the victim herself. Until we have one or the other, we're at a standstill."

"Then let's see if we can't resolve the impasse. Which way to Miss Sako's room?"

"Down this hall on the right-hand side." Lotz pointed. "But the Admin agents aren't going to let you through."

"We'll see about that. Lieutenant, would you mind accompanying us?"

"Not at all."

The three of them headed down the curving hall until a Wolverine drone blocked their path.

"You have entered an exclusionary zone," warned the drone. "Move back or I will be forced to subdue you."

"You can ignore the dumb thing," Lotz said. "It won't actually attack."

"Ten, nine, eight."

Isaac transmitted his new DTI investigator badge.

"Sev..."

Lotz gave the drone a confused look. "Why'd it stop counting?"

"Drone, stand aside," Isaac ordered.

The drone sidestepped out of their way.

"The *hell*?" Lotz breathed.

Interesting, Isaac thought to himself. *That actually worked.*

"It seems we may proceed," he said, then continued down the corridor.

"What just happened?" Lotz asked, stealing a glance back at the motionless drone.

"Exactly what it looked like," Isaac explained. "The Admin drone recognized our authority in this situation." He flashed a wry grin at Lotz. "Flip-flops or no."

"But how?"

A big, gray-skinned, yellow-eyed synthoid saw them coming and hurried over.

"Stop!" he barked.

Isaac sent his investigator badge.

The synthoid stopped in his tracks. He opened the badge over his palm, scrutinized it for long seconds, then looked Isaac over.

"In flip-flops?"

"We were diverted on short notice," Isaac explained again.

"Huh." The synthoid studied the file once more, then murmured to himself, "Approved by Director Shigeki? Doesn't get much more official than that."

He closed the file then clasped his hands behind his back and stood up straight.

"Sir!" he snapped with rigid formality. "How may I be of assistance?"

"The *hell*?"

The synthoid's eyes caught sight of Susan, and his mouth cracked open in surprise.

"Agent Cantrell?" he asked, his expression warming in her presence.

"Agent Pérez," she replied with a slim smile.

"You two know each other?" Isaac asked.

"We do," Susan said, then shrugged. "It's a long story. Perhaps later?"

"Of course." Isaac turned back to Pérez. "Agent, I'll be taking the lead of this investigation. Do you have any problems with this?"

"None at all."

"What is going *on* here?" Lotz asked. "Did I miss something? What kind of magic are you working?"

"The kind that comes with a badge," Isaac replied.

"Sir," Pérez began, "do you have any orders for me and my team?"

"A SysPol forensics specialist is on her way. I'd like your team to stand aside and grant her and her drones full access to the crime scene. While I'm sure your team is quite capable, our specialists have substantially more experience with SysGov infosystems, such as the printer in question. Do you have any concerns with this approach?"

"No, sir. I'll take care of that right now." Pérez opened a comm window and transmitted a quick text message. A few moments later, a pair of synthoids stepped out of what Isaac presumed to be Elena Sako's hotel room. "Done."

"Thank you, Agent." Isaac turned to Lotz.

"The *hell*?"

"Lieutenant, the matter of competing jurisdictions has been resolved, at least for the moment. As you heard, a SysPol specialist will be granted access to the crime scene. I believe that addresses the immediate concerns voiced in your support request. Wouldn't you agree?"

"I—well, yes." He rubbed the back of his neck with a perplexed expression on his face. "Yes, you seem to have everything moving in the right direction. *Somehow.*"

"Then I believe your team is clear to stand down from this case. We will, of course, keep you informed of our progress and will let you know if we require any additional support. Do you see any issues with this course of action?"

"Uhh, no. No, that's, uhh, quite all right."

"Then, Lieutenant, I thank you for your time and for bringing this issue to SysPol's attention. We'll take it from here."

"Sure thing. No problem."

Lotz backed away, swinging his arms aimlessly. He took one last look at the detectives in their swimwear, then frowned and headed back the way they came. Shortly after he disappeared around the bend, Isaac heard a faint:

"The *hell*?"

"We're using the Cutlass as our command center for tournament security," Pérez explained, leading them into the Petal Four hangar after two synthoids posted at the entrance finished checking their documentation.

Isaac was almost disappointed they didn't react to his flip-flops, but he assumed Pérez had alerted his team of what to expect from the new arrivals.

Chronoport *Defender-Prime* sat offset to one side with enough room for two or three more within the spacious, enclosed hangar. Modular weapon and equipment pods hung from its thick delta wing, and the long spike of its chronoton impeller extended out the rear. A wide ramp led up into the craft's belly, while a smaller ramp connected to one of its modular pods.

Most of the pods were gun or missile launcher mounts, but this pod was a thick wedge with a pair of ports for its own thruster and the ramp leading to a hollow interior.

"The Cutlass?" Isaac asked.

"A Type-6 drone hangar," Susan explained. "Can also detach from the chronoport to serve as a troo—" She made a show of unnecessarily clearing her throat. "A *personnel* transport."

The pod interior was brightly lit with four inert Wolverines docked into charging stations along one wall. Two synthoids sat at what appeared to be the pilot and copilot positions under different circumstances, their eyes and hands dancing across unseen displays and controls.

"I don't seem to be able to access the local infostructure," Isaac remarked.

"Right. Give us a moment," Pérez said. "We'll fix that for you."

He stepped over to the two other agents and leaned down to speak into one of their ears. The agent nodded and—from Isaac's perspective—mimed opening a window and fiddling with the controls. A few moments passed, and the room erupted with densely packed virtual screens showing static-position surveillance video, direct feeds from the eyes of security personnel, and the results from algorithmic monitoring software.

Nothing sentient, though, if Isaac was to hazard a guess.

I wonder if any of them will have issues with Cephalie, he thought.

"How's it look now, sir?" Pérez asked.

"That'll do. Thank you."

Pérez nodded and rejoined them.

"It's good to see you, Miguel," Susan said, speaking less formally than when they were in the presence of the LSP lieutenant.

"Likewise." He cracked a thin smile.

"Should I assume the two of you have worked together in the past?" Isaac asked.

"Oh, yes!" Susan turned to him. "Miguel was my mentor when I joined STAND," she added, referring to the Admin's Special Training And Nonorganic Deployment command. "We served together during my first few years in the DTI."

"A period," Pérez added, "in which she went from a very green rookie to surpassing this grizzled, old veteran in many ways."

"Well..." Susan smiled bashfully. "I wouldn't go *that* far."

"That said, I seem to recall a few growing pains along the way. Remember the Doctor Quiet case, where you blew up—"

Susan made a quick cutoff gesture across her throat.

Isaac glanced over to her and raised an inquisitive eyebrow. She smiled and shrugged back at him.

"Right," Pérez said. "Perhaps we can reminisce another time."

"Agent Pérez," Isaac said. "I'd like you to start by providing your take on events so far."

"Certainly, sir, though there's honestly not much to tell. Elly Sako reported receiving a death threat earlier this morning in the form of a fake severed head, and we've been unable to ascertain who sent it or how." He swept an arm across the arrayed virtual screens. "As you can see, we maintain full surveillance coverage across the occupied sections of this hotel floor as well as the path between our three player suites and the hangar."

"Do you monitor the suite interiors?"

"No, sir. We don't intrude further than the hallway outside their rooms."

"Has all that surveillance picked up anything?"

"Unfortunately not, though we cannot rule out infiltration of her room by a sophisticated drone or some form of abstract intrusion."

"Did anything unusual happen prior to Sako reporting the death threat?"

"Just one thing." Pérez paused with a grimace. "She did have a rather heated argument with GW Lacan."

"Who's he?"

"Another one of our finalists."

"And what was the nature of their argument?"

"It revolved around Miss Sako having sexual relations with another man. Lacan didn't take it well."

Isaac and Susan exchanged a brief glance to each other.

"He's already denied any involvement," Pérez added.

"You've spoken with him?"

"I have. He was the last person to speak with Miss Sako, and he was visibly upset with her. It seemed a logical place to start."

"Did you speak with anyone else?"

"Besides Sako and Lacan? No."

"Anything else noteworthy about their argument or your interviews with the players?"

"Nothing comes to mind."

"Do you have a surveillance recording of their argument?"

"We do." He turned back to the seated synthoids. "Agent Arlot?"

"I heard, sir. One moment." The agent brought up a fixed-position angle of the two players standing near a hotel suite doorway. He selected a timestamp just before Sako opened her door, fast forwarded to when Lacan left, then selected the ending timestamp. He presented the new file to Isaac. "Here you are, sir."

"Thank you." Isaac transmitted the files to a new Themis case folder. "How long after their argument did Sako report the death threat?"

"Not long. Less than ten minutes. We can pull up the exact timestamps, if you like."

"Please do. That'll help us establish a definitive timeline."

Pérez nodded to Arlot, who began trawling through the surveillance video again.

"How would you characterize Sako's emotional state when she reported the threat?"

"Shocked and rattled," Pérez said. "Her response struck me as genuine, if that's what you're asking."

"It was."

"What are you thinking?" Susan asked.

"Just checking some of the basics," Isaac said. "It's not unheard of for a celebrity to fake death threats like this for any number of reasons. If we can rule it out, then that's one less avenue to chase down. Agent Pérez?"

"Sir?"

"I'd like to interview Miss Sako next." He grimaced, glancing down. "Once our uniforms have arrived."

"Of course, sir. I'll arrange it."

"Also, we'll need to perform a forensic analysis on the severed head. Where is it?"

"We haven't moved it yet. It's still in the printer where she found it."

"Then I'll leave its handling to our specialist."

"Also, there is one other matter I feel I should make sure you're aware of," Pérez said. "A second chronoport has been dispatched to the Crimson Flower. It should be here in about four hours. I understand they're being sent to bulk up the player security."

"I see. That seems like a reasonable precaution, given what we currently know." An alert blinked in his virtual sight, and he opened it. "Ah, good. Cephalie stopped by the local station—the CFPD First—and already has some new uniforms for us. She's still waiting on the more complicated gear like her LENS, but uniforms are good enough for starters. We should head there next."

"Mind if I stick around for a few minutes?" Susan asked. "It's been months since Miguel and I spoke."

"Not at all, but don't take too long. I'll see you at the station."

❖   ❖   ❖

"It's been a while, hasn't it?" Pérez put a hand on her shoulder and entered into a closed-circuit chat. "I don't think we've talked since before the Dynasty Crisis."

"Yeah, that sounds about right," Susan said.

"Were you involved in the assault?"

"No, and I consider myself fortunate to have missed that one, given how many people we lost." She let out a slow, sad sigh. "I volunteered to go with the fleet but didn't get picked."

"Almost all of STAND did," Pérez noted, "but they only took so many. Which made sense, I suppose. There was always the chance of a boarding action, but our superiors considered it remote, and STAND numbers in the fleet reflected that."

"Were you there?"

"Yeah," he said, and something struck her as haunted in his tone. "Yeah, I saw it. Watched as another Earth got eaten up by...hell, I still haven't got a clue what it was, even after it was explained to me."

"The tear in the Dynasty universe."

"It was like the darkest, most voracious abyss you'd ever laid eyes on, and it drew their Earth in. I never thought I'd see a planet warp like that, become egg-shaped, but"—he shrugged—"that's what happened. A whole planet, with untold billions of stories on it, just... gone. Devoured by out-of-control physics."

"You okay?" Susan asked, a little worried about her friend.

"Yeah, but... changed, you know?" He shook his head. "And tired. The Crisis made me realize I've been doing this shit for a long fucking time, and it's worn me down. I'm *tired* of it all."

"Hey." She nudged him in the chest. "You're not going to join the Last STANDers, are you?"

The customary STAND service contract was for a twenty-year term, with each follow-up contract lasting ten years, and while STAND retention was exceedingly high, there were those among the elite force who grew weary of their synthetic existence while also having no desire to return to civilian life. Some STANDs opted for self-deletion, which was an accepted way for a STAND to exit service and would normally be preceded by a farewell ceremony and celebration given in their honor by their closest friends and comrades. However, that was sometimes too passive for the kind of people who signed up as STANDS, and for those individuals, there were the "Last STANDers."

The Last STANDers were an informal group within STAND where individuals actively request assignments with the lowest chances of survival, basically choosing to commit suicide through combat. Although the practice was well known amongst the Peacekeeper hierarchy, it was neither encouraged nor discouraged. It was *accepted* and generally considered an effective way for STANDs to self-regulate their own ranks and to weed out individuals who might be edging toward instability.

"Oh, hell no!" Pérez assured her, laughing. "There's plenty of fight still left in me, you'll see. Not only am I not going anywhere, but I'm going to have your back through whatever this mess is. You deserve nothing less from me."

"All right." She smiled at him. "Good to hear."

"Hey, Susan." He clapped her on the shoulder. "It's great seeing you again. It really is."

"Good to see you too. You take care of yourself, all right?"

CHAPTER SEVEN

THE PROG-STEEL DOOR SPLIT OPEN, AND ISAAC AND SUSAN STEPPED into the conference room, once again in their uniforms, Isaac in the dark blue of SysPol and Susan in the lighter blue of a Peacekeeper. He didn't have a LENS yet, and Cephalie was still at the CFPD station, but he felt *considerably* more comfortable with just the uniform. It also helped that Nina had arrived and had begun her work on the problematic food printer.

Elly Sako sat at one end of a long, rectangular table made of smoked glass, arms hugging her chest as if she were cold. She looked up as they entered, and Isaac noted her eyes: slightly reddened as if she'd been crying, but still sharp and in control. She wore a tight pink shirt and matching skirt while a pair of abstract angel wings floated behind her back.

He would have preferred to conduct this interview in a setting comfortable for the victim, but she couldn't return to her hotel room yet, and even if she could, that's where she'd found the severed head.

A neutral location would have to do.

"Hello, Miss Sako," Isaac said. "I'm Detective Cho, and this is Agent Cantrell. Thank you for agreeing to speak with us."

"Oh, it's no trouble." She chuckled without humor. "It's been that kind of day, you know?"

"Of course." Isaac took the seat near the corner, diagonal from her, and Susan sat down next to him. "Let's start with the threat itself. Do you have any idea who might have sent it?"

"No." She shook her head. "Could be anyone, though."

"Why do you say that?"

"Because I'm Lunarian and I'm from the Admin."

"Why do you believe that could lead to a broad list of suspects?"

"Well, let's see here." She put an elbow on the table and leaned forward. "I'm a citizen of the Admin, so I'm already on some people's shit list. And yeah, I've seen those League protesters outside. Our ActionStream hosts tried to keep a lid on it, but they *clearly* didn't pay off the right people in your government. Those protests were all over the news."

"Our news outlets aren't government controlled."

"Oh." She backed away and blinked. "Really? They're not?"

"No."

"I guess that explains a lot, then." She shrugged as if the revelation didn't matter. "Anyway, you can see the protesters as clearly as I can. What a bunch of idiots, right? We're here to compete, but they're acting like we intend to, I don't know"—she threw up her hands in frustration—"eat their babies, or some shit like that."

"You believe the protesters could be the source of the threat?"

"Look at it this way. They *definitely* want me to leave."

"Have you had any confrontations with League protesters?"

"No, but they're not being let onto the premises, as far as I've seen, so they haven't had the chance."

"Have you received any threatening messages besides the obvious one?"

"No again, but that might be because my mail is going through a DTI 'filter,' if you catch my meaning. They might not be letting me see the disturbing stuff, if there *is* disturbing stuff. You'd have to ask them."

"I see." Isaac opened his case log and made a note to do just that. "Is there anything besides what you've seen on the news that leads you to believe League protesters are threatening you?"

"No, but I'm not accusing them of anything either. I just think they're one of the parties the head *could* have come from. That's all."

"What other parties do you consider suspect?"

"No one specifically. At least on the SysGov side of the transverse.

Those LAST idiots are the loudest bunch, but that doesn't mean there aren't others who silently agree with them. In fact, I think it's obvious there *are* people like that. I haven't been here long, but I get this impression some of you hate us because we're different. Because we're not as sophisticated or enlightened as you, or whatever. We're treated like the weird new neighbor you secretly suspect is a serial killer. A lot of people have already made up their minds about us, even without looking past the surface." She held up a hand and gestured toward him. "No offense."

"None taken," Isaac assured her. "You indicated there's no one else you suspect within SysGov. Does this mean you believe someone within the Admin might be threatening you?"

"Oh, absolutely!"

"Why would that be?"

"Because I'm Lunarian, of course. Admin Lunarian. Not"—she swirled her finger to indicate their surroundings—"the other one." She smiled apologetically. "Sorry. It's weird having to specify that."

"Why would you being from the Admin's Luna matter?"

"Shouldn't that be obvious?" she asked, but then frowned. "Right. Yeah. Guess it wouldn't be for you."

"Again, why would your place of origin matter in this case?"

"The Admin versions of Earth and Luna share something of a troubled history," Susan explained. "The Admin was formed over two centuries ago in response to the Yanluo Massacre, where a rogue AI destroyed most of China, Mongolia, and parts of Russia. Our government's primary purpose is to prevent a similar catastrophe by enforcing a set of technological Restrictions upon the member states. Some governments joined the Admin willingly, but others, such as the Lunar Federation, resisted."

"Then we're talking about some very old, very bad blood between Earth and Luna, correct?" Isaac asked.

"That's right," Susan said. "Luna has resisted attempts to integrate its populace within the greater Admin, and Lunar terrorists are a frequent thorn in our side. While Martian terrorists are often better equipped, the proximity between Earth and Luna makes terror cells like Free Luna the more immediate threat."

"Which all boils down to people hating me because I'm Lunarian," Sako finished.

"Have any members of the DTI disparaged your home in your presence?"

"Not really, no."

"Not really or not at all?"

"Not at all," Sako clarified.

"Are you aware of any of them speaking ill of Luna to others?"

"Again, no. They're a rather stoic bunch, and Pérez keeps them in line." She leaned back in her seat. "Even if they did believe I'm nothing more than a troublemaker from a moon full of troublemakers, they wouldn't be dumb enough to say it out loud. At least not with Pérez in earshot."

"What about the other two players?"

"No, nothing there either." She sighed with a frown. "Not with my background, at least."

"I see." Isaac made a note regarding her Lunar heritage. "Moving on, I'd like to discuss your argument with Lacan."

"Yeah, I thought you might bring that up."

"Please explain what started the argument."

"Yeah, that." Sako slouched a little in her chair and blew out a long breath. "How to put this delicately..."

"Please be as direct as you like."

"Fine." She sat back up. "He was mad because I wasn't putting out."

"Had you engaged in sexual relations with Lacan in the past?"

"*Yes.*" She looked away, avoiding eye contact, visibly uncomfortable with the topic.

"Recently?"

"Yeah. About a week ago."

"Were the two of you in a formal relationship?"

"*No.*"

"Did Lacan believe you two were in a relationship?"

"*Probably.*"

"Why do you say that?"

"Because he used the L-word."

"Love?"

"Yeah, that one."

"Before the argument, did you make it clear to him you were no longer interested in having sex?"

"*Yes.*"

"When did you make this clear to him?"

"On the flight over."

"And how did he take the news?"

"Like an immature little man-baby."

"Did he threaten you on the flight over?"

"No."

"Was the argument outside your room the only time he threatened you?"

"Yeah, but I wouldn't call that a *threat*."

"I believe"—Isaac swiped to a separate sheet of his notes—"that he said he would rip off another man's genitalia and then assault you with it. Is this correct?"

"*Yes.*"

"Why didn't you consider this a threat?"

"Because he was talking nonsense. Just lashing out because his dick was sad." Sako shook her head. "Fucking idiot."

"How long have you known Lacan?"

"About a year."

"How did the two of you meet?"

"We'd run into each other here and there at different events, and we kept in touch while we both traveled, but there was nothing serious until the last Weltall qualifier. Well, the parties *after* the qualifier. We both had a few drinks and hooked up that night."

"Where did the qualifier take place?"

"Byrgius University on Luna. *Our* Luna, obviously."

"What prompted you to stop having sex with him?"

"Well . . ." Sako gazed off to the side, and her face took on an almost dreamlike quality. "I'm seeing this guy."

"Would you please confirm who it is you're seeing?"

"Wong Fei."

"That would be the star SysGov player and, according to some, the tournament favorite."

"Yep. That's him."

"Are you in a relationship with Wong Fei?"

"Yes. Oh, definitely."

"Do you consider it a serious relationship?"

"I . . ." She smiled coyly. "I'd prefer not to answer."

"When did you first meet him?"

"At Byrgius, actually. The SysGov players and some of the ActionStream staff were on hand for the qualifier. They even brought the trophy over with them. Anyway, he came up to me after I won, and we chatted for a while. And I do mean a *while*." She smiled in pleasant reminiscence. "We talked for *hours!*"

"This would be before the parties that night?"

"Yes, that's right."

"What did you talk about?"

"Anything and everything. SysGov. The Admin. The tournament. Games. Ourselves. Our dreams. Our futures. Anything that came to mind, really. It was, I don't know, just so *easy* talking with him."

"Then, if I understand the situation correctly, you were being actively courted by two men at the same time, one from the Admin and one from SysGov, starting shortly after the universal qualifier."

"Yeah, I guess you could say that." She flashed a sly grin. "And, before you ask, yes, I had sex with both of them over the past month."

"Are you sure that was wise?"

"What do you mean?"

"You've admitted to having sexual relations with two men." Isaac sat forward. "Both of which are involved in the same high-profile tournament you're in and are your direct competitors. That suggests to me, at a minimum, the potential for conflicts of interest."

"You're wondering if one or the other was trying to manipulate my feelings? Maybe to gain an edge in the tournament?"

"That's one possibility, yes."

Sako scoffed and rolled her eyes. "Then I don't think you 'get' us gamers."

"How so?"

"Okay, yeah, I've slept with them, but try to look at it from our perspective. We're always on the move, always bouncing from one venue to the next. And between events, we sink most of our waking hours into these games, studying and practicing and refining our craft. Who besides other gamers understands this lifestyle and how lonely it can be? Who else do we see on a regular basis? You think I'd prefer to sleep with *fans*?" She shuddered briefly. "So yeah. Gamers like to hook up with other gamers, and we all know the relationships stop when we're in-game. We *are* professionals, after all."

"But two of them at once?"

"Look, I realize I could have handled that better. I would have broken things off with Lacan sooner, but he's just so *dumb*! He couldn't take a hint!"

"Which is why you made matters clear to him on the flight over."

"Got that right!"

"What are your thoughts on the message itself? Specifically, the 'leave or die' wording."

"Seems obvious to me. Someone wants me out of here and wants it bad enough to send me a severed head." She sat up and planted defiant hands on her armrests. "But I'm not going anywhere, I can tell you that much!"

"Understood." Isaac swiped to the next sheet. "There's just one other matter I'd like to ask you about. Please describe what you were doing between the end of your argument with Lacan and when you discovered the fake head."

"Oh, there's not much really. I placed an order at the food printer, then watched some news while I waited. As soon as the head popped out instead of my meal, I called Pérez."

Which lines up with the timetable we've put together so far, Isaac thought. *A few minutes' delay between the end of her argument and her call to Pérez.*

"Thank you for your time, Miss Sako." Isaac rose from his seat. "That'll be all for now. We'll be in touch if we have any more questions."

✧　　✧　　✧

Susan joined Isaac in the hallway outside the conference room.

"I sort of got the impression you don't buy her story," Susan said, using security chat for privacy. "The way you kept pressing her for information."

"It's not that." Isaac started down the hallway with her. "It's more about us staying alert for something out of place. For example, Raviv and I worked this one celebrity death threat case that burned a lot more time than it should have. The victim, a well-known speedrunner named Jay Jei Story, had us running around in circles before we finally took a hard second look at his testimony, and then we spotted the cracks. So far, I haven't noticed anything like that with Miss Sako, and I'm not sure what the motive would be to fake the threat or how she would even do it, given her lack of experience with SysGov infosystems." He turned to Susan as they walked. "How about you? Any thoughts?"

"Same here. Just wasn't sure we were on the same page so far."

"We are."

"What are our next steps?"

"We'll question Lacan and then Wong Fei."

"It seems unlikely Lacan could have done it," Susan said. "He has the same lack of experience as Sako."

"True, but it's the only lead we have, at least until Nina finishes sifting through that printer. Then, perhaps, we'll have a better sense for where to take this case."

They reached Lacan's hotel suite, and Isaac glanced over the abstract label by the door.

"'Grafton Wisdom Lacan,'" he read. "Rather unusual name."

"Says the guy who recently attended a Markie Flavor-Sparkle concert," Susan said with a half-smile.

"Point taken. Let's see what he has to say."

He palmed the buzzer.

"Are you really an Admin investigator?" Lacan asked pointedly, slouched at an angle against the sofa opposite Isaac and Susan, who had pulled over separate chairs to sit across from him in the middle of the suite's first floor.

"That's correct," Isaac answered. "I've been granted temporary authority as an Admin investigator to pursue this case."

"Is this really necessary? Pérez already questioned me."

"I'm aware of that. Nevertheless, we will be conducting our own investigation."

"And you think I'm involved?"

"Mister Lacan, it would be best if you leave the questioning to me." Isaac opened his virtual notes. "The process will go more smoothly that way."

"Fine," he huffed, slouching even deeper into the sofa's prog-foam. He tossed his braid, which was blonde with a single streak of black running clear through it, off his shoulder.

Do I think Lacan did it? Isaac asked himself as he spent a few moments arranging his notes. *Now that is an interesting question.*

It was hard not to notice Lacan's fidgeting. He did it constantly and his amateurish attempts to avoid notice or mask the fidgeting as normal—often by scratching himself—only served to draw attention to the tic. But that told Isaac very little, beyond the obvious fact Lacan was nervous.

But *why* was he nervous? Was it because he'd committed a crime? Or because he was sitting across from two detectives who—he might assume, correctly—considered him a suspect?

"Hey, can I clear something up?" Lacan asked suddenly.

"You're welcome to make a statement for the record, if you wish."

"Look, I know I said some nasty stuff to Elly." He sat up. "But I didn't mean it, all right? It was all in the heat of the moment. You got that? Heat of the moment."

Isaac glanced to Susan and spoke to her in security chat.

"I'm getting the impression his word choice carries some added weight in the Admin."

"It does. He's using the 'heat of the moment' defense."

"What's that mean in this situation?"

"His words to Elly could be construed as a threat of physical violence in and of themselves. From a legal perspective, I mean. However, we would have to show the words were premeditated. A 'heat of the moment' claim is a common defense in such situations."

"Got it." Isaac faced Lacan and returned to normal speech. "Thank you for clarifying that. Continuing on, I'd like to start with your confrontation this morning with Elly Sako."

"I don't deny it," Lacan stated. "I was mad, and we fought. But that's *all* it was, okay?"

"What prompted the fight?"

"The bi—" Lacan bit off the word, his face twisting in anger. He grunted and crossed his arms before continuing. "She broke up with me."

"Why did she break up with you?"

"How the hell should I know?" he snapped. "I'm done trying to figure out how her head works!"

"Did she give you a reason?"

"Well, yeah."

"And what was that reason?"

"Because, *apparently*, she prefers synthetic dick over the real thing."

"Is that how she worded it?"

"No."

"How did she word it, then?"

Lacan bit the inside of his lip and slouched back. "She told me she was seeing another man."

"When did she tell you this?"

"On the way over from the Admin."

"Do you know who?"

"Yeah. That 'star' SysGov player, Wong Fei." He sat up and leaned forward. "You know, I bet that's what's going on here."

"What do you believe is going on?"

"I bet he's manipulating Elly," Lacan said, emphasizing his case with a pointed finger. "Yeah, that's got to be it. He's using her to gain an edge. Maybe trying to get her to spill her plan prior to the finals. Hell, she might even spill *my* plan to him!"

"Did you tell Elly your planned strategy for the finals?"

"Yeah, but I'm not stupid." He crossed his arms again. "I have a backup strategy no one knows about. If those two think I can be fooled so easily, they're in for a rude awakening!"

"Why did you share your strategy with her?"

"I don't know. Because I thought it was worth sharing, and I thought I could trust her." He shrugged his shoulders. "How was I supposed to know she was being manipulated by that fleshless freak?"

Isaac glanced over to Susan after Lacan used the anti-synthoid slur, but she remained as cool and collected as ever.

"Did she tell you hers?" he continued.

Lacan blinked. "What?"

"Did Miss Sako tell you her strategy for the upcoming finals?"

"She..." He looked down and his jaw tightened.

"Mister Lacan?"

"No," he said, his voice soft. "No, she didn't."

"I see." Isaac jotted down a quick note.

Lacan began chewing on the end of his braid. He then realized what he was doing and tried to switch to combing the ends with his fingers.

"Why do you believe Miss Sako is being manipulated?"

"Isn't it obvious?" He tossed his braid aside.

"Please state your thoughts plainly for the record."

"Because it's so bizarre!" Lacan shifted forward, sitting on the edge of the sofa. "Those two just met, what? A month ago? Back at our universal qualifier? And now he has her wrapped around his little finger!"

"A month hardly seems like a stretch for a change of heart."

"But the bloodless freak is from another *universe*!" Lacan snapped. "It makes no fucking sense!"

"Did you ever tell Miss Sako you loved her?"

"Of course!"

"Did she ever reciprocate?"

"She..." Lacan paused for a while. Then he shook his head. "No, she didn't."

Everything's matching up so far, Isaac thought as he reviewed his notes. *Besides Lacan's accusations, I haven't spotted a single difference between his and Elly's stories.*

He glanced to Susan, who gave him a little shoulder shrug, as if to say "what next?"

What next, indeed, he thought. *This interview isn't going anywhere. I think we'll wrap this up and move on for now.*

"Did you send the severed head to Miss Sako?"

"No."

"Do you know who sent it?"

"No."

"Do you suspect anyone of threatening her?"

"Haven't got a clue. I'm new here, all right?" He raised a forearm and tapped the infosystem on his wrist. "I can't even order a meal without this thing. And someone thinks I hacked a printer here? That's just stupid!"

"Do you want Miss Sako to go back to the Admin?"

"I..." He hesitated with an uncomfortable look on his face.

"Mister Lacan?"

"What does it matter what I want?"

"Mister Lacan, please answer the question."

"Fine!" he snapped. "Yeah, I want her to go home. I want her to get as far away from that metal freak as possible! Doesn't mean I threatened her!"

"Noted." Isaac closed his virtual screens and rose from his seat. "Thank you for your time. We'll let you know if—"

He paused when a high-priority message intruded on his virtual sight, sent from Lieutenant Lotz. Its header flashed urgently, and when he opened the message, he understood why.

The text read: *Come quick. A protester has been murdered.*

CHAPTER EIGHT

ISAAC AND SUSAN EXITED THE CRIMSON FLOWER THROUGH ONE of several doorways on the ground floor. They followed the sidewalk around the League protest zone to a cluster of dark gray trailers set up near the back of the crowd. Simple virtual signs hovered over the trailers, listing the services provided by each portable building: food printers, field office, public restrooms, and so on.

Two LSP quadcopters and half a dozen stern-faced state troopers formed a protective semicircle around the entrance to the men's restroom, augmented by virtual police tape and the copters' strobing lights. League protesters pressed in as close as they dared, and Isaac detected a dangerous mixture of curiosity and defiance simmering within the crowd.

One of the protesters spotted Susan's Admin uniform, and the crowd's attention shifted in her direction.

"Monster!"

"Fascist!"

"Go slink back home, you snake!"

Susan marched forward, back straight, her face an impassive mask as they neared the crime scene.

"You okay?" Isaac asked quietly.

"Of course. I'm not about to let them bother—"

Her arm flashed up in a blur of motion, and she caught something speeding toward Isaac's face. He flinched back, but quickly recovered as Susan opened her hand to reveal a rough moon rock.

He let out a sharp breath and checked the crowd. One of the protesters stood with his arm outstretched in the obvious aftermath of an overhanded throw. His black cap and scarf covered his entire face except for a narrow slit around the eyes.

Those eyes locked with Isaac's, then widened.

"Oh shit!"

"You!" Isaac pointed at the man. "Stop right there!"

The protester dashed into the crowd.

"What going on out here?" Lotz shouted from the restroom entrance. He strode over to the detectives. "Something wrong?"

"Just this." Susan presented the rock then bobbed her head toward Isaac. "It almost clubbed him in the head, though I believe I was the intended target."

"Aw, hell. You catch who threw it?"

"I did." Cephalie appeared on Isaac's shoulder, and the LENS hovered up to eye level. "Caught the throw on video, and I'm tracking his current position in the crowd. Want me to nab him?"

"Thanks, but we'll take care of this." Lotz turned back to the troopers clustered around the restroom. "O'Leary!"

"Sir?" A fresh-faced trooper hurried over.

"We've got another troublemaker to take care of. Get the perp's ID from the LENS and then send out some drones to bring him in. Charge him with assault on an officer."

"Yes, sir. Right away."

"Let's get you back from the crowd." Lotz put a hand on Susan's shoulder and urged her toward the two copters. "Before something worse gets tossed our way."

"Good idea," Isaac agreed, and they followed the lieutenant through the police cordon.

"Sorry about that." Lotz shook his head once they had the reassuring bulk of a police vehicle between them and the crowd. "Guess I didn't make the connection when I messaged you."

"What connection would that be?" Isaac asked, though he already suspected the answer.

"Her in that uniform." Lotz gestured to Susan with an open hand. "Sorry, I should have expected your presence might rile up these idiots."

"It's quite all right." Susan clasped her hands behind her back. "I've dealt with worse."

"What's the situation, Lieutenant?" Isaac asked.

"Well, we've got a fresh corpse inside"—Lotz pointed a thumb over his shoulder at the restroom entrance—"and an unruly crowd outside. I've had worse days, but not by much."

Isaac checked the entrance, which was obstructed by a combination of virtual police barriers and a large OUT OF ORDER sign hovering in front of the privacy bend.

"What do we know so far?"

"Not much." Lotz summoned a file over his palm. "We pulled an ID from what's left of the victim's wetware. Name was Pablo Evons. Lunarian, age twenty-six. Lived all the way out in Armstrong Landing. No criminal record. We'll need some time before we can say more, but he's dressed all in black like the rest of these troublemakers, so I'm pretty sure we'll find he was a member."

"What's 'left' of his wetware?" Susan asked.

"You'll see," Lotz warned. "It's a mess in there."

"Who found the body?" Isaac asked.

"One of the technicians from the toilet company," Lotz said. "The League rents this and the other trailers from an outfit called Party Logistics. The reclamation unit in the men's room backed up about half an hour ago and sent a fault to their nearest satellite office. One of their ACs, a gentleman named Asepsis, transmitted into an on-site support drone and entered the restroom to service it. He discovered the body."

"Was he the one who put up the out-of-order sign?" Isaac asked.

"No. According to him, the sign was active when he arrived. Though, the interesting bit is he says the sign is wrong. The font and coloring are off, and it lacks a link to their service techs. Based on that, I'm wondering if the killer put up a fake sign to delay the body's discovery."

"If so, then it's noteworthy the killer failed to account for the fault message. Anything else?"

"Just the body and the crime scene itself. Let me show you."

Lotz led them around the bend at the front of the restroom to a long interior lined with burnished metal sinks, urinals, and stalls. The body lay facedown in a pool of blood centered around the head, its limbs spread to either side at the base of a wall-mounted reclamation unit. The unit's protective handguard had been bashed aside, and blood streaked down the front.

"Where's the top half of his head?" Susan asked with a grimace.

Lotz pointed to the reclamation unit. "Down the chute in a million pieces. We have a forensics team on the way. It'll be their job to search the trailer's waste reservoir."

Isaac knelt and rested his forearm across his thigh. What remained of Pablo Evon's head resembled a top-down cross-section of a human skull, albeit one where the top half had been chewed off by grinders designed to break down waste.

"We arrived with a medical team," Lotz added, "and they would have tried to revive him, or pull his connectome, but..."

"Not enough of the brain left."

"Nope."

"The killer wanted him to stay dead. That's for sure." Isaac pushed off his knee and rose to his feet. He swept his eyes across the crime scene, soaking it in. "Blood splatters on the third sink over, and a dented basin."

"Signs of struggle?" Susan suggested.

"Very likely. The forensics report will tell us more, but if I were to guess, I'd say the killer and Mister Evons fought each other around here." Isaac gestured vaguely near the third sink. "The killer managed to subdue Evons, then dragged him over to the reclamation unit, bashed the handguard aside, and shoved his head in."

"He may have been trying to dispose of Evons entirely," Lotz said. "The unit's wide enough for a body to fit."

"Right. But the grinders seized up before they made much progress," Isaac finished, his eyes intense and focused.

"What are you thinking?" Susan prompted. "You have that look."

"I'm thinking this crime scene is an awful, sloppy mess. Whatever transpired here wasn't planned."

"Then you don't think this is related to the death threat?"

"I'm not willing to go that far," Isaac cautioned. "Given where this crime took place, the killer is either a League member or disguised as one, and the League is one potential source for the threat against Miss Sako. That means this crime could be related in some way we can't see yet. Furthermore, we're dealing with an individual who isn't afraid to go for a permanent kill. He didn't just defeat Evons; he ground up the man's brain to finish the job."

"I see what you're saying," Susan said. "And Sako would be even more vulnerable."

"How so?" Lotz asked.

"There are only two types of people in the Admin who have their connectomes extracted: STANDs like me and criminals."

"Criminals?" Lotz's eyes widened. "Wait a second. Then it's *true*? Your government rips people's minds right out of their skulls?"

"If they're guilty of certain crimes," Susan replied matter-of-factly.

"But..." Lotz shook his head. "I mean, are people over there *okay* with that?"

"I suppose most are."

"Are *you* okay with it?"

"Of course. I'm a sworn agent of the Admin, after all."

Lotz's face twisted in disgust. "But doesn't that practice bother you at least a—"

"Lieutenant Lotz," Isaac interrupted. "I believe we're getting distracted here."

"I... You're right." He sighed and gave Susan an apologetic smile. "Sorry. I'm sure you're sick of hearing stuff like that."

"It's all right." She shrugged. "At least you didn't throw anything at me."

"The important point to realize, Lieutenant," Isaac began, "is the Admin's here—both through the exchange program and in this tournament—because they *want* to be here. They want to peacefully coexist with us, despite all our differences. Despite the ways *our* culture and technology can sometimes terrify *them*."

"Such as how your president's an AI," Susan offered.

"You find that unusual?" Lotz asked.

"Oh yeah! I'm not really bothered by it, personally, but a lot of people freaked out when they learned about her."

"And there are plenty more examples where that came from," Isaac said.

"It's been a learning experience working over here, adapting to how SysPol operates. We've had our share of disagreements." Susan patted her sidearm, and her eyes twinkled with mirth. "He doesn't even like me carrying around a lethal weapon, and you should see his face every time I suggest using my combat frame."

Isaac gave her a profound grimace.

"That," she said, her eyes still laughing. "That face right there."

"It *is* a tad on the excessive side." Isaac let out a brief sigh. "Moving on, I believe we can leave this investigation in your hands." He raised an eyebrow to Lotz. "Unless you feel SysPol should take a more active role."

"No, we can handle it for now. And I'll be sure to let you know the moment something unusual pops up."

"I appreciate that." He faced Susan. "Well?"

"Where to next?"

"Back to our interviews. We still need to speak with Wong Fei."

✧   ✧   ✧

Wong Fei sat opposite Isaac and Susan in an expansive cushioned chair with an easy, confident smile on his face. His posture was formal as he cradled a teacup in his hand, yet not so rigid as to be unapproachable. His dark hair was neat and trim, and he wore a crisp brown business suit complemented by a dynamic scarf animated with falling cherry blossom petals.

"Can I offer either of you some refreshments?" Wong Fei asked, setting his tea down on the low glass table between their chairs. "I just finished brewing a pot of my favorite Darjeeling blend. There's plenty if either of you would like a cup."

"No, thank you," Isaac said, and Susan shook her head.

"Of course. Business first, then." Wong Fei sat attentively in his chair. "I imagine this is about the severed head in Elly's suite." He shook his head. "Such a terrible way to greet a visitor. This sort of pigheaded behavior isn't constructive at all."

"How did you learn about the death threat?"

"Elly called me shortly after she reported it to her security detail."

Interesting, Isaac thought, making a quick note. *Elly didn't mention talking to him. This could be nothing more than an oversight on her part, though.*

"Describe her reaction."

"Emotional. Shaken." Wong Fei smiled sadly. "About what you'd expect after being shown your own severed head. I did what I could to soothe her. I would have headed to her room, but I wasn't sure how her security would react to my presence, so I settled for keeping on the call until she sounded more composed."

"What is the nature of your relationship with Miss Sako?"

"We've grown very close in a short span of time." He smiled coyly. "Romantically close. I'm excited to see where it leads."

"Why do you say that?"

"Because, as strange as it might sound, we have a great deal in common, and I find that very appealing in a woman."

"There's a lot different between the two of you," Isaac pointed out. "Young versus centennial. Organic versus synthetic." He paused for emphasis. "Admin versus SysGov."

"Oh, certainly!" Wong Fei grinned. "But think for a moment about the differences you just described. Do those really paint a portrait of who someone is? No, they don't. They're broad brush-strokes. Categories to lump this or that person into. They don't speak to the unique beauty of the individual. And that's what I feel attracted to here. Not a young, organic, Admin woman. Not a category. But Elly Sako, the one-of-a-kind human being."

"Describe your relationship with Mister Lacan."

"Icy, to say the least." Wong Fei chuckled. "I suppose he considers me something of a rival." He raised a hand. "In both a romantic and professional sense, I mean."

"Do you consider him a rival, romantically?"

"No."

"And why's that?"

"Because Elly broke up with him, of course."

"Then you feel the two were in a relationship."

"Yes, even if she denies it."

"Did you encourage her to break up with Lacan?"

"I did, though perhaps not for the reasons you might be thinking."

"Why do you say that?"

"Two reasons, really. First, I could see how unbalanced and unhealthy their relationship had become, with Lacan obsessing over her while she viewed it as a purely physical dalliance. The sooner she ended it the better, in my mind. For both of them, really. Second, our relationship was becoming more serious, and so I felt this was an important step for her to take if we were to continue seeing each other."

"I see." Isaac expanded a highlighted section of his notes.

"Moving on, I'd like to discuss your criminal history. Specifically, your attempt to sabotage and intimidate your opponents at various tournaments between late 2955 and early 2956."

"Ah." Wong Fei frowned ever so slightly. "That. Well, if you'll permit me to clear the air, Detective...?"

"Go ahead."

"I'd like to point out I pled guilty during my sentencing and have paid my debt to society. Also, it *was* a long time ago. Over three decades and counting. I'm not the same person I was back then."

"I understand all that," Isaac assured him. "I'm more interested in hearing your motive for the crime."

"Simple. I wanted to win. At any cost. I was obsessed with victory back then."

"And now?"

"I've...mellowed, I guess you could say." He smiled disarmingly. "Winning isn't as important to me as it used to be."

"Your record indicates it is. You regularly reach at least the semifinals of any competition you're in, and you have an impressive number of victories to your name."

"Well, *yes*," Wong Fei agreed. "I do like to win, of course. But I earned those victories through hard work and dedication to my craft. And I'd like you to note, Detective, there isn't even a sniff of illegal activity in my record since the '50s."

"Of course." Isaac glanced over his notes. "Do you have an IC at present?"

"Yes. Nezha. We met about ten years ago, I think, at a *Solar Descent* tournament and really hit it off. Our personalities clicked, and it didn't hurt we were in the same line of work."

"Where is he now?"

"On Earth visiting some old friends. Some *very* old friends, even by our society's standards." Wong Fei flashed a crooked smile. "He doesn't like it when I make fun of his age."

"He's not on Luna?"

"He'll transmit back from Earth before the tournament starts so he can watch it live, though he'll be staying off-site."

"Why's that?"

"Too many issues with the Admin, especially since I had to travel there recently. The Admin puts heavy restrictions on our abstract citizens, you see. Nezha would have had to switch to a synthoid body, amongst other limitations, and he wasn't feeling up to it. He's spent his entire life in the abstract and wasn't about to start messing with the physical now.

"I miss him, but it's not like I *need* him for this tournament. The two of us will team up sometimes, depending on the entry requirements for a given tournament. We heavily integrate our connectomes for unlimited tournaments and go our separate ways for limited venues, such as this one."

Isaac jotted down a follow-up note to confirm Nezha's whereabouts.

"And the other SysGov players?"

"Both of them are going it solo. One of the stipulations for the Weltall Tournament is no abstract citizens or anything that could be construed as an artificial connectome may enter. I guess you could say the contestants for this tournament are 'restricted,' though that's a bit of a loaded term with the Admin. Anything else, Detective?"

"Just a few more questions, then we should be on our way," Isaac said. "Do you know who threatened Miss Sako?"

"No."

"Do you suspect anyone of threatening her?"

"No."

"Do you want her to leave SysGov for any reason?"

"No, of course not."

"Understood. Thank you for answering our questions." Isaac rose from his seat. "We'll let you know if we need anything else."

✧   ✧   ✧

"I'll have Cephalie check with the Ministry of Transportation," Isaac said in security chat once they were outside Wong Fei's hotel suite. "I want to see if Nezha really is on Earth."

"Suspicious of something?" Susan asked him. "Or just checking?"

"Just checking, but it doesn't hurt to be thorough while we wait for Nina's findings."

"By the way..."

"Yes?"

"I'm sorry to say I missed Wong Fei's old crimes when I looked over his records."

"That's all right. We've been playing catch up from the start."

"True, but it made me wonder." She turned to him as they walked. "*How* exactly did Wong Fei pressure his rivals?"

"Ah, that. Most of the intimidation was done through anonymous messages, but not always." Isaac held out a palm, and an evidence file appeared.

Susan winced.

"In the incident that led to his arrest, one rival received a replica of their own severed hand. Complete with a bloody message carved into the flesh."

CHAPTER NINE

THE COUNTER-GRAV TUBE FROM THE GENTLE RAIN HOTEL IN Petal Four deposited Isaac and Susan on the circumference of a wide, circular plaza. The thin, green core of Pistil Tower sprouted from its center and ballooned outward as it rose. Dozens of spindly, paler supports arched upward from the plaza's edge to meet it overhead, and sunlight shone through the transparent gaps between them.

A polished expanse of prog-steel stylized as crimson stonework stretched out before them, veined with clear platforms built over pathways for flowing water. The area bustled with foot traffic as guests partook of the many shops, restaurants, and entertainment venues ringing the Pistil Plaza.

Isaac and Susan followed navigational arrows to a dark gray, many-leveled structure pressed into the plaza's outer wall below the glowing virtual letters "CFPD." A waterfall next to the station produced a soft mist that kissed and cooled their skins as they approached.

They walked in and stepped up to one of the waiting desk sergeants, an abstract uniformed woman with a blue-skinned avatar and golden glowing eyes.

"Hello, Sergeant," Isaac began. "We're looking for Specialist Nina Cho."

"Detective Cho and Agent Cantrell, I presume?"

"That'd be us."

"Specialist Cho arrived a few minutes ago. She's in waiting room 105." A blue pulsing trail appeared, leading into the station. "Just back and around the corner. Can't miss it."

"Thank you."

They followed the guide arrows inside, turned a corner, and stepped through the opening prog-steel door. Nina reclined in a chair with her boots propped up on the table and three separate screens hovering around her. She swiped the screens closed and sat up when they entered.

"Hey, Nina." Isaac dropped into one of the chairs with a sigh.

"Hey, yourself. How'd the interviews go?"

"They went," he sighed. "Nothing unusual so far. Just a love triangle that may or may not be relevant. How about you? Got anything good for us?"

"Cephalie brought these."

A spherical drone slightly larger than Nina's head floated up into view beside her. Its outer shell resembled a silver lidless eyeball, encapsulating its internal systems within fast-reacting prog-steel.

"Hey, kiddos." Cephalie's avatar appeared atop the drone and waved at them daintily.

"My new LENS." Isaac nodded. "Good to have one again. Thanks, Cephalie."

"No problem."

"Anything for me?" Susan asked.

"Why, as a matter of fact..." Nina reached down beside her chair and retrieved a huge pistol and magazine belt. She placed them on the table and slid them over to Susan. "One anti-synthoid hand cannon and accessories for the lady."

"Nice!"

"How about you?" Isaac asked. "Find anything?"

"Maybe. Probably." Nina transmitted copies of her report, which all four of them opened. "This is a preliminary version, mind you. No complaining to Raviv about how I haven't dotted my t's or cross my i's."

"Don't you have that backwards?"

"I know what I said."

"You sure about that?"

"I'll clean it up later, but this should get you moving in the right direction." She expanded the first table. "Okay, let's start with the printer and the surrounding area. Tons of different DNA all over the place." She shrugged. "No surprise there. It's a hotel. Still, I ran it through the criminal database and got a few hits. Some people with minor offenses in their history. Nothing that stands out to me, but I've attached the full list anyway."

Isaac opened the file and skimmed down the names. Wong Fei's name wasn't on the list, but his synthoid wouldn't show up in a DNA search.

"Thanks," he said. "Always worth a check."

"Right. Moving on to the printer itself, I sifted through its infostructure and found remnants of malicious code. You can find the breakdown in tab two."

Isaac expanded the tab, and technical data unfolded in his virtual sight.

"I can't be a hundred percent sure," Nina cautioned, "but I think we're looking at a common piece of prankware."

"Prankware?" Susan asked.

"A program people use to disable the limits on a printer," Cephalie explained, "in order to produce something it normally wouldn't, such as an obscene shape or disgusting flavors."

"We're not talking about strict, secure settings to begin with," Nina added. "After all, sometimes a guy really wants his birthday cake shaped like a pair of boobies, you know? It doesn't take much to open up a food printer's limits, even in a legit manner."

"Then this prankware," Susan asked, "disabled certain limits on the printer and allowed it to produce the head?"

"That's what I suspect happened, yes. Also, if I'm right, the hacked pattern was queued up in such a way that it replaced whatever was ordered next."

"Why aren't you sure it's prankware?" Isaac asked.

"Because I can't confirm when the printer was infected," Nina admitted. "There's a chance I'm looking at junk code from an older, unreported incident. I checked with LSP to see if they had any related complaints from the hotel or its guests for this suite, but I didn't turn up anything. Ergo, that leaves us with either an unreported incident or the severed head. I can't be certain, but my Esteem's on the severed head."

"Makes sense to me," Isaac said. "What about an infection vector?"

"That's where it gets tricky," Nina said. "The printer, a DynaFood model Delta-7, isn't doing us any favors. Lots of high-end features, as you'd expect from a hotel in the Crimson Flower, but these models have security holes from here to Saturn. Anyone who was within the printer's command range could have hacked it."

"How far is its command range?" Susan asked.

"Typically, it'll be limited to the hotel suite," Isaac said.

"Which this one is," Nina confirmed.

"What about someone standing in the doorway?" Susan asked. "Like when Lacan and Sako were arguing."

"That would work, too," Nina said.

"Could the hack have originated from an Admin wearable?" Isaac asked.

"I don't see why not. If they can order food at the printer, they can hack it, provided they have a copy of the prankware."

"Doesn't sound like it'd be hard for someone to get ahold of, either," Susan noted.

"Correct," Nina affirmed with a nod.

"Which means the threat could have been sent by anyone in the suite recently," Isaac sighed. "Players, security agents, hotel staff, previous guests, you name it."

"Sorry." Nina shrugged her arms in a genuine apology. "I wish I had something more solid for you."

"At least it gives us a starting point," Isaac said. "I'll take it."

"What about the head itself?" Susan asked.

"Nothing remarkable about it," Nina said. "Just customized food from a food printer. Colored meat inside an edible waxy skin. Sugar strands for hair. Syrup with food coloring for blood. It's all perfectly edible, if unappetizing."

Isaac cringed. "You didn't taste it, did you?"

"No way!" Nina shooed the idea aside. "Come on! I'm a professional!"

"Right."

"Got one more thing to add." Cephalie's avatar walked to the center of the table and pushed her glasses up the bridge of her nose. "I received feedback from the Ministry of Transportation."

"And?"

"Nezha's been on Earth for the past month."

"Then that's one name we can check off the list." Isaac turned to Susan. "I think we have our next stop."

"Which is?" Susan asked.

"Whoever sent the message was in the room recently. Let's go have a chat with Pérez. He should be able to provide us with a list of people who've been in the suite since his security took over."

✧   ✧   ✧

"Susan?" Isaac asked as they crossed the Admin hangar, heading toward the Cutlass transport docked under the chronoport's delta wing. Cephalie guided the LENS a few paces behind them.

"Yes?"

"What's your opinion of Pérez?"

"I'd trust him with my life. We kept each other safe on plenty of missions together. Also"—she leaned toward him and spoke softer—"he may not look it, but he's a big softy at heart. He just has this tough Peacekeeper exterior you need to break through first."

"You think highly of him, don't you?"

"He taught me what it means to be a Peacekeeper and pounded some important lessons into my head. I owe a lot to him."

"Sounds like it."

"That said, he's a bit old-school in his beliefs. A lot of the older STANDs are."

"How so?"

"Very much against the chief executor's push for reforms, such as the outreach to terrorist havens like Luna. He considers it a sign of weakness."

"He prefers a strong, centralized Admin?"

"Exactly. One that tells the states what to do rather than asks them." Susan shrugged. "It's a frequent topic of debate back home."

"What's your take on those reforms?"

"Well, I'm of two minds when it comes to them. On the one hand, I'm not a big fan of being nice to terrorists and their sympathizers."

"Naturally. And on the other hand?"

"What we've been doing so far doesn't seem to have worked all that well, so maybe it's time to try a different approach."

They stepped through the transport's open back and saw Pérez hunched over two synthoids at the transport's controls. He looked over his shoulder and nodded to them.

"We're putting together the full list for you now. Just double-checking to make sure we're not missing any names."

"How long is it?" Isaac asked.

"Fairly short, to be honest." Pérez stepped away from the other synthoids and joined them by the transport's docked Wolverine drones. "From the players, there's Sako and Lacan, of course, and also Wong Fei. He visited her room shortly after we arrived, though he was gone before Lacan visited to have his little chat. A few other agents were in there as well as a few housekeeping drones. And me, of course. I had to perform one last inspection of her suite, since she opened the door to talk with Lacan." He shook his head. "Didn't spot anything unusual."

"Checked and double-checked, sir." Agent Arlot swiveled in his chair.

Cephalie saved the file to the LENS then provided links to Susan and Isaac. They both opened the list.

"No surprises here," Isaac remarked, glancing over the names.

"Where do you want to start?" Susan asked.

"With Lacan and Wong Fei. Their rooms and wearables. We'll search for any evidence that might tie them to the death threat. If we don't get any hits there, we'll go through the DTI agents on the list."

"That won't be a problem, sir," Pérez said, clasping his hands in the small of his back. "You'll have our full cooperation."

"Cephalie," Isaac said, "put in requests for the search warrants we'll need for Wong Fei and for Lacan's room."

"Already one step ahead of you."

"Great." Isaac grimaced and turned to Susan. "That leaves Lacan's wearables. I've been concerned about this, so we might as well deal with it now."

"Concerned about what?" Susan asked.

"Getting a search warrant valid for an Admin citizen. Is there someone currently in SysGov who can legally issue one, or do we need to contact the Admin directly? If so, when's the next chronoport depart, and how long will it take for us to get an answer?"

"Oh, right!" Susan turned to Pérez. "Miguel, do you have a copy? I didn't bring the file with me when I started over here three months ago."

"Sure. Give me a sec." Pérez opened a virtual interface.

"A copy of what?" Isaac asked.

"The search warrant, of course."

"You mean a warrant request form, don't you?"

"No." Susan shook her head. "I mean the actual warrant."

Isaac's brow furrowed. "That can't be right."

"Here you go." Pérez offered the file, which Isaac pulled over to his palm and read once his Admin English translator kicked in. The document was surprisingly short and direct.

"Am I reading this right?" he asked.

"I don't see why not," Susan said. "Is there a translation error?"

"It's not that. I mean is this how search warrants work in the Admin? As a simple fill-in-the-blanks form any Peacekeeper can copy?"

"Not quite," Susan clarified. "Miguel and I would only use a warrant like this under very specific circumstances. Typically, when trying to collect information on a suspected terrorist. And even then, we can get audited."

"Then we *do* need higher approval to search Lacan's wearables?"

"Well…" She smiled guiltily. "Not really."

"You've lost me."

"I said Miguel and I can't on our own," she added carefully. "That's because we're just agents. However, that's not true for all positions."

She gave Isaac a meaningful look. He squinted at her with a confused expression, but then realization dawned on him, and his eyes widened.

"Oh, no," he breathed.

"Because DTI investigators can make all the copies they want," she finished.

"You mean to tell me I'll be filling out my own search warrants on this case?"

"It *is* simpler this way."

"That's not the issue!" Isaac looked over the form. "Does it really have to be me who does this?"

"Yes," she said firmly. "Unless you want me to be audited and then reprimanded. Possibly even discharged from the Peacekeepers."

"Well, we don't want that." He huffed out a breath and shook his head. "Fine, I'll take care of it."

"Then I think we're done here?" Susan asked more than stated.

Isaac closed the search warrant and nodded to her.

"Thanks for the help, Miguel."

"My pleasure."

Susan followed Isaac out.

"Is it really that shocking a difference?" she asked him with genuine curiosity.

"I suppose not."

They exited the hangar and nodded to the sentries as they passed. Isaac opened a comm window to Nina.

"Need something?" Nina answered.

"Got some more work for you. Cephalie is in the process of rounding up search warrants for Wong Fei's and GW Lacan's rooms as well as any wearables Wong Fei's might have."

"But not Lacan's wearables?"

"I . . . already have that one covered."

"How'd you manage that?"

"I'll explain later. In the meantime, would you mind getting in touch with a Lieutenant Cameron Lotz? Once all the documentation is in order, we'll want LSP to help us sift through those rooms."

"Good idea. I'll get the cavalry lined up."

"We're heading your way next. See you in a few."

Isaac and Susan stepped through the open threshold into Wong Fei's room to find several LSP troopers tearing the walls apart, literally. Decorative panels lay in uneven stacks while state troopers ran hardwired cables to the infosystem nodes underneath.

A pair of drones roughly the size of Isaac's LENS floated nearby with a rack of infosystem nodes suspended from their pseudopods. The rack resembled an enlarged metal honeycomb, and they set it in one of several piles of hardware, then floated back to another room.

Lieutenant Lotz spotted the detectives as they entered and hurried over.

"Looks like you're making good progress, Lieutenant," Isaac remarked, surveying the activity.

"That we are. I've got a dozen troopers and their support drones working through this suite and I placed another dozen under Specialist Cho's command in the other room. We're finishing up this floor, and the other two should go faster now that all the paneling is off."

"That's good to hear. Find anything so far?"

"Not yet," Lotz said. "At least nothing malicious, but we have a lot of nodes to check. We're going to be at this all night."

"What about Wong Fei's synthoid and wearables?"

"We checked him over before he left. He didn't have any wearables, which made sense since his synthoid is set up with plenty of internal storage."

"And his synthoid itself?"

"Clean. Nothing beyond his UAM gaming collection."

"He own any other synthoids besides the primary?"

"Not that we've seen, and not anywhere in the suite," Lotz said. "He only has registration for the one body, so if there's another, it's not legit."

"Did he give you any problems?"

"Not a one. He was perfectly behaved the whole time."

Isaac looked around. "Where is he now?"

"At some gala near the top of Pistil Tower that ActionStream is putting on before the tournament starts. The other players are there, too."

"It's where you'd be," Cephalie commented, materializing on his shoulder, "if you hadn't been dragged into this case."

"What a shame," Isaac said dryly.

"I've got several troopers up there as well, keeping an eye on things in case someone tries to bolt or do something equally stupid." Lotz shrugged. "Not that they'd get far, but..."

"No, that's good thinking. Best to play it safe."

"Also, I have an update for you on the Evons murder. We pulled the most recent contacts from his wetware, which led us to a lot of explicit material being sent back and forth with another League member. A young lady named Miyuki Saga. We reached out to her for an interview, and she came in without a fuss. Everything was playing out like you'd expect until all of a sudden she starts blubbering like crazy, going on about how his death was her fault. Turns out her *husband* is *another* League member named Togashi Saga, and she hasn't seen or heard from him since the murder. We're trying to track him down now."

"Sounds like you have the matter well in hand."

Isaac had worked with a variety of state troopers over the years, and they ran the gamut from superstars to incompetent walking disasters. He was pleased to see Lotz leaned toward the former category. He could tell the man took his job seriously and had an instinct for how to tackle problems and keep his team pushing forward.

Isaac turned in a slow circle, looking around the partially disassembled suite.

"Everything appears to be in order over here, as well," Isaac said. "Lieutenant, if there's nothing you need from us, we're going to check on Lacan's room next."

"Sure thing, Detective. I'll give you a call once we're finished."

Isaac glanced up at Susan. "Shall we?"

"Let's."

They headed out, took a grav tube to the Admin floor, and walked down a curved corridor until they reached Lacan's room. A pair of DTI agents checked their IDs before letting them in.

Lacan's room was in a state similar to Wong Fei's, with troopers and drones pulling panels, running cables, and stacking infosystem nodes. He spotted Nina in the kitchen staring at something on the counter. One of her forensics drones floated nearby, thin tendrils of prog-steel connecting it to a trio of objects on the counter.

"Nina?" he said, walking over.

She looked up and, when she saw him, started to grin ear to ear.

"Now that's a good sign," Susan commented.

"Oh, it is!" Nina pushed a blue wristband forward.

"What's this?" Isaac asked.

"One of Lacan's wearables. Guess what I found on it?"

"Suspicious prankware?"

"Yup! He tried to delete the program, but that won't cut it when you're up against me."

"You sure this is the one he was wearing when he confronted Sako?" Susan asked.

"I am." Nina tapped the wristband. "I checked its styling against the DTI's security video. This is the one he had on this morning, and he was still wearing it when the troopers issued the warrant."

"Did he give you any trouble when you asked for the wristband?" Isaac asked.

"No. He must believe deleting the prankware is enough." She shook her head. "Ah, the poor, naive mind of a criminal. Thinking he can delete his sins away. So blissfully ignorant."

"Then, that's it." Susan turned to Isaac. "Looks like we have means, motive, and opportunity."

"Indeed," Isaac agreed. "The prankware, the ugly breakup, and him stepping just far enough into the room to connect with the printer. It all fits."

"He even said he wants Sako to leave," Susan noted. "And if she did, *he'd* have no romantic competition."

"For what little good that'd do him." Isaac opened a comm window to Lotz.

"Yes, Detective?"

"We have the evidence we need. We found it in Lacan's room."

"And?"

"Lacan was the one threatening her. Your troopers can move in to arrest him on charges of unlawful coercion whenever you like, but you might want to wait until the gala quiets down. No need to make a scene."

"Understood. We'll take care of it, Detective."

CHAPTER TEN

ISAAC STOOD IN THE SHADOW OF *DEFENDER-PRIME*'S WING BESIDE Susan and Pérez, waiting for . . . some reason he was not yet clear on. He'd left Cephalie and the LENS back at the CFPD on Susan's recommendation.

"Who's on his way again?" he asked quietly.

"Special Agent James Noxon," Susan replied. "He's bringing us additional security personnel aboard *Pathfinder-Prime*."

"He's an agent like you and Pérez?"

"Umm, yes and no."

"That's not very helpful, Susan."

"Sorry. It's a little difficult to explain if you haven't worked in the DTI. He's more important than his rank would lead you to believe."

"Why's that?"

"Because he's part of Director Shigeki's 'inner circle.'"

"Then he works in Foreign Affairs?"

"What?" She shook her head. "No, sorry. Not Jonas Shigeki. His father, *Csaba* Shigeki, the director-general."

"Ah. Then he reports directly to the man in charge of the whole DTI."

"That's right."

"Why didn't you say so?"

"Because, technically, he doesn't."

Isaac lowered his head and rubbed his temples.

"You see, *technically*, he's just another agent."

"Which is why I'm confused about the three of us standing here"—he gestured to Susan and Pérez—"waiting for his chronoport to arrive."

"Look at it this way. He's been a part of the Shigeki family's security detail since before there was a DTI. The Shigekis come from a long line of Peacekeepers, and Noxon has served them since . . . well, since the beginning, I think."

"The beginning of . . . ?"

"The Admin."

"That would make him quite old," Isaac noted.

"Very old." She nodded to Pérez. "Maybe even as old as Miguel."

"Older, actually," Pérez commented.

"And he's still an agent after all this time?" Isaac asked.

"That's the role he wants," Susan explained. "I don't think *anyone* is going to tell him otherwise. Besides, us STANDs tend to find our niche and stick to it."

Pérez nodded in agreement.

"I see."

"There are very few people in the DTI," Susan continued, "who have the director-general's ear and trust. Who he discusses the *really* high-level stuff with. Noxon is one of them. He might as well be an under-director, given the level of sway he has in our organization."

"Which makes him part of the inner circle you mentioned."

"That's right."

"Hmm."

The top of the hangar split open, and Isaac gazed upward. The approaching silhouette of the chronoport was a dark, tailed arrow against the clear, blue sky. Susan stiffened her posture, and even Pérez tensed up as he tugged his uniform straight.

"Are you nervous?" Isaac asked her.

"A little," Susan confided.

"Should I be?"

"Probably not. I've worked with Noxon a few times in the past. Never had any issues with him, nor him with me that I'm aware of, but his presence still gives me the jitters."

"Huh."

"At least it's not Director Kloss we're dealing with."

"Too true," Pérez agreed.

Susan had once faced down an army of weaponized construction drones with nothing but her pistol and whatever she could scrounge off their crashed aircraft. She'd engaged them during a torrential downpour of liquid methane that was slowly freezing her to death, fending them off until help finally arrived.

That hadn't fazed her. She'd actually been *modest* about her heroics afterward, all while Isaac had slumped in the cockpit, unconscious from his injuries. He hadn't witnessed the battle in person, obviously, but Cephalie had shown him the highlight clips later, and so he knew for certain Susan had sprung into action without the slightest hesitation.

She's charged into impossible odds without question, he considered. *But this James Noxon makes her nervous.*

The huge craft began its descent, and Isaac turned at the sound of footfalls coming down *Defender-Prime*'s ramp. The new Peacekeeper joined them at Isaac's side. He was a tall man with a long ponytail who wore his uniform as if it were a part of him. Not a crease in sight.

"Good." The newcomer removed his peaked cap and brushed off the top. "He's not here yet."

Pérez pointed up, and the newcomer's eyes followed upward.

"All that matters is we're here first." He fitted his cap back on, then extended a hand to Isaac. "Captain Jason Elifritz. A pleasure to finally meet you, Detective. I would have introduced myself sooner, but it seemed better to stay out of your way while you worked the case."

"I appreciate that, Captain," Isaac replied, returning the man's firm handshake. "I take it *Defender-Prime* is your ship."

"That's right." He nodded to Susan. "Agent Cantrell."

"Long time no see, Captain."

"Too long. Good to see you're doing well for yourself."

"You two know each other?" Isaac asked.

"Since just after Cantrell became a STAND," Elifritz said. "She and Pérez served under my command for a while." He flashed a disarming smile. "We blew up a *lot* of terrorists together."

"Is that so?" Isaac replied neutrally.

The line of Peacekeepers-plus-Isaac settled into an uneasy silence as the chronoport descended into the hangar. Thruster exhaust blew past them, hot against Isaac's face even at this distance. His skin beaded with sudden perspiration, but the torrent of dry air absorbed the moisture almost instantly.

A docking cradle morphed out of the floor, and *Pathfinder-Prime* came to rest in it. Its fusion thrusters switched off and their vectored nozzles irised closed. A ramp opened and extruded outward from the craft's belly, and over a dozen Peacekeepers marched out. Isaac guessed they were all synthoids, since most of them possessed the typical gray skin and yellow eyes of Admin STANDs, though a few of them exhibited more realistic exteriors.

One of the gray-skinned synthoids walked toward them, and as one the Peacekeepers beside Isaac tensed up, standing rigidly at attention. Isaac couldn't help but feel out of place. He wore the only SysPol uniform in a sea of the lighter blue Peacekeepers. He wondered if Susan ever felt awkward like this.

Probably not, he thought. *That uniform might as well be a part of her, which seems to be a rather common trait among the Peacekeepers, now that I think about it.*

The synthoid walked over and stopped in front of Isaac.

"Detective Cho, I presume," he said in a deep, resonant voice.

"That's right."

"Agent James Noxon." He extended a hand, which Isaac shook. "I understand we have you to thank for sorting out our little problem."

"I wouldn't go that far. It was a team effort."

"Of course." He faced Elifritz. "Captain, I'll be taking command of the STANDs assigned to *Defender-Prime*."

"Yes, Agent. I've seen the orders. You'll have my full support."

"Good to hear. Agent Pérez?"

"Sir."

"Before I make any changes to your team, I'll need to be briefed on the current status of our security coverage."

"Yes, sir." Pérez gestured to the docked transport under *Defender-Prime*'s wing. "We're using the Cutlass as our command center. We can review our coverage plan for you there."

"Very good." He turned to Susan, then to Isaac. "Agent Cantrell, Detective Cho, I'd also like to review the charges and evidence against our...troublesome citizen."

Isaac opened his mouth to speak, but Susan beat him to it.

"Yes, sir!" she snapped with rigid formality.

"Excellent." Noxon nodded to the Cutlass. "Then let's get to it."

"Right this way, sir," Pérez said.

The meeting in the Cutlass started with Pérez providing a detailed overview of the players' protective coverage, the surveillance setup in the hotel floor and hangar, inspection processes and schedules for their rooms, and entry admittance procedures for hotel staff and other guests to the Admin floor.

Noxon stayed quiet through most of it, arms folded as Pérez walked him through the current situation. When Pérez finished, Noxon unfolded his arms.

"Most of that looks good," he began. "With the additional agents I brought and now only two players instead of three requiring active protection, I want coverage doubled whenever the players are on the move or outside our floor, understood?"

"Yes, sir, but do you still think that's necessary?" Pérez asked. "With the death threat against Sako resolved, there doesn't seem to be a need for heightened security. Also, there is some local . . . sensitivity to our presence here."

"I've read your reports on the protests," Noxon said neutrally.

"Then you should understand my concerns about an increase in how visible our presence here is."

"Maybe so, but the additional resources are here, so we'll put them to use. I don't want any other embarrassments on the DTI's watch, and neither do the directors."

"Understood, sir. In that case, I'll put together a revised coverage schedule."

"Furthermore, I want you to shift command and control over to *Pathfinder-Prime*. We'll coordinate all our efforts from its bridge moving forward. Any objections?"

"No, sir," Pérez said.

"Captain?"

"None here," Elifritz replied. He'd let Pérez do most of the talking so far, pitching in only to clarify or expound upon a few points during the briefing.

"Good." Noxon turned to Susan and Isaac, and his face soured. "Now, about our wayward citizen. Where is he now?"

"Lacan is confined to a cell in the Crimson Flower First Precinct Building," Isaac said. "He's been charged with unlawful coercion, a category of crimes which can include death threats like the one sent to Miss Sako. Do you want to see the prisoner?"

"That won't be necessary," Noxon said. "You're confident in the evidence against him?"

"We are, for several reasons, but the big one is we found deleted remnants of prankware on one of Lacan's wearables."

"This is the software you believe he used to corrupt the printer?"

"That's correct."

"How confident are you it's a match?"

"Very. Since arresting Lacan, our forensic specialist has gone over the evidence more thoroughly and was able to match the program on his wearable with garbage code fragments in the printer. In short, all the evidence matches up. A copy of the prankware found in his possession caused the printer to produce the severed head."

"You said a copy of that program," Noxon noted. "I take it there's no way to be certain *his* copy was what caused it."

"Correct, unfortunately," Isaac admitted. "The prankware is generic in that respect, with no identifiers for a particular copy, but that's where the other evidence comes into play."

"He had access to the printer just before it produced the threat," Susan pointed out, "and he certainly had a motive."

"True enough," Noxon agreed, "but how did he get his hands on it in the first place?"

"It's possible one of the SysGov players or a staff member for ActionStream provided him with it," Isaac said. "Possession and distribution of prankware are fairly minor crimes, so LSP—the Lunar State Police—will follow up. SysPol will provide additional support if requested, but I consider that unlikely. The program's distribution is an issue for local law enforcement."

"What does the accused have to say for himself?" Noxon asked.

"I believe LSP is conducting an interrogation now," Isaac said. "Last I checked, he hadn't confessed."

Noxon harrumphed. "I suppose that's to be expected."

"Why do you say that?"

"Because he threatened to kill Miss Sako."

"Yes," Isaac said, "but why do you believe he wouldn't confess?"

Noxon's brow creased in confusion.

"Allow me to explain, sir," Susan stepped in. "Death threats are handled a bit differently in the Admin."

"Yes, I remember you mentioning the heat of the moment defense."

"Right. But that won't cover a severed head. A threat like that, requiring preparation to deliver, is classified as a premeditated message."

"And a premeditated death threat indicates intent," Noxon added, "in a legally relevant sense. With severe consequences."

"Oh," Isaac said. "I see."

"Threatening to kill someone in a premeditated fashion," Susan explained, "isn't too far away from actually committing murder, in terms of the punishments in the Admin."

"Okay, yes, I see your concern now," Isaac said.

"On top of that," Noxon added, "SysGov, unlike the Admin, has a death penalty."

"I'm not sure I see why that's relevant."

"Because I need to ask...is Lacan to be executed?"

"What?" Isaac blurted. "No! I mean, yes, we do have the death penalty! But no, he's not going to be executed for *threatening* someone!"

"Good." Noxon nodded, visibly relieved. "That's one less worry, then."

Isaac sighed and shook his head.

"Then, if not execution, what's to be his punishment?"

"I don't know. That'll be up to the judge."

"Don't you have a say in this?"

"Sure, I do. I can pass a recommendation on to the prosecutor. In fact, I was planning to do that already."

"And what will you recommend?" Noxon pressed.

"I was going to suggest leniency," Isaac said. "First, because Lacan strikes me as a lovesick fool. Second, because no one was hurt, and nothing was damaged. Even the printer's fine. And third, I don't see the point in throwing *our* book at him. He's an Admin citizen who threatened another Admin citizen. He just happened to do it in our jurisdiction."

Isaac tried to read Noxon's face, but it might as well have been chiseled from stone.

"Why?" Isaac asked finally. "Do you *want* us to throw the book at him?"

"Depends how heavy the book is," Noxon said matter-of-factly. Isaac couldn't tell if he was joking or not.

✧   ✧   ✧

"*That* was unexpected," Isaac exclaimed as they left the Petal Four hangar.

"Actually, I think it went quite well." Susan patted him on the shoulder. "Congratulations. You just survived your first encounter with the inner circle." She smiled slyly. "Mister DTI Investigator."

"I don't plan to make a habit of this. Honestly, Noxon didn't seem so bad to me. The way everyone was acting made me expect...I don't know. Someone who brought a little more fire and brimstone to the conversation."

"It's not so much how he acts as the power he represents. *And* the people you don't want to cross."

"Plenty of those in the DTI?"

"Oh, you wouldn't believe!"

"I think every large organization has members like that. People in positions of authority you simply *do not* mess with."

"Yep. That's the inner circle for you."

"SysPol has those too." He wagged his finger. "Like Mitch."

"Mitch who?"

"Just Mitch. No last name. He's the Themis superintendent back at Saturn, which makes him Raviv's direct superior. Something of an eccentric AC, as I understand it. I've never spoken to him myself, but I know he drives Raviv up the wall sometimes."

"Eccentric how?"

"He's very opinionated. And very vocal about his opinions."

"That doesn't sound so bad. What sort of opinions?"

"*Everything.* And if you get on his bad side, your reward is listening to him pontificate at you for *hours.* Once, Raviv was on the receiving end of an epic rant about how disgusting biological sex is and how everyone should go post-physical and be done with it."

"Yikes!" Susan cringed. "Yeah, that sounds eccentric."

"Which is why sometimes it's best to simply keep your head down and put in an honest day's work for an honest day's pay."

"I hear that," Susan agreed. "Where to next?"

"The hotel lobby to check in. The finals start tomorrow, and we'll be back on our original schedule. I don't know about you, but I could use a good night's sleep." He rubbed his palm against an eye. "I figure we can take care of any loose ends with the state troopers after the tournament winds down for the day. Lacan's not going anywhere."

"Sounds good to me." She smiled. "It should be quite the show tomorrow."

"Should be."

"You don't sound excited."

"Well..." He shrugged.

"Aren't you looking forward to the tournament?"

"Yeah, sure." He shrugged again. "Guess so."

"Who do you think will win?"

"Oh, I don't know."

"Come on, give me a n—"

"Wong Fei."

"Really?" Susan raised an eyebrow. "You sound rather confident there. You sure he'll be the winner?"

"Pretty darn sure. Remember, I've actually seen him play. He's going to chew up the competition and spit them out." Isaac let out a sad sigh. "It's a shame, really."

"What is?"

"Sako and...who's the other Admin player?"

"Shingo Masuda."

"Right. The two of them came all this way to another universe." He shook his head. "Only to have their butts kicked tomorrow."

"You really think so?" Susan asked with a lopsided smile.

"Yeah." He shook his head. "It really is sad how badly your team is going to lose tomorrow."

"Well"—Susan put her hands on her hips—"I think Elly's going to win it all. Care to make a wager?"

"I don't bet."

"Aww." She frowned at him. "You're no fun."

"People have said worse things about me."

CHAPTER ELEVEN

THE NEXT MORNING, ISAAC SAT AT A SMALL TABLE IN THE FERTILE Ground restaurant attached to the Gentle Rain hotel's bottom floor. The table was stylized so that its base seemed to grow out of the ground like a thin but gnarled tree, expanding out into an interlocking weave of branches to support the glass tabletop.

The rest of the establishment continued the faux-natural décor with water trickling down stone walls and drones stylized as oversized beetles fluttering over, their glowing abdomens providing soft illumination.

Isaac leaned back in his chair and watched the other patrons, who were a mix of people from both the Admin and SysGov. He didn't see either of the Admin players, but a few DTI synthoids were hanging out with some of the chronoport's organic crew. One adventurous SysGov girl with a too-long yellow scarf flowing behind her—perhaps six or seven years old—actually went up to a DTI agent and asked him to pose for a picture. Her mother hurried over and apologized to the agent, who waved the matter aside. And then he actually posed for the girl! He even smiled for it!

Isaac wasn't sure posing with his sidearm drawn was the best look for the Admin, but matters between the two peoples could have been far, *far* worse. At least the agent declined—politely but firmly—when the little girl begged to hold his weapon.

His waitress came back with a beetle drone levitating her food tray over her shoulder. The drone dropped off a traditional Lunarian breakfast while the waitress freshened his cup of coffee. The breakfast consisted of steamed dumplings filled with finely minced meats and vegetables, a side dish of yama sauce for dipping, a bowl of barange wedges, and a perspiring glass of barange juice.

Lunarian cuisine had originally developed as something of a counterculture response to the prevalence of printed foodstuffs, which had led Lunarian cooking to utilize a wide selection of genetically engineered produce, designed with convenience in mind. The yama pepper, for instance, grew to contain a thick, spreadable paste, while the barange combined the easy peeling of a banana with flavor and texture similar to an orange.

The anti-printer aspect of Lunarian cuisine had faded in the ensuing centuries, but its unique ingredients and recipes persisted to form a popular niche within the wider realm of SysGov culinary arts.

"You've been looking forward to this, haven't you?" Cephalie took a seat on the edge of the fruit bowl.

"You better believe I have. There isn't a single ingredient on this plate that came from a printer." Isaac dipped one of the dumplings in yama sauce and took a bite. The sauce's sweetly spicy profile mixed perfectly with the savory meats inside.

He finished off the dumpling and spotted Elly Sako's arrival with a pair of security synthoids close behind. She passed one of the Admin tables and took the time to exchange words with the agents. She signed their virtual notebooks and even gave out a few hugs when the chronoport crew asked her.

Doug Chowder showed up shortly after Sako, now fully in his Neon Caravaggio persona. He stepped around the restaurant with an aloof, uninterested air about him, sniffing at the amateurish décor before joining the SysGov players at their private table up in one of the balconies. His girlfriend Ito Tomoe was also present, but she kept to herself, probably to make it easier for him to stay in character.

Markie Flavor-Sparkle was enjoying his breakfast in the balcony opposite the players. Or at least Isaac assumed so. He couldn't see the celebrity himself, but the colorful undulating streamers peeking over the edge and the muffled giggles of his female companions painted a clear enough picture.

"It's nice," Isaac declared, skewering a second dumpling.

"What's nice?" Cephalie asked.

"This." He indicated the restaurant and all its patrons. "Our two peoples hanging out, getting to know each other, and learning that—despite all our differences—we also have tons in common."

"I guess."

"You don't approve?"

"Nah, it's not that. Just being a realist." She pointed around the room with her cane. "You wouldn't see a scene like this in the Admin, that's for sure. Not with an 'artificial intelligence' like me floating around," she added, using the Admin term for abstract citizens with synthetic origins like her.

"True. But I think we're looking at real progress here. And the more positive exposure they get to ACs, the more likely they'll be to overcome their prejudices."

"Oh, I certainly agree with that. All I'm saying is we're looking at a small step in the right direction, not a paradigm shift. The people here are outliers in the Admin, not the new norm."

"Gotta start somewhere." He forked another dumpling into his mouth and chewed. "Hmm," he murmured disapprovingly.

"Not enough heat?" Cephalie asked.

"Not *quite* enough." Isaac added a dollop of yama paste to the sauce dish and mixed it in, resulting in a reddish slurry.

"You're going to kill what few taste buds you have left."

"So you keep telling me."

"Good morning, Isaac."

He looked up to see Susan join him at the table. She wore a black dress with long sleeves, a tall collar, and a shield-shaped pin at her throat. Isaac had also forgone his uniform for a black business suit and a scarf crackling with purple lightning.

"Good morning to you, too. Sleep well?"

"I did. And you?"

"Eh." He waffled one hand back and forth. "Had trouble getting to sleep. Kept thinking about the case last night."

"Why's that? We solved it, didn't we?"

"I know. But I still have this feeling that we missed something." He bit into a dumpling. "Not sure what, though."

Cephalie floated up to Susan's shoulder.

"He's just like this sometimes," she whispered into her ear. "Especially with the easy cases."

"Am not," he protested.

"We can head over to the CFPD if you want," Susan offered. "I doubt either of our superiors would be bothered with us being more thorough."

"*Psst!*" Cephalie hissed. "Don't encourage him!"

"Oh hush." Isaac dunked the half-eaten dumpling in yama sauce and finished it off. "But Cephalie's right. Sometimes I overthink the simple ones. Sometimes a love triangle gone bad is just what it appears to be. And occasionally the perp really is dumb enough not to scrub his own infosystems."

"'Never underestimate the stupidity of the criminal mind,'" Susan quoted.

"Too true. And speaking of which, we received an update from Lotz on the Pablo Evons murder."

"And?"

"Togashi Saga turned himself in last night and confessed to the whole thing. Sounds like he intends to throw himself at the mercy of the courts. According to him, he confronted Evons in the League restroom and tried to intimidate him into staying away from his wife. The other man refused to back down, and their confrontation turned violent."

Susan shook her head. "I don't even know her, but she hardly sounds worth it. A marriage is like any other oath. Why say the words if you had no intention of living by them?"

"Ultimately, we all choose who we build meaningful relationships with." He let out a long exhale. "Not everyone chooses well."

"You've got that right."

"That said, *this* relationship is one worth pursuing." Isaac tapped his fingers on the table.

"It is?" Susan squeaked, sounding startled.

"What?" He blinked in bewilderment.

"*Our* relationship?"

"Certainly. It's important for all our futures that SysGov and the Admin learn how to coexist together."

"I—" She paused, then seemed to calm down, almost deflating in the process. "Right. SysGov and Admin. Of course."

"Is something wrong?"

She shook her head, back to her usual self.

"You sure?"

"I must have misheard you at first. Don't worry about it."

"Okay," he replied, satisfied. "I won't, then."

He checked his abstract clock.

"We still have over an hour," Susan informed him.

"Yeah, but I figure they might want us to show up early. Either way, plenty of time till we need to go." He looked up from his food. "You still think Elly Sako will win?"

"Absolutely. You?"

"Wong Fei all the way."

"Oh really?" She raised a playful eyebrow at him. "Why so confident?"

"My keen detective instincts tell me so."

"*Zhù hào yún.*"

Isaac glanced over to her, and this time it was his turn to raise an eyebrow at her flawless use of the SysGov phrase.

"You're going to need it," she added with a wry grin.

◇　　◇　　◇

The Markie Flavor-Sparkle preshow was already underway when they arrived at Pistil Stadium, situated beneath a clear dome atop Pistil Tower. Bright colors and musical rhythms rioted through the bowl-shaped stadium, and Isaac muted the sensory deluge. The venue had a maximum capacity of over five thousand physical beings, and it was already close to that threshold, even though the preshow had yet to finish. The rising sun shone through the domed bubble canopy, casting long shadows across one side of the bleachers.

They followed the nav arrows to their assigned seats beside the large circular stage and sat down, at which point Isaac dropped his abstract filters.

He immediately regretted the decision. It was as if someone had taken all the colors in existence, swirled them into a ribboned slushy, then unscrewed his skull cap and poured the sludge directly into his brain pan.

"Uhh," he groaned, and checked his clock to see how long he'd have to endure the spectral onslaught.

"The show's much more tasteful when he leaves his shirt on," Susan commented, using a period of relative calm between songs.

"Sure," he grunted noncommittally.

As if on cue, Markie Flavor-Sparkle grabbed his shirt with both hands and ripped the front open, to the approving screams of his fans. He then threw the tattered garment into the crowd and began to sing "Love Hurts (And I'm a Masochist)."

"Never mind," Susan sighed.

"It's his thing."

"Where's your sister?"

"Umm, not sure." Isaac looked around. He ran a search, and an arrow blinked in his abstract vision, denoting Nina's seat far up the sloped sides of the stadium. She was standing atop her seat and waving at the singer with both arms. "Behind us near the exits."

"Guess her ticket didn't come with a seat near ours."

"Guess so."

A tall man in a crisp mauve business suit sat down on the edge of the seat next to Isaac, as if he intended to get back up soon. The sides of his head were shaved down to a buzz, while he'd grown the top and back long, pulling it into a braid that tailed halfway down his back. Impossible architecture morphed across his scarf in black and white, apparently inspired by Escher paintings with looping pathways that always led down, stairs that connected to the wrong place on upper levels, and other optical illusions.

"Detective Cho!" The man in the purplish suit extended his hand. "A pleasure to meet you!"

"Hello?" Isaac shook the man's hand, filtering out the concert once more. "And you are?"

"Sven Kohlberg, ActionStream senior publicist and chief coordinator for the Weltall Tournament. I wanted to stop by and thank you for bringing the 'you know what' to a swift conclusion."

"Just doing our job."

"For which I'm quite grateful." He leaned closer. "Trying to promote our latest product while visiting players threaten to kill one another is ... less than ideal, shall we say?"

"Certainly."

"Though, I was surprised when Lacan was arrested. My first guess, after I heard word of the incident, was Wong Fei would be the guilty party."

"Why do you say that?"

"Well, I'm sure you're better informed about this than me, but he's had run-ins with the law before. You know, the whole incident where he sent severed hands to his rivals." Kohlberg shook his head. "From the sound of it, the message sent to poor Elly had a similar feel."

"You're correct, of course, that we knew about Wong Fei's

history. And yes, the incidents do share some similarities, but we found no evidence linking the two."

"Oh, I see. I see." Kohlberg nodded. "That's reassuring to hear. Perhaps I was jumping to conclusions." He patted his chest and smiled. "I'm not an experienced detective, after all. Good to hear our side's star player is in the clear."

"Mister Kohlberg?" Susan asked, leaning over. "Speaking of star players, who do you think will win?"

"Oh, it's tough to say. *Very* tough. Wong Fei's the favorite, and for good reasons. I know some people say his strategies are boring and predictable, but the difference comes in the execution. Yes, his opponents tend to know what he'll do, but he performs so consistently and cleanly it really doesn't matter.

"So yes, Wong Fei is the favorite, but let me share a little tidbit with you. I officiated the universal qualifier in the Admin, and Elly Sako's performance really caught my eye over there. Much more so than Lacan's or Masuda's. Her approach was as unorthodox as it was impressive. If nothing else, I expect she'll hit the other players with unexpected strategies. Whether they'll be *effective* or not"—he shrugged—"who can say?"

"See?" Susan nudged Isaac with her elbow. "Elly has a chance."

"I never said she didn't."

Markie Flavor-Sparkle's performance of "Love Hurts (And I'm a Masochist)" reached its color-spurting climax, and Kohlberg edged forward in his seat.

"I'll be up soon. A pleasure speaking with you."

"Before you go," Isaac said, "do you have time for a quick question?"

"Oh, of course, Detective. Of course. What can I help you with?"

"I was wondering why the finals were being held on Luna. It seems an unusual choice, since both governments are centered on their respective Earths."

"Simple. The Admin insisted, and we saw no reason to deny the request."

"Why would they do that?"

"Politics, I believe. As a form of outreach between Earth and Luna over there. They wanted to elevate Luna's role throughout the Million Handshake Initiative."

"Makes sense," Susan added. "Improving relations between

Earth and Luna was a major pillar of the chief executor's election campaign."

"Ah," Isaac said.

Markie's song ended. He spread his arms, took a knee, and bowed to the audience, sweat dripping off his ripped chest.

A hole opened in a nearby aisle and a pathway extruded out to meet with the stage. Markie Flavor-Sparkle and his dancers filed out, waving at the cheering audience, and the path retracted behind them.

Another hole opened in the center of the stage, and a mirror-finished plinth rose as spotlights swiveled to focus on it. A gleaming trophy of frosted glass sat atop the plinth, stylized as a crashing meteor as big as the average head.

"Why a meteor?" Susan asked.

"It's the ActionStream logo," Isaac replied. "Though I'm surprised there's a physical trophy for the finals."

"Normally we don't have one," Kohlberg added. "But this tournament presented a few...unique challenges, shall we say? Assume for the moment an Admin player won. Any UAM we gave the winner would face compatibility issues over there. Plus, we would be sending them home empty-handed, which seemed lame to me. A physical trophy made the most sense for this event." He rose from the seat. "Anyway, that's my cue. Please enjoy the rest of the tournament."

"Thank you," Isaac said. "I'm sure we will."

Stairs formed on the side of the stage. Kohlberg ascended them and walked over to the trophy. He placed a hand beside the trophy and swept his gaze across the crowded stadium.

"Who's ready for some *Weltall*?" he asked in a voice that boomed across the room's shared abstract senses.

The dense crowd cheered its approval.

"All right! Then let's get to it!"

Five depressions formed on the stage, opening up to reveal spherical isolation pods, though Isaac noticed the distribution of the pods was not equidistant. Instead, an empty patch existed where an imaginary sixth pod would have completed the ring.

A side entrance yawned open, and beams of light focused to illuminate it.

"From the Admin's Lunar Federation," Kohlberg announced, "please welcome Elly Sako!"

Sako walked out, clad in Admin blue and silver, though her attire was a far cry from a Peacekeeper uniform. She wore a blue crisscrossed halter top with matching miniskirt connected by silver suspenders, along with blue leggings and silver boots. Abstract angelic wings unfurled behind her back. She raised her arms and waved as the crowd welcomed her warmly.

"And from the Admin's Earth, put your hands together for Shingo Masuda!"

Masuda stepped out into the open, his unsmiling expression focused and severe. His clothing shared the same Admin colors as Elly's but possessed a more formal flair, almost but not quite matching a Peacekeeper uniform. A flaming abstract snake spun in a circle behind him, consuming its own tail. He took hold of Elly's hand, and they raised their arms together, but while Elly smiled broadly, Masuda only nodded to a few individuals in acknowledgement of the crowd. Colorful abstract shapes, animated emojis, and brief messages streamed by overhead, sent from the tournament's off-site viewers.

"And now, from SysGov's European Cooperative. Please welcome Gomako Grim!"

An entrance on the far side of the stadium opened, the path ahead formed, and the first SysGov player stepped out, clad in a brilliantly white gown with white gloves and a flowing train that continued forward to curl around her ankles like a cloth serpent.

She raised her hands together, forming two mirrored letter G's with her fingers.

"Marry me, Gomako!" someone yelled close enough for Isaac to hear over the background applause.

Susan leaned over and spoke into Isaac's ear.

"Didn't Doug design her uniform?" she asked.

"So he said. Seems rather plain for him, though."

"Next, hailing from the state of One Asia, here's Yoo Ji-hoon!"

The next player stepped into the light, also dressed all in white, though his attire consisted of a long coat open in the front and a pair of baggy pants, showing off his chiseled abs and pectorals. He brushed back his shaggy hair, which transitioned dynamically from his natural black to the same pure white of his clothes.

"And last but certainly not least! Joining us from the L4 Lagrange Republic, here's Wong Fei!"

Wong Fei's attire reminded Isaac of Masuda's uniform but all in white to match his fellow SysGov players. He wore a calm, confident smile as he stepped up beside the other two. Once in position, all the players approached the stage, two from one side, and three from the other. Streamers unfurled from behind the SysGov trio, glowing brighter than the reflective white of their attire and whipping behind them. Abstract energy crackled between the streamers, growing more intense whenever the players closed with one another.

"Okay, now that's a neat touch," Isaac commented.

The players each took position next to an isolation pod.

"Format will be a standard configuration, free-for-all deathmatch," Kohlberg announced. "Each player must seek out and destroy his or her opponents' avatar cores. Today's session will conclude either when all but two players have been eliminated or at the end of the timer."

A three-hour countdown appeared overhead.

"Either way, the second session will start at the same time tomorrow. Game state will be preserved between sessions, and the tournament will continue each day in this manner until only one player's core remains. Any questions?"

None of the players spoke up.

"Players, are you ready?"

Everyone nodded.

"Then step into your pods!"

The five pods split in half like walnut shells. Each player climbed in, and the pods sealed them inside.

"Everyone, a quick demonstration before we begin!" Kohlberg walked up to Gomako Grim's pod and banged on the shell. "They can't hear a thing inside these! So if you see a sneaky tactic, cheer away! You won't alert the other players!"

Kohlberg hustled off the stage.

All the spotlights switched off, and a vast, abstract expanse of space materialized overhead. The stadium grew quiet. Markers appeared over five star systems, and tiny icons blipped into existence. Each player may have had their perception and commands limited by the speed of light, but the audience's spectator mode displayed all events simultaneously unless focused on a specific player's point of view.

Isaac and Susan watched the initial stages of the match unfold.

"A simple enough start," Susan said after a while. "Everyone's sending out their scouts, trying to locate the other players."

"Not everyone," Isaac noted. "Wong Fei isn't."

"Really? Hadn't noticed. I wonder why."

"Hmm." Isaac opened a private view of Wong Fei's home system over his lap. "He's placed most of his starting fleet around his sun."

"To do what?"

"To build something. Can't really tell what it'll be, though."

"Whatever it is, he's got an industrial head start on the other players, but not a huge one. And he's giving up a lot of situational awareness. Honestly, I don't think the tradeoff is worth it. He'll be in trouble if one of the other players catches him with his pants down."

"You could be right." Isaac zoomed out a bit. "And Masuda's home star isn't too far from his."

"Plus, the map is a tight one. Most stars have multiple neighbors within two light-years."

"They probably did that to speed up the game. It gives the players more resource options and also pits them against each other sooner."

"How do you think my girl Elly's doing?"

"Your 'girl'?" Isaac asked, giving her a sideways glance.

She smiled and shrugged.

"Let me see," he sighed, then zoomed over to Sako's starting system to find it almost devoid of activity. "This can't be right. Her home planet has less than half its starting industry."

"Would you widen the view, please?"

"Sure." He pulled back, and icons appeared sprinkled around her star's Oort cloud. "She's spreading herself thin. *And* she's lifted most of her planetary industry into space, along with her avatar core."

"Why would she do that?"

"To move them elsewhere, I'd assume. That's going to slow down her early game, but I'm sure she has something in mind. There *are* resources between stars, but they're harder to find and not nearly as plentiful."

"See how she's sent out three times the scouts of any other player?" Susan observed. "She's planning something, all right."

"Question is what."

"Masuda, Gomako, and Yoo all seem to have opted for standard openers. Scout their surroundings and build their core industries and fleet."

"But Masuda's leaning more heavily into military craft," Isaac said. "I think he might have spotted Wong Fei, hence why he's preparing for an offensive."

"Any sign Wong Fei knows he's been spotted?"

"Not that I can see. He's still focused on building his home industry, with a heavy focus on solar megastructures. Though it seems like he's *finally* started to scout the neighboring systems."

"Any scouts heading to Masuda's system?"

"Umm." Isaac shifted the private view. "Yes."

"Then there's a chance he'll spot the attack."

"Could be too late by then, though. Look." Isaac highlighted the frame of a new megastructure in Masuda's system.

"Oh, nice!" Susan grinned. "Masuda's building an interstellar mass driver."

"And it's oriented toward Wong Fei's system." Isaac grimaced. "I think we can agree he's been spotted."

"You worried?" she poked him with her elbow.

Isaac gave her a dismissive look.

"Just asking. It'd be a shame if your boy was taken out this early."

"First of all, he's not my 'boy.' Second, you realize we could both lose this..." He paused, struggling to find the appropriate word.

"Wager?" Susan suggested.

"No."

"What should we call it then?"

"I don't know. A pair of friendly predictions?"

"Fine by me." She reclined leisurely in her seat. "What happens when I win?"

"*If* you win."

Her eyes gleamed. "So, it *is* a wager?"

"I..." Isaac frowned. "Fine. It's a wager. Happy now?"

"Only once I win. What'll be my prize?"

"How about we all go to the beach after this?"

"Weren't we going to do that anyway?"

"...yes."

"Then what happens if you win? Do we go somewhere else?"

"No. The beach again."

"And if we both lose?"

"We still go to the beach."

"Hmm." Susan furrowed her brow and crossed her arms. "This is sounding less and less like a wager."

"Well, you made it clear you want to see a Lunar beach, so there you have it."

"I think you've missed the point."

"Probably."

The game unfolded and began to escalate, with light skirmishes occurring on the fringes of each player's territory. Gomako Grim and Yoo Ji-hoon both began to colonize second star systems, while Elly Sako's forces spread out in the cold expanse between stars, scrounging for dark planetoids ejected from their orbits.

Meanwhile, Masuda mustered his forces for an invasion of Wong Fei's star, and even though the elite SysGov player should have spotted the attack by now, he remained almost obsessively focused on expanding his industry. Several massive megastructures began to take form near his star, but Isaac couldn't tell what they were, since Wong Fei had built thin, reflective shells around each, masking the devices underneath.

"Looks like Wong Fei's time is running out," Susan mentioned.

"You might be right."

❖   ❖   ❖

Shingo Masuda wasn't sure which player he'd zeroed in on, but he appreciated the player's greedy approach: focus on economy and sprint ahead toward a macro endgame, overwhelming the opposition with a combination of superior tech and greater numbers. Calculated greed could propel a player far in this profession, and Masuda possessed a sense for when to press his luck and when to play it safe. It was one of the reasons he'd made it to the finals.

This was not a play-it-safe moment.

He'd studied the default starting position density before the match and calculated the odds of his home system spawning close to another player. Those odds were in favor of at least one other player being dangerously close.

Which was why he'd chosen an aggressive opener rather than a greedy one. Sure, it might put him behind later in terms of macroeconomics, but it also gave him more options in the early game, and some well-placed attacks could take out another player before he or she surpassed his temporary force advantage. That would leave him with two home systems rich in resources and one less foe to deal with later. Not a bad achievement for this early in the match.

Fortunately for him, he'd spotted his victim, who'd gone for an extra greedy opener heavy in solar megastructures. But all those massive orbiting satellites occluded the star's light, painting a giant bullseye on the system, and Masuda happened to be close enough to capitalize on his opponent's misfortune. He wasn't sure which megastructures the other player had constructed because of the thin, reflective shells masking them. There were a *lot* of options within *Weltall*'s tech tree, but judging by the player's other actions, he guessed they were for star lifting, meant to accelerate his or her early game advantage by converting the star matter into resources.

Masuda's scouts would soon report back with a detailed breakdown of the other player's system and might even spot the enemy avatar core. Either way, their battle would be over before it started since his interstellar superweapon would soon be primed and ready to fire. It would only take a few shots to decimate all those expensive megastructures, and then his fleet could swoop in and mop up whatever scattered forces remained.

Not a bad way to start the match. Not bad at all.

Events sped along at 2,102,400 seconds per second, equating to one simulated year every fifteen seconds of in-game time. He tweaked the parameters and build queues on some of his factories while he waited for the scouts' reports, then he started a few research projects to push him deeper into the tech tree.

The report came back a few minutes later, and he grinned wolfishly. It contained *exactly* the information he needed.

He loaded the coordinates into the superweapon and engaged its firing program. He couldn't see what he was shooting at in real time but was instead firing on projected positions of the planets and megastructures. This was one of the things he liked about *Weltall*. The developers had used the real-world limits of light to create the classic "fog of war" feel for their strategy game.

Still, even though he couldn't *see* the planets, orbits were predictable, and the time it took each kinetic projectile from the superweapon to reach them was also predictable, along with any curvature caused by nearby gravitation. The mathematics took place automatically within the game's interface; all he had to do was call the shots. His superweapon finished its salvo, and then Masuda ordered half his fleet to cross the interstellar gap between their two systems.

A part of him hoped Sako wasn't in the neighboring system.

It would be a shame if he took out the only other Admin player, especially after Lacan had humiliated all of them by getting arrested because, as Sako had put it, "His dick was sad." But Masuda was also a professional, and he intended to give this competition his all regardless of who he faced. He hoped the first casualty was a SysGov player, but a win was a win.

He opened a chart that summarized the progress of his attack, and then watched the salvo timer reach zero.

That was it. His mass driver attack had struck. He couldn't see the evidence yet, but his kinetic weapons had surely decimated his opponent's home system. He started a second, identical timer, counting down the time for when he'd be able to observe the first evidence of his attack.

And then he waited some more, eager to see all those gutted megastructures as he fleet moved closer.

But something else happened shortly before his second timer finished.

First, a report came back identifying Wong Fei's avatar core among the megastructures. The tough, triangular craft could take a surprising amount of damage for its size, giving it potential applications in early game rush tactics, but tough though it was, it couldn't withstand the output of his mass driver!

Masuda chuckled at this. He was about to take out the tournament's favorite in his opening engagement!

But then the occlusion pattern around the star changed, indicating Wong Fei was relocating those mysterious megastructures. Masuda frowned at this; that would leave more work for his fleet, and probably more losses in the mop up, but he'd still win, just not as decisively as he'd hoped.

He was tempted to adjust the orders to his fleet, but they'd be in Wong Fei's system by the time those orders arrived, and so he held back and waited some more—

—until Wong Fei's home star began to move.

"*What?*" he blurted, sitting up in his isolation pod.

The star accelerated to the side, and its gravity well dragged all the planets with it, altering their projected positions.

Masuda checked the superweapon's firing calculations.

"No!" he exclaimed.

All of his kinetic shots had missed. Wong Fei had dodged a near light-speed barrage at interstellar distances by *moving his star!*

More information came back, and now he could see the exposed megastructures were stellar engines! Lots of them! The star's path shifted, no longer to the side, but now accelerating directly toward Masuda's system.

His attack had failed, and now Wong Fei was coming toward him!

"I'm not out of this yet!" He queued up even more kinetic attacks.

His attacks sped across space, and this time he hit some of the planets, but Wong Fei had clustered not just the stellar engines, but *all* his megastructures behind his star! He was using his own star as a shield! It was almost like he'd converted his starting system into a mobile fortress!

Masuda's fleet reached the approaching star, and dire reports came back as his losses piled up.

"Not as greedy as I thought," he hissed.

He switched his entire industrial base over to the production of more ships, and even began cannibalizing the superweapon for materials. He needed every asset under his command switched to a war footing if he were to survive this, because he wasn't up against another player's fleet, with all the sloppy, long-distance control delay that entailed.

No, Wong Fei was bringing the heart of his industrial might with him for this attack! His star closed in, shrinking as the stellar engines converted its mass into thrust. Then, one by one, Wong Fei's fleet latched onto the megastructures and began decelerating them.

But the shrunken star continued to barrel forward.

"Oh no!"

Wong Fei's star shot through Masuda's system. It didn't even need to hit anything; its gravitation force alone distorted the orbits of planets, flinging some into deep space while sending others along scorching paths too close to his own star. All those resources that he desperately needed! Gone! Or, at best, temporarily out of reach! He needed every scrap he could muster, and this was not helping!

Wong Fei's fleet charged in, forming a protective shell ahead of his megastructures, and Masuda rallied his forces for what he feared would be his final showdown.

He tensed for the inevitable, fingers dancing across his controls.

But then the interface locked up suddenly and without warning, jittering between two frozen animation frames, and a reddish blot appeared before him. The blot expanded to either side, and viscous lines dripped from the stain. Its liquid flowed unnaturally, as if filling unseen containers with its murk.

And then those containers took form.

Or rather, their letters did.

The message before him read: LEAVE OR DIE.

It looked like blood.

He took a few heavy, unsteady breaths, unsure what to do next.

And then the words burst at him. Abstract blood gushed into his isolation pod, splashing all over him and flooding the interior. It wasn't real, couldn't be real. He felt no physical pressure from the stream of crimson, but he heard and saw it.

He signaled the pod to open, but nothing happened. He signaled it again, but his PIN couldn't locate the connection anymore.

"Help!" he cried, banging on the pod door. "Someone, get me out of here!"

No one answered. He could hear nothing outside the pod, and nothing could hear him.

The virtual fluid rose past his head. Blood stained his vision, and his breath quickened.

"Help! I can't see! Someone help me!"

He fumbled against the pod's arched interior with his hands, blinded by the grotesque visual data. His fingers clawed across a ridge near the top, and he remembered.

The manual release! They were shown how to use it during orientation!

He wrapped his fingers around the handle and pulled on it with all his might.

CHAPTER TWELVE

"AND THEN THERE WERE FOUR," SUSAN SAID.

"Hmm," Isaac replied, not really listening as he leaned forward in his seat.

What exactly just happened? he thought.

He knew the game well enough from the trial version to know what had occurred mechanically. Wong Fei's forces had swept through Masuda's home system where they'd blasted everything in sight, including Masuda's core. After that, Wong Fei had maneuvered his megastructures into orbit around Masuda's star, claiming the untapped stellar body as his own.

That much was clear.

But *why* had it happened?

"Seems like your boy's still in it," Susan added.

"Did you notice how Masuda froze up at the end?"

"Not really. I was focused on all the exploding spaceships."

"He hardly put up a fight. He didn't even try to evacuate his core to another system. Doesn't that seem odd to you?"

"Maybe he didn't see a way out?" Susan suggested, not sounding confident in her reasoning.

Masuda's pod split open, and he flopped out onto his hands and knees. He crawled across the stage on all fours, picked himself up, then stumbled over the edge when stairs formed too slowly. His knee cracked against the hard floor below the stage, and he winced and rose again.

He limped down one of the aisles, which gaped open and extruded a path down into the understage. Kohlberg hurried after him with a concerned look on his face.

"What's going on?" Isaac asked.

"I don't know," Susan said, "but it doesn't look good."

Both of them rose from their seats at the same time and headed after Masuda. They took the same path down into the understage, which opened into a circular space with tunnels leading off in eight directions and a central column supporting the stage. Thick beams hung low off the ceiling, spreading out under the stage in a radial pattern, and hexagonal containers lined the walls, their contents ready to be hauled up onto the stage by automated systems depending on how the venue was to be utilized.

Kohlberg stood near Masuda by one of the exits, which a pair of DTI agents hustled out of, alert but unsure of the nature of the crisis.

"I'm sorry. What happened again?" Kohlberg asked urgently.

"Someone hacked the game!" Masuda cried out.

"Detective Cho, SysPol Themis," Isaac said, pinging everyone nearby with his badge. "Mister Masuda, are you all right?"

"No, I'm not all right!" he spat, his brow creased with worry. He pointed at the ramp leading up to the stadium. "There was a message in the game!"

"A message?" Isaac asked. "What kind? What did it say?"

"There were bleeding letters in the interface, and they read as 'leave or die.'"

"But that's..." Isaac paused and bowed his head in thought.

It was the same message Elly Sako had received. But Lacan couldn't have delivered it, right? He was locked up in the CFPD, and besides, manipulating a complicated abstraction like *Weltall* was leagues different from pranking a hotel printer. Furthermore, Masuda had no connection to the dispute between Sako and Lacan, other than being a fellow Admin player participating in the same tournament. At least, no connection they'd come across so far.

What's going on here? he wondered.

He looked over to Susan, who shook her head as if to say she didn't have a clue either.

"Blood letters?" Kohlberg scoffed. "That can't be right."

"I know what I saw," Masuda stressed. "Don't try to tell me otherwise!"

"I—" Kohlberg stopped himself. "Yes, of course. I'm very sorry, Mister Masuda. I didn't mean to imply you were lying."

"You two!" Masuda snapped at the DTI agents. "I'm leaving!"

"Back to your room, sir?" asked one of the agents.

"Absolutely not!" he snapped. "Didn't you hear me? Someone wants me dead! So fuck this tournament and fuck going back to my room! You're to take me straight to the chronoport, because I'm not leaving it until we're safely back in the Admin, you hear me?"

"Understood, sir."

"Now hang on a minute," Kohlberg urged. "Let's not be hasty. If what you say is true, perhaps we can make an exception to your loss."

"*If?!*"

"I'm not saying you're wrong, mind you, only that we'll need to check the software first. As long as we do find tampering, we could invalidate your loss. For instance, we could reinstate you into the competition with a new core, or perhaps restart the entire match. Given the unusual circumstances we find ourselves in, I'm more than willing to entertain—"

"Forget it!"

"But—"

"Save it!" Masuda pointed to the two agents. "We're leaving!" He turned on his heel without another word and marched down the nearest corridor. The two agents took up positions in his wake.

"Oh dear," Kohlberg moaned as the trio disappeared around a corner, following an abstract sign to the grav chutes.

"What the *hell* is going on?" Pérez demanded, hurrying down the ramp to the understage. He strode over to Isaac and the others with fire in his eyes.

"Someone sent Masuda a death threat while within the game," Isaac recapped. "Same message as before. 'Leave or die.' He's being taken back to the chronoport."

"Is this true?" Pérez stepped up to Kohlberg by the corridor mouth.

"That's what Masuda said happened to him," Kohlberg answered. "I can't say more until someone looks at the UAM."

"Damn it!" Pérez growled, slamming a fist into the wall. Isaac assumed his strength limiters were engaged because he didn't punch *through* it.

"Miguel?" Susan asked.

"I—" He seemed to collect himself. He lowered his fist and

straightened his posture. "Sorry. I shouldn't have reacted like this. I'm just upset that—I'm just upset." He turned to Isaac. "Detective, looks like this mess is back on your lap."

"That it is, unfortunately."

"How should we proceed?"

"First, we need to look at that program. Mister Kohlberg?"

"Yes?"

"I need you to halt the tournament."

"But—"

"No buts. We need to look at the UAM files loaded into their pods, because that's the only lead we have right now. Either pause the tournament willingly or we come back with a court order shutting you down. Do we have an understanding?"

"Uhh, no. I mean, yes. Yes, we have an understanding, but—"

Kohlberg stopped at the sound of the two synthoids hurrying down the ramp: a silver-skinned man and a woman with a faceted, ruby-like face. Both wore mauve clothing similar to Kohlberg's business suit.

"Who are they?" Isaac asked pointedly.

"My superiors," Kohlberg said, moments before the avatar of a flaming wheel materialized behind the new arrivals. "And one of our lawyers. I'll need their permission to shut the tournament down. They'll want to see that court order."

"Then they'll have it. Cephalie?"

She appeared on Isaac's shoulder.

"See to it. Make it clear to the judge we need this expedited."

"Right away!"

She vanished.

"I'll, uhh, go break the bad news to them." Kohlberg donned a forced smile and started up the ramp to join the two synthoids and their abstract lawyer.

Isaac opened a comm window.

"Hey, Isaac," Nina responded. "Why do I get the feeling this isn't good news?"

"Because it's not. Meet us beneath the stage. Looks like we have a busy day ahead of us."

✧   ✧   ✧

"What do you have for us?" Isaac asked Nina.

The stadium was empty except for the SysPol officers and their drones while virtual police cordons glowed across each of the exits. Cephalie had returned with a court order granting SysPol Themis the authority to suspend the tournament as part of their investigation, and Kohlberg—after reviewing the documentation with the ActionStream lawyer—canceled the remaining tournament events for the day. The players had all returned to their respective rooms, with Masuda being the only exception.

"Well, Cephalie and I can confirm Masuda's story." She propped a leg up on the stage next to Masuda's pod and leaned over her knee. A pair of her forensics drones floated behind her, giving her an official air despite her baby blue dress. "The pod's infostructure recorded the message, and it played out like he said with letters written in blood. Same threat as before. 'Leave or die.'"

"SysGov English?" Susan asked. "Or the Admin version?"

"The Admin's," Cephalie said from atop the LENS. "Identical to what came with Sako's 'head.'"

"Hmm." Isaac stepped up to the pod and gazed in. "Anything else?"

"No," Nina said. "Or, at least, not yet. We collected a save-state off the pod and uploaded it to Panoptes. We'll have to wait for the analysis."

"Did you—"

"*And*," Nina cut in, "because I know my little brother so well, I already filed a request for it to be expedited. It's near the top of their job queue."

"Thanks. That's what I was about to ask."

"Can I call it or what?" Nina told Susan.

"But what about Lacan?" Susan asked.

"That's the question, isn't it?" Isaac stepped away from the pod, head bowed in thought. "We have two threats now, the first of which we *believe* Lacan sent. But now I'm not so sure. Have we arrested an innocent man?"

"The evidence fingered him as the perp," Nina stated.

"I know, but perhaps we need to dig deeper." He looked up at Nina. "I'd like you to go over his wearable again. Go over it *hard*. Look for anything out of place. Anything suspicious."

"You've got it."

"Do you think we might be dealing with two criminals?" Susan asked. "Lacan with the first and someone copying him for the second?"

"Perhaps. But if so, why? What would this theoretical second criminal gain by mimicking the first message? Not only is Lacan stuck in a cell, but he lacks the experience to alter a SysGov UAM file. If someone's trying to pin the second death threat on him, they're going about it all wrong."

"Or perhaps both messages were sent by the same person," Susan suggested, "and we arrested Lacan in error."

"I'm more inclined to believe that scenario," Isaac said, "as much as I hate to admit we messed up."

"Either way, I think we need to talk to Masuda next," Susan suggested. "Perhaps there's a link between the two incidents. Beyond the obvious fact they're both Admin players."

"Agreed. Nina?"

"I know the drill. I'll finish up here then head back to CFPD to take another look at Lacan's wearable."

"Thanks. Let me know as soon as you find something."

"Will do."

He joined Susan by the edge of the stage. "Let's go, then."

✧   ✧   ✧

"Thank you for agreeing to speak with us, Mister Masuda."

"It's no problem, Investigator," Masuda replied, fidgeting as he settled into his chair. "Or should I call you a detective?"

"Either will do, I suppose."

Masuda sat across from the two detectives in *Defender-Prime*'s cramped mess hall, which doubled as a conference room when needed.

"I . . ." Masuda wrung his hands and put on a forced smile. "I've calmed down a bit since I got that message. Having a couple thousand tons of military hardware between me and the outside is reassuring."

"I'm sure it is." Isaac opened his abstract notes. "We'd like to ask you a few questions, if you don't mind. Mostly to look for any connections between this incident and the first. Beyond the obvious, of course."

"Of course. I'll help you any way I can."

"That's good to hear." Isaac swiped to a new page. "I'd like to start by going over some of your background. You're from the Admin's Earth, correct?"

"That's right. My whole family is. My dad works in the Department of Blight Restoration, though he's just a superintendent, unfortunately. Nothing too special."

Isaac glanced over to Susan. "Where do superintendents fit into the Admin hierarchy?"

"They're one tier below directors."

"Ah."

Nothing special, huh? Isaac thought.

"Why did you say 'unfortunately' when you referred to your father's position?"

"Well, Dad's been after an under-director slot for years, but there's a *lot* of competition for those." Masuda leaned forward and spoke softly. "Lots of backroom politics. Lots of backstabbing, too. The infighting gets vicious whenever a slot opens. He would have the position on merit alone if it wasn't for all that needless backroom drama."

"What about your mother?"

"Department of Public Relations. She's the one who recommended I compete in the Weltall Tournament, even though I wasn't too thrilled about this whole transdimensional travel thing. I don't like to leave Earth if I can avoid it, but now look at me." He chuckled. "Here I am, getting death threats in another universe. Anyway, Mom worked on the publicity campaign for the Million Handshake Initiative. The Weltall Tournament, specifically. She's been busy commissioning adverts, running publicity events. That sort of thing. Loves her job. Both of them do, really."

"And yourself?"

"I know my parents would have liked to see me in the Admin, and I did have my eye on a position in the DBR for a while. Even took classes in self-replicator theory and containment strategy, though I never experienced that spark of enthusiasm I have with games. Looking back, I think I was blindly following Dad's footsteps until I realized my path led elsewhere.

"I'd be lying if I said my parents were fully supportive. There was some...pushback, at least at the outset. But in the end, they realized—and *accepted*—that my passions lay elsewhere." He flashed a self-congratulatory smile. "And, to be honest, they're *quite* happy with the money I'm raking in from the tournament circuit. Plus, I think Mom likes having a family member in the tournament. I've been featured in a few recent adverts, if I'm not mistaken."

"Does your family have a long history of service in the Admin?"

"Oh, yes!" His eyes lit up. "It all began with my great-great-great..." He started counting with his fingers, but then stopped and frowned. "You know, I seem to have forgotten how many greats it was. Anyway, it began with my something-great grandfather back in the 2700s. Kentaro Masuda. Perhaps you've heard of him?"

Isaac glanced over to Susan again.

"He's...umm?" She shrugged and shook her head. "No, sorry."

"He served in the Violations War. Even fought in the Battle of Phobos Command. Our family's been a part of the Admin ever since. It's one of the reasons Mom and Dad resisted my career choice at first. But it's not like the line's at risk of being broken anytime soon. My little brother already accepted a commission in the Peacekeepers, and my little sister is studying chronometrics in the hopes of joining the DTI, though competition for those slots is *fierce* these days."

Isaac considered the differences in background between Sako and Masuda. There wasn't much common ground between the two, besides the fact they were both from the Admin. Sako was the clear outsider with her Lunarian heritage and the moon's troubled history, while Masuda hailed from a line rich in service to the Admin.

So far, there's only the one link, he thought. *They're both from the Admin.*

"Moving on," Isaac began, "please describe your relationship with GW Lacan."

"I wouldn't call it a relationship, really. We first met in person at Byrgius University during the universal qualifiers, and he didn't make much of an impression, though that certainly changed!"

"How so?"

"Let me put it this way. We're here as representatives, whether we like it or not. Our actions reflect upon the Admin as a whole, for better or for worse, but that's a responsibility Lacan either didn't realize he had or simply chose to ignore. I'm not sure which is worse. *I'm* certainly aware of my responsibilities here, and I assure you I take them very seriously."

"What about Elly Sako?"

"She..." Masuda frowned and hesitated.

"Yes?"

"I'm sorry. Is this really necessary? She received a threat, too. Does my opinion of her really matter?"

"It might. It's impossible to say whether a fact is relevant to the case when it remains unknown."

"Of course, but..."

"Why the hesitation, Mister Masuda?"

"It's just..." He sighed. "You know the saying, 'If you can't say something nice...'"

"'Don't say anything at all,'" Isaac finished. "Of course, I do."

"*That's* why I'd rather not speak ill of her behind her back."

"Mister Masuda—"

"But, I understand your position." He huffed out a breath again. "Look, I don't want to sound like a bigot here, but she makes me uneasy."

"Why's that?"

"Well, she's Lunarian."

"And?"

"And nothing. She's a Lunarian, and I get nervous around her because of it. Look, I know this sounds bad. I know not every Lunarian is a terrorist. There are good ones and bad ones just like people from every other corner of the system. It's just Luna has a *lot* more troublemakers than Earth does. They're a constant thorn in the Admin's side, and I've heard some insider stories that will churn your stomach. So, because of that, she puts me on edge." He sat back. "I know her background shouldn't have that kind of effect on me. I'm just being straight with you here, okay?"

"And I appreciate your honesty, Mister Masuda. Is there anything else about her besides her lineage that makes you uneasy?"

"No. Not really."

"Not really or not at all?"

"The latter."

"Very well." Isaac made a few notes. "What about Wong Fei? What's your relationship with him?"

"I've spoken to him a few times. Same with Grim and Yoo. Didn't have any problems with any of them, though Wong Fei struck me as the most approachable."

"Anything of note from your interactions with SysGov citizens, the other players included? Anything unusual or strangely confrontational?"

"Nothing comes to mind, sorry." He smiled faintly and let out a brief, sad chuckle. "Besides the message in blood, I have nothing but praise for our hosts."

"What about your thoughts on how Wong Fei took you out of the tournament?"

"He outplayed me, simple as that. I'm man enough to admit when I've been beaten. But I'm not sore about it, if that's what you mean. The good thing about being a professional gamer is there's always another tournament."

"What about your security detail?" Isaac asked, grasping for any lead at this point. "Anything out of the ordinary there?"

"No. They've been superb. I have nothing but praise for Pérez and his team."

"I see. Finally, I want to loop back to Lacan. Do you believe he was the one who threatened you and Miss Sako?"

"I can only speak for myself, but no, I don't see why he would have threatened me like that." Masuda shrugged. "Or *how* he could have."

"Is there anyone you suspect of threatening you?"

"No." Masuda shook his head. "No idea. Sorry."

"That's quite all right, Mister Masuda." Isaac closed his notes and rose from his seat. "That'll be all for now. Thank you for your time."

CHAPTER THIRTEEN

"SO, WHAT DO YOU THINK IS GOING ON HERE?" ISAAC ASKED. HE and Susan sat at a corner table in the Fertile Ground restaurant while they nursed their drinks. They'd changed back into their uniforms—*again*—and had stopped at the restaurant for a quick lunch break. His LENS floated nearby, and Cephalie's avatar sat on his shoulder.

"My guess is a simple one," Susan began. "We have two death threats against two Admin players. Seems to me the obvious explanation is the most likely one. Someone in SysGov doesn't want the Admin around, and they're using this tournament to make their point."

"What do you make of Lacan?"

"Framed. We'll know more once Nina gets back to us, but I'm guessing she'll find some well-hidden holes in the evidence."

"Which she should have spotted at the outset," Isaac grumped. "Assuming Lacan *was* framed."

"You upset with her?"

"Maybe a little. Either way, we know someone other than Lacan is causing trouble, whether he's involved or not."

"The question is who."

"Right," Isaac sighed. He took a sip of his coffee. "That's the question."

"Do you think LAST might be involved?"

"I suppose it's a possibility. Cephalie?"

"Hmm?" She glanced up from his shoulder.

"What's going on with the protests outside? Have they calmed down at all?"

"The exact opposite." She shook her head like a disapproving parent. "The crowd has doubled in size while the rate of incidents has *tripled*."

"That's what I was afraid of," Isaac said. "If anything, the protest shows not everyone is happy with the Million Handshake Initiative. We know a vocal minority wants all this burgeoning goodwill to go away and for both sides to stay clear of each other. As for whether they're *involved* in any of this"—he shrugged his shoulders—"who can say?"

"LAST's involvement," Susan said, "or the involvement of someone sympathetic to their cause, could explain why Lacan was framed. If someone wants the Admin out, why not create an Admin scapegoat while you're at it?"

"Sorry, but I have to disagree with you there," Isaac said.

"Why's that?"

"Recall our reactions when we pinned the crime on Lacan. All our tension melted away because we thought he was nothing more than a lovesick fool causing trouble. If the criminal's goal is to make the players leave, like the messages say, then framing Lacan *hurt* that goal instead of helping it."

"Perhaps there's another motive for framing him?"

"Maybe. But then why make it so obviously *not* him for the second threat?" Isaac asked. "That's the part I can't figure out, no matter how hard I try. On the surface, the two incidents bear plenty in common. But look a little deeper, and it's like they conflict with one another. It doesn't make sense to me. Why go through the trouble of framing someone if you don't plan to follow through with that fiction?"

"Yeah, I see your point." Susan stirred her barange soda with the straw. "Where do we take this from here?"

"ActionStream. Kohlberg headed back to the office after we brought a halt to the tournament, and Cephalie's already set up a meeting there. The UAM's theirs, so we look at who had access to it and when. We'll head up Pistil Tower after we finish lunch." He looked over to see their waitress returning. "Speaking of which."

"Here you go, sir." The waitress's beetle drone set a plate down with his "kroppkakor torpedo." The long roll was stuffed with round dumplings, each filled with minced bacon, onions, and potatoes, and all of it drizzled in a thick yama sauce that oozed out the sides.

"Thanks." Isaac licked his lips and sent her a generous tip, which she acknowledged with a polite nod.

"Is there anything else you need, sir?"

Isaac shook his head and tried to find a good way to pick up the huge sandwich. He slipped his fingers underneath the bottom.

"How about you, ma'am? Anything for you? Perhaps I can top off your drink?"

"Oh, no. I'm fine." Susan raised her soda. "Still plenty left."

"Just let me know if you need anything, then." The waitress left with the beetle drone buzzing in the air behind her.

"You sure that thing'll hold together?" Susan asked as Isaac struggled with his sandwich.

"What makes you say that?" he asked moments before half the sandwich slipped out the back and plopped onto his plate. "Aww." He set the deflated sandwich down and used a fork to shovel the innards back between the slices.

"Might want to cut that monster in half first."

"I think you're right." He finished reassembling his sandwich and was about to cut it down the middle when an alert blinked in his abstract vision. He checked the sender and toggled the alert with his elbow. "Go ahead, Nina."

The comm window expanded. "Hey, Isaac. Did I catch you at a bad time?"

"Just refueling," he said, cutting the sandwich in half. "What do you have for us?"

"The forensics report on the *Weltall* program came back."

"That was fast."

"Hey, I'm not complaining. I sent you the full version, but figured you'd like me to walk you through the summary." She tilted her head. "Should I wait until you finish?"

"Now's fine." Isaac raised the sandwich to his lips, only to accidentally squeeze the dumplings out the back again. They *splorshed* onto his plate and splattered his uniform with yama sauce. He grunted something incoherent under his breath, then picked up his napkin and unfurled it with a snap of the wrist. His uniform's smart fabric became waterproof, and he sopped up the sauce with his napkin.

"You having trouble over there?" Nina tittered.

"No more than usual." He picked up his knife and fork with a sigh and cut off a bite-sized chunk of the sandwich. "What's the brief from Panoptes?"

"First, they compared the save-state from Masuda's pod to an unaltered copy of the UAM ActionStream provided. From there, they identified the changes and reverse engineered them. The changes were simple and easy to spot, residing in a task running parallel to the main UAM runtime. Even someone with a basic understanding of UAM architecture could pull this off. Hell, *I* could probably have whipped this together, and UAMs aren't really my thing."

"Assuming you had access to the original file," Isaac said, "which could be the tricky part."

"Everyone on the guest list has an advanced copy," Susan noted.

"Hmm. Good point. Never mind."

"Anyway," Nina continued. "That parallel task targeted Masuda specifically, keying in on his PIN's connection string. Again, not difficult to get ahold of for people involved in the tournament."

"Then he wasn't targeted at random." Isaac nodded. "Good to know. Anything else?"

"Just the audio and visual abstraction itself. Letters in blood and all that."

"Did the report find anything that *shrinks* the list of suspects?" Isaac asked.

"Sorry, nope."

"I suppose it was too much to hope for," he complained. "How about you and Lacan's wearable?"

"I'm at CFPD, and my drones are tearing it apart, layer by layer, both from a physical and a data perspective. If there's anything fishy inside, I'll find it, but it won't be fast. I'm being extra, *extra* thorough this time, given what we expect to find."

"Understood. Keep at it."

"Will do."

"Would someone on Pérez's team be able to help?" Susan suggested. "Especially since it's Admin hardware instead of what you're most familiar with? That might even be why you missed something the first time."

"Maybe. It's worth a shot. I'll give him a call."

"Let us know as soon as you have something," Isaac said.

"Of course."

Nina closed out of the call.

Isaac began to cut off another bite from his sandwich, but the innards slipped out before he finished and landed in a puddle of yama sauce.

Susan drained her barange soda and set it down. "To Action-Stream?"

"In a minute," Isaac said, grimacing at the culinary warzone on his plate.

✧　　✧　　✧

The grav tube dropped them off in a stylish foyer with couches to either side of translucent red doors. Vines climbed up the walls, and the meteor logo of ActionStream glowed overhead, its long tail burning a diagonal path.

The doors split open, and Isaac led the way over to the receptionist's half-moon desk, which hardly seemed necessary, since the receptionist was an AC. The avatar floated up as they approached, manifesting as a burning meteor with a broad, friendly face composed of craters and a flaming top.

"May I assist you?" the receptionist asked in a deep, masculine voice.

"Yes," Isaac said. "I'm Detective Cho. This is my deputy, Agent Cantrell, and my IC, Encephalon. We have an appointment with Sven Kohlberg."

"Of course, Detective. I see you on the schedule right here." The receptionist detached a portion of the meteor's burning exterior and tapped through one of his virtual screens, prompting a comm window to open.

"Yeah?" Kohlberg asked in audio only.

"Detective Cho and company here to see you, sir."

"Oh, good! I'll be right out."

The meteor-receptionist closed the comm window.

"He should be with you shortly. Is there anything else I can do for you, Detective? Refreshments perhaps?" Fragments of the meteor formed a hand-shape, and he gestured toward an expensive-looking food printer built into the wall near a quartet of abstraction recliners.

"No, thank you."

"Perhaps I can entice you with you a sampling of our company's abstractions, then? Those recliners have access to our entire software library, as well as a few upcoming releases, such as *Weltall*. All available for you to sample free of charge."

"That's quite all right," Isaac declined. "We'll wait here, if it's all the same."

"Of course, sir." The meteor-receptionist tipped his fiery top hat. "Please let me know if there's anything you need."

"Is your avatar always a talking logo?" Susan asked.

"Only during business hours," the receptionist said with a craggy smile. The meteor-face flashed into a hulking barbarian in a loin cloth with a pair of sword handles sticking up over his shoulder. He shrugged then flashed back to the meteor-face. "It's part of my dress code."

"Ah."

Kohlberg walked into the reception area a few minutes later.

"Detective Cho! Agent Cantrell!" He beamed at the two of them before the avatar on the LENS caught his eye. "And..."

"Call me Cephalie," his IC added from atop the LENS.

"Cephalie, nice to meet you." He rubbed his hands together. "Any news on the case, Detective? Can we start the tournament back up?"

"Is there somewhere we can talk in private?" Isaac asked.

"Certainly. We can use my office. Right this way."

He led the way down a long hallway. Office spaces sprawled out to either side, separated from the corridor by tall glass walls. Men and women in business suits mingled with AC avatars of space pirates, dragons, wizards, witches, cyber-knights, amazons in bikini chainmail, soldiers from both World Wars, war-synthoids from the Colonial Wars, a variety of real and fantastical space-ships, and a cute, tiny pig in striped pajamas.

"Our abstract employees can use models from our products," Kohlberg explained without being prompted. "Makes a meat bag like me a little jealous sometimes."

"Which one would you pick?" Susan asked.

"Pardon?" Kohlberg turned halfway around as they continued down the hall.

"Which model? If you were an AC, I mean."

"You know, no one's ever asked me that." He rubbed his chin in thought. "I suppose I'd have to go with Jack Danger."

"Who's that?"

"A swashbuckling vagabond with a heart of gold."

"He's a character from *Sky Pirates of Venus*," Isaac said as they moved beyond the larger work areas and entered an area of smaller, more private offices.

"Which is still our most lucrative property, even after all these years," Kohlberg added. "Not as big as the *Solar Descent* juggernaut, but then again, what is? Back then, I was still a programming grunt. Are you a fan of the property, Detective?"

"I...may have played it once or twice."

"Well, just say the word. I'd be happy to give you an advanced copy of the next expansion once this business with the tournament settles down."

"Thank you for the offer, but no."

"Fair enough. Here we are." Kohlberg palmed an abstract interface, and the glass wall split open. He stepped into the spacious office, rounded the black glass desk with the ActionStream meteor logo, and sank into the recliner behind it. The desktop looked unusually thick, leading Isaac to assume it contained a powerful infosystem.

A pair of chairs formed out of the floor, and Isaac and Susan sat down. The glass office wall closed and frosted over for privacy.

"Now." Kohlberg knitted his fingers on the desk. "When can we restart the tournament?"

"I'm afraid that won't be anytime soon."

"Why not?" Kohlberg asked pointedly. "You have the save-state from their pods, correct? What more do you need?"

"Mister Kohlberg, I understand your interest in getting the tournament back on schedule, but *my* interest is identifying who's sending these messages and bringing them to justice. For now, the stage is a crime scene, and until I have a better understanding of how that program was altered, it will remain off-limits."

"But—"

"Mister Kohlberg," Isaac interrupted, "I'd appreciate it if you let me ask the questions here."

"Yes, of course. Sorry. It's just I've been tense around here. The CEO is riled up over this fiasco. If you ask me, he's gearing up our legal team to contest the order."

"He's certainly welcome to try."

"Either way, *that* one's not my fight." Kohlberg sat up. "Go ahead and ask your questions, Detective. What do you want to know?"

"First, who loaded the UAM into the pods?"

"Easy. I took care of that. Loaded the latest version myself."

"Did anyone else have access to the pods?"

"No. They were sealed and submerged just below the stage. We had to make way for Flavor-Sparkle's crew and his opening act."

"What about from the understage?"

"No, the pods weren't low enough. They were still in the stage, not stored in an understage container. You'd have to either raise the pod to the stage or place it in storage in order to access it."

"Then do you believe anyone could have accessed the pods between the time you loaded the program and the players began their match?"

"No, I don't see how. And even if someone did, they would have been in plain view of the concert crew."

"Then what about Flavor-Sparkle's roadies?"

"Same answer. Anyone trying to access the pods from up top would have to raise them first."

"Cephalie?" Isaac said.

"Yes?" Her avatar appeared on the desktop.

"Check in with the Crimson Flower's management. See if we can get access to the stadium's surveillance records and the understage logistical records."

"You thinking we might get lucky and spot someone messing with Masuda's pod?" she asked. "Maybe while Flavor-Sparkle's crew was setting up? Or perhaps down in the understage?"

"It's worth a shot."

"I'll get the ball rolling, then." She vanished.

"Moving on, Mister Kohlberg," Isaac continued, "did you make any changes to the UAM after you received the latest version?"

"No, of course not." He chuckled. "Why would I?"

"How did you receive the file?"

"Right here." He tapped his desk. "It was sent to my office infosystem."

"Did you forward the file to the pods from here?"

"No, I took it down in person. Had to because the pods won't accept remote updates. Used a secure wearable, too. The company discourages us from transmitting full versions of the game before publication. An infraction like that comes out of my yearly bonus, which means I walked the file over."

"Did you go straight to the stage from here?"

"No, I received the file yesterday, so I took it home with me—again, on a wearable—then loaded it early this morning. Why do you ask?"

"Who sent it to you?"

"An AC named Ergon."

"And who's that?"

"He's the owner of Unreality Disconnect, one of our software development subsidiaries. UD is the team who coded *Weltall*, with Ergon developing the initial concept. It's a small team. Maybe five or six ACs, last I checked. ActionStream is acting as the publisher in this arrangement."

"Do you know if Ergon was involved in coding the program?"

"Oh, most definitely! He's very hands-on with the products he and his team deliver. I'd venture to say he coded thirty or forty percent of *Weltall* all on his own, and his team worked through the rest under his direction. *Very* talented AC, that one, though a bit odd. He used to work for us directly. Even coded part of *Sky Pirates* before branching out to found his own company. That's one of the reasons we do business with him so often."

"Then is it likely Ergon made coding changes prior to sending you the latest version?"

"Likely? I'd stay it's almost a *certainty*! He's always adjusting features and making balance changes up to the last minute. You know what they say, right?"

"What do they say?"

"First rule to finishing a project is to shoot all the programmers!" Kohlberg laughed as if he'd told a fabulously funny joke, but when neither Isaac nor Susan joined him, he cleared his throat awkwardly. "Umm, because they'll, you know, keep tweaking the code until the end of time? Sorry, it's just a joke. Probably funnier if you work in the industry."

"I would assume so," Isaac agreed dryly. "Mister Kohlberg, do you have an IC?"

"How is that relevant?"

"Please answer the question."

"Well, no," Kohlberg frowned. "Not presently. I'm between companions at the moment. Been separated from my last IC for a couple years. Still searching for a new special someone. Besides, it's better that way. At least in the short term."

"Why do you say that?"

"Because of my travel to and from the Admin, obviously. It's easier not having one right now."

"Who was your last IC?"

"That would be Claudia Siebert. Originally organic, but she abstracted about . . . oh, fifteen years ago, I think? Nice enough person, but we weren't a good enough fit."

"What was the deepest level of integration you tried?"

"Low. Surface thoughts only. Didn't go deeper than that." Kohlberg shrugged. "We gave it an honest try, but it didn't work out. I don't blame her for the breakup, and as far as I know she doesn't blame me."

"Do you have her connection string?"

"Of course. Why?"

"Can you provide it?"

"Sure." Kohlberg opened a comm window, searched through his contacts, and transmitted the string to Isaac. "There you go."

"Thank you." Isaac saved the string to his notes.

"Look, Detective, I'm okay with sharing, but mind telling me where the sudden interest in my background is coming from?"

"It's quite simple, Mister Kohlberg," Isaac said. "You were the last person in possession of the UAM before it was loaded into Shingo Masuda's pod."

Kohlberg's brow furrowed and it stayed that way for long seconds, but then realization dawned on his face and his eyes widened.

"But that would mean— Are you suggesting what I think you're suggesting?"

"The sequence of possession over the program passed through you, Mister Kohlberg."

"But I wouldn't *change* it!" he defended. "And besides, I received the program directly from Ergon!"

"Yes. Which makes *both* of you suspects."

CHAPTER FOURTEEN

"NOW, HOLD ON A SECOND!" KOHLBERG BLURTED, STANDING UP. "You can't possibly believe I had anything to do with this!"

"What I believe doesn't really matter." Isaac rose from his own seat and looked Kohlberg in the eyes. "It's possible you're involved, and it's our job to either show the scenario to be true or false. If you're innocent, then you have nothing to fear."

"But my involvement makes no sense! ActionStream is *profiting* from the tournament! There's a whole new market on the other side of the transverse just waiting to be tapped, and we're in position to capitalize on it! I'm all set to rake in some serious bonuses if *Weltall* hits it big over there. Never mind that's it's my *fucking job* to make sure this event goes smoothly! Why would I shoot my own foot off like this?"

"As I said," Isaac stressed patiently, "if you're innocent, then you have nothing to worry about."

"But you don't even have a warrant!" He paused and creased his brow. "Do you have a warrant?"

"Not at present, though I'll have no difficulty obtaining one. As you said, the program was in your possession prior to the tournament, and you loaded it yourself. That makes you a clear suspect."

"But—"

"Mister Kohlberg, we can do this one of two ways," Isaac continued matter-of-factly. "Either you grant us the access to your office we need, or I can return with a search warrant. It's your call, but I recommend the first option."

"But I can't give you access to it now!" He spread his hands over the desk. "There's confidential material in here! Not to mention..." He trailed off.

"Not to mention...what exactly?" Isaac asked with a raised eyebrow.

"Look, can you at least give me a few minutes to clean up?"

"Absolutely not!" Isaac snapped. "If you so much as delete a single file, I'll charge you with obstruction of justice and arrest you on the spot. You'll grant us access to this office, either now or when I return with a warrant, and it will be in an *unaltered* state from this point forward. Am I making myself perfectly clear?"

"I..." Kohlberg's mouth twisted, and his head drooped. "Yeah, you've made your point." He palmed an abstract interface over his desk, and the infostructure unlocked. "Happy now?"

"Where's the secure wearable you stored the UAM on?"

"Here." He unfastened his collar, reached in, and pulled out a trio of meteor-shaped pendants on a chain. He looked at virtual labels on their backs, unclipped one from the chain, and placed it on the desktop. "Anything else?"

"Does this represent the complete path?" Isaac pointed to the pendant. "From your desk, to the wearable, to the pods?"

"Yes, that's right."

"Then I believe we have everything we need for now."

"Okay. I'll wait outside, if it's all the same to you."

"That would be preferrable."

"Just don't judge." He gave Isaac a nervous grin. "Okay?"

"As long as no crimes have been committed, I really don't care what else we find."

"All right. I'll hold you to that." Kohlberg let out a calming breath and nodded, appearing somewhat more comfortable with the situation after Isaac's reassurance. "I'll leave you to it, then."

He stepped out into the hall, and the glass wall sealed shut again.

"That was more contentious than I thought it'd be," Susan observed, switching to security chat.

"Same here, but he didn't force us to obtain a warrant. That's a good sign. Cephalie, you back yet?"

"Here." She appeared back on the desk.

"How'd it go with the Flower's management?"

"Friendly and helpful, which is a nice change of pace sometimes. We should have the surveillance files and understage records later today."

"Nice. Good work."

Cephalie tapped the black desktop with her cane. "Want me to grab copies of everything?"

"If you don't mind. Copy everything off the desk, then forward it to Nina. We'll take the pendant with us."

"Processing. There's a lot here, so I'll need to send it in chunks. Lots of fat UAM files. Also, I think I found what made Kohlberg uncomfortable."

"Is there any chance it's related to this case?"

"Can't see how."

"Even a remote chance?"

"Nope. Zero percent, if you ask me."

"Then it's none of our business."

"File transfer underway." Cephalie paced across the desk and twirled her cane as the LENS scooped up the pendant with a pseudopod. "You realize Nina's going to forward all this to Panoptes, right? You know, since she's still busy with *Lacan*'s wearable."

"That's her call to make." Isaac sat down in Kohlberg's recliner and activated the desk's main interface. Multiple windows materialized around him. "Event Schedule, My Mail, Project Status, Opportunities, Trash, Personal, Miscellaneous."

Isaac expanded the My Mail tab and searched for "Weltall." Over two thousand hits came back, so he added "Ergon" to the filter. That dropped the count down to three hundred. He skimmed over the most recent entries and found the version update for the tournament.

"Just like Kohlberg said. He received the file yesterday from Unreality Disconnect."

"Did you expect anything else?" Susan asked.

"Not after he unlocked the desk without a warrant." Isaac switched off the interface and stood up. "Though we'll need Nina or help from Themis data forensics to tell us more. Still, we've—"

An incoming call blinked in his virtual vision. It was from Nina.

"That was fast," Isaac remarked, eyeing the incoming call with a confused expression.

"Maybe it's good news?" Susan suggested.

"One can hope." Isaac answered the call. "Hello, Nina."

"*Isaac*," she replied, sounding mischievous for some reason.

"Good timing. I was just about to call you and—"

"Isaac, what *are* you and Cephalie doing?"

"I'm sorry?"

"My inbox obscenity filters tripped a few moments ago. Mind explaining why you're mailing me exabytes of porn?"

"We didn't..." He frowned, his eyes tracing back to Kohlberg's folders, especially the one marked Personal. "Oh."

"Care to explain yourself?"

"Okay, first, I didn't know they were porn, and second, those files should be tagged as evidence."

"Well, they're not. So, as far as Themis is concerned, you just sent me a mountain of porn across our work mail."

Susan put a hand over her mouth and started shaking in silent laughter.

"One of them's titled *Wild Vixens of the Oort Cloud, Part Eighteen*. You branching out from baseline human, Isaac?"

Susan's face pinched up and she squinted her eyes shut.

"Umm, Cephalie?" Isaac asked. "Didn't you tag those files?"

The small woman snapped her fingers. "Knew I'd forgotten something."

Isaac glowered at her.

"I hope Raviv doesn't find out about this," Nina chortled.

"Raviv's not going to care. Look, just tag them yourself, okay? This is all work related."

"Could have fooled me."

"Well, it *should* have been marked as evidence." He gave Cephalie a fierce eye. "Anyway, while you're on, do you have an update on Lacan's wearable?"

"Not yet. Still working on it. Why?"

"I've got another wearable for you to look at, plus the image from Kohlberg's office infosystem. The, ah, segmented save-state with all the porn. The *Weltall* UAM passed through both."

"Great." She blew out a tired breath. "I'll keep the two wearables and forward the save-state to Panoptes. That should help keep the turnaround time down for all this work you keep piling on me."

"Sounds like a plan. There's another location we need to check before we meet up with you, but let me know if you can break free and start on the second wearable early."

"Sure, but don't get your hopes up."

"All right. Talk to you later."

"Later. Oh, and Isaac?"

"Yes?"

"There's an advertisement here for *Part Nineteen*. Want me to order you a copy?"

He closed the call with an indistinct grunt, then turned to Susan.

"You okay?" he asked.

She straightened up, a bemused grin on her face, and gave him a thumbs-up.

"Then let's go." He palmed the wall open and stepped out to find Kohlberg waiting along the opposite wall with a worried expression.

"I get lonely, okay!" he blurted out. "It's not easy, what with all the travel this job demands, and all the—"

"Mister Kohlberg," Isaac cut in, "frankly, I don't care."

"Did you at least see what you needed?"

"For now, yes."

"Then, are we done here?"

"Not quite, I'm afraid."

"What else do you want to see?" Kohlberg sighed in a resigned manner.

"The other location the file passed through, of course."

"But I've shown you that. From my desk to the wearable to the pods, just like I said."

"Yes, but you also said you took the wearable home with you last night."

"Well, yeah, but..." Kohlberg's lips twitched in horror and his shoulders slumped. "Oh *no*."

"Oh, yes." Isaac cracked a thin smile. "Tell me, how close is your residence?"

✧   ✧   ✧

Kohlberg's apartment was located in Petal Six near the bottom of a downward-hanging castle turret overlooking the crater slopes. The grav tube dropped them off in a circular lobby with four doors leading to four quarter-circle apartments.

Kohlberg reached for the door interface, but then paused and turned back to Isaac.

"Is this really necessary?" he pleaded once more.

"It is," Isaac insisted.

"But there's...you know, private stuff in my home."

"And it will stay private. I assure you that whatever it is, I've seen worse. I'm only interested in material relevant to the case. You have my word nothing else will appear in my final report."

"Yes, but can I at least change the abstract décor to something more . . . suitable for guests?"

"No," Isaac replied bluntly. "Now, if you don't mind? The sooner we get this over with, the better."

"Fine." Kohlberg palmed the door, sidestepped, and gestured for them to enter. "Go on in, then."

"Please wait outside." Isaac led the way in, and Susan palmed the door shut once she and the LENS were inside.

"Wow." She looked around. "I'm not sure what I expected, but . . . wow."

"Quite."

The walls were coated in animated artwork exhibiting life-size female subjects in various states of dress . . . or undress, as it were, and posed in an even wider variety of suggestive positions. But not just any women. *Fantasy* women.

There were ladies with cat ears and fluffy tails, ladies with blue skin and glowing eyes, ladies with serpentine tails, black leathery wings, and horns, mermaids, translucent water nymphs, a pair of the more buxom *Solar Descent* characters, and on and on it went across every square meter of wall, plus a few spots on the ceiling. They came in all shapes and colors, with sizes ranging from the petite to the voluptuous, while their expressions took advantage of the entire spectrum between shy and sultry.

"I can see why he wanted to change the décor," Susan remarked.

"Let's get this over with," Isaac grumped, marching deeper into Kohlberg's den. "Cephalie?"

"I've already started." She shook her head from atop the LENS. "See? This is why I do my best to avoid meat-sack drama."

"Actually, some of this artwork isn't half bad." Susan pointed to a wall where a lustful demon-woman held a reserved angelic woman in her arms. The angel-woman closed her eyes and sighed as the demon-woman nibbled down her neck. "Do you see how these two are—"

"I'm *really* trying not to, Susan," Isaac stressed.

"Right. Sorry!"

They passed through a rounded lounge with soft lighting and curved sofas encircling a dynamic prog-steel sculpture of a nude woman pole dancing. More 2D fantasy women writhed along the walls. Isaac turned down a short hallway beyond the sculpture room, followed it to a T-junction, and then gazed down at the forested slopes through the arched windows.

"Does he have a home office in here?" Isaac asked.

"To the left," Cephalie said. "At least, if the infostructure's any indication."

Isaac took a left and came face-to-face with a very solid-looking door that appeared to have been added to the apartment's original floorplan. He palmed the interface, but the door bleeped at him and refused to open.

"Cephalie, the door?"

"Give me a second. There's some security software here, but it's nothing I can't handle."

The interface blinked green, and the door split open to reveal a large but dimly lit room. Isaac took one step inside—

—and then froze as the lights switched.

"Yay! Master's home!" said the naked catgirl sprawled luxuriously across the expansive bed next to half a dozen otherworldly women with more strewn across the floor. All of them together probably possessed enough clothing to cover *one* person, and even then, not cover her very well.

"Oh dear," Isaac breathed.

"Is something wrong? What's going on in there?" Susan peeked her head in. "Oh, wow."

"Whoops, sorry!" The catgirl's pink, fluffy tail twitched happily, and her pale ears perked up. "You're not Master! Did Master send you here? Would you like to be *entertained*?" She rose onto all fours and wiggled her well-rounded buttocks.

"No," Isaac replied bluntly.

"Aww," she cooed. "You sound angry. Haven't I been naughty enough? Would you like me to try *harder*?"

"Are you sentient?" Isaac asked.

The catgirl juddered to a halt mid-wiggle. The expression on her face melted away, and she sat back atop her feet.

"Slutty Servant Roleplay Mode suspended," the catgirl said in a dull monotone. "Entering Standby Mode. Please make your selection from the available options." An abstract menu appeared next to her.

"Guess not," Susan said. "Kohlberg should really get out more."

"Not our problem." Isaac walked over to the desk set up next to the bed. He kept his eyes down because the tangle of bare limbs and tails spread across the floor created a formidable pedestrian hazard.

He dropped into the recliner and summoned the interface—

—which autoplayed a fully immersive abstraction through *all* his virtual senses. He almost fell out of the recliner and aborted out of the abstraction immediately.

"What's wrong?" Susan asked from the other side of the bed. "You okay?"

"Yeah," Isaac said weakly. He swallowed, his throat suddenly dry. "I don't think Kohlberg works at this desk."

"Why do you say that?" she asked, surveying the tangled mass of inert bodies.

"Just a wild guess." He rose from the recliner, steadying his hand on the desk because his legs had transformed into noodles. "Cephalie, would you mind checking all these synthoids?"

"You want me to go *inside* these things?"

"If it's not too much trouble."

"*Fine.*" She pushed her glasses up and vanished from the LENS.

Susan put her hands on her hips and stared intently at one of the pleasure synthoids.

"Find something?" Isaac asked.

"Maybe. Do any of these look familiar to you? The non-fantasy ones, I mean."

"I haven't been paying close attention, to be honest."

"Take a look at this one." Susan rolled the body over, so the woman's face gazed vacantly up at the ceiling. "Remind you of anyone?"

"It does, actually," Isaac said. "That's Gomako Grim. Or at least a synthoid copy of her." He frowned down at it. "A very *detailed* copy."

"And this one here." Susan turned over another one. "Don't you think it looks like Sako?"

"Somewhat. I can see the resemblance in the face, but the skin tone is darker. The hair length and eye coloring are different, too. It's not an exact match."

"None of the synthoids have connectomes," Cephalie announced, reappearing atop the LENS, "in case you were wondering. Just shells with some basic, nonsentient programming."

"Is any of this illegal?" Susan asked. "Copying other people's looks into synthoids and having sex with them?"

"Depends," Isaac said.

"On what?"

"On whether Kohlberg has the correct permits for all of this. Some celebrities sell replication permits for their looks, with varying restrictions depending on the specific permit, and some do allow all *this*." He gestured to the bodies on the bed. "Any applicable permits should be stored locally, so we shouldn't have a problem checking them."

"They're local," Cephalie said. "And I see one here purchased from Gomako Grim. An expensive one, too. The synthoid cosmetic pattern is part of her 'Grim Intimacy VIP Bundle.' It includes a UAM module for her body and allows for both physical and abstract replications."

"Then he's legally allowed to make a sex doll of her."

"What about the Elly look-alike?" Susan asked.

"It's not a match, so it would fall under a legal gray area," Isaac explained. "If Sako was from SysGov, and she found out about this, then she could sue for illegal use of her likeness. After that, it would be up to a jury to say if Kohlberg had infringed upon her rights."

"But since she's from the Admin?"

"There's nothing she can do," Isaac said with a shrug. "There's no legal framework between the two superpowers to sort out disputes like this."

"It's still creepy."

"Agreed. But not illegal, which is our concern in the matter." He put his hands on his hips and surveyed the room.

"Does he have permits for *all* of them?" Susan asked.

"He does," Cephalie said. "Every synthoid here has a legit permit, though the Elly look-alike's background is a bit different from the others."

"How so?"

"Most of these were custom built, but he bought that one secondhand. From the receipts, looks like the seller was ditching an old security synthoid body. He bought it, then had it, ahh, *modified* to his specifications. There are receipts for that too." She flashed a wry grin. "Want me to look into the changes he asked for?"

"I don't think we need those kinds of details," Isaac replied. "Anything else?"

"There's no way I can tell if the UAM passed through the apartment's infostructure."

"Why not?"

"Because he installed a slew of automated programs to scrub his temporary files on a regular basis."

"Were these programs added recently?" Susan asked.

"Not according to their activity logs," Cephalie said. "As far as I can tell, they've been running in the background for years."

"Hmm." Isaac huffed out a breath. "Then we can't tell if the *Weltall* program passed through here?"

"Nope, sorry. I doubt Nina would have much luck here either. Those scrubber programs look *very* thorough."

"All the same, take images from everything and send them to her."

"On it."

"And make sure they're properly tagged as evidence this time," Isaac stressed.

"Of *course*, Master," she quipped, then vanished.

"You see any point in staying here?" Isaac asked.

"Did you check out this menu? The catgirl has a mode called Blushing Virgin Roleplay."

"*Susan.*"

"No, I don't see the point in staying."

"Me neither." He took one last look around the room's debauched spectacle. "All right. Let's go."

Isaac navigated through the walking hazards on the floor, almost tripped on a jutting thigh, sidestepped around what his mind chose to categorize as a two-person pretzel, then strode through the door and down the windowed hallway. They backtracked through the apartment and met Kohlberg by the floor's grav tube.

"Well?" Kohlberg asked, barely daring to look up.

Isaac stepped over to him with a deep grimace. He opened his mouth and was sorely tempted to say something. But what the man did with his free time was his own business, so long as it held no relevance to the case. There was no "Nubile Catgirl" angle to the case, and Isaac considered the chances of one popping up to be close to zero.

He closed his jaw with a soft click, shook his head at Kohlberg, and walked into the grav chute without saying another word.

CHAPTER FIFTEEN

ISAAC AND SUSAN TOOK THEIR SEATS IN THE CFPD CONFERENCE room opposite Ergon, who'd recently transmitted over from Earth via connectome laser. His avatar took the form of a dark, spherical void with hot, swirling matter falling into it. He floated on the other side of the table, expressionless without a face or body.

"Thank you for agreeing to speak with us on such short notice," Isaac said. "I'm Detective Cho, and this is my deputy, Agent Cantrell."

"Hmm?" Ergon murmured in a vaguely male tone of voice. The dark void remained motionless except for the constant swirling motion. It didn't even bob up and down.

"I said—"

"I heard you."

Isaac blinked at the abrupt reply.

"Yes, well," he said, recovering, "we have a few questions we'd like to ask you."

"Hmm?"

"First, I'd like to confirm a few facts. Would you please state your name and occupation for the rec—"

"This room is tiny."

"I'm sorry?" Isaac asked.

"This room," Ergon repeated. "Is tiny."

Isaac turned to Susan, who shrugged. He then made a show of looking around the room.

"It doesn't seem tiny to me."

"Could you adjust the scale, please?"

"The scale?"

"Yes."

"What scale?"

"Of the room."

"I'm sorry, but I have no idea what you're talking about."

"I feel cramped in here. It's making me uncomfortable. Please make the room bigger."

"You feel cramped?" Isaac asked skeptically.

"Mmhmm."

"But you're an AC."

"Hmm?"

"You don't take up any space."

"Yes, I do. My avatar has a radius of twelve million kilometers."

"I'm afraid we don't have a room that big."

"But it's so cramped in here. I had to shrink my avatar down to fit inside. It's quite awkward, you see. Can't you change the scale?"

"No, I can't change the room's scale. It's fixed by this thing called reality."

"Mmm," Ergon murmured. "Mind if I fix it then?"

"I . . ." Isaac let out a slow exhale. "You're welcome to try."

"Thanks."

An invite to an abstraction blinked in Isaac's virtual sight.

"Done. I'll meet you inside," Ergon said, and vanished.

"What an unusual fellow," Susan commented.

"Let's just go along with this." Isaac allowed the abstraction to unfold around him, only to discover it was a one-to-one replica of the conference room. Out of curiosity, he checked the dimensions, and found the virtual room to be over a hundred million kilometers long. He waved his hand in front of his face and saw the action instantly, which told him the speed of light was not being obeyed in this simulation.

"Much better!" Ergon declared.

"How often do you leave the abstract?" Isaac said.

"Why do you ask?"

"Professional curiosity."

"Not much. I try to avoid the physical whenever possible."

"I see." Isaac opened his notes, which now measured millions of kilometers across but looked exactly the same to him. "Now, Ergon, you're the owner of Unreality Disconnect, is that right?"

"Mmhmm."

"And you're also the lead programmer for *Weltall*, correct?"

"Mmhmm."

"Did you send an updated version of *Weltall* to Sven Kohlberg yesterday?"

"Hmm?"

"I'm sorry. Are you asking me something? Or are you confused by the question? I can't tell."

"Hmm."

"That's not an answer."

The dark swirl floated behind the table, unresponsive.

"Here, let me handle this." Cephalie appeared on the table and walked over to the dark void. "Hey, Ergon!" she shouted.

"Hmm?"

Cephalie pointed at Isaac and Susan. "They're curious about your new game!"

The dark void burst with light so intense Isaac squinted and flinched back.

"Why didn't you say so?" Ergon declared, his radiant aura pulsating with excitement. "I'm always happy to converse with fans!"

"Yes. Sure," Isaac said, shielding his eyes with a hand. "We're fans. Now would you please answer our questions?"

"Certainly! What would you like to know?"

Isaac was about to speak up, but Susan cleared her throat. He shot her a quick glance, saw she was silently asking to take the lead. He gestured with an open hand for her to proceed.

"Mister Ergon," Susan began.

"Please, just Ergon, if you don't mind. It's short for Ergosphere. Mister Ergon sounds so pretentious."

"Of course. I was curious about a mechanic that seems to be missing from your game."

"A missing mechanic?" The swirl pulsed more rapidly for a few moments. "Whatever do you mean?"

"Well, I've noticed that *Weltall* utilizes real-world physics for most of its gameplay fundamentals, but one branch of physics doesn't seem to be represented at all."

"Ah! I think I see where you're going with this."

"You give the player access to a wide range of methods to manipulate the matter and energy in the game space. They can build all sorts of structures and vessels to accomplish this, but the one thing they *can't* do is travel through time or visit other universes. Why is that?"

"Oh, how very astute of you!" Ergon commended. "Yes, that was a problem we didn't know we'd face during the game's development. You see, we've been working on *Weltall* for over four years now, long before anyone knew about transdimensional travel. In fact, we originally included a few temporal mechanics into the core gameplay loop, but they were based on our old, disproven theories of time travel. The ones that said branches in the timeline were impossible to create. Obviously, we couldn't leave them in, so out they came!"

"But why not replace them with gameplay based on our newest theoretical models?" Susan asked. "Why abandon time travel as a game mechanic entirely? You've certainly taken some theoretical leaps with the inclusion of large-scale exotic matter megastructures in the game. Why not do the same for time and transdimensional travel?"

Isaac wasn't sure where Susan was going with this, but she and Cephalie had maneuvered Ergon into a more talkative mood, so he sat back and allowed the interview to play out without interruption.

"A few reasons," Ergon answered. "The first—and arguably most important—reason is we didn't think it would be fun. At the end of the day, *Weltall* needs to be an enjoyable experience for our customers that keeps them coming back for more. And while some of them might enjoy the mind-bending aspects of fighting across multiple universes or triggering branching time-lines, that was not the game we set out to create.

"We wanted to craft a play experience with a broad tapestry for player expression, true, but it also needed to have a certain amount of focus. That focus took the form of one universe and real-world physics. Within reason, of course. We've made adjustments here and there for balance purposes, but always in service of the core game. For example, our stellar engines are *significantly* more effective than the real thing would be.

"The second reason is time, strangely enough. We could have spent more time in development, certainly, but a unique

opportunity had arrived, and we needed to go after it! Funda-
mentally redesigning the core gameplay experience at the same
time would have been foolish, to say the least!"

"And this opportunity you speak of," Susan said. "What was it?"

"Why, the interest in our product from the Admin, of course!"
Ergon said. "ActionStream put us in contact with Director Jonas
Shigeki, who had expressed interest in an early version of *Weltall*.
He'd been looking for a product to bring over to the Admin, and
he considered our game a prime contender! But he also wanted
to release it within a few months, so we knew we had to make
some hard choices, choose a final direction, and pull the product
together. Though, in an odd way, we were still able to keep our
physics true to the real world."

"But how can that be without transdimensional combat in
the game?" Susan asked.

"Yes, I know what you're saying." The swirl dimmed slightly.
"We were originally going to make up a vague fictional excuse
that involved a lot of hand-waving, but then we had the good
fortune of discussing our problem with Doctor Andover-Chen of
the Gordian Division. It turns out, he believes there are universes
out there in the transverse that have vastly different properties
than our own, perhaps even different speeds of light, stronger
gravitational constants, or more intense chronoton barriers around
the True Present. We simply hold that *Weltall* takes place in a
universe with chronoton barriers so intense they *instantly* destroy
anyone who tries to activate a time drive while inside!"

"That sounds like quite the elegant solution," Susan remarked.

"Oh, thank you! Thank you!" Ergon replied. "We thought so,
too. He also helped us settle on a title, strangely enough. We
were calling it *Universe* all throughout its development, but then
I hit on the idea of changing it to *Weltall*, as a small nod to the
Gordian Division. In case you didn't know, it's an Old German
word for 'universe.' The doctor said his boss would like that."

"Was Director Shigeki pleased with how you held to his
requested timeline?"

"I'm not entirely sure, to be honest. We didn't deal with him
much after the initial meetings. We worked through ActionStream
mostly, but the feedback we received through them was overwhelm-
ingly positive. We pour a lot of pride into our products, and I
personally put in a *ton* of extra hours tuning game balance for

the latest version." The swirl pulsed proudly. "I think it's some of my finest work."

"That would be the version in use at the tournament?"

"Yes, correct."

"Were you the last AC to work on it?"

"That's right. I transmitted it to Sven yesterday."

"It sounds like you're quite excited to see if the game is well received in the Admin."

"Oh, absolutely! I think we have the makings of a genuine hit here, but one can never be certain until the product is out in the public's hands."

"Then I take it you'd be upset if someone altered the game file to make it threaten Admin players."

"Oh, good grief, yes!" Ergon declared. "Why, I'd be livid! Why would anyone...wait a second." The swirling mass dimmed to a ruddy color. "Did someone do that?"

"Yes." Susan nodded gravely. "I'm afraid so."

"THEY DID WHAT?!"

The swirl exploded with flame and fury so strong it threatened to blow their virtual forms out of their seats. The table rattled against the floor, and Isaac grabbed hold of the table leg while Susan braced herself with a foot against the back wall. She waited for the eruption to die down, and even when it finally did, the swirl continued to undulate with the equivalent of heaving, angry breaths.

"So, to confirm," she said at last, "you were the last AC at your company to handle the game file."

"I was," Ergon replied, his livid rage contained for the moment.

"And you sent it straight to Sven Kohlberg."

"Yes," he simmered.

"Do you have any idea who might have altered it?"

"I wish I did," he seethed, "but no. I have no idea who fucked with my game."

"He seemed quite passionate about his work," Susan said as they headed down the corridor to the CFPD forensics labs.

"And unlikely to be involved," Isaac said. "But appearances can be deceiving when it comes to the abstract. Many ACs lack the neural chemistry—simulated or otherwise—behind emotions, and that can make them difficult to read. No shifty eyes or shuffling feet to clue us in to what lies beneath the surface."

"No eyes or feet at *all*, this time."

"True enough." Isaac gave her a thin smile. "Fortunately, we happen to know an expert on AC behavior."

Cephalie's avatar appeared atop the LENS. "You rang?"

"Any thoughts on Ergon?"

"Plenty. I've seen his type before. Some ACs become detached from reality, and he struck me as one of the types who live their lives almost exclusively within the abstractions they select. If that's accurate—and I think it is—then he wouldn't care enough about the politics at play here to threaten either Sako or Masuda."

"Not to mention he'd be alienating potential customers," Susan added.

"My thoughts as well," Isaac said. "And we're faced with the same gap when considering Kohlberg. Why harm your own company when you're positioned to profit from its success?"

Isaac palmed the door to Forensics Lab Two. It split open, and he walked inside.

"Hey, everyone." Nina nodded from her seat at a workbench, alone except for her drones. The disassembled components of Lacan's wearable floated within a sterile glass-fronted chamber set in the wall, suspended in a thin and almost invisible prog-steel mesh so that the pieces appeared frozen in air, mid explosion.

"I come bearing gifts," Cephalie declared from atop the LENS. A pseudopod morphed out of the side and presented Nina with Kohlberg's pendant in an evidence capsule.

"Yay," Nina moaned halfheartedly. "More work." She waved absently to her drones. One of them took the capsule and fed it into the next workbench. "Anyway, what brings you down here?"

"We finished our interview with Ergon," Isaac said. "It seemed like a good time to regroup."

"Impressions?" Nina asked.

"He's even less likely to be involved than Kohlberg. How about you? Got anything for us?"

"I do. Check this out." Nina expanded part of her interface and sent them copies. "I think I found where I slipped up. Or rather, where I *might* have slipped up. I'm not certain either way yet."

"That's not an encouraging start."

"I know, but bear with me." She highlighted a nodule within the wearable's schematics. "See this here? It's on the underside of the wristband and is designed to connect with a person's PIN, or

Personal Implant Network. Basically, that's the Admin equivalent of our wetware implants. Anyway, the component maintains its own activity log file independent of the wearable as a whole, and that log doesn't match up with *other* logs."

"Sounds suspicious," Susan said.

"It is, but here's where it gets interesting. If we assume this sub-log is unaltered, then the prankware was loaded into the wearable from Lacan's *PIN*! Not an external device!"

She grinned and spread her arms grandly, but then frowned when both Isaac and Susan didn't acknowledge the revelation.

"Do I need to spell it out for you?" she asked.

"That'd be best," Isaac said.

"Okay." She scooched forward in her seat. "Recall what the wearable does. It's a translator for SysGov infostructure. But if I'm right, Lacan didn't load the prankware onto it directly. He loaded it through his PIN. Which means the prankware was copied to his PIN *without* the wearable's help. And *that* means the prankware came to him through an *Admin* interface! Not a SysGov one!"

"I see now." Isaac nodded. "Given what you've discovered so far, do you think the prankware was planted on him?"

"It's a distinct possibility." She gestured to the disassembled device. "Unfortunately, that's about all I can say. It's a possibility."

"Has anyone talked to Lacan about this?" Susan asked.

"LSP interrogated him again. He still maintains that he's innocent. No new information, though."

"Did the file come directly from Lacan's PIN?" Susan asked. "Or was another device using his PIN to connect with the wearable?"

"Don't know," Nina admitted. "I could probably figure that out if I analyzed Lacan's implants, but Susan, you know how those implants are secure little buggers. I'd have to cut him open and take them out to get a good look at them, and I don't think we're quite there yet. Not while you two have less squicky avenues to explore."

"This is still a promising development," Isaac said. "If I understand you correctly, this limits who could have planted the evidence to either another Admin player or part of the chrono-port's crew."

"Not really," Nina cautioned. "Remember, the SysGov finalists and ActionStream reps were all in the Admin recently, and all of them had wearables to translate Admin infostructure."

"Hmm." Isaac grimaced.

"Sorry." Nina shrugged her arms. "But that's what we're dealing with."

"What about Pérez?" Susan asked. "Did he or his team help you out with analyzing the wearable?"

"I asked him, but he apologized and said he didn't have anyone. None of the people on his security team are infostructure specialists. They're more the run-and-gun variety."

"Makes sense," Isaac said. "They're here to guard the players, not conduct an investigation."

"Well, sometimes we get lucky," Nina said with indifference, "and sometimes we don't. It was worth a shot."

"What should we do with Lacan, then?" Susan asked.

"Nina?" Isaac asked. "Your recommendation?"

"I say we hold onto him for now. Even with what I found, it's still possible he's involved. There's not enough evidence one way or the other to be sure. You want to risk releasing him and then have it blow up in your face later?"

"No."

"Then have LSP hold onto him until we know for certain."

"All right," Isaac said. "We'll go with that for now. Anything else?"

"Yep. Panoptes got back to me regarding your exaton of smut."

"I think you mean exa*byte*," Isaac corrected.

"I know what I said." Nina leaned back. "Anyway, they didn't find anything unusual on the image from Kohlberg's desk. The only copy of the UAM they found matched the unaltered version ActionStream provided us earlier."

"What about his apartment?"

"Preliminary report is the UAM never touched that system."

"Preliminary?"

"I've been expediting every request, but it's not like we're the only case in the queue. This stuff takes time. They're moving forward with a deeper analysis, but their rep told me—as one specialist to another—not to get my hopes up."

"Then that leaves Kohlberg's pendant," Susan noted.

"Which I'll start on as soon as we're done here," Nina said. "I don't think Lacan's wearable has anything else to tell us."

"Where does this leave us?" Susan asked Isaac.

"Nowhere good. Cephalie? How about you?"

The small woman floated down from the LENS to Nina's workbench.

"A few things to report," she began, "I spoke with Claudia Siebert, Kohlberg's old AC."

"And?"

"She's been on Earth this whole time, so she's not involved. I also pumped her for potential dirt on Kohlberg. Gave her every window I could think of for her to drop a bombshell, but she wouldn't. Her story matches Kohlberg's; they went their separate ways amicably."

"Did she have anything to say about his . . . umm"—Susan smiled bashfully—"colorful interests?"

"She knew about them. She didn't spell it out for me, but I got the impression she joined in from time to time."

"Ah."

"Also"—Cephalie pointed her cane at the pendant—"I took a peek inside Kohlberg's secure wearable. Nothing too invasive, but enough to scope out the contents."

"Anything interesting?" Isaac asked.

"Only the unaltered version of the program. Nothing else."

"Then that's the entire transfer path." Isaac put his hands on his hips and shook his head. "From Ergon to Kohlberg to the pod. We've seen the correct version all the way through."

"Has Crimson Flower management gotten back to you with the surveillance video?" Susan asked.

"They did, and I've already looked through it and the logistics records. They sent me three close, unobstructed angles of the stage and two more for the understage. None of them saw anything out of the ordinary. Kohlberg showed up, loaded the program into each of the pods, then submerged the pods and left. After that, Flavor-Sparkle's roadies began to set up. Understage cameras and the logistical record all confirm the pods remained in the stage the whole time, which means no one—roadies or otherwise—could have accessed them. First time the pods came back up was for the players."

"Hmm," Isaac grumbled.

"But there's one other possibility you might want to look into," Cephalie said.

"What's that?" Isaac asked.

"The pods themselves. Or rather, the *installer*."

Isaac's eyebrows raised at the possibility.

"You're suggesting the program was loaded correctly but then altered by something malicious in the pod itself?"

"Just saying it's a possibility. We've checked the software side of things. Maybe we need to dig into the hardware side. That's all I'm saying."

"Worth a look." Isaac opened a comm window and waited for Kohlberg to answer.

"Yes, Detective?" Kohlberg said, sounding a touch annoyed.

"Mister Kohlberg, can you tell me who provided the isolation pods?"

"Easy. The company's name is Avalanche. We contract all our infostructure install work to them. Their offices are in Petal Five."

"Do you know who at Avalanche was in charge of the stage install?"

"That would be Ian Zou, one of their senior technicians. Why would you . . . oh."

"Mister Kohlberg?"

"You know, don't you?"

"Know what?"

"This is about his League membership, isn't it?"

Ian Zou is a member of LAST? Isaac thought. *Now that is interesting.*

"It might be," Isaac replied neutrally.

"Well, of course it is. I suppose it *does* look bad, and perhaps we should have chosen our contractors better for this project. I can send you his contact string if you like."

"Please do."

"Anything else, Detective?"

"Not at present. Thank you." He closed the window.

"Someone from LAST worked on those pods," Susan noted with a thin smile.

"*Definitely* worth a check now." He turned to Nina.

"You're going to ask me to root around those pods, aren't you?" she said.

"You know it."

"Then pick." She tapped the glass in front of Kohlberg's floating pendant. "This or the pods first."

"The pods," Isaac said without hesitation. "It's only a matter of time before ActionStream's lawyers start pressuring us to release the crime scene. Let's finish any open business there first."

"All right, then." Nina rose from her seat and motioned for her drones. "Come on, kids. Those pods won't diagnose themselves."

"What about us?" Susan asked.

"We're going to pay Mister Zou a visit, and we may have a few pointed questions about his activities with LAST."

CHAPTER SIXTEEN

ISAAC APPROACHED THE RECEPTIONIST'S DESK IN THE AVALANCHE lobby. She wore a white business suit with a white scarf twinkling with hints of digital data. The company's logo animated overhead as an avalanche of ones and zeros thundering down a mountainside to sweep through an unsuspecting town in the valley.

"Can I help you, sir?" the receptionist asked.

"Detective Cho, SysPol Themis." He transmitted his badge. "We're looking for Ian Zou."

"Mister Zou?" Her eyes widened in surprise.

"Yes. Is that a problem?"

"Uh, no. Of course not," she recovered, "but why would you need to see him, sir? Can I get someone else for you to speak with?"

"I'm afraid our business is with Mister Zou specifically."

"And what business might that be?"

"I'm not at liberty to say."

"I see, sir." The receptionist frowned.

"Is he here? We tried calling ahead, but he didn't answer."

"Umm, let me look over the check-in log." She pulled up a new interface and scrolled through it. "Yes, sir. He's here. Checked in this morning, right on time. Should be at his desk. Would you like me to call him over? If you need to speak privately, we have a meeting room off the lobby you can use."

A door split open along the side of the lobby, revealing a rectangular table surrounded by chairs. Rotating abstractions of Avalanche infosystem products covered the walls.

"That'll work for us. We'll wait there for him."

Isaac and Susan walked in and picked their seats, the LENS floating in after them.

"She became nervous when you asked for Zou," Susan noted once the door was closed, speaking in security chat.

"Mmhmm," Isaac agreed. "Wonder why."

The door split open again twelve minutes later, and a gaunt man with wispy white hair shuffled in. His face was somber and unfriendly with prominent bags under his eyes. He wore all black accented with a dynamic scarf roiling with dark thunderheads and held a Halley Water brand bottle in one hand.

"Yes?" he wheezed.

Isaac could almost picture dust puffing from his mouth. Or perhaps a moth flying free. The words "desiccated" and "embalmed" came to mind when gazing upon the man.

"Ian Zou, I presume?"

"That's me." He took hold of a chair with a skeletal hand, pulled it out, then dropped into it with a pained sigh. He took a swig from his water bottle and set it on the table. "Need something?"

"We'd like to ask you a few questions concerning your involvement with the Weltall Tournament."

"Our last ActionStream job?" He nodded, then hacked up a few phlegm-rattling coughs into his fist. "What do you want to know?"

"Mister Zou, are you all right?" Isaac asked, genuinely concerned for the man's health.

"I'll transition when I'm damned well ready to!" he snapped with surprising energy. "You hear me? When I'm good and ready, and not a moment sooner!"

"I didn't say anything about you transitioning."

"But you were thinking it," he accused, "weren't you?"

"The thought may have crossed my—"

"You people are all the same! Did Jennifer put you up to this? I bet she did. Well, whatever she told you, it's nothing but a pack of lies! There ain't a thing wrong with my health! Why, I've never felt more alive. It's like I'm entering my second prime!"

Zou thumped his chest proudly, but then doubled over and started coughing again.

If this is your prime, Isaac thought, *I'd hate to see what a slump looks like.*

"Mister Zou, we have no interest in when—or if—you choose to transition into a synthetic body. We're here to discuss your involvement with the Weltall Tournament. Nothing else."

Zou let out one more weak cough.

"Is that so?"

"It is."

"Fine," he wheezed, eyes drooping as the previous burst of energy oozed out of him. "What do you want to know?"

"Perhaps you could start with the technical specifications of the install."

"Six Polar Bear abstraction pods, modified with extra sound-proofing, and a supporting infostructure. That would be six Iceberg-XL meganodes, per ActionStream's specifications."

Isaac raised an eyebrow. "You knew that off the top of your head?"

"What of it?"

"I'm just a little surprised."

"It's the last big job I worked on. Finished it yesterday, about an hour before Kohlberg said he was going to load the game files. Why wouldn't I have it fresh in my head?"

"I suppose that's a fair explanation."

"You think I'm going senile, don't you?"

"I implied no such thing, Mister Zou."

"Well, I'm not. You hear me? I'm not!" He began coughing again.

"Perhaps we could get you a medibot injection for that cough? My LENS has a small supply for emergency use."

"Hell, no!" he growled, his eyes lighting up. "I'm not putting that crap in my body! You know what medibots do after they're finished?"

"What might that be?"

"Nothing! You inject yourself with all sorts of unnatural metal filth, and afterward you've got millions of little, broken machines floating around your innards. Now you tell me, does that sound healthy?"

"I'm not sure your explanation is entirely accurate, Mister Zou."

"My body is a temple!" He thumped his chest again. "And I pamper it. I'll have you know I take a daily regimen of all-natural herbs and supplements. Very healthy! Very natural! Much better than any medibot pattern on the market. All I need is another carbon pill, and I'll be good as new!"

"A . . . carbon pill?"

"They contain activated charcoal. Carbon is a wonderful purifying agent. Cleans me right out!"

"Soot?" Isaac filled in. "You medicate yourself with soot?"

"Activated charcoal!" Zou corrected. "But not alone. I have a whole regimen a certified LunaCare wellness expert put together for me. I take mint and aloe supplements twice a day, plus the CT pill in the morning. All very natural and healthy. No medibots or any other artificial crap."

"I'm almost afraid to ask, but what's in the CT pill?"

"Concentrated topsoil."

"Seriously?"

"All-natural topsoil. Processed, filtrated, and concentrated into pill form. They're expensive, too. I have to import them from Earth."

"Dirt," Isaac said dully. "You eat dirt."

"Concentrated—"

"Yes, concentrated topsoil. I heard you the first time."

"It's an all-natural way to filter out the body's toxins. Works great in tandem with the carbon. This combination has been proven to be effective by no less than *two* studies, conducted by former members of the Southern Nectaris Medical Institute."

"Only two?" Isaac asked, despite his better judgment.

"*Former* members?" Susan added.

"They quit to found LunaCare. They're the ones who got me started on Halley Water." He took a swig from his water bottle. "This stuff is amazing! I drink at least three liters every day."

"And what," Isaac began, "if I may ask, is so special about the water?"

I know I should get this interview back on track, he thought, *but I can't seem to stop gawking at this man-sized shipwreck.*

"Halley Water is the purest water in existence," Zou explained.

"Because it's been filtered through carbon and dirt?" Susan ventured.

"No, don't be silly! This is *comet* water!"

"Oh, good grief." Isaac put his head in his hands.

"Don't you realize the water you drink used to be someone's

piss? Or worse, was squeezed out of their poop? Do you like the idea of drinking someone's poop water?"

"Not when you put it like that," Susan replied with a grimace.

"Exactly! That's why I drink nothing but certified comet water. Each delicious, refreshing sip has been plucked from the dawn of the solar system, having never passed through a person's bowels before mine." He picked up the bottle. "See, it says so right here on the label."

"I'll take your word for it." Isaac cleared his throat. "Mister Zou, perhaps we could return to the matter at hand?"

"Sure, sure." He set the bottle down and crossed his scrawny arms. "The *Weltall* job, right."

"Did anything unusual or unexpected happen on the job?" Isaac asked. "Receive any unusual requests from the customer? Anything of that nature?"

"Yeah, there was one. Kohlberg made it clear I couldn't bring my companion with me. Said the installation couldn't be performed with the help of any ACs. I argued with him, but he said the requirement came from the Admin itself, so there you have it. The customer is always right. Made the job such a hassle. Had to guide all the drones myself. Normally, Ebullience takes care of that."

"Ebullience?" Isaac repeated. "Your companion's name means cheerful and full of life?"

"Yeah? So? Why does everyone act like it's such a strange thing?"

"I can't think of a single reason, Mister Zou."

"He took some time off. I think he found the requirement offensive, so I'm here all alone right now." Zou shook his head. "Such a damn hassle. Should have told Kohlberg to shove it."

"Where is Ebullience now?"

"Earth somewhere, I think." Zou shrugged. "He'll come back when he's good and ready."

"I'd like a copy of his connection string."

"What for?"

"To verify his whereabouts."

"If you say so." Zou transmitted a copy of the string. "There you go."

"Thank you. Moving on, did you have any other disagreements with Mister Kohlberg?"

"No. Just the stupid requirement from the Admin."

"And what is your opinion of the Admin?"

"Oh, I see." Zou paused to regard the two detectives more carefully. "You think I'm like those bigoted morons protesting outside, don't you?"

"Are you, Mister Zou?"

"Can I be honest with you?"

"That would be preferable."

"I've been a member of LAST for a while." Zou leaned forward. "Long before joining was the 'in' thing to do. I joined back when it was still the League Against Stupid Time Travel, when all we protested against were those idiots in the Antiquities Rescue Trust and how their idea of archeology was to go back in time to the Great Library of Alexandria, ransack all the books, and shoot anyone who tried to stop them!"

Isaac wasn't sure being a member of LAST was currently—or had ever been—an "in" thing, but he supposed it was a matter of perspective.

"Nowadays," Zou continued, "I hardly recognize the organization. Yeah, I'm still a dues-paying member, but that's because all this multiverse nonsense makes me jittery. Just look at the Gordian Knot or—*good grief*—the Dynasty Crisis! How many times do we have to almost destroy all of reality before someone fires the braking thrusters? There's nothing stupid about wanting to keep our universe from going *poof* one day.

"I guess you could say I agree with their concerns, but I'm not so sure about their methods. What would kicking out everyone from the Admin accomplish? Maybe it'll make League members feel good because they're doing something tangible? Hell if I know, but the Admin's not some physical manifestation of evil. Like you." He gestured to Susan. "Are you here to herald the destruction of all realities?"

"Not that I'm aware of," she said evenly.

"Right! And no one else from the Admin is either. You know why? Because it's *stupid*! The Admin wants to keep existing, same as we do."

"Thank you for the detailed answer," Isaac said. "Moving on, are you aware of any way the infostructure you installed could have been used to modify the game files?"

"You mean in order to send a player a death threat?" Zou asked.

"That's right."

"The answer's no. At least not initially. Not at the time I handed them over. Those units were blank slates when I finished. Any software put on them came later."

"Could someone have loaded them with malicious code before they were installed at the stage?"

"Sure, I suppose that's possible, but it wouldn't have mattered."

"Why not?"

"Because of our install process. You see, my drones loaded those units straight from our factory, and I performed a wipe once they were installed. If someone had snuck malicious code onto them beforehand, it was gone by the time Kohlberg arrived."

"Why would a wipe be necessary on new units?"

"To clear out the diagnostics we install after printing the units. A wipe is standard procedure. It clears up a little extra memory, and it manages our liability. No software means no software problems can be blamed on us."

"What about LAST? Do you have any reason to believe they might be involved?"

"Like I said, I'm not active in the group anymore." Zou sighed, then hacked up a wet cough. "I suppose there are some people in the group crazy enough to try, but I have no idea how they'd pull it off. Other than to have access to the units after I installed them."

"I see." Isaac saw an incoming message blink in his periphery. It was from Agent Noxon. He expanded and skimmed through it.

Wonderful, Isaac thought sarcastically. *The Admin's top man on site would like to have a word with us back in the hangar. And I don't have a lick of progress to report.*

He closed the interface.

"That'll be all, Mister Zou. We appreciate your time."

Susan led the way through *Pathfinder-Prime*'s cramped, twisting corridors. Unlike a SysGov craft, the chronoport possessed no artificial gravity, and therefore was designed to operate under three different modes: free fall, local gravity from underneath the vessel, and acceleration in the direction of travel. The interior reflected this need with frequent handholds, ladders traversing the walls sideways, and walls that doubled as floors under different flight conditions.

Susan guided Isaac and the LENS through an open door to the craft's bridge, where bulky acceleration-compensation seats sat in rows of three. Noxon and Pérez stood at the front of the bridge with what might have been patrol timetables and routes hovering nearby.

Both synthoids had changed as well. Or rather, their gear had. They'd clad themselves in full-body armor with deployable helmets retracted into their collars and assault rifles slung from their shoulders. The armor and weapons were coated in variskin, currently set to display Peacekeeper blue.

"Cantrell, Cho." Noxon nodded to each of them as they walked over. "Good. Thank you for coming."

"You wished to speak with us?" Isaac said.

"Yes. I thought it important we keep up with each other's progress. You with your investigation and us with securing the players' safety."

"Good idea. Where'd you like to start?"

"Pérez?" Noxon prompted.

"Sirs, the additional agents and drones brought here on *Pathfinder-Prime* have allowed us to effectively double our existing coverage. The hangar, hotel floor, and the path between them are as secure as we can make them. We've employed a mix of stationary and roaming patrols to guard all active ingress points. There are also some locations"—he pointed at a map of Petal Four—"such as here on both sides of the hangar, and here along the perimeter of the hotel floor, that can act as auxiliary entrance points. We've sealed all of them and inspect them regularly.

"Shingo Masuda is currently housed in *Defender-Prime*, and Elly Sako is in her hotel room. We've dedicated a two-agent team to protecting Sako at all times, and we've designated a second team to escort Masuda, should he choose to leave the hangar. Additionally, we've outfitted several of our Wolverines with hazard detection modules and have them searching for weapons, bombs, biohazards, hostile self-replicators, and other potential threats. One Wolverine will accompany each player when on the move, sweeping ahead for any potential dangers.

"We've also coordinated with Crimson Flower management, and they've permitted us to expand our search area temporarily and equip our agents with heavier gear as an additional deterrent. Six agents and two Wolverines are currently working their way through Pistil Stadium. They're staying in contact with Specialist Cho, which should keep us from interfering with her work. At the same time, we have another team checking the full route from Petal Four to Pistil Stadium."

"Sounds thorough," Isaac remarked. "Find anything yet?"

"No, but we'll keep at it."

"It's possible the death threats are pure bluster," Noxon commented, "but we'll proceed on the assumption they're not. For now, that's all we can do, though there is one development we want to bring to your attention."

"And that is?"

"Are you aware of the recent incident with the League?" Pérez asked.

"No, I haven't been following the protests."

"Here," Pérez said. "Take a look."

An abstraction unfolded between them, detailing the base of the Crimson Flower and the gathered protesters. The crowd was over three times the size Isaac recalled from when he and Susan had slipped in.

"This was taken less than an hour ago," Pérez said softly.

At first, Isaac wasn't sure what to look for. A trio of LAST leaders atop counter-grav platforms led the protesters in song and chant. The crowd struck him as more agitated and energetic than before, more likely to test the bounds of what authorities would tolerate, but not dangerously so. Not yet, at least.

He was about to ask what he should be looking for when he saw them.

Several balloons, each about the size of a car, inflated along the front of the crowd. They took the forms of various Admin-theme objects, all with compressed, cartoonish proportions: overly serious synthoids, drones that looked a little too doglike, and comical representations of the three players.

Once fully inflated, attendants released the balloons to bob over the crowd, who batted them into the air at first, then began to attack them more aggressively. A Wolverine was the first to deflate, followed by two synthoids. Someone slashed the butt of the Masuda-balloon, causing it to careen over the crowd on a fart-propelled trajectory until it slammed headfirst into the Elly-balloon's exaggerated breasts.

The Masuda-balloon pooted out the last of its thrust while

the Elly-balloon pirouetted over the crowd, bleeding air from an unknown attack. It caved in to drape flaccidly over the crowd, which scurried out from under it.

After that, someone had the bright idea to set the balloons on fire.

Because of course that's what the crowd would do next.

One by one, the protesters ignited the cartoonish effigies. Black smoke billowed into the air, and flaming abstract swirls formed in above the crowd, morphing into the phrase LEAVE NOW. The message burned overhead, and the crowd cheered.

Isaac groaned.

Why do the bad protests always end with something on fire? he wondered.

"It seems to me," Noxon started, "that suspending the tournament has emboldened LAST."

"You could be right," Isaac sighed.

"I'd like your permission to change that."

"Well, I can't arrest them, if that's what you're asking."

"Of course not," Noxon replied. "And that's not what I'm after. I want your permission to restart the tournament."

"Are you sure that's wise?"

"Perhaps not, but look at it this way. We Peacekeepers are no strangers to hostile reactions, and though it's unfortunate to see them here in SysGov, we're accustomed to these sorts of... impotent displays. But if people here think a little bonfire will scare us, then it's time we showed them the truth." He pointed to the crowd's recording. "We do *not* back down to trash like this."

"There's no guarantee you can keep Sako safe."

"I'm well aware of that," Noxon said. "But our two peoples have a tournament to hold, and I'll be damned if I'll let fear of criminal scum stop us. Besides"—he flashed a smile—"I want to see who wins."

"I understand your position, and I sympathize with it, but let me check something first before I give an answer." He opened a comm window and called Nina.

"Fishing for an update?" she answered.

"You know it."

"Well, as far as I can tell, Avalanche did a first-class job. I haven't found *anything* weird here, and I've been looking awfully deep into their hardware."

"How far along are you?"

"Past the halfway mark. I'll wrap up here soonish."

"Can you give me something a little more concrete than 'soonish'?"

"Oh, I don't know. Call it an hour. Maybe two tops if I hit a snag."

"Two hours then. Got it."

"You getting pressure to restart the tournament?"

"Something like that. Any concerns on your end?"

"Nope. I'll be out of everyone's way soon enough."

"Call if you need more time."

"Will do."

Isaac closed out of the window.

"All right," he said to Noxon. "I'll give Kohlberg a call after we're done here and tell him he can restart the tournament in two hours."

"Thank you, Detective. Leave protecting our citizens in our capable hands. As for hunting down the criminal trash threatening our citizens...?"

"Unfortunately, the hunt isn't going well. We're not sure how the program was altered or who might have done it, and we still don't know if Lacan was involved or not."

"I see." Noxon nodded gravely. "Is there anything we can do to assist?"

"Not at present. If something comes up, I'll let you know."

"What about LAST?" Noxon asked. "Is there any indication they're involved?"

"Not at present, but..." Isaac eyed the paused model of the crowd outside.

"Thoughts?" Susan prompted.

"Just pondering where we go next." Isaac opened an interface and ran a quick search. "Looks like LAST's Lunarian chapter is led by a man named Brian Reed. His office isn't too far from here, actually. Perhaps we should pay him a visit."

"Sounds like a long shot," Susan said.

"True," Isaac admitted. "But I see two angles that might benefit us. First, it'll be a clear sign that SysPol is keeping a stern eye on his organization. *And* the protests here. It could prompt him to send word down the chain to lower the volume a few notches. Second, we can see if Reed knows of any troublemakers in his organization."

"You think he'd actually rat out his own people like that?"

"Maybe. He might if he's interested in staying on the right side of the law and suspects someone is about to break it." Isaac shrugged. "It's not ideal, but I think it's worth a shot, especially given how agitated that crowd is becoming."

"Then I won't take any more of your time, Detective," Noxon said. "Good luck. To both of you."

CHAPTER SEVENTEEN

THE SYSPOL VARIABLE-WING AIRCRAFT SLOWED TO A HOVER ON a gentle stream of gravitons. The Lunarian branch of LAST—a huge, white-walled building—sat on a lonely peninsula jutting into the Crisium Sea, its silhouette leaning out over the waters at a slight diagonal to form a tilted rhombus.

The V-wing settled onto a landing pad near the building's midpoint. The prog-steel hull split open, steps formed down the side, and Isaac walked out of the tandem cockpit. He rounded the V-wing and joined Susan on the other side. She was staring out across the vast, crystal clear waters.

"You did want to go to the beach," he said. The LENS floated out to join them.

"Not quite what I had in mind."

"Come on." He bobbed his head toward the entrance. "Let's go see Reed."

They crossed the landing pad to the building access, where two League security guards waited for them. The two men wore all black body armor with sidearms at their hips. One of them stepped into their path and held up a hand in front of Susan.

"You can come in, Detective," the guard said, his eyes locked on Susan, "but the Peacekeeper isn't allowed inside."

"Agent Cantrell?" Isaac said. "Would you please show them your badge?"

"Sure." She pinged everyone nearby with her credentials.

The security guard didn't bother to look away from her.

"As you can see," Isaac said, "we're *both* SysPol detectives. Please stand aside."

"Doesn't matter what she is in SysPol. She's still a Peacekeeper, and we're not letting her inside."

"It's all right," Susan said, switching to security chat.

"No, it isn't all right, Susan."

"I can wait in the V-wing. There's no need to cause a scene."

"I beg to differ." He switched back to normal speech and faced the guard. "You. What's your name?"

"Me?" The guard pointed to his chest. "Why would you need to know?"

"Is it unusual for me to ask a person I just met for his name? Don't you think that's rude not to introduce yourself? Or could there be more to it than that? Is there some reason you feel uncomfortable providing your name to a detective?"

"Uhh, no. No reason, I guess. It's Lester Tolk."

"Well, then, Mister Tolk. Allow me to explain how precarious your situation is. Agent Cantrell holds the rank of deputy detective in SysPol Themis Division, which means you're impeding her in the execution of her duties. Have I made myself sufficiently clear?"

"We're not letting her in."

"Apparently not, then. Do you own this building?"

"What?"

"I asked if you own this building?"

"No, of course not."

"Then are you a legal representative of the owner," Isaac continued, "who, by the way, has agreed to be interviewed by us?"

"Uhh, no. Don't think so."

"Then by what authority are you impeding our progress?"

"Not your progress. Just *hers*." He pointed at Susan. "She can't go in. Doesn't matter what fancy excuses you make."

"Mister Tolk, let me be *extra* clear with you, because your thick head seems to require it. I'm a hair's breadth away from charging you with obstructing an officer of the law. Now stand aside or I will have my LENS *make* you stand aside."

"You wouldn't do that!" Tolk challenged. "You're bluffing!"

"As you wish." Isaac gestured the LENS forward. "Cephalie! Restraint Mode!"

The LENS's outer shell morphed into a teardrop. Its small graviton thruster powered up, and it sped forward as a streak of silver aimed at Tolk's stomach. The man barely had time to raise his hands when the LENS's shell blossomed into four pseudopods that connected with his wrists and ankles. The force of the impact pitched him back so hard his head *almost* cracked against the ground. The LENS morphed a fifth appendage behind him and used it like a spring to ease him down onto the floor.

"What the *fuck*!" Tolk yelled, now on his back and pinned to the floor.

"And you?" Isaac turned sharply toward the second guard. "What's *your* name?"

"I'm Mister Not-Standing-In-Your-Way!" He scurried to the side and pressed himself against the wall.

"That's what I thought." Isaac glanced back over his shoulder. "Agent Cantrell, looks like we're both free to enter."

"So it would seem," she said with a wry grin.

"Cephalie?"

"Yeah." She materialized on Tolk's chest.

"Would you be so kind as to call Dispatch and have them arrange for Tolk's pickup?"

"Sure thing." She pushed up her glasses. "I'll take care of it."

"Thank you."

"Why the *fuck* did you do that?" Tolk spat.

"It always surprises me." Isaac shook his head as he walked past the restrained guard. "I say I'm going to do a thing, and then people act shocked when I do it."

"Fuck you!" Tolk raged. "Fuck both of you!"

Isaac let out a weary sigh. He sent a destination request to the grav tube and stepped in. The chute whisked him upward and dropped him off outside the penthouse. He waited for Susan to join him, and they both entered Reed's office together.

The penthouse was mostly empty space lined with one-way windows gazing out across the glittering blue waves. Chairs, sofas, and plants dotted the penthouse office, most arranged to afford a view through the windows, though one corner appeared to be dedicated to an automated kitchen and bar.

Brian Reed sat behind an expansive desk with his back turned to them, his whole body hidden behind a high chairback except for one hand hanging limply over the armrest. Virtual screens concealed half the windows along one wall, displaying live feeds from news organizations based on Earth, Luna, L4, and L5. A trio of windows contained what appeared to be civilian streams from the protest outside the Crimson Flower, another showed a countdown to when the Weltall Tournament would resume. Finally, one curious window showed a fuzzy, zoomed-in shot of what appeared to be a hangar door on the surface of Argus Station.

"Allow me to apologize for the greeting you received, Detectives." Reed spun his chair around to face them. He was a tall man with a shaved head and narrow eyes. He wore a business suit decorated with a stepping pattern of dark grays and blacks along with a static black neck scarf. The dark cloudlike avatar of his IC floated over one shoulder. "Mister Tolk's actions do not represent LAST as a whole. If I had known he'd react so negatively, I would have seen to it that other personnel greeted you."

Somehow I doubt that, Isaac thought. *One look at this office tells me you lord over this entire branch. If you'd wanted us to come in without a hassle, that's what would have happened. And if you wanted us to be hazed on the way here, well...*

"The matter at the door is resolved and behind us," Isaac said. "Frankly, Tolk's behavior isn't my problem. We're here to discuss a far more serious matter with you."

"I can imagine." Reed stood up and paced across the virtual screens. "Before we begin, would you mind if I show the two of you something?"

"If you wish."

"Here. Take a look at this one." Reed expanded the camera view from Argus Station. "This is an external shot of the DTI hangar on Argus Station. Our people keep an eye on the Admin's comings and goings, and we're aware of a series of high-level meetings between the Gordian Division and the DTI. We're confident both Commissioner Schröder and Director-General Shigeki are involved, and the latter isn't here for a brief visit. Instead, the heads of each organization seem to be *integral* to whatever is being discussed. A troubling sign, indeed?"

"Our leaders meeting to talk isn't such a bad thing," Susan defended. "It wasn't long ago both sides were worried our differences might lead to war. Now look at us."

"You do have a point, Agent Cantrell. The current situation is far from the worst it could be. But how far, I wonder? The last time the Gordian Division and the DTI collaborated on a large scale, it ended in the destruction of an entire universe. The so-called 'Dynasty Crisis.' The people in these meetings have enough authority and firepower to rend whole *realities*! And yet these meetings aren't even on an official schedule. Why the secrecy? What are they hiding from the public?

"Our members have asked around, but all we've learned is a single word. 'Providence.' God's protection. Now what could that mean, I wonder. Do these people consider themselves gods? Who are they to decide the fates of whole universes? No one elected Schröder!"

"But he," Isaac countered, "along with all the other division commissioners, work under the chief of police, who reports directly to the president."

"A small comfort. Between the Dynasty 'Crisis' and the Gordian Knot, we've dodged two nearly fatal bullets, and what's been the response? *More* travel. *More* cooperation." He gestured to Susan. "No offense, Agent Cantrell. I'm sure you're a decent enough person, but I don't like your presence here one bit. Nor what it represents for the future."

"Mister Reed," Isaac said firmly, intent on getting the conversation back on track. "We're here to discuss the death threats leveled against citizens of the Admin."

"Yes, of course." Reed paced back to his desk and rested a hand atop the chairback. "I wondered how long it would take someone from SysPol or LSP to show an interest in our activities. Ask your questions, Detective. I won't flinch away from any of them."

"Do you know who sent the death threats to Elly Sako and Shingo Masuda?"

"No. If I did, I would have immediately reported this information to the police."

"Do you suspect anyone in LAST could be involved?"

"No."

"The threat the players received is very similar to the rhetoric of the protesters."

"Similar, but not the same. We're telling the Admin to leave, not leave or die."

"Are you aware of any illegal activity occurring or being plotted within LAST?"

"To the best of my knowledge, no."

"Please clarify that answer."

"LAST is a large organization, Detective. You know that as well as I do. And while I'm the head of the Lunar branch, there's no way I could possibly track everything every member does or intends to do. On top of that, there are plenty of people who claim to be members of LAST because they share our beliefs but who are not dues-paying members of our organization. They have no official ties to LAST, but their actions can still color public perception of us.

"Obviously, we're heavily involved in the protest outside the Crimson Flower, which includes a mix of official members and people who joined the protest organically. This is a legitimate and important demonstration, and we intend to make our point as strongly and loudly as possible. Within the confines of the law, of course.

"But, as I pointed out, not everyone in that crowd is a member, and even for the ones who are, how much control do you realistically think I have? League membership is priced to be accessible, and penalties for members who make fools of themselves are almost nonexistent. What punishments do I have to dole out, other than revoking their member status?"

"Still," Isaac said, "your word surely has some measure of influence." He nodded to the live feed of the protest. "You've seen the escalating tension just as I have. That crowd is edging toward unstable. One strong push in the wrong direction, and it could turn violent."

"You raise a valid point, Detective," Reed conceded. "How about this? I'll send out a message to all League members on Luna urging them to keep the *Weltall* protest safe and professional. I'll even copy you on the message so that you can evaluate for yourself whether I'm stoking the fires or trying to quench them. How does that sound?"

"We'd appreciate that."

"Then I'll start drafting the message immediately." He tapped his desk with a finger. "Is there anything else you need from me, Detective? Or is our business here concluded?"

Isaac paused to consider that very question. Reed had a point about any large organization and how unwieldy it could be to exert control from the top, and that went double for something as loosely organized as a political movement.

I knew the LAST angle was a long shot when I suggested it,
he thought. *I suppose it's something that Reed agrees the crowd
is getting too rowdy. And he might be able to calm them down.
We're not leaving empty-handed... but it still feels that way.*

He glanced to Susan, who gave him a subtle shake of her
head, then turned his gaze to Reed.

"We're done here, Mister Reed," he said at last.

"Was that a waste of our time?" Susan asked, dropping into
her seat in the V-wing.

"Probably," Isaac said. Cephalie secured the LENS behind
their tandem seats, and the canopy sealed shut.

"Where to next?"

"Back to the Crimson Flower. After that... not sure."

"We could head for the stadium," she suggested. "The tournament's about to start."

"Susan, we're still on the case."

"I know that. What I mean is if something's going to happen,
it'll be near the players, right?" She shrugged. "Wouldn't hurt to
be close by, just in case. Plus, it'll give us time to think. Or *you*
time to think. You're better at this than I am."

"Thanks." He gave her a lopsided grin.

"So? Back to the stadium?"

"Sure."

"All right, then." Susan inputted their destination. The V-wing
lifted off the landing pad, spun to a new heading, and powered
away from the League building.

The tournament was well underway when they took their former
seats near the stage. Only four isolation pods were in view, with Elly's
lonely capsule across from the pods for the three SysGov players.

The game abstraction hovered over their heads with each
player's forces and territory marked as color-coded clouds sprinkled
with icons. Wong Fei had consolidated control over Masuda's
conquered system and fortified his position around its sun, while
Gomako Grim and Yoo Ji-hoon dispatched surgical strikes at
each other, though neither player seemed ready to commit to a
major offensive. Both Grim and Yoo now controlled two systems
each and were maneuvering to take a third, but they'd set their
sights on the *same* system, and that was drawing them into tenser

conflict while Wong Fei reignited his stellar engines to drive his star toward them.

Meanwhile, Elly didn't control *any* systems, her meager forces thin and scattered in the void between stars. Yoo's scouts had caught her scent, and he'd dispatched a sizable fleet to hunt her avatar core down.

"Still think Elly's going to win this?" Isaac asked.

"I don't know," Susan said. "Let's just say I'm having doubts."

Isaac altered the shared abstractions around them, dimming the game map overhead and muting the sound.

"Have you heard back from Nina?" Susan asked, speaking in security chat.

"No. She would have called already if she'd found anything with the hardware. I assume she's back at CFPD looking over Kohlberg's pendant."

"Unless she hits upon a surprise break, that's it for the file transfer angle."

"*Someone* altered the program."

"I know, but we don't have any evidence pointing to a guilty party."

"Yeah." Isaac crossed his arms and dug his back into the seat. "Maybe we need to approach this problem from a different angle."

"Any thoughts?"

"Not sure yet. Let me start with a question. Who benefits the most from these two crimes?"

"Someone who hates the Admin," Susan said without hesitation.

"That's the obvious takeaway, but I'm not so sure anymore. What if the Admin-hate is a ruse? What if the criminal's objective is something else?"

"Such as?"

"Let's look at what the two crimes have accomplished. Lacan is in jail, and Masuda's locked himself in the chronoport. That's two players down in a competition with a lot of prestige at stake."

"You mean the perp might be another player?"

"The thought had crossed my mind."

"I don't know." Susan gazed over the isolation pods. "Would that make all four of them suspects?"

"Perhaps not. Let's consider the printer in Sako's room again, and let's assume we're correct that someone had to be in the room to corrupt it."

"That could be a dangerous assumption," Susan noted. "Given what we've seen so far, we could be up against a very skilled hacker. Someone talented enough to circumvent normal requirements and issue orders to the printer from outside the room."

"I agree, but let's see where this trail takes us. If we limit ourselves to players, who does that leave us with?"

"Wong Fei and Elly Sako."

"Exactly."

"You think one of *them* is behind this?" Susan asked incredulously.

"All I'm saying is it's possible. Any player stands to gain from having less competition, and both of them were in the room prior to the printer spitting out a severed head."

"But it was *Elly's* head," Susan stressed.

"Which she could have sent to herself. Plus, either player could have planted the evidence on Lacan's wearable, though it would have been easier for Sako to pull that off, given their earlier intimacy."

"I know, but..."

"I'm not accusing anyone right now." Isaac smiled humorlessly. "We both know there's not enough evidence for us to do anything. I only think it's a possibility we should consider."

"But what about the threat to Masuda?" Susan asked. "None of the players could have done that, right?"

"Perhaps the criminal has a coconspirator," Isaac suggested. "The skilled hacker you theorized."

"That seems like a stretch."

"But is it, really?" Isaac leaned over. "Remember, Nina said the Lacan evidence got planted through an Admin-type access. But modifying the *Weltall* UAM required SysGov expertise. Therefore, it makes sense for us to be dealing with at least two people, one knowledgeable in Admin infostructure, and one for the SysGov side of things."

"Hmm. I hadn't thought of that." Susan stared off in thought, then began to nod her head. "Makes sense, though. And these sorts of threats do fit in with Wong Fei's old run-ins with the law."

"Yes, but I consider him the less likely of the two."

"Why's that?"

"Because he was already the favorite going into this tournament. And he's doing quite well, while Sako is struggling to gain a foothold."

"The message sent to Masuda came at a convenient time," Susan noted. "Arriving right before his and Wong Fei's fleets clashed."

"Yes, but Wong Fei was about to overrun him anyway," Isaac dismissed.

"Yeah, you're right about that," Susan agreed. "Though, given Masuda's reaction, if Wong Fei *hadn't* taken him out, he would have quit the tournament on his own."

"Agreed."

"But do you really think it's Sako?"

"It *could* be," he stressed. "The way I see it, we have two possibilities. One, Sako is indeed a victim in all this, and I've missed the mark entirely. Or two, she threatened herself while framing her ex-lover. If so, a second person threatened Masuda with the goal of thinning out her competition."

"If you're right, then she's already established herself as the top Admin player," Susan observed. "Even if she doesn't win it all, she's already hit it big."

"Yeah," Isaac sighed, not satisfied with his own line of thinking.

"What's wrong?"

"Nothing"—he shrugged—"beyond the fact that my theory is filled with guesswork patched on top of guesswork, with no real evidence to back it up."

"Not much else we can do without a lucky break."

"I prefer to make my own luck," Isaac growled, sitting up in his seat. "Is there a way we can access Sako's records from the Admin? Would the Admin have performed a background check before allowing someone to enter the tournament?"

"Of course. And Sako would have received extra scrutiny because she's a Lunarian."

"Would Pérez have access to that report?"

"I doubt it. He wouldn't need access to a background check to run the security detail. Any documentation like that would be saved back at DTI headquarters, under the control of Kloss' group in DTI Espionage."

"Is there a way for us to get copies of her background check?"

"Sure. As an investigator, you can request access to them. Plus, we happen to have two chronoports sitting in the hangar. We can ask Noxon to dispatch one back to the Admin and collect the files for us. Transit time is one hour one way, so the

whole process should take less than three hours, even allowing
for some bureaucratic delays."

"Can't the chronoport message the DTI from here?" Isaac
asked. "I thought those ships came with multiverse transceivers
or something."

"Chronometric telegraphs," Susan corrected. "They don't have
the range to reach the Admin from SysGov, and besides, the
bandwidth is *terrible*."

"How terrible?"

"Better hope the report doesn't have pictures, and if there's
video, then just forget it."

"I see."

"It's easier and faster to head back in person."

"Got it. Mind giving Noxon a call?"

"No problem," Susan said. "Let me take care of that right now."

She opened a comm window as Isaac leaned back in his seat
and stared up at the game. Elly Sako's dispersed forces drew his
eye, and he wondered if he was on the right trail or not.

Gomako Grim ran her eyes across the status charts and build
queues hovering around her and considered her position stable,
for the moment. She'd been nervous going into this tournament.
Of course, she always struggled with her nerves before *any* tournament, but this one had been worse.

This one was against the Admin.

She faced her fellow SysGov players, too, but they were
known quantities. She'd battled both countless times before
in other tournaments, had racked up her share of wins and
losses, and knew—more or less—what to expect from them.
Wong Fei was as predictable as he was terrifying, executing his
plans with almost mechanical precision. Yoo Ji-hoon was more
of a wildcard, prone to unpredictable and dangerous shifts in
strategy from match to match.

So far, both were sticking to the familiar. Wong Fei was
turtled up in a single system utilizing the defensive stance he
often favored, while Yoo played a more standard game of ter-
ritorial and economic expansion, similar to her own approach.
She knew she could beat both. She'd done so before, though in
different games.

This one was no different.

No, the difference was the *Admin*. She'd been there during the Admin's universal qualifier, but one event was hardly enough time to gauge an opponent's preferences. The three foreign players represented a terrifying unknown to her in the highest profile event of her life.

She'd thrown up in her room last night.

It seemed silly to her now that she'd calmed down and the tournament was underway. The Admin players had blundered their way forward, both inside and outside the game. Lacan had landed himself in jail, and Masuda barely put up a fight before Wong Fei annihilated him. He was sulking back in the Admin hangar, while Sako was doing...something on the edge of the map. Hiding, maybe? Perhaps to let the other players wear each other down before swooping in at the end?

Whatever Sako's plan was, it didn't appear to be an effective one.

She must be starving for resources by now, Gomako thought. *Oh, well.*

Sure, two of their players had received death threats, but so what? She'd received a few over the years herself; it came with stepping into the public sphere. She'd reported them to the police and moved on with her life. None of those incidents had ever amounted to anything, anyway.

Though, Gomako supposed, a guest player being threatened while in a foreign *universe* was a bit different than an angry fan blowing up at her over an avoidable loss. Still, it seemed like such a small thing to get worked up over. No one had been *hurt*, after all.

So one hotel printer and the game file got hacked, she thought. *So what? Big deal.*

Gomako noticed a shift in Yoo's fleet movements. He was pulling back from the system she'd tagged as Expansion Three, the one he'd seemed intent on contesting up until a few moments ago.

Perhaps he's finally tracked down Sako and smells blood in the water, she wondered. Whatever the reason, it was an opening, and she intended to capitalize on it. She mobilized the bulk of her home fleet and sent it toward Expansion Three. Wong Fei's mobile star was still closing in, but she had time before he arrived.

She didn't think she could *hold* Expansion Three, but she didn't need to in the long run. Instead, she intended to fortify the system with military installations backed up by minimal industry. She would then use it as a buffer to wear down Wong Fei's concentrated might before he reached her two core systems.

Yoo's forces continued to pull back along their entire contested border, and she felt a twinge of nervousness at this development. Shifting his forces away from Expansion Three was one thing, but he was abandoning huge swaths of territory between their stars without so much as a skirmish.

Why? What was going on?

Yoo wasn't known for his passivity. He preferred to go for the throat when he saw an opening, and she wondered once again what Sako was doing on the far side of Yoo's star systems.

Her fleet arrived in Expansion Three and swept through it, searching for ambushes or hidden forces.

Nothing. Yoo had *completely* abandoned the system.

Odd, she thought to herself. *Very odd.*

She set her fleet to work on the construction of an interstellar mass driver and several weapon platforms to support her mobile force, then launched another wave of scouts to find out what the hell was going on in Yoo's territory.

She watched Wong Fei's approach with trepidation for several minutes, concentrating on it, girding the defenses of Expansion Three for the inevitable battle, when an alert arrived from her scouts.

Yoo's systems were empty.

Not abandoned.

Empty.

No ships. No factories. Not even the planets remained.

Everything was gone.

Or rather, had been *consumed.*

She knew this to be true when the first hostile blip appeared near her scouts.

The machine wasn't very large in the overall scheme of *Weltall.* It measured about two kilometers long and vaguely resembled an old, terrestrial trilobite, far smaller than the fifty-kilometer bulk of her scout craft, which destroyed the attacker in a single shot.

But it wasn't alone. More appeared from the edges of space, swarming toward her scouts. Not hundreds or thousands or even millions, but *billions* of them! There were more enemies than her scout fleet had ordnance! The fleet followed her last orders and began to retreat in the face of overwhelming opposition, but the swarm overtook them, destroyed them—

—and then *ate* them to produce more.

Because that's what the All-Predator did. Gorge on everything to make more of itself in a vicious cycle of death by creation.

Sako! she thought urgently as she abandoned Expansion Three and pulled all her forces back to her two core systems. *She must have released an All-Predator! But how? That exists at the end of a lengthy tech tree! Did she pour all her resources into blitzing into late-game tech just to unlock the* All-Predator?!

It suddenly made perfect, brutal sense. The All-Predator was the ultimate endgame equalizer, incapable of distinguishing between friend and foe. Individually they were weak, but together they formed a nigh unstoppable hegemonizing swarm. They couldn't eat stars—thank goodness—but they'd eat just about everything else!

That's it! Gomako thought. *She's using her nomadic fleet to seed the All-Predator in as many systems as she can. And while she remains relatively safe in dark space, the All-Predators are going to eat the rest of us alive! If that happens, she wins!*

She must have already finished Yoo off. Which means there aren't any other players between me and that swarm!

Gomako focused all her energy on preparing for the onslaught. The entire industries of two star systems churned out weapons and ships at a prodigious rate, and her forces consolidated in mighty swarms of their own, from humble scout corvettes all the way up to dreadstars nearly as large as Earth's moon.

The All-Predators arrived in her second system as a blizzard of metal snowflakes that turned her scopes red from edge to edge. Her fleet hardly needed to aim as it fired lasers and dumped waves of missiles into the onrushing horde. Millions of All-Predators died, but millions more swarmed in, oblivious to the losses, only knowing their insatiable hunger.

She commanded her fleet through a fighting withdrawal, abandoning the system while inflicting as much damage as she could, all while micromanaging her industry in a desperate attempt to fortify her final bastion. Some of the All-Predators descended upon the planets and moons of her second system and began to feast, while even more raced after her fleet, now on final approach to her home system—

—and her avatar core.

She assembled her defenses and waited.

The All-Predators arrived, and mines obliterated scores of them, but more poured into her home system. Always more in a never-ending tide. She scoured their ranks with lasers and kinetics, then sortied her fleet forward for one final stand.

But it wasn't enough. The All-Predators advanced across the system with ravenous, implacable abandon, eating her ships, her megastructures, her planets.

And finally her avatar core.

The interface switched over to spectator mode and zoomed out, revealing the terrifying extent of the All-Predator swarm.

She never stood a chance.

"Good game," she said with a shake of her head. "Well played, Elly. Well played."

CHAPTER EIGHTEEN

"SO *THAT'S* HOW YOU USE THE ALL-PREDATOR!" SUSAN WHISPERED. "We thought it was useless."

"Apparently not," Isaac said. "I wonder if Nina was watching."

The game state paused, the player pods opened, and Kohlberg strode onto the stage.

"Wow!" Kohlberg exclaimed, spreading his arms. "What an upset! What a comeback! Who could have seen it coming?" He waved Sako and Wong Fei to join him while other ActionStream attendants guided the two defeated players down into the under-stage. "What a finale tomorrow promises to be! Elly Sako versus Wong Fei! The sneaky assassin versus the defensive powerhouse! The Admin versus SysGov!"

Susan leaned over as Kohlberg continued his post-match wrap-up for the day.

"I heard back from Noxon," she said. "*Defender-Prime* departed for the Admin a few minutes ago. We should have her background check sometime after midnight."

"Good. Did he voice any concerns about our request?"

"None. Why would he?"

"I don't know. I half-expected there to be some pushback to us wanting Sako's background material, either with our access to the DTI files or the use of a chronoport."

"Seemed straightforward enough to me," Susan said. "You're an investigator. The request was well within your authority."

"Guess I'm still getting used to what this role means."

The event began to break up after that. Highlights from the match played overhead while attendees filed out through the exits along the upper rows. A pair of armored DTI agents met Sako at the base of the stage and escorted her down into the understage.

Isaac stayed in his seat, watching the flow of the crowd and waiting for the rush to die down before making his own break for the exits. A second pair of DTI agents drew his eye, and his brow creased when he saw who they were protecting.

"Wait a second." Isaac nudged Susan in the shoulder.

"What?"

"Look there." He pointed. "What's *Masuda* doing here? Shouldn't he be on his way back to the Admin?"

"Don't know. Want to find out?"

"I do." Isaac rose from his chair.

"Mister Masuda," Isaac said, approaching the player from the other side of the ramp down to the understage. His pair of DTI synthoids parted to allow Isaac and Susan through.

"Why, Investigator, good to see you," Masuda replied, then nodded to Susan. "Agent. What can I do for you two?"

"I was surprised to see you in attendance today."

"Ah, yes." Masuda smiled bashfully. "I suppose you would be."

"Last we spoke, you made it clear you had no intention to return. You seemed quite emphatic on that point."

"Yes, I was," Masuda admitted.

"What changed, if you don't mind me asking?"

"Oh, I don't mind. Not one bit, though I get the impression you're wondering if my change of heart might have some relevance to the case."

"It's my job to be on the lookout for potential connections," Isaac defended. "And you *are* acting in a way inconsistent with your testimony."

"Then let me do my best to reassure you. The reason is quite simple. Sako asked me to come."

"She *did*?"

"Yes. She stopped by the chronoport after the match was rescheduled."

"Just to ask you to attend?"

"More or less. We talked a bit about the tournament and the threats we've both received, our reactions to them. Those sorts of things. Then later she asked me to join her for the tournament tonight."

"Did she give you a reason?"

"Not specifically, though I could guess." Masuda smiled. "She's the only Admin player left, after all. It's only natural to want some moral support while she faced down all three of SysGov's top players."

"That's it, then?" Isaac asked. "She wanted you to come here and cheer her on?"

"Just so."

"Did you tell her you'd attend?"

"At first, no. I gave her the same answer you heard from me, that I had no plans to leave the chronoport."

"How did she react?"

"I could tell she was disappointed, but she didn't press the point or argue over my decision, even though she clearly didn't agree with it."

"What changed your mind?"

"Why, the fine men and women of the DTI, of course!" Masuda slapped one of the agents on the shoulder, who seemed oblivious to the gesture while he continued to scan their surroundings for threats. "I spoke to Pérez after Sako left, and he walked me through all their enhanced security measures. I was quite impressed! Plus, a drone leads the way wherever I go! These countermeasures show the DTI is taking the death threats *very* seriously. It helped put me at ease. Not completely, mind you, but enough for me to come out tonight and support a fellow player. I hope you find that a satisfactory explanation."

"I do. Thank you."

"Is there anything else I can assist you with?"

"Not at this time, no."

"Then, if you'll excuse me, I'd like to have a word with her before we go our separate ways."

"Of course." Isaac stepped aside.

Masuda and his escort headed down the ramp.

"How's this fit into your Sako theory?" Susan asked.

"It doesn't," Isaac groused.

"Thanks for coming, Shingo!" Sako gave Masuda a warm, full-body hug, then released him and held him at arm's length. "I knew you'd show!"

"That makes one of us," Masuda replied. "Those were quite the moves you pulled off, by the way."

"Thanks! I started practicing with the All-Predator back during the Byrgius qualifier."

"But I never recall you using them before."

"Right you are!" She winked at him. "I've been saving it for the finals."

"That took guts," Masuda commended.

"But it paid off. Grim and Yoo never saw it coming!"

"You would have caught me off guard, too, had I still been in the match."

"Aww, don't be like that." She patted him on the shoulder. "Trust me, this trick could have blown up in my face a dozen different ways. It's hellishly difficult to pull off."

"I'd imagine so. I try to stay clear of self-harming weapons myself."

"To be honest, keeping clear of the All-Predator is the easy part once you have access to endgame tech. The *real* trick is having enough resources to unlock it while at the same time avoiding other players who are *much* stronger than you."

"You made it look easy, somehow."

"That's what I was going for!" she declared brightly. She nodded down the corridor. "You turning in for the day?"

"Yes. You?"

"Over to the Pollen Mixer for some drinks. Wong Fei'll be there, too. You're welcome to join us."

"You're having drinks with him?" Masuda asked. "But you two still need to fight it out tomorrow."

"So?" she defended. "Doesn't mean I can't have a drink with the guy."

"No, I suppose not," Masuda conceded.

"Interested? You're welcome to join us. Some of these SysGov mixed drinks are *amazing*!"

"Thanks, but no. I'd rather not stay out any longer than I have to." He leaned closer and spoke softly for emphasis. "And I suggest you do the same."

Sako shook her head. "Not going to happen."

"But the death threats—"

"Whoever made them can go fuck themselves," she declared firmly. "I'm not going to let them rule *my* life."

"Well, try not to stay out too late. You want to be fresh for tomorrow."

"No promises." She winked at him again, then tugged on the sleeve of one of her guards. "Come on guys! Let's hit the Pollen Mixer!"

Masuda watched them disappear around the bend, then he turned to one of his own escorts. Agents Arlot and Duncan both stood alert and attentive a few paces back.

"Arlot?"

"Sir?"

"I'd like to return to the hangar now."

"Of course. Please follow me."

Arlot led the way down one of the understage passages in the opposite direction Sako's party took, guiding Masuda to a small grav tube transfer station restricted to Crimson Flower staff and guests. A Wolverine drone waited for them, crouched by the entrance. It sat up on all fours when it saw them coming.

Arlot loaded their destination and let the drone go through first. He waited one minute and then he stepped in himself.

When it was Masuda's turn, he paused ever so slightly. Antigravity was one of the SysGov marvels he struggled with. It was an empty, open tube, after all! Even in the low Lunar gravity, the fall would be fatal under normal conditions. But people walked in and out of these tubes as if it were the most normal thing to do!

Why couldn't they use elevators like sane people? he wondered.

"Sir?" asked Agent Duncan, standing behind him.

Masuda hadn't realized how long he'd delayed.

"I'm fine."

He walked forward onto nothing and felt the low gravity of Luna vanish, replaced with the sensation of free fall. The graviton current whisked him down through a short passage filled with flashing rings of light before depositing him in a larger public transfer station located many levels below the stadium. His escort guided him to another tube, and they climbed in once more and sped further down the tower.

Masuda supposed, of all the wonders he'd experienced over in SysGov, antigravity was the most impressive. Certainly, the terraformed moon itself was quite the spectacle as well, but he believed the same could be achieved in the Admin with enough resources and patience.

The politics of Luna—and violent tendencies of its most radical citizens—made such a project difficult to justify. Why pour so much effort into creating and nurturing a biome on the airless moon when its inhabitants seemed more inclined to sabotage progress than welcome it?

In that regard, SysGov held a powerful edge over the Admin. Not only did this society possess the *technical* mastery to achieve great works across the solar system, but its people possessed the *will* to collectively see them through.

SysGov had terraformed both Luna and Mars and had even begun to remake hellholes like *Venus*! What had the Admin done with its own version of the solar system? Nothing, beyond preserving the status quo.

In that light, he thought dimly as he transited down the tube, *I wonder if they view us like we view the Lunarians. As troublemakers one should keep a wary eye on.*

The public tube delivered them to the wide plaza at the base of Pistil Tower. He stepped away from the exit and looked across the red, polished flagstones. He would have preferred a more private route back to the hangar, but the Crimson Flower wasn't laid out with his convenience in mind. Every path from the stadium to the Admin hangar passed through the central plaza.

The Wolverine trotted across the open expanse, halfway to the other side, its head swiveling back and forth as it worked to verify the route ahead.

Masuda began to cross the plaza with Arlot ahead of him and Duncan behind, passing clusters of SysGov citizens along the way. A few locals turned to take in the curious foreigners and their mechanical guard dog, but most headed about their business with barely a glance, if that.

They had almost reached the Petal Four tubes along the outer circumference of the plaza when Arlot stopped in his tracks. He held out his palm as if reading an abstract message, but Masuda couldn't see anything. The agent was keeping the message private.

"Is something wrong?" Masuda asked.

"Yes," Arlot replied brusquely. "League protesters have broken into the Crimson Flower."

"They've *what*?" Masuda blurted. "How many? Where are they now?"

"One moment, sir."

Masuda gathered the impression the agent was trying to hold two conversations at once. He looked urgently around the plaza, but everything appeared normal to him. It was just another day in the Crimson Flower, except...

"Over a hundred protesters," Arlot reported, "with more flooding in, and they're making faster progress through the building than we projected. It's like the Flower's internal security isn't even slowing them down. Either someone's opening the checkpoints for them or they got their hands on some high level keycodes. Either way, we're to head directly for the hangar. Duncan?"

"Ready!"

Arlot urged Masuda forward with a hand on his shoulder, and together they sprinted to the Petal Four transfer station. Someone shouted behind them, and Masuda turned to see a cluster of black-clad protesters pour out of a nearby transfer station.

"There he is!" one of the protesters shouted, pointing at Masuda. "After him!"

The protester must have manipulated the local infostructure, because a giant, abstract arrow materialized over Masuda's head. It bobbed up and down, flashing between red and white while emitting a two-toned siren.

"Uh oh," Masuda breathed.

Arlot grabbed a smoke grenade off his equipment harness and threw it so hard it traveled almost horizontally into the crowd. The compact cylinder sparked against the ground like a stone skipping across water, and jets of white smoke billowed out of both ends.

The thick cloud disoriented a few League protesters, but others raced through the smoke, homing in on the abstract marker over Masuda's head. A large man wearing a black helmet with a reflective visor kicked the smoke grenade to the side.

"I don't think nonlethal's going to cut it," Duncan said, placing a hand on his slung rifle.

"Those are the orders," Arlot snapped. "Now into the tube! Go, go, go!"

Duncan grabbed Masuda by the shoulders and manhandled him into the tube, all while keeping his armored bulk interposed between the player and the advancing protesters. Arlot planted a second smoke grenade on the wall next to the grav tube, then backed into it. The graviton current whisked them away at a diagonal into Petal Four.

Masuda let out a long, calming exhale.

"That was a bit too exciting for my tastes."

"Uh huh," Duncan grunted, holding onto him and gazing up.

"At least they're behind us."

"I wouldn't be so sure, sir."

"Huh?" Masuda asked, then gulped and followed the agent's line of sight up along the tube's path.

"Stick close to us," Duncan said. "We'll get you through this."

"What's wrong?"

"Not sure, sir."

The grav tube dropped them off in a circular room with a central fountain and a dozen public access tubes—

—which protesters were already pouring out of.

"You have entered an exclusionary zone," their Wolverine warned, standing between the intruders and the arriving agents. "Move back or I will—"

A burly man with black pants, a black scarf, and a bare chest with LEAVE written across it in greasy black paint tackled the drone to the ground while the others rushed toward Masuda. One of the protesters pulled some sort of round device from his pocket and tried to push past Arlot, readying a throw, but Arlot grabbed the man by his shirt and flung him back with enough force to bowl over two others.

"Ouch! That hurt!" whined one of the downed protesters.

"To the hangar!" Arlot snapped. "*Move it!*"

The pair hustled Masuda down a curving corridor lined with hotel suites. Behind them, black-clad protesters stumbled over their fallen brethren before advancing down the hall in a wild mass, though one of their number had stopped to paint huge black words on the side of the fountain.

"Should one of us break off and delay them?" Duncan asked.

"No! We stick with Masuda!" Arlot ordered.

They hurried down the arcing corridor and were about to pass a T-junction when shouting up ahead prompted Arlot to slow down. Another group of protesters hurried into view from around the bend, abstract arrows guiding them straight to Masuda.

"How'd they get ahead of us?" Duncan asked.

"Forget it! Left!" Arlot shouted. "Go left!"

They turned at the junction and sprinted down a straight hallway while the two mobs converged and poured in after them. The agents guided Masuda through several more turns before coming into view of the hangar entrance, where two more agents stood watch.

"Seal it behind us!" Arlot called out. "We've got company!"

"Yes, sir!"

They filed into the expansive hangar where *Pathfinder-Prime* sat in its docking cradle, belly ramp open. The two hangar guards backpedaled through the hangar entrance, even as protesters came into sight at the far end of the corridor. One of the agents palmed the interface, and the prog-steel door snapped shut.

"Locked, sir."

"Good job."

"Whew!" Masuda exhaled. His knees quavered like jelly, and he dropped to a crouch to steady himself.

"Report!" Noxon snapped, hurrying down the ramp with Pérez and three more agents.

"League protesters have reached the hangar exterior," Arlot said. "However, Masuda's inside here with us and the entrance is sec—"

The interface to the hangar entrance chimed. Prog-steel split open, and the first of many protesters stumbled in. Another clambered over the first, and more flooded through after him.

"Oh, hell," Arlot breathed.

"But we locked that door!"

Virtual chimes sounded off from both hangar side entrances. Prog-steel yawned open, and more protesters flooded in from either direction. One of the protesters, a heavyset man with a black bandana and triumphant gleam in his eyes, flung a spherical device at the gathered agents. It burst open before impact and splattered Arlot with a black, tarlike substance.

The tar writhed around him, creeping across his armor. He tried to scrape it off but that only joined his hands to his torso via thick strands of the strange goop.

"Oh, shit!" cried Arlot, the fear and urgency palpable in his voice. "What *is* this stuff?!"

"Self-replicators!" Noxon snapped. "Purge your armor, agent! Do it now!"

"Shit! Here goes!"

"Get down, sir!" Duncan grabbed Masuda and shielded him with his body.

Arlot triggered a controlled detonation underneath his armor's corrupted malmetal plates, which blew the front half of his suit off and sent pieces scything through the air. One hexagonal plate struck the heavyset protester with the bandana in the head. Blood sprayed into the air, and he dropped to a heap on the floor.

The advance of protesters slowed, then halted as all eyes turned to their downed comrade. The whole hangar seemed to hold its collective breath while a pool of blood gathered underneath the man's head, soaking his bandana.

"Oh God," uttered one of the protesters. "Is he dead?"

Arlot patted himself down, checking himself for infection points.

"See any more of that shit on me?" he asked urgently.

"You're clean!" Duncan gave him a thumbs-up.

"They drew first blood!" shouted one protester with a black scarf pulled up over his mouth. "Get them!"

An angry throaty roar rose from the League members, and all three clusters charged in at once.

"Orders, sir?" Pérez asked.

"Neutralize them!" Noxon snapped. "Nonlethal suppression!"

"Yes, *sir!*"

"And someone get Masuda into the damn chronoport!"

Arlot grabbed Masuda while the other DTI agents charged into the advancing mob.

Isaac didn't know what he expected to find when he reached the Admin hangar. All manner of blood-soaked worst-case scenarios played out in his mind as he rushed to the Admin's aid. The League mob had moved through the Crimson Flower with startling rapidity, and local law enforcement had only begun to mobilize. Even then, so many protesters had entered the Flower and gone off in so many directions that it would take the state troopers valuable time to corral and subdue them.

Too much time, in Isaac's estimation, which was why he and Susan had joined up with Nina, and together they'd headed straight for the Petal Four hangar.

They found the first sign of conflict immediately in front of the grav tubes where a damaged Wolverine stood triumphantly over an unconscious protester with black paint smeared across his bare chest. He was drooling on the carpet.

"You!" Isaac snapped. "Come with us!"

The drone trotted after them as they hurried to the hangar. Navigation arrows pulsed in his virtual vision, but he didn't need them. He could have found the hangar *blindfolded.*

A raucous melee raged within the hangar. Outnumbered DTI agents fought against an angry mob of black-clad protesters, beating them back with their hands and feet and the butts of their rifles. They were living weapons clad in armor, and unconscious protesters littered the ground. He could almost *feel* the crunch of their impacts as synthetic fists broke ribs and cracked skulls.

But the protesters kept coming at them, and they had a few synthoids of their own, evident in the DTI agents and busted drones on the ground. One agent lay sprawled on the floor while a protester hammered the back of her head with her own severed arm.

Isaac's LENS tracked the weapons in the room and highlighted them in his virtual vision: a few knives and smart-paint grenades on the protesters and the (as yet unfired) rifles belonging to the agents. One of the protesters had somehow claimed a rifle, but it was little more than a bludgeon without the authorization codes.

The situation was bad, but it wasn't worst-case bad. This wasn't the scenario where the Admin fought back with intent to kill. They'd busted heads and shattered bones, sure, but no one had *died* as far as Isaac could see. Every injury could be mended with the right care.

But that would have to wait.

Right now, he needed to restore order.

"Cephalie!" Isaac pointed at the man beating the downed agent with her own arm. "Crowd control mode!"

"You've got it!"

The LENS morphed into a teardrop and burst forward. It clipped the protester in his raised arm, ensnaring it in a globule of morphing prog-steel. He dropped the severed limb, his eyes growing wide, mouth forming an O as the force of the impact drove him back. The LENS angled down and struck the floor with a loud clang. It left a piece of itself spiked into the floor, then darted after its next target.

The protester yanked on his bound wrist but couldn't pull it free.

"Nina!" Isaac faced her. "You, too!"

"All drones forward!" she shouted. "Crowd control mode!"

Her six forensics drones morphed into aerodynamic shapes and shot into the crowd. Together, their combined forces ricocheted through the mob like angry streaks of silver, bouncing from one protester to the next, binding wrists and ankles to the floor before speeding off in a new direction. Their shells shrank with more immobilizations as the drones expended pieces of themselves with each restraint.

One of the protesters saw the drone attack and decided to charge at Isaac, which almost made him roll his eyes at the futility. The man's attire made him look like a mummy wrapped in black cloth strips with ragged streamers billowing behind him. Susan stepped in the protester's path, dodged the sluggish punch he threw at her, grabbed his arm, twisted it behind his back, and tackled him to the ground, all in one fluid motion.

"Thanks," Isaac said.

"Anytime," Susan replied, binding the prisoner with a prog-steel cuff.

The mob's numbers were too great for their drones to incapacitate everyone, but the shock of seeing so many League members incapacitated so easily rippled through their ranks, and many halted there, unsure what to do next, now that their supporting numbers were stripped down.

A few protesters continued to fight, especially those closest to the agents and, therefore, unlikely to have witnessed the culling their numbers had received. However, the DTI agents knew an opening when they saw one, and they went on the offensive, clobbering the few remaining fighters.

It was quick, brutal, and efficient. Just what Isaac had come to expect from the Admin, and soon every protester was either incapacitated or had ceased to fight.

"This is the System Police!" Isaac shouted, his voice amplified over the room's shared virtual senses. "You are engaged in an illegal assembly and are under arrest!"

"They started it!" whined one of the protesters. She pulled her scarf down from her mouth and pointed at the DTI agents.

"Sit down and wait your turn to be processed!"

"But—"

"Sit *down!*"

The whiny protester dropped onto her butt, and soon others followed her example.

"Are we under arrest, too?" one of the DTI agents asked. He didn't recognize which.

"Don't be dense." Isaac opened a comm window. "Dispatch."

"Themis Dispatch here. We're seeing a lot of activity at your location, Detective. Do you require assistance?"

"You could say that. I need all available LSP units to converge on my position." He surveyed the bloodied protesters littering the floor. "As well as all available medical responders. Same location."

"Most of the CFPD is currently occupied with a multitude of crimes spread all over the Crimson Flower, but I see a few units available to support you. Routing them to your location now. Same with the medical teams. The first should arrive at your location in under ten minutes. Do you need anything else, Detective?"

"Not right now. I think the worst is over. Thanks, Dispatch."

He closed the window, then stepped forward until he was near the middle of the carnage.

"Didn't your branch president tell all of you to take it down a few notches?" he asked.

None of the protesters would meet his gaze.

CHAPTER NINETEEN

ISAAC NURSED HIS THIRD CUP OF COFFEE AS HE STARED OUT THE window. Or was it his fourth? He couldn't quite remember at this point. Either way, it had been a *long* night, and it wasn't over yet. Stars twinkled overhead in a clear sky, partially obstructed by the overhanging mass of Petal Three.

The Wellspring Hospital drooped from the underside of Petal Three like a complex, upside-down castle. Its exterior matched the rest of the Crimson Flower in its loud brilliance, but the interior was a pleasant pastel green. The silhouettes of tree branches rustled along the walls amidst animated gusts of wind.

He turned from the window at the sound of footsteps.

"How are you holding up?" Susan asked, the LENS following her with its restored outer shell.

"Tired," Isaac confessed. "But it's nothing caffeine can't solve. You?"

"Fully charged. My connectome will need some downtime eventually, but I'm still good to go for a while."

"I wish I felt the same." He took another sip of the black, scalding elixir.

"This can wait until tomorrow, you know."

"It can, but at the same time it won't. This is the first indication we've had the threats against the players are credible, and we need to know how these protesters fit into this mess."

"You think they're connected?"

"I'd be shocked if they're not." Isaac took another sip. "We don't have any evidence linking them. *Yet.* However, the League cut through Crimson Flower security like management left the door open. That's an interesting parallel to some of what we've already seen."

"Our mystery hacker?"

"Exactly." Isaac drained his cup, then walked over to a reclamation chute stylized as a hollow tree trunk and tossed it in. "Either way, we need to know how they pulled it off."

The two walked down the curving hallway, full-length windows on one side and a series of doors on the other, until they came to a door guarded by a state trooper. An abstract medical chart glowed next to the entrance with the green header glowing at the top.

It read: ROBERT SOUTHWORTH (STABLE / DATA ISOLATED)

"Is he awake?" Isaac asked.

"Last I checked," the state trooper replied. "Said he couldn't sleep."

"And he's been informed of his rights?"

"Yes, sir. Took care of it myself." The trooper shook his head disapprovingly. "I don't think he realizes how much trouble he's in."

"Good."

"Why this one?" Susan asked. "The state troopers have over two hundred protesters in custody, either here or back at the station."

"True, but most of them—the ones directly involved in the hangar ruckus at least—are keeping quiet. They know they're in deep trouble. Mister Southworth, however, is a different story. Not only did he throw a smart-paint grenade at Agent Arlot, which escalated the confrontation, but the agent's purged armor knocked him out. He has no idea what happened between that moment and when he woke up at Wellspring."

"I'm not sure I follow, but okay. How do you want to handle this?"

"Actually, about that. I know this isn't typical for us, but would you mind waiting outside for this one? At least until I've warmed up the witness?"

"Sure, but why?"

"I have a hunch as to how this'll play out, and I'd like you to barge in at the right moment." He tapped his temple. "I'll leave a link open for you to watch."

"Okay, but how will I know when to come in?" She shrugged her arms. "Shouldn't we decide on a signal or code phrase or something like that?"

"Oh, you'll know," he said with a crooked smile. "I have faith in you." He indicated the door. "Trooper, if you would be so kind?"

"Yes, sir." The trooper sent the door the unlock code, and Isaac stepped in with the LENS following close behind.

Robert Southworth was a large, stout man with small, beady eyes and a wide mouth over a lantern jaw. He wore a pastel green medical gown, and his bloody bandana had been replaced with a medibot wrap, which trickled a steady stream of the microscopic machines into his injury site. He lay in a bed curved into a gentle sine wave, elevating his head.

Under normal circumstances, he might have been watching a show or playing games to pass the time using the room's infostructure, but LSP had imposed a selective data isolation that denied his access to information not related to his recovery.

"Finally!" Southworth shifted higher in the bed. "I wondered when someone from SysPol would show up. I've been so excited to share my story, I haven't been able to sleep!"

"Mister Southworth, I'm Detective Cho from SysPol Themis. I'd like to ask you a few questions, if you're feeling up to it."

"Oh, of course, Detective! Of course! It's no trouble at all!"

"Thank you." A chair formed out of the floor near the side of the bed. Isaac sat down and opened his notes.

"Also, please call me Robby. All my friends do."

"Mister Southworth," Isaac continued without missing a beat, "I gather you have some information you're keen to share with me?"

"Oh, I do, Detective! I do!" he rubbed his meaty hands together. "You see, we finally got them!"

"'Them'?"

"Why, the Admin, of course! We're going to reveal to the worlds how barbaric these brutes are. I mean, just look what they did to me!" He touched the medibot wrap on his head.

"Would you describe the event for me, please?"

"All I remember was a loud bang and then...pressure. Something exploded off one of those Admin thugs. I'm not sure what, though. Could have been a hidden weapon. Took me right out!" He waved around the room. "Next thing I know, I'm here."

"Ah yes." Isaac opened the man's medical chart. "According

to the doctors, you suffered a rather nasty concussion. However, the medibots seem to have stabilized the brain injury. How do you feel?"

"Got a bit of a headache."

"I mean in terms of your mental acuity."

"Oh, that? I feel great! My memory of the event is crystal clear!"

"Excellent. However, I can't fail to notice your description appears to be incomplete."

"Uhh, no, that was it. An explosion, pow to the head, then sleepy time."

"Yes, but before that."

"Before?" Southworth seemed confused. "What do you mean?"

"I'm talking about what led you to be in the hangar in the first place."

"I don't see how that's relevant. I didn't reach those thugs until we were all in the hangar, so I can't bear witness to whatever crimes they committed elsewhere. I can only speak to events in the hangar."

"Which you were trespassing in."

"Oh, *pfft!*" He waved a dismissive hand. "Yes, fine. I was trespassing. I confess. But don't you see? That was a small price to pay for us to catch those thugs red-handed."

"You confess?" Isaac raised an eyebrow. "To being in the hangar without the permission of the Admin?"

"Yes, yes." Southworth gave the issue another wave. "I committed a teeny, tiny pipsqueak of a crime in the service of the greater good, and I'm more than happy to pay whatever fines come up. I won't even contest them!"

"I *see.*" Isaac took his time jotting down this particular note.

"Umm, Detective?"

"Yes?"

"What are you doing there?"

"Annotating your confession."

"Umm. Why?"

"Because I'll need to turn it over to my counterpart in the Admin for processing."

"Your . . . counterpart?" Southworth blinked in bewilderment. "Why would you need to do that?"

"Unfortunately, the matter of how to process your crime is much more complex than you realize."

"*My* crime?" He shifted awkwardly in the bed. "I hardly see how trespassing is any concern to a SysPol detective." He swallowed. "Don't you people normally deal with murder and stuff like that? I've already told you how those thugs brutalized me."

"Then perhaps you misunderstand the purpose of my visit." Isaac looked up from his notes. "I'm not here to discuss what the agents did to you."

"You're not?"

"No. I'm here because of what *you* did to *them*."

"But I didn't do anything!" he protested.

"I beg to differ." Isaac opened a virtual slide and removed his privacy filter. "Do you recognize this?"

"Of course, I do. It's a smart-paint grenade. We use them in demonstrations all the time."

"This is *your* paint grenade, to be precise. The one you lobbed at Agent Stanford Arlot of the DTI."

"So, I threw paint at him. So what?"

"But that's not all. You or one of your accomplices loaded a very specific pattern into the grenade. One you had reason to suspect would provoke a strong response."

"Well . . ."

"A pattern the grenade began to replicate as soon as its microbots splashed against Agent Arlot's armor. A pattern recognizable to many in the Admin. A black, swirling pattern mimicking a real weapon called 'ravenous pitch.' That's why Agent Noxon registered it as a self-replicating threat and why he ordered Agent Arlot to purge his armor. He was trying to save Arlot's life."

"Hey, they threw grenades at us, too!" Southworth defended. "I remember seeing one go off in the plaza!"

"Which was a harmless smoke grenade. One of the softest responses to an out-of-control mob in existence."

"So is a paint grenade!"

"Not one designed to fake a deadly weapon."

"I—" Southworth threw up his hands. "Fine. We suckered the Admin into baring their fangs. So what? It didn't *hurt* them! I'm the victim here!"

"In more ways than you realize, I'm afraid." Isaac leaned back. "And that brings us to the crux of your problem."

"*My* problem?"

"You assaulted a Peacekeeper with a look-alike weapon."

"Then I'll pay that fine, too!"

"But that's just it, Mister Southworth. We're not talking fines anymore."

"For throwing some paint?"

"Not because of what you did, but *where* you did it. Tell me, do you know where you were when you threw that grenade?"

"In the hangar, of course."

"That's right. The *Admin* hangar."

"So? I don't see why that matters."

"It matters because of the legal framework established between SysGov and the Admin." Isaac opened a copy of the relevant law and presented it to Southworth. "It's not widely known—I had to read up on the law myself—but the short version is SysGov recognizes the interior of a chronoport to be sovereign Admin territory."

"We weren't inside the chronoport."

"No, but the law extends to the chronoport's immediate surroundings when it's not in flight. In this case, that encapsulates all the space between the hangar walls."

Isaac watched a terrible realization dawn on Southworth's face. The man's lower lip quivered as the full weight of his error bore down on him.

"And that means," he summarized, "you were standing in Admin territory when you assaulted one of their agents."

He'd made a few other discoveries while reviewing the new law, such as how he'd broken it himself by taking counter-grav equipment—namely the thruster in his LENS—into the chronoport. The law enumerated a short list of technology that could not be brought into the Admin, and now he had to include his own infraction in the case file.

He wasn't looking forward to explaining his error to Raviv.

"Umm." Southworth gulped after a lengthy delay. "Is that bad?"

"Very."

"How bad?"

"Bad enough that the Admin may request your extradition."

"What for?"

"To stand trial in their courts."

"Oh, *shit!*" Southworth twisted the bedsheets with white-knuckled hands, and the blood drained from his face. "What's going to happen to me?" he squeaked.

"I don't know."

"You won't let them take me, will you?"

"It's not for me to decide. It's out of my hands."

"Then whose hands is it in?" he demanded. "Who do I need to talk to? I don't want the Admin to take me! They'll suck my thoughts right out of my brain! Please don't let them take me! I'll do anything!"

"Actually, there *is* someone you can talk to."

"There is!" Hope blossomed on his face.

"Yes. In fact, I believe she might already be—"

The door split open, and Susan walked in with the coldest, meanest expression he'd ever seen on her face. She stopped at the foot of the bed, hands clasped in the small of her back as she scowled down at Southworth.

"—on her way," Isaac finished.

"Oh, fuck," Southworth trembled, staring up at her, his face contorted by fresh fear.

"Is this *him*?" Susan asked in one of the best bad cop voices he'd ever heard.

"It is."

"And has he been cooperative?"

"Not especially." Isaac sighed, rising from his seat. "Though I did make some progress. He confessed to trespassing in your hangar, and he knew the paint would provoke your agents."

"Excellent." Susan flashed a sinister grin. "That should be more than enough."

"No, wait!" Southworth quivered. "You don't want me! I'm a pathetic nobody! I swear!"

"Maybe." She leaned forward and placed her fingertips on the footboard. "But if it's a choice between nothing and you, I'll take *you*."

"But that's just it! I can help you there! I can help you find who you're really looking for!"

"Then you'd better start talking."

"How'd you break into the Crimson Flower?" Isaac prompted.

"Someone sent us the keycodes. I don't know who."

"Is this your idea of help?" Susan glared down at him. "Because I'm not impressed."

"I'm being straight with you! Here, I'll show you the message."

Southworth held out his open palm, but nothing appeared over it.

"Uhh."

"Cephalie," Isaac said. "Open a hole in the firewall for South-worth to access his private mail."

"Pathway opened," Cephalie said.

A menu materialized over Southworth's hand, and he expanded one of the top threads.

"See?" He shifted the virtual screen forward. "A lot of us received the same message. It came with the keycode that let us into the Crimson Flower."

The correspondence was a thread dozens of messages long, mostly from one League member to another. Two messages were sent from an unidentified source, and the timestamps for those two messages came immediately before and immediately after the most recent *Weltall* match. The keycode was attached to the second anonymous message.

"Cephalie, would you grab a copy, please?" Isaac said.

"Got it."

Susan opened the attached keycode over her left hand. It materialized as a red flower with silvery lines of cursive script underneath it.

"This isn't a general access keycode," she noted. "This is a copy of the *Admin*'s keycode. The one Crimson Flower management set up for us. The one we use to lock down the hangar and hotel floor."

"Which also grants free access to most of the Flower," Isaac added. "That would explain how the protesters busted in so easily. They used a valid keycode to open the doors in their way, even ones the Admin sealed."

"What about the player?" Susan asked. "Shingo Masuda. How'd you people find him so easily?"

"We were watching the live stream when we were sent the keycode. We figured the players would be on their way back to the hotel, so that's where we headed. Whoever sent us the keycode let us know it was coming right before the tournament started. We weren't sure what to make of it, but enough of us thought it was legit to put a plan together. Sure enough, we received the keycode shortly after the tournament ended. One of us tested it on a side door, it worked, and the next thing I knew we were storming the place."

"What would have happened if you'd caught Masuda?"

"We were going to douse the players with paint."

Susan crossed her arms and scowled at him.

"Look, that's it, I swear! Just scare them with paint made to look like an Admin weapon. You see? Harmless."

"Except for all the broken bones and traumatized organs," Isaac countered gruffly.

"Is there a reason you went after Masuda and not Sako?" Susan asked.

"We didn't go after one or the other. We found that Masuda guy first, is all."

"Then you don't know where Sako was after the tournament?"

"No. Like I said, we figured they'd both head back to the hotel."

"Do you know who sent you the keycode?" Isaac asked.

"No, sorry. I'd tell you if I did."

"Suspect anyone?"

"Not a clue. Figured we had a sympathizer on the inside."

"What about the death threats leveled against the two players?" Susan asked. "Know anything about those?"

"Uh-uh." Southworth shook his head.

"If you're lying..."

"I'm not, I swear! I don't know anything about the death threats! The League has nothing to do with those!"

"Then I guess that covers it." Isaac rose.

"Are we done here?" Susan asked.

"I believe we are." He palmed the door open.

"Hold it!" Southworth cried out. "What about me? You're not going to send me to the Admin, are you? I helped you out just like you asked! Please don't send me away!"

"We'll let you know when a decision is made," Isaac said.

He and Susan left without another word. The state trooper locked the door behind them.

✧　　✧　　✧

"You're not actually going to extradite that punk," Susan asked, "are you?"

"Nah. Like Southworth said, he's a nobody. And no one from your government's made the request, anyway. All in all, not worth our time." Isaac paused in thought. "Wait a second. Do I actually have that sort of authority?"

"You can certainly request it."

He shook his head in disbelief as they headed back to the transfer station.

"The keycode is an interesting find," Susan said.

"Yeah, no kidding. Cephalie?"

"Here." The LENS accelerated beside him and Cephalie appeared atop it.

"Forward the exchange Southworth provided to Nina. See if she can figure out where it came from."

"I will, but I doubt she'll have much luck. Most likely all the routing codes are fake."

"The chance of her finding something isn't zero."

"Fair enough. I'll take care of it." She vanished.

"Who would have had access to a copy?" Isaac asked Susan.

"All the DTI agents and the Admin players. Probably Action-Stream reps, too, since they're the event coordinators. I can check with Pérez for the full list."

"The players..." Isaac murmured.

"You wondering about Sako again?"

"I am. She's the one who asked Masuda to be at the tournament, *and* she had an excuse that kept her clear of the protesters."

"Those could be coincidences."

"Perhaps," Isaac said noncommittally. "But you're right. The Sako theory is a house of cards. I don't have *anything* solid in the foundation."

"Here's another thing. Why would Sako encourage Masuda to attend the tournament when he'd already lost? That goes against your notion this is about one player thinning out the competition."

"You're right." He shook his head. "Unless I'm wrong about the motive. Let's consider for the moment all three incidents are related. The severed head, the message in blood, and leaking the keycode to the League. What's been accomplished? And, more importantly, who benefits from that?"

"I don't see any common threads," Susan admitted. "Except they're all acts against the Admin."

"Same here," Isaac agreed, nodding. "Maybe that's it, then. Maybe it really is that simple and we've been trying to overthink it this whole time."

"What? Someone just wants the Admin to leave?" Susan asked. "Like the League members?"

"Yes, but I'm more inclined to believe the League are pawns in all this."

"What makes you say that?"

"If they had someone on the inside who could orchestrate the two death threats, why would they need to receive that keycode from an anonymous source?"

"Ah, I see your point. They'd already have stolen it by now."

"Exactly. Which implies that while their goals might overlap with whoever the guilty party is, they're not...in league with each other."

Susan chuckled. "Was that a joke?"

"Not an intentional one." He gave her a halfhearted smile. "Anyway, all three events place stress on SysGov-Admin relations. Is that the goal in and of itself? Maybe it is. There are plenty of people who'd like to sour that relationship. We just finished talking to one, after all."

"Same could be said about radicals from Admin Luna," Susan suggested.

"True, but Sako's heritage as a Lunarian is hardly proof of anything, which is why I'm more interested than ever to see the results of her background check."

"Oh, almost forgot. Captain Elifritz called while you were chatting up the prisoner. *Defender-Prime* returned with Sako's files. He doesn't want to transmit files this sensitive to us, so we'll need to stop by the hangar to pick them up in person."

"Okay. We'll head there next."

"Not back to the hotel?"

"Not yet. I'm curious to see if those files hold the answers we're looking for. Besides, I've got too much caffeine in my system right now." He let out a long, weary sigh. "And if Sako *is* involved, it's still an open question who her coconspirator is. She couldn't have done all this—"

Isaac stopped midsentence, even though he and Susan were conversing in security chat, because Elly Sako and Wong Fei rounded the bend with a pair of DTI agents behind them.

"Oh!" Sako remarked, eyes widening. "Detectives!"

"Miss Sako," Isaac said smoothly, switching back to normal speech. "And Wong Fei. What brings you to the hospital?"

"A goodwill visit," Wong Fei said.

"We're handing out health sigils to the injured protesters," Sako said.

"I'm not sure you being in close proximity to League members is a bright idea," Isaac observed.

"We understand that," Wong Fei agreed. "Which is why I'm here as well."

"We're trying to demonstrate a unified front of goodwill," Sako added. "You know, to show these people we're not so bad after all."

Isaac found his eye drawn to the agents behind the pair.

"Oh, they wait outside," Sako reassured him. "And we make sure the state troopers are okay with us going into each room beforehand. They turned us away from a few of the more... troublesome guests."

"That's probably for the best," Isaac said. "What is it you're handing out exactly?"

"Here. See for yourself." She held both her hands out, and an abstraction appeared in the space above them. It was like someone had taken a snake, chopped off its head and tail, and then sewn the two new ends together to form a circle.

"That's..." Isaac frowned at it. "That's a flesh wheel. Covered in snakeskin."

"Mmhmm!" Sako nodded brightly.

"And you're giving copies of this to the protesters?"

"Of course!"

"The wheel carries a great deal of hopeful symbolism in Admin culture," Wong Fei explained, tracing the flesh wheel with a finger. "Fortune follows misfortune. Happiness follows grief. That sort of thing."

Susan gave Isaac a brief but emphatic nod as if to tell him, yes, this was a thing in the Admin.

"Life has its share of ups and downs?" Isaac ventured.

"That's right," Wong Fei said.

"But why a snake?"

"It's the *caduceus* snake," Sako explained. "A symbol of medical wisdom."

Right, Isaac thought to himself. *With its head chopped off and the throat sewn to its own behind.*

"Don't fret, Detective," Wong Fei reassured. "We've had to explain this to everyone."

"I'm not surprised."

"We're on our way to see a man named"—Sako summoned a virtual list—"Robert Southworth. Do you think the state trooper will let us in to see him?"

"I do." Isaac glanced back down the hall. "And I suspect he'll be in a...receptive mood."

"Oh, good." Sako smiled at the news. "Well, we'll be heading his way then. Didn't mean to take too much of your time."

"No trouble at all. Good night." He checked his abstract clock. "Or morning, as it were."

The two players and their escorts disappeared down the curved hallway.

"How's *this* fit into your theory?" Susan asked at last.

"I'll tell you when I figure that out."

CHAPTER TWENTY

"INVESTIGATOR, AGENT." CAPTAIN ELIFRITZ GREETED THEM WITH curt nods as they entered *Defender-Prime*'s bridge. "Good to see the two of you are well. Heard you had some excitement while we were out."

"You could say that," Isaac replied. "The League protest got a little rambunctious."

"So I've been told." He shook his head with a slim smile. "We leave the hangar for a few hours, and look what happens."

"Do you have the background files for us?"

"I do. If you'll follow me."

Elifritz led them down the chronoport's central corridor to a side door. He palmed the door open and ducked into a cramped office with a desk jutting out of the wall and two chairs bolted to the floor. One wall was covered with service medals and abstract pictures of Peacekeepers grouped together in front of what might have been earlier versions of the chronoport.

Isaac found his eye drawn to a second, smaller set of pictures close to the desk. They featured Elifritz alongside a tall, attractive woman with a playful glint in her eyes. One of the pictures showed them walking across a red desert in white pressure suits while others were in more earthlike settings, often around a wide variety of animals.

"Let me unlock the access for you," Elifritz said, "then I'll get out of your way."

"You've been to Mars?" Isaac asked conversationally.

"I was stationed there for a while. That's where I met my wife Michelle."

"Your wife is Martian?"

"She is. You sound surprised."

"Maybe a little. I understand Earth and Mars don't get along over there."

"I know we form a rather unlikely couple. The Peacekeeper and the Martian. I met her while stationed in the Solis Planum."

"Our biggest base on the planet," Susan filled in.

"Ah."

"I was suffering from a bad case of homesickness," Elifritz continue, "so I thought a trip to the zoo might help. Michelle was working there as a veterinarian." He smiled with warm remembrance. "She's always loved being around animals."

He pressed his hand against a closed-circuit interface on the desk, and a folder appeared in the space above it. The translator in Isaac's wetware interpreted the title as:

DEPARTMENT OF TEMPORAL INVESTIGATION
CITIZEN BACKGROUND ANALYSIS
ELENA SAKO

"You can use my office as long as you like." Elifritz side-stepped back into the corridor and gestured inside. "Please make yourselves at home. Let me know if there's anything you need."

"Are we allowed to take copies of the files with us?" Isaac asked.

"Absolutely. As an investigator, you can take the files and use them however you like. I only asked you to come here because I didn't want to transmit something like this over an unsecured, foreign infostructure."

"I see your point. We should be good for now."

Susan slid in first and sat down in the chair opposite the desk, which left the captain's chair for Isaac. He dropped into it and spread the file headers in the space between them.

"Where do you want to start?" Susan asked.

"Not sure." Isaac perused the headers. "Do you see a summary?"

"Here." Susan highlighted a subfolder, then created a copy of her own.

Isaac opened the subfolder and began reading.

✧   ✧   ✧

"It certainly sounds like the DTI thought Sako might have been radicalized." Isaac took a sip from his latest cup of coffee. "They performed a *lot* of background interviews. Around five times what they held for most of the other players."

"That by itself isn't noteworthy," Susan explained. "Anyone not from Earth gets extra scrutiny, and that goes double for Lunarians and Martians. That said, they didn't find anything."

"Not anything *conclusive*," Isaac stressed. "But we already knew that. Otherwise, she wouldn't be here."

"Still, the interview list *is* quite extensive," Susan admitted. "They interviewed her parents, numerous friends and classmates going back to grade school, former coworkers and bosses, gaming sponsors, and so on."

"Have you come across what she did before going pro?"

"Let me see..." Susan frowned. "Social studies teacher for two years, straight out of college. Both years were spent in Block F9 High, Tycho Crater City."

"Something jump out at you?"

"Only that I've heard of the block before. It's called the Niner Slums. And it became the Niner Slums after the Niner Riots. It's not a nice place to live."

"That would explain the quick career change, though it's an odd leap from teacher to gamer." Isaac grouped the interviews by area. "Seems the DTI focused a lot of their attention on both the F9 high school and her time at Tycho State University, where she earned her degree."

"Makes sense if we're worried she might have been radicalized."

"By terrorists?"

"Or their sympathizers."

"Hmm." Isaac found a tab titled "Radicalization Analysis" and opened it. "Sako has a radicalization quotient of 3.7. What's that mean?"

"It's the lower end of what's considered safe. Three point seven out of ten. It measures the risk of radicalization against the Admin based on a person's known associations and actions." Susan opened the same summary. "In her case, it means she associated with radicalized people, both in college and during her first job, but there were no signs she adopted any of those views."

"Exposure but not acceptance?" Isaac summarized.

"That's what they concluded."

"And by exposure, we're talking extreme views like violently supporting Lunar independence, right?"

"Yeah. Stuff like that."

"What about her family?"

"Let me see." Susan shifted her current sheet aside and expanded the interview page for Sako's parents. "No siblings; just her two parents. The agents conducted a single interview with each parent then moved on. Guess they didn't see much point in a deeper look. Her mother works in the Department of Energy, so that might have contributed. It's a low-tier analyst position, but her reviews are solid."

Isaac swiped through the radicalization subfolders and saw headers for "Media Consumption Analysis," "Socialization Analysis," and "Private Message Analysis," among others.

"The DTI went through her private mail?" Isaac asked, surprised and a little disgusted.

"Yep."

"Is this normal?"

"For Lunarians it is."

Isaac shook his head and closed the radicalization tab. It contained a wealth of information on Sako, but he suspected he'd come to the same conclusions as the DTI agents, that Sako had been exposed to radical points of view but had shown no signs of adopting them. Perhaps the information in those interviews would prove useful later, but right now he lacked the key to deciphering them in a new way.

Instead, he opened Sako's history as a professional gamer.

"Says here, Sako got her start as a gamer in local *Legions of Patriots* tournaments while she still worked as a social studies teacher. Isn't that the game you used to play competitively?"

"It is," Susan replied. "How'd she do?"

"Rocky at first, but the victories ramped up quickly. Her team decimated the competition during the regional qualifier for something called the Lunar Patriot Cup."

"Oh, nice. That's a big one. How'd they do at it?"

"They pulled a major upset and won first place. After that, she quit her teaching job."

"Makes sense. The prize money from the Cup would make her teacher salary look like a rounding error. Anything else?"

"Nothing that stands out to me. After that, we've got a breakdown of her three years as a pro. Some ups and downs, but part of that can be tied to her play style. She's not afraid to experiment. All in all, she's made quite the name for herself."

"Here's something interesting." Susan leaned toward him and turned a spreadsheet around.

"What do you have?"

"Her finances."

"What's an 'Escudo'? Admin currency?"

"Yeah. Our equivalent of SysGov Esteem. Often abbreviated as something-E. Like kilo-E or giga-E."

"Got it," Isaac said, nodding. "What caught your eye?"

"Check out these entries here." Susan highlighted several rows. "She's been giving a *lot* of money to three charities, especially in the last year."

"'Mothers of Luna,'" Isaac read, "'Tycho Rebirth,' and the 'Heller Foundation.'"

"All three are involved in Block F9 revitalization projects."

"Which makes sense, given her professional success and her previous work in the slum."

"Yes, but where it gets interesting is with the Heller Foundation, named after Debra Anne Heller, a former principal at the same school Sako taught at. She started up the foundation last year, and Sako has been a huge benefactor."

"Heller quit to form the charity?"

"No. She was fired. For distributing what amounts to Free Luna propaganda."

"Does Heller have a criminal record?"

"Umm." Susan opened a linked page. "She participated in the Niner Riots and was arrested for property damage and theft. That was over twenty years ago, and her record has been clean since."

"How many people were involved in that riot?"

"About half a million."

"Hmm." Isaac rubbed his chin. "Interesting, though hardly conclusive. You could just as easily say Sako donated the money because she knows and trusts Heller from the school."

"True," Susan admitted. "And the agents performing Sako's background check thought the same. From what I've read, they dug through the money transfers but couldn't find any ties to illegal activity. If the Heller Foundation is a front for Free Luna or one of the other terror groups, its true nature has been well concealed."

"*But.*" Isaac raised a finger. "This does fit my theory."

"It's still a house of cards."

"I know."

"Next steps?"

"Confront Sako directly. We'll ask her some hard questions and see how she reacts."

"Before we head out, why don't we talk to the captain again?" Susan suggested.

"What for?"

"He and his crew have been transporting key people back and forth in the lead-up to the finals." She shrugged. "Wouldn't hurt to ask if he noticed anything unusual."

"Good thinking. I'll give him a call."

"You wished to speak with me?" Elifritz said, sliding through the door to his office.

"We did," Isaac said. "Can you give us an overview of *Defender-Prime*'s recent activities?"

"Sure, though I imagine you know most of it already." Elifritz took off his peaked cap and smoothed out his hair. "This chronoport and its crew have been allocated to the Million Handshake Initiative for the foreseeable future, and as such, our responsibilities involve transporting citizens from both universes back and forth as needed. We haven't been assigned a typical DTI mission in months.

"At the moment, we're supporting the Weltall Tournament with transportation for players and other key personnel, such as ActionStream employees and representatives from a few other SysGov companies. Other software publishers, mostly. We shuttled the SysGov citizens—again players and company employees—to the Byrgius qualifier, provided in-universe transportation for their tour of the Admin, and brought them back along with our own players."

"Why didn't the SysGov citizens use a Gordian TTV?" Isaac asked.

"I can't be certain," Elifritz emphasized, fitting his cap back on. "I wasn't party to those talks, but it's my understanding the DTI offered to handle all transport requirements for the event, and our offer was accepted by your government."

"Makes sense," Susan added. "Fostering cooperation is the

main point of this tournament, after all." She frowned ever so slightly. "Even if it's gone a bit off course."

"You mentioned other SysGov companies. Which ones?"

"Oh, let me think." Elifritz looked up. "Titan Omni, Abstract Artists Agency, Checksum Error, YesWeStillMakeShmups, Drake Gaming. A few others, all of them software publishers and competitors of ActionStream's. I can get you the full list of companies and representatives, if you like."

"Please do."

Elifritz nodded. He opened a virtual interface, searched through it for a file, and copied it over to Isaac.

"Thank you. What were their visits to the Admin for?"

"Negotiations with DOS. That's our Department of Software, which ActionStream worked with to secure their publications rights. So far, ActionStream is the only company to have locked in a distribution contract. The rest are working toward the same."

"Are any of these companies at the tournament?"

"Some." Elifritz opened another sheet. "Both Wyverian Gaming and Titan Omni are in attendance. We're scheduled to take a few of their people back with us after the tournament."

"Have passengers from those companies caused you trouble or acted in an unusual way?"

"No, sir." Elifritz shook his head. "Nothing of the sort."

"What about the SysGov players?"

"No complaints there."

"The Admin players?"

"Same. No issues."

"What about the ActionStream reps?"

"They..." Elifritz grimaced and let out a slow sigh. "No, there were no problems on my ship."

"Captain?" Isaac raised an eyebrow. "I'm detecting some hesitancy there."

"I know. But it's also accurate to say there were no problems."

"Yes. 'On your ship,'" Isaac repeated. "Were there problems elsewhere?"

Elifritz shuffled from one foot to the other. The man didn't strike Isaac as nervous so much as uncomfortable.

Is this it? he thought, excitement building despite his calm exterior. *Have we stumbled upon the key to this case? Are we about to crack it wide open?*

"I would rather not cast aspersions where I have no business doing so," Elifritz said finally.

"I understand and appreciate that," Isaac said, choosing his words carefully, "but if you have information that might be relevant to our case, then I really need you to tell us about it."

"But that's just it. I don't *know* anything. I simply heard a rumor. A rather ugly one at that."

"Captain, you have my word this rumor—whatever it is—will be treated as such. We deal with facts in Themis Division. And while rumors can sometimes lead to facts, anything you heard will need to be verified."

This must be one juicy rumor if it's making him this *uncomfortable!* he thought excitedly. *Come on, Captain! Out with it!*

"Very well." Elifritz straightened. "The rumor involves Sven Kohlberg from ActionStream."

"Yes?" Isaac prompted, even more curious upon hearing the name.

"You see, we weren't just transporting him. He brought along a great deal of cargo for one man. Over five hundred kilograms in total, which we delivered to his temporary residence at Byrgius University."

"What was the additional cargo?"

"They were . . ." Elifritz sighed and shook his head.

"Yes, Captain?"

"They were *sex synthoids*!"

Isaac's excitement deflated like a balloon farting out the last of its air.

"Oh. *That.*"

"Yes! That!" Elifritz continued, his discomfort with the topic boiling over. "And not just him! He met with DOS reps and college faculty and who knows who else during the qualifier where—as the rumor goes—everyone partook, if you catch my meaning."

"Yes, I believe I do," Isaac replied dully.

"I apologize, sir, but I hope you can see why I was hesitant to share this. Surely, this can't be true. He must have brought those synthoids for another purpose."

"I don't know. Seems to me the rumor mill hit its mark this time."

"What?" Elifritz regarded Isaac and his unsurprised expression, then noted the same face on Susan. "Wait a second. You two knew about this?"

"We came across his synthoid harem earlier," Susan sighed with a shake of her head.

"Is something like that *legal* over here?" Elifritz asked with a disgusted expression.

"If you have the right permits, it is," Isaac replied simply. "Any other juicy rumors? Or just the one?"

"Just the one, thankfully."

"What about weird activity on your ship? Anything to share?"

"No, sir. All our trips were uneventful, and none of our passengers caused us problems."

"Then I believe we're done here. Thank you for your time, Captain."

"No trouble at all."

Elifritz left, and the door closed behind him.

"Off to interview Sako again?" Susan asked.

Isaac yawned into his fist, then rubbed one of his eyes with his palm.

"Or perhaps the hotel first?"

"Hotel. We can talk to Sako in the morning."

"It *is* morning."

"After breakfast, then," Isaac corrected. "At least let me catch a few winks first."

CHAPTER TWENTY-ONE

"WHAT I CAN DO FOR YOU TWO?" SAKO DROPPED INTO THE MASSIVE couch near the front of her hotel room. Her DTI bodyguards remained outside. "Your AC said you wanted to speak with me?"

"That's right," Isaac answered. He and Susan sat down in chairs across from her. "We have some follow-up points we'd like to clarify with you."

"Is this about the League mob?"

"Partially, but we can start there." Isaac opened his notes. "Where were you during the attack?"

"At the Pollen Mixer. We went straight there after the tournament."

"And what were you doing at the Mixer?"

"You know, celebrating."

"Were you with anyone else?"

"My tagalongs, obviously." She bobbed her head toward the door where two DTI agents stood watch. "And Wong Fei."

"Were all three with you the whole time?"

"Sure."

"In the same room? In visual contact?"

"Uh no, actually. Wong Fei rented a private room for us, and I told the agents to wait outside." Her brow creased. "What's this about?"

"What were you doing in the private room?"

255

"Celebrating."

"How?"

"Do you really need to know?"

"Please answer the question."

"Fine." She shook her head. "We were making out. It probably would have led to sex—and some really good sex at that—but then the agents barged in and told me to be ready to move." She sighed. "That *thoroughly* killed the mood, and all for nothing. None of the protesters headed up the Pistil. All we did was hunker down in the Mixer and wait it out. Shingo had it way worse than me."

"Did you ask Masuda to attend the tournament's second session?"

"Yes."

"Why?"

"I don't know." She leaned back and looked away. "I kind of did it on a whim. Thought it'd be nice to have him in the audience."

"What was his response?"

"He told me no but then showed up anyway." She shrugged. "Go figure."

"Whose idea was it to head to the Pollen Mixer?"

"Mine."

"Weren't you concerned about your safety?"

"Maybe a little. But I'm not about to let fear rule my life." She leaned forward and flashed a grin. "Besides, it worked out in my favor. Those protesters never guessed I was still up in the Pistil!"

Yes, Isaac thought. *Isn't it strange how that all worked out for you?*

"Moving on, I have a few questions regarding your finances."

"Oh? What does that have to do with anything?"

"Perhaps nothing," Isaac admitted. "You donate heavily to a few charities, correct?"

"That's right."

"And the charity you donate the most to is the Heller Foundation."

"Correct again." She smirked at him. "Sounds like someone has access to my background check."

"Why that one in particular?"

"Because I know the founder and I trust her. The others I donate to fund Lunar revitalization projects. But you know how it is with charities, right? How much of the money ends up being put to good use and how much goes to 'overhead'? The other two—Mothers of Luna and Tycho Rebirth—both have good reputations, but with Debra, I *know* my money is making a difference. That's why her foundation gets the most."

"What's the nature of your relationship with Debra Heller?"

"I used to work for her back when I was a teacher. Why are you asking me these questions?"

"What kind of boss was she?"

"An *excellent* one," Sako stressed in a defensive tone. "*Very* supportive. Truly cared about the kids."

"Are you aware she was fired from her principal position?"

"*Yes.*"

"Did that affect your opinion of her?"

"*No.*"

"Why not?"

"Because it was a stupid, overblown scandal brought on by morons who wanted to force her out. That's why."

"Why do you say it's—"

"Look, Detective," Sako huffed, "why don't you cut straight to the questions you *really* want to ask?" She gave him a come-at-me gesture with both hands. "I'm a big girl. I can take it."

"And what questions might those be?"

"The ones where you ask if I'm a Lunar terrorist."

Isaac grimaced, taken aback by her directness. He glanced over to Susan, who looked surprised by the answer.

"Fuck!" Sako stood up and rounded the couch. "I fucking knew it! I had to put up with this shit back home, but I thought this place was different! I thought *you'd* be different!"

"Please calm down, Miss Sako."

"You're such a fucking disappointment! You know that?"

"I don't care whether I disappoint you or not," Isaac replied with equal bluntness. "The only matter that concerns me is solving these crimes."

"And you think *I'm* involved?" She splayed a hand over her chest.

For better or worse, at least she's talking, Isaac thought. *She's angry and unbalanced. She might slip up if I press her further. If she's involved, that is.*

"I wouldn't be asking these questions if the possibility didn't exist," he replied.

"Why? Because I was born on Luna and give some of my hard-earned money to charities there? Does that somehow make me terrorist material?"

"Of course not."

"Then why are you here asking me these questions?"

All right, here goes, Isaac thought. *Let's see what happens when I turn up the heat.*

"Because I can't help but notice how you've acted recently."

"What's that supposed to mean? I'm one of the victims!"

"Yes, but you're not acting like one, and I want to know why. Someone has threatened to kill you. Someone threatened Masuda as well. Someone helped those protesters break into the Flower. And yet with all that, what have you been doing? Partying at the Pollen Mixer? Visiting protesters at the hospital?"

"I already told you I'm not going to live my life in fear!"

"You also encouraged Masuda to leave the safety of the chronoport."

"What? Are you implying I *knew* the League would break in?"

"Did you?"

"Oh, fuck you!" she snapped, cheeks reddening. "What a load of shit! Is *this* what I have to look forward to?"

Isaac paused to ponder her words.

"What did you mean by that? Looking forward to what, exactly?"

"None of your business!" she raged. "You going to charge me with a crime?"

"I'm not here to charge you."

"Then get out!" She pointed at the door.

"Miss Sako—"

"Get the hell out! We are *done!*"

Isaac locked eyes with her, and she stared back at him, arm outstretched and finger pointing. He was tempted to press harder just to see where it led, but he also knew he had no evidence she'd committed a crime. This was an interview, not an interrogation, and he respected the difference, even if the line between the two could become gray on some cases.

He closed his notes, rose from his seat, and walked out the door without saying another word. Susan came up beside him, and they headed back to the grav tubes.

"That could have gone better," she commented in security chat.

"Bit of an understatement there."

"Did you notice how she dodged your question?"

"The one about the League's break-in and her knowing about it? I did, though it's hard to say what that means, if anything." He frowned and shook his head. "Maybe I pushed too hard."

"The tournament's almost over. If someone intends to strike, it'll be soon. I'd say a little pushing might be just what we need."

"Maybe so, but push *where*? That's the problem. We still have no idea who's behind this, beyond one flimsy theory."

They'd almost reached the grav tubes when a call came in. Isaac checked who it was and answered it immediately.

"Hello, Nina."

"Hey. Are you two free? Can you stop by the stadium?"

"Sure. Got something for us?"

"Maybe. Whatever I've got, it's at least more than nothing. Come by the stadium and I'll walk you through it."

"Understood. We're on our way."

✧   ✧   ✧

They found Nina near the tall archway that served as one of several upper entrances to the stadium. Abstract police cordons hovered in wide circles around the arch, and wall paneling on one side had been removed and stacked, revealing dense racks of infostructure nodes.

Nina sat on one of her drones while she reviewed a virtual report. Another two drones floated beside the exposed wall, their pseudopods connected to the largest node on the rack.

"I thought you were looking into that anonymous message sent to the League," Isaac said, stopping next to her.

"I did. Led me here."

"What did you find?" Susan asked.

"First, let me get you two caught up." Nina pushed off her drone seat. "Data forensics sent me the final reports for both Kohlberg's office and home infosystems, and I finished going over the man's pendant. There are copies of the reports in your mail."

"Is there any point in me looking at them?" Isaac asked.

"Not unless you want to bore yourself to sleep. In short, all three analyses turned up nothing." Nina shrugged with a sly smile. "Except for porn. Someone needs to find that man a girlfriend."

"Not our problem," Isaac replied dryly.

"Yeah, well, you didn't get an earful from an AC complaining about all the sex scenes she had to sift through while looking for data anomalies." Nina chuckled. "Kind of makes me want to send in even more of Kohlberg's garbage."

Susan cleared her throat. "You mentioned the League message?"

"Just about to get there." Nina patted a fat infostructure node. "So, at first, I took one look at those messages and almost gave up, because I could tell the routing codes were fake."

"How did you know?"

"Well, for one, whatever program generated the fake codes wasn't very creative. They were randomly generated strings, which means most of them don't even exist." She chuckled and leaned against the node she'd been resting her hand on. "Though, it turns out, one matched up with an address on Ganymede. I'm sure that's nothing more than a weird coincidence. It's not like the Crimson Flower has any infostructure in Jovian orbit!"

"Then what brought you here?" Isaac asked.

"Don't get ahead of me," Nina warned. "And no, before you ask, I didn't ignore your request, even if I thought it was fruitless. I started by going down to the Flower's base and spot-checking the nodes near the protesters. You know, ones our anonymous message might have passed through."

"Did the League give you any trouble?"

"Nah." Nina waved the concern aside. "They have other problems now, like a whole line of state troopers in riot gear glowering at them. They didn't so much as *look* at me funny. And the trip paid off because I found two nodes those messages passed through."

"Which would have also shown fake routing codes," Isaac noted.

"Yes, but then I had a hunch." She waggled her eyebrows at him. "What if I could guess where the messages came from and check *those* nodes? I thought to myself, 'Nina? Where have you spent too much time recently? A place that *must* be tied to this case, somehow?'"

"Pistil Stadium?" Isaac ventured.

"Right you are!" Nina knocked on the node she was leaning on. "And then I lucked upon the messages. Both passed through this node!"

"Can you tell who sent them?" Susan asked.

"No, but I *do* know it was someone in the stadium. That much I'm certain of."

"That doesn't narrow it down much." Isaac crossed his arms. "Were the players in the pods at the time?"

"No," Nina said. "I already cross-checked the timestamps with the tournament stream. All five players were outside the isolation pods for both messages."

"Then one of the players could have sent them."

"No way for me to rule it out," Nina confirmed.

"But it could have been *anyone* in attendance," Susan noted.

"I know," Isaac sighed.

"Sorry." Nina shrugged. "I wish I had more for you."

"No, it's all right," Isaac said. "This is solid work. It's just… we need more."

Isaac sat down on the edge of the stage, leaned forward and propped his elbows on his knees, and placed his chin atop laced fingers. He stared at the floor, deep in thought. Susan took a seat in the row in front of him, Cephalie appeared atop the LENS, and Nina used the top of one of her drones for a mobile chair.

They were the only people in the stadium. It was dead silent except for the distant hum of ventilation and the occasional *clank* of Nina's drones replacing wall panels.

"Where do we take our investigation from here?" Susan asked after a while.

"I don't know," Isaac said quietly, still staring at the floor. "There has to be something we've missed."

"That's pretty obvious, Isaac," Cephalie tittered.

He gave her a sour look.

"Sorry."

"Let's look at the facts again." Isaac held up a finger. "We have three crimes so far. Number one, the severed head in Sako's hotel room."

"Produced by the same kind of prankware found on Lacan's wearable," Nina said.

"Which we suspect was planted there by someone using an Admin PIN," Susan added.

"Right," Isaac said, nodding.

"And there aren't many people who could have pranked the printer," Susan continued. "From the players, we have Lacan, Sako, and Wong Fei."

"For non-players, Pérez and his agents round out the list." Isaac held up a second finger. "Then we have the message in the game."

"With no idea how it got there," Nina said. "Every infosystem the UAM file passed through came up clean, and the hardware checks out as well. Nothing unusual to report."

"We have the surveillance video and records from the stage and understage." Cephalie summoned a trio of windows. "Plenty of clear, unbroken views all around. After Kohlberg loaded the files, no one touched the pods until the players arrived."

"Which is where our theoretical hacker comes into play," Susan said.

"That'd have to be some hacker to get past all our scrutiny," Nina sighed, "but I suppose it's possible. Unlikely, but possible."

"And he or she would have to be a *SysGov* software expert," Susan added. "Someone from the Admin wouldn't have the necessary skills."

"Finally"—Isaac held up a third finger—"we have the message to the League with the keycode."

"The *Admin's* keycode," Susan emphasized. "Pérez sent me the list of people who had a copy: all three players and his entire security team, basically."

"Plus whoever provided it to them," Isaac noted.

"Which is ActionStream."

"Three crimes." Isaac rested his chin on his fingers again and stared down at the floor. "Three crimes that don't seem to point to one place."

"You still think we're dealing with more than one criminal?" Susan asked.

"I do. I don't see how one person could have pulled all of this off. Or at least done it so cleanly as to leave us scratching our heads. Two parts of the crimes—framing Lacan and altering the *Weltall* UAM—stand out as requiring different skillsets." He pointed to his IC. "Cephalie, you're good at hacking."

"Well, I don't like to brag..." She twirled her cane with a wolfish grin.

"Could you have pulled this off?"

"Some of it. Modifying *Weltall* would be a breeze for me, though there's no way I'd be able to cover my tracks like this. Getting the keycode to the protesters wouldn't be hard. I know a few good ways to generate fake routing codes."

"What about framing Lacan?"

"Doubtful. Admin systems are too different. I *might* have

been able to pull off something similar, but Nina would have caught it, I'm sure."

"And the same holds true if we look at it from the other side," Isaac said. "Right, Susan?"

"Absolutely. None of the players—or anyone at the DTI for that matter—has much experience with SysGov infosystems. Not on the level we're talking."

"Which brings us back to at least two people." Isaac sat up on the stage. "One from the Admin and one from SysGov."

"But who?" Nina asked.

"Still considering Sako?" Susan asked.

"I am. But if it's her, who would the coconspirator be?"

"What about Wong Fei?" Susan suggested.

"Our star player?" Nina asked incredulously.

"He's committed intimidation crimes in the past," Susan noted. "Sending replica severed hands to people? Sounds similar enough to me. Plus, he and Sako have grown close in a very short period of time."

"You raise a good point with those past crimes," Isaac agreed. "And while his career as a gamer doesn't exactly cover the skills we're looking for, his criminal record tells us he already has them."

"But, come on!" Nina protested. "Wong Fei? I don't buy it."

"We have to consider all possibilities," Isaac replied.

"If Sako has been radicalized," Susan went on, "then it's possible she recruited Wong Fei's aid at some point."

"Kohlberg seems the more likely helper to me," Nina offered. "Just imagine it. A lonely guy like that gets approached by a hot foreigner asking for favors. She shakes a little ass, shows a little cleavage, and next thing you know he's helping her sabotage the entire political landscape."

"What would he need Sako's ass for when he can go home to his synthoid harem?" Susan countered.

"Plus, he'd be hurting his own company," Isaac noted. "That's been my problem with the Kohlberg angle from the start. Sure, perhaps he could fool all of us and alter the UAM somehow, but *why*? What's in it for him?"

"Sweet. Admin. Ass," Nina repeated.

Susan shook her head.

"Hell, I bet if *I* shook my ass at him, he'd commit a few crimes," Nina continued with a quirky smile.

"Please don't," Isaac grumbled.

"Just saying. You know, as a hypothetical."

"Cephalie?" Isaac asked. "How about you? Any thoughts?"

"Sort of. It's more of an approach than an idea."

"I'm all ears. Let's hear it."

"Okay." Cephalie opened Sako's background report and produced a timetable of her actions prior to arriving in SysGov. "Let's say we keep going with the Sako angle. Speculating who she might have partnered with is all well and good, but the question then becomes *where* did this conspiracy form?"

"It would have to be in the Admin," Susan said. "This is Sako's first time in SysGov."

"Right." Cephalie highlighted one entry in the timetable. "And that brings us to where she first came into contact with potential coconspirators."

"The universal qualifier at Byrgius University," Isaac said.

"Exactly. And even if Sako's not the one we're looking for, the conspiracy had to form somewhere. *This* is where all the people we've been looking at—all the players and the people in their orbits—began to mingle."

"That's a very good point," Isaac said, "but unfortunately Byrgius is in the Admin."

"Why's that a problem?" Susan asked.

"Well, it's . . ." He frowned at her. "It's in the Admin."

"True." She nodded. "So?"

"It's in the *Admin*, Susan," he repeated, unsure how to make the problem clearer.

"But they made you an investigator. Your authority extends that far."

"Yes, I suppose you're right." Isaac let out a weary sigh. "Point taken. We can talk to Noxon. It's not ideal, but we should be able to put together a list of material for them to collect and bring back."

"I'm sorry, but I think you've misunderstood me," Susan said.

"How so?" Isaac asked, confused.

"You're an *investigator*," she stressed. "And we have two *chronoports* sitting in the hangar."

"Wait a second." He gulped. "You don't mean . . ."

"That you should requisition one?" she finished with a bright smile. "Why not?"

CHAPTER TWENTY-TWO

"LET ME GET THIS STRAIGHT," NOXON SAID ONCE THEY'D ALL gathered on *Pathfinder-Prime*'s bridge. "You believe *yet another* one of our players might be involved in these crimes—in addition to the one still stuck in a cell—and you want me to authorize the use of one of our chronoports so you can take it back to the Admin to expand your investigation, starting with Byrgius University. Does that summarize the situation?"

"Yes, that about sums it up." Isaac sighed. "I'm sure this request must seem—"

"Excuse me for a moment." Noxon placed his hand on a PIN interface.

Isaac waited in silence on the bridge, then glanced over at Susan, who flashed a quick smile his way. He returned his attention to Noxon, who hadn't moved.

"I'm sorry. What are you doing?"

"Calling to approve your requisition, of course."

✧   ✧   ✧

Director-General Csaba Shigeki didn't like negotiations.

It wasn't that he was bad at them. Quite the opposite in fact; he considered himself a skilled negotiator, since his natural talent for reading people allowed him to peer through the masks worn when arguing over finite pools of resources. He thought that personal assessment was accurate, because he had to be at least *somewhat* competent at negotiation in this line of work. How else could he have navigated and manipulated the levers of governance to form the DTI and ensure it had enough resources to thrive?

No, he wasn't bad at negotiating. He simply preferred the more comfortable, pleasurable task of *running* the organization he'd created. There was simplicity in the arrangement—an elegant beauty to the hierarchy—even if the DTI's tasks were anything but simple. He received directives from the chief executor, and in turn he gave directives to his underlings. Hierarchies were straightforward, and they worked more often than they didn't. More than that, he *enjoyed* his job and the larger role it played in keeping the Admin safe and prosperous.

Negotiations were . . . messy, in comparison.

"No, I can't accept that," declared Commissioner Klaus-Wilhelm von Schröder. "If this is to be a joint venture, then it's a joint venture right down the line. And that means both SysGov and the Admin contribute the same quantity of exotic matter to Providence."

Shigeki put on a brave face, but inside his mind he wanted to scream. Negotiating with Schröder was like banging his head against a fortified malmetal barrier. Worse, in fact, because he could probably bust through the barrier eventually.

On the surface, one might believe Schröder lacked the duplicity to navigate a contentious negotiation. He wore no masks, for one. There were no falsehoods in his position, no scummy manipulations. He shot straight and he demanded the same from the other side of the table. If they'd been playing cards, his entire hand would be faceup. In theory, that *should* be a crippling disadvantage, but the man possessed an uncanny second sense for sniffing out the pressure points—

—and then jabbing them with a hot poker.

"I only suggested a modest reallocation," Shigeki countered. "Sixty-forty with SysGov taking the larger share. Your exotic matter industry greatly outstrips our own, after all. Both in terms of quantity and quality."

"A fair enough point," Schröder admitted. "But what do I get in return?"

"I hold that sixty-forty is a reasonable distribution, given the differences in our production capacity."

"Which I can't accept. It's either a fifty-fifty split or you make concessions elsewhere."

Do you have any idea how expensive *exotic matter is for us to produce?* Shigeki thought glumly. *Actually, you probably do, which is why you're going to squeeze as much out of me as you can. There's no way I'll convince the chief executor to front fifty percent of the exotic material. Hell, I'm not even sure he'll accept* forty!

He glanced around the long conference table, across the assembled faces that made up both the Gordian Division's and DTI's senior staff, and his eyes paused on Doctor Andover-Chen, and then Doctor Hinnerkopf.

He let out a short, inward snort.

It's not that the project doesn't have merit, he thought. *It has* tremendous *merit, but you technical types always fixate on one question and one question only: Can it be done? Well, sure, it can, but did you ever consider the limitations of time, budget, and personnel? No, of course you didn't. You saw it was possible, and so you leaped forward at the opportunity.*

But there's a major problem someone has to deal with, and by "someone" I mean me. Our fleet won't be back to pre-Crisis strength for at least another year. Securing the resources and budget for those new ships was a painful, grueling experience, but now you want me to go back in front of the chief executor with outstretched hands and say the equivalent of "Please, sir. I want some more."

I can already hear his answer.

Shigeki returned his attention to Schröder.

Fine, he thought. *I need him to agree with sixty-forty. Time to figure out what we can spare.*

To his right, Jonas cleared his throat, and Shigeki gave him a nod to proceed.

"There's a piece of tech we could potentially put on the table," he suggested.

"You mean in addition to your impeller designs?" Andover-Chen asked.

"It's something we have in development. We recently started practical tests, and the tech shows a great deal of potential."

Damn, not that, Shigeki thought. He knew exactly what his son was about to propose, and a part of him wanted to cut him off right then and there. *I'd hoped to keep that technology to ourselves. But Jonas probably sees the same problem I do. The truth is what else can we offer that's worth enough to offset the exotic matter costs? We can't afford to let the negotiations fall apart, not with SysGov's counter-grav tech as the all-too-tempting prize. They may not realize how much that piece alone is worth to us.*

"What are you offering?" Schröder asked.

Jonas looked to Shigeki, and he waved for his son to continue.

"Go ahead. Give them the project brief. Let them have a good look at it."

Jonas placed his hand on the conference table, and an abstract diagram materialized, showing the slender spike of a chronoton impeller. Though *this* one thickened near the base. The diagram began a cycling animation, and the base widened until it resembled a cylindrical exhaust port with a thick spike down the center.

"A *new* style of impeller?" Andover-Chen asked, smiling with the glee of a child who might soon receive a new toy.

"More of a refinement to our existing designs," Hinnerkopf clarified. "The impeller is a rotating type, same as all of ours, but we've injected some SysGov-inspired features into the design, most notably through active changes to the exotic matter's permeability."

"This morphing section at the base." Schröder pointed to it. "What's it for?"

"Think of it as a jet engine's afterburner," Jonas suggested. "It allows us to temporarily exceed the impeller's maximum speed."

Shigeki wasn't sure why Jonas had chosen that analogy, but dealing with Schröder was always an adventure. The man had been plucked from the Admin's 1950s, after all, and sometimes archaic comparisons worked better, which seemed to be the case this time as Schröder nodded his understanding, visibly intrigued by the offer.

"This can go faster than ninety-five kilofactors?"

"Oh yes." Jonas grinned like an eager salesman. "And at almost no cost to maneuverability."

"Why not have it active all the time, then?"

"The modification places significant strain on the impeller," Hinnerkopf explained. "It's not suitable for extended cruising. Also"—she continued indignantly—"it's *not* an afterburner."

"But what about—"

A priority alert blinked in Shigeki's peripheral vision, and he expanded it to see an incoming call from Noxon. He checked the time.

"Everyone, sorry to interrupt," Shigeki began. "We've been at this for almost two hours today, and I think we're due for a lunch break. Besides, Klaus, I'd like to give you and your team some time to consider our latest offer in private."

"Sounds good," Schröder said, rising from his seat. "Meet back in an hour?"

"An hour it is," Shigeki agreed.

The meeting began to break up. Kloss and Jonas headed over to one end of the room, where a wall panel split open and a massive catering shelf extended out, laden with drinks, snacks, and do-it-yourself sandwich materials. Both of them picked up plates and began assembling their lunches.

Shigeki placed his hand on the table and established a link with Noxon.

"Nox. Shigeki here," he began, his real lips not moving. "Sorry it took me so long to answer."

Noxon didn't respond for a few seconds.

"Not a problem, sir."

"Where are you? There's some delay on the call."

"I'm on Luna."

"What are you doing all the way out there?"

"Your son sent me here," he answered dryly.

"Oh." Shigeki shrugged. "Is this about the gaming tournament he was talking about?"

"It is. I have a related requisition that needs your review. Transmitting it now."

"I see it." Shigeki opened the file and began reading through it. "One of our investigators needs to use a chronoport?"

"That's correct. We have two over here right now, *Defender-Prime* and *Pathfinder-Prime*. With your permission, I intend to take *Defender-Prime* back to the Admin, where it will serve as a support craft for the investigator. *Pathfinder-Prime* will remain here as our command center for event security."

"What's the chronoport needed for?"

"Two of our visiting civilians have received death threats, and the root of these crimes might be back home."

"Got it. You heading out or staying?"

"Heading out. I intend to leave the original lead, Agent Miguel Pérez, in charge of event security. Unless you want me to stay."

"No, that's all right. I trust your judgment." Shigeki traced down the virtual document with a finger then paused at a line near the bottom. "What the hell?"

"Sir?"

"Did you know we had a rank called 'junior provisional investigator'?"

"I don't pay much attention to what Kloss does in Espionage."

"Hmm." Shigeki took another look at the form then shook his head. "Hold on. I need to confirm something. Be right back." He muted the call and twisted in his seat until he faced the catering table. "Kloss!"

His subordinate looked up, plate in one hand, half-eaten sandwich in the other, his cheeks stuffed like a chipmunk.

Shigeki beckoned him over with a stern finger.

Kloss hurried to his side, balancing the plate atop his fingers while also trying to jam the second half of his sandwich into his mouth. Pieces of shredded lettuce fluttered down to the floor, and sub dressing dripped down his fingers.

"Ea, osh?" he mumbled, which Shigeki assumed translated into "Yeah, boss?"

"Mind if I ask you something?"

"Ea?" He chewed and swallowed before taking another large bite in an effort to inhale the meal as fast as possible.

"What, pray tell, is a 'junior provisional investigator'?"

Kloss froze, the sandwich partially shoved into his gaping mouth.

"Kloss?" Shigeki raised an eyebrow. "Something wrong?"

The man held up a finger with the sandwich braced in his jaw. He grabbed hold of it again, took another bite, and began to leisurely masticate the food. Behind him at the catering table, Jonas became utterly enthralled by the dessert selection, a change in disposition his father did not fail to notice.

"Because," Shigeki continued, "as far as I know, there's nothing junior or provisional about *any* of our investigators. They're all lifers with ten years' field experience, minimum. That's a requirement you set, by the way."

Kloss set his plate down on the conference table, unfurled a napkin and began to methodically wipe down each finger, all while chewing in slow motion.

"I'm still waiting." Shigeki leaned away from his subordinate and draped an arm over the chair back.

Kloss swallowed, then proceeded to inspect the front of his teeth with his tongue. Once satisfied he'd scoured them clear of debris, he cleared his throat and spoke up.

"It is a ... new rank."

"How new? Within the past year?"

"Yes." Kloss gave him a few deliberate nods. "We did add it within the past year."

"What for?"

"We discovered an ... administrative gap in Espionage that needed to be filled. The ... new rank fills that gap."

Back at the catering table, Jonas seemed to be having a hell of a time deciding between the chocolate pudding and the vanilla pudding.

"Kloss?" Shigeki sighed.

"Yeah, boss?"

"Why are you bullshitting me?"

"I'm not—"

"Never mind. Hold that thought." Shigeki reopened the call with Noxon and expanded it to include Kloss. "Nox, you there?"

"Right where you left me, sir."

"This 'Isaac Cho' person. You trust him?"

"I wouldn't have forwarded his request to you otherwise."

"And you." Shigeki pointed a stern finger at Kloss. "You trust him?"

"Well..."

"He *is* one of your investigators."

"Yeah, but"—Kloss shrugged his shoulders—"there's no way I can keep track of everyone who works in Espionage."

"I *see.*" Shigeki drummed his fingers on the table. "Nox, who's captain of the chronoport you want?"

"That would be Jason Elifritz."

"Elifritz ..." Shigeki repeated, considering the name. "Ah, now I remember him. Solid. Dependable. Has a very sweet Martian for a wife. He's on the short list for one of the new Hammerheads, if I'm not mistaken."

"That would be him, sir."

"Okay, I'm going to authorize this one, but only because both you and Elifritz are on board. Support the investigator, but know that either of you can take over on a moment's notice, understood?"

"Understood, sir."

"Otherwise, keep to our normal operating parameters. Nothing too far into the past." Shigeki annotated the requisition and approved it. "There. Done."

"Thank you, sir. We'll be heading out soon."

Noxon closed the call.

Shigeki glared up at Kloss, who tried to put on a brave face. "Have a seat, Kloss," he said with a mirthless smile. "Let's talk."

◆   ◆   ◆

"There you have it." Noxon took his hand off the PIN interface.

"I get the impression my 'investigator' status isn't exactly official," Isaac noted.

"It's official enough."

"I'm surprised we received time travel authorization, too," Susan said.

"Excuse me?" Isaac blinked. "Time travel? Did I miss that part?"

"It falls under 'normal operating parameters,'" Susan explained. "Which nowadays means we can go back up to negative-one year from the True Present." She shrugged. "Might prove useful."

"Let's not get carried away here," Isaac cautioned. "Agent Noxon, thank you for pushing the requisition through. When will *Defender-Prime* be ready to depart?"

"I'll need to coordinate with Pérez, and Elifritz may need to recall key personnel back to the ship, but other than that nothing comes to mind. We sent *Defender-Prime* out recently, so I don't expect any surprises. Give us half an hour to sort everything out, and we should be good to go."

"That'll do nicely, though before we leave . . ."

"Yes?"

"In addition to Agent Cantrell and myself, I'd like Specialist Cho to join us as well. Her expertise could prove useful, depending on what we find."

"Of course. She's welcome to come along."

"I'd also like Encephalon to join us, though I'm aware this is a more sensitive request."

"Ah, yes," Noxon said, a measure of stiffness infiltrating his tone. "Your AI can come along, but it must follow the approved restrictions. Its connectome must be limited to a synthoid body, and that body cannot be capable of connectome transmission."

"I understand." He glanced over to his shoulder where Cephalie's avatar popped into being. Her connectome remained outside the hangar, but her connection to his wetware allowed her to watch and participate when needed. "Well?"

"You're going to make me switch to physical, aren't you?" Cephalie moped. She flopped down onto her butt and kicked out her legs.

"I'm not making you do anything," Isaac protested.

"You know how long it's been since I strutted around in a body?"

"No. I've known you for five years, and I've never seen you in a body before. Unless you count the LENS."

"Which I don't." She hugged her knees to her chest. "Seventeen years. I've enjoyed a seventeen-year bodiless streak, and you're telling me to break it by going to a place that is . . . less than friendly to my kind?"

"I'm not telling you. This is completely your decis—"

"Fine, you talked me into it." Cephalie stood up. "I'll go see what LSP has in the way of spare bodies."

She vanished from his shoulder.

"Well, that was easier than expected," Susan commented.

"There's one last problem we need to address before we leave," Susan said ten minutes before their scheduled departure.

She'd brought Isaac to a large maintenance bay through a door near the chronoport's boarding ramp. Printers and storage lockers lined the walls of the brightly lit room, and the Peacekeeper blue container holding Susan's combat frame sat against the back wall. Crimson Flower logistics had delivered the container a few minutes ago.

One of the printers hummed with quiet activity.

"I already said I'm fine with you bringing the frame," Isaac protested. "I don't see the point, but it hasn't delayed our departure, so it's a nonissue."

"No, that isn't it." She sighed. "Noxon brought this one to my attention. Though honestly, I should have seen it coming given the whole investigator thing. You're not going to like this."

"Will I like it less than us lugging around your Admin death machine?"

"Yeah, probably."

"All right." Isaac sighed and waved for her to continue. "Hit me with it."

"This isn't coming from me, you understand? Please don't get upset."

"Susan, just tell me what's wrong. I can't fix a problem if I don't know what it is."

"Hey, kiddos!" A fresh-faced woman with freckled cheeks and blonde hair cut high and tight waved as she entered the bay. She wore a dark gray state trooper uniform with the cap stuffed through her shoulder strap.

"Hi, Cephalie," Isaac replied, almost automatically.

"Well, that's disappointing," Cephalie pouted, putting her fists on her hips. "I thought you'd take at least a *few* seconds to figure out it was me."

"Cephalie, you're the only person I know who says 'hey, kiddos' when greeting us. And besides, which other strange woman was going to walk in here?"

"You'd better not mean me." Nina strode in wearing a heavy backpack. She unslung the pack and put it on the floor.

"Hey, Nina," Isaac said. "And no, I wasn't talking about you. What's in the backpack?"

"Forensics gear. Because *someone*"—she shot Isaac a fierce eye—"insisted I leave my drones behind at the station."

"The rules are the rules."

"Says the guy who doesn't have equipment to lug around." She rubbed her left shoulder.

"This feels so *weird*." Cephalie stretched out a hand and wiggled her fingers. "How do you meat sacks stand it?"

"We manage somehow," Isaac replied dryly. "I'm surprised you picked one that looks so young."

"Why do you say that?" Cephalie asked, now inspecting her own legs.

"I thought you'd try to match your avatar more closely."

"I did, but this was the only female synthoid they could spare on short notice." She shook out her arms and bounced up and down on her toes. "I suppose I could have gone with one of the guys, but that would have been even weirder. Not that gender matters a whole lot to me, but I like my avatar's aesthetics. Besides, men have all that unnecessary crotch baggage."

Isaac put a hand to his face. "If I ever hear the phrase 'crotch baggage' again, it'll be too soon."

"Hey, she's *your* IC," Nina said.

"I *know*."

"You should have stuck to the single life like me."

"I'm considering it." He looked over to find Cephalie's new body grinning like a shark. "LSP okay with you running around in one of their uniforms?"

"They removed the insignia and badge before lending me the body." Cephalie ran both hands down her chest. "Which, I have to say, has some *nice* torso baggage."

"That's someone else's spare synthoid you're fondling," Isaac pointed out.

"I'll return it in good order."

"Not what I meant," he sighed.

"Speaking of uniforms," Susan cut in. "The 'issue' we were discussing?"

"Right. What about it?"

"Do you recall a conversation we had when I first arrived in SysGov? You said detectives don't have a strict uniform code."

"Sure, I remember that. Why?"

"Admin Peacekeepers don't enjoy the same level of flexibility, and that includes investigators. Our dress code while on duty is very strict."

"But I'm not a Peacekeeper."

"Well..." Susan glanced away. "You *are* a DTI investigator, and DTI investigators *are* Peacekeepers, so..."

"But I'm not really an investigator either." He paused, beginning to doubt his own answer. "Am I?"

"*Technically,*" Susan said, "you are."

"But this is temporary."

"'The rules are the rules,'" Susan echoed with an apologetic smile. "Even for junior provisional investigators."

The lone active printer stopped humming and beeped. The output tray extended, revealing a freshly printed Peacekeeper uniform folded into a square with a peaked cap resting on top.

Susan retrieved the uniform and cap.

"You're serious," Isaac said, "aren't you?"

"I'm sorry." Susan lowered her head and presented him with his new uniform.

"I have to?"

She nodded.

"It's the rules?"

She nodded again.

Isaac took hold of the uniform and frowned at it. He wasn't

sure how he felt about this. He'd spent the past ten years of his life in SysPol, with five years at the Academy and another five in the field as a probationary detective. He'd dedicated a third of his life to earning the right to wear his uniform, and now someone was telling him he had to don the colors of a foreign power because of *rules*?

It made him uneasy and didn't feel right, almost like wearing an Admin uniform was a betrayal of some kind, though a betrayal of *what*, he couldn't say. But despite his discomfort, one guiding principle shone brighter than all others in his mind.

"Whatever it takes to solve the case," he said at last.

"Glad you understand," Susan said.

"What about us?" Nina put a hand on Cephalie's shoulder.

"You're not Peacekeepers," Susan replied, "so you can wear whatever you like."

"Nice!"

"I miss my hat," Cephalie groused, rubbing the loaner body's head of short blonde hair.

"We'll print one out for you!" Isaac snapped.

CHAPTER TWENTY-THREE

DEFENDER-PRIME ROSE FROM THE PETAL FOUR HANGAR. IT CLEARED the Crimson Flower and continued climbing until it reached an altitude of five hundred meters. Once there, it held its position and began the process of slipping through the outer wall of the SysGov universe and entering the transverse.

Chronotons passed through the chronoport in two directions. Not *physical* directions, but temporal ones, with half the surrounding particles moving into the past and half rushing forward, building the future. These were particles with closed-loop histories, oscillating backward and forward through time, and they slipped through the empty space between atoms as if the ship wasn't there at all.

Additionally, those chronotons exhibited "side-to-side" motion on axes beyond the familiar X, Y, and Z. It was this side-to-side motion the chronoport was about to tap into.

The impeller spun up to one hundred twenty cycles per second, and the twin fusion thrusters idled, ready to flood the spike with the tremendous energies required to push through the outer wall of a universe.

"Chronometric environment stable," announced the temporal navigator. "Impeller spin stable. All systems configured for transdimensional flight. We are ready for phase-out, Captain."

"Execute," Elifritz ordered.

Energy from the fusion reactors flooded through the spike's exotic matter. Pulses drove through the matter in sync with the rotational speed, and chronotons passing through the spike began to bounce off along a single transdimensional axis, generating chronometric pressure on the drive system. That pressure built until it reached a critical threshold, pushing the chronoport into the transverse.

The effect this process had on the crew was less impressive than one might expect.

Isaac's stomach lurched into his throat before bouncing back down. He braced himself for more, but none came. They were underway and in freefall.

Nina sat next to him on the bridge, her fingers digging into the armrests.

"Was that it?" she asked.

"So it would seem."

✧   ✧   ✧

Defender-Prime phased through the outer wall of the Admin universe and appeared above Luna. Mild gravity replaced the free fall of transdimensional flight, and Susan found herself tugged deeper into her seat on the bridge. She released her harness and sat up.

"It's so . . . gray," Nina whispered from two seats over, watching a live feed from one of the chronoport's external cameras.

"Of course it is," Isaac said matter-of-factly. "It hasn't been terraformed."

Defender-Prime eased power into its twin fusion thrusters and hovered over an airless expanse of plains and craters dotted by domes molded out of lunar rock and the thin capillaries of shielded tunnels. The chronoport hovered near a large cluster of domes butted against a glassy, elliptical scar over half a kilometer thick and three times as long.

"We're reaching out to the university now," Elifritz reported from his seat near the front of the bridge. "We should have landing clearance shortly."

Susan gazed at the mutilated landscape below and let out a slow, sad exhale.

"Something wrong?" Isaac asked quietly.

"Nothing," she deflected. "It's been a while, is all."

"You've been to Byrgius before?"

"You could say that." She gave him a halfhearted smile. "I went to school here before I dropped out and enlisted."

"Oh." Isaac took in the view. "Then this is where you decided to become a Peacekeeper?"

"That's right. About ten years ago." She pointed at the screen. "See the scar? This part here used to be Cushwa Dome. Over there were Moser and Williamson Domes. You can still see a few pieces of Kilcawkley Dome along the edge of the scar. Some of my classes were in those domes." She sighed. "Now they're all gone."

"What happened?"

"Free Luna happened. They released a self-replicating weapon inside the Lunarian dormitory. It ate everyone and everything in its path. Almost eleven thousand people, in the end."

"They released it in the *Lunarian* dorms?" Nina asked.

"Yeah. I was asleep in Lyden Dome at the time. You can still see remnants of it along the edge of the scar here and here."

Nina shook her head. "But isn't Free Luna—I don't know—trying to *free* Lunarians?"

"You're expecting barbarous monsters to think like rational people," Susan said, almost clinically. "To them, Lunarians who won't fight back or who've accepted the Admin are simply another enemy. Worse in some ways because they've 'betrayed' their homeland. That sort of mindless hatred is why they were targeted first, and one of the reasons why I'm still alive."

She sat gazing into the screen, and despite her almost distant tone, her eyes were dark. Not distant at all, Isaac thought, watching her profile. She didn't seem to notice him as she looked back into her own past.

"I learned a lot that day," she continued. "About hate and hearts and how some problems can't be solved with words. So many young lives were snuffed out that day, but so many more got to live on, and that was because of the Peacekeepers—and especially the STANDs. They went into that campus over and over again, despite the nanoweapon. SysGov hasn't seen anything like that. I know that. But it was like walking into Hell itself for anyone from the Admin, and that's exactly what they did, again and again. They lost seven of their own that day, but they saved my life. And not just mine. They pulled a lot of others—almost two hundred of us—out before they were forced to pull back. Before they were *ordered* to pull back, really, because they were *still* ready to go back in, even though they knew damned well how few of them would come out again. But Director Shigeki personally ordered them out, and nobody bucks him. So they did, and then their cruiser razed the blight with sustained laser fire."

She paused, and silence hovered as the SysGov visitors looked at the savage scar.

"That's one of the reasons I enlisted," she said finally. "To protect those who can't protect themselves." She sighed. "And to never again be someone who can't protect herself."

"Well"—Isaac touched her on the shoulder—"I can safely say you ticked that box." She looked at him, and he smiled almost gently, then squeezed her shoulder. "In fact"—his smile segued into a grin—"I'd have to say it's possible—*remotely* possible—you may have overcompensated just a bit."

"And when he says 'just a bit,' he means 'quite a lot,' actually," Nina said, and Susan surprised herself with a snort of amusement.

"Maybe just a bit," she said, and smiled back at them both.

"Landing clearance received," reported the pilot. "Heading in."

The chronoport floated sideways until it was positioned above a crater with artificially extended walls. A ring of lights blinked along the lip and more lights on the crater floor strobed in a contracting cross that repeated its animation loop every few seconds.

The end of the chronoport's impeller almost grazed one wall as it eased into the crater, but the pilot kept the craft stable and centered, and it touched down on the landing pad without incident. Its fusion thrusters throttled back, and a boarding tunnel extended out of the crater wall.

"Thrusters off," reported the pilot. "Docking seal secure."

"Very good," Elifritz said.

Noxon stood up and walked back to Isaac and the others.

"Detective, this is your show now. We've requested a meeting with the university's chief archivist, a man named Ethan Tunstall. He'll be waiting for you in his office."

"Thank you, Captain. Agent Cantrell and I will head out. We'll contact the ship if we need anyone else to join us."

Susan stood up and sidestepped out of the row to let Isaac through. He slid out and put on his peaked cap.

"Which way to the exit?" Isaac asked quietly.

"Follow me."

Susan led him down the chronoport's central corridor, then

took a twisting side passage until they reached the side docking hatch. She pressed her palm against the interface, and heavy malmetal plating shifted out of the way to reveal a long tunnel. Ribbed, retractable supports gave way to a wide view of the star-filled Lunarian sky.

They crossed the metal walkway and checked in at the security kiosk on the far end. A pair of campus security officers verified their IDs while a Wolverine sat nearby, its gun-head swinging back and forth like a metronome.

They took a ramp down from the security kiosk to the upper level of a bright, two-tiered concourse with a modest green hilltop and tree ringed by a few benches. Over a dozen tunnels connected with the concourse on both levels, leading away to Byrgius University's many domes. Labels and simplistic symbols floated in the air above each tunnel, and a grand map of the whole university glowed in the air above the park.

Students passed them by, some glancing curiously in their direction, others intent on *not* looking their way. A Wolverine paced past them, tracing a slow, leisurely patrol around the concourse.

Susan set her hands on the railing and gazed at the map. She remembered passing through this space hundreds of times in what felt like another life, each time hurrying from one class to the other, but she'd never stopped to soak in the place.

Isaac leaned onto the railing next to her.

"How's the wearable working out?" she asked.

"Seems fine." He pulled back his cuff to reveal a wristband. "I can see and read the big campus map and the signs by each tunnel. Anything else I'm missing?"

"No. That's about it."

"Good." Isaac looked up at the map. "Tunstall is in Meshel Dome. Seems like we need to get down to the bottom level first."

"Yeah." She gazed at the campus map, and one location along the scar caught her eye.

"You okay? You seem out of it."

"It's a strange homecoming. I never thought I'd be here again. I'm not even the same person anymore." She chuckled without humor. "In more ways than one. Susan the bright-eyed, idealist student is a distant memory nowadays. Same with Susan the squishy, flesh-and-blood human."

"Need a minute?"

"No, I'm fine. Just...contemplating."

"Come on, then." Isaac placed a hand on her shoulder. "Let's go see the archivist."

"Right..."

He pushed off the railing and headed for the nearby stairs.

"Isaac?"

"Hmm?" He turned back to her.

"Would you mind if we take a quick detour first?"

"What for?"

"It's just a place I'd like to visit. It won't take long, I promise."

"Sure, Susan. Sure."

She led them down the stairs to an exit marked with KILCAWK-LEY and a symbol showing numerous concentric rings. Despite the number of students and staff passing through the concourse, they were the only people in the tunnel.

"Didn't you say Kilcawkley Dome was destroyed during the attack?" Isaac asked.

"I did."

The tunnel dipped down, then climbed back up, opening onto the blasted remains of Kilcawkley Dome, its skeletal supports arching high overhead. They stood in a small space at the end of the tunnel, protected behind a transparent bubble that afforded a clear view of the starry sky and the flat, glassy expanse of the blight scar.

Hundreds of narrow, identical gravestones of lunar rock stood beneath the ruins of the dome, arranged in ever widening rings. Abstract displays hovered in the air, and Susan walked up to one and skimmed through the long list of names.

"Circles," Isaac observed.

"Yes."

"Good follows bad?"

"That's right."

"Anyone you know?" he asked, watching her scroll through the listed dead.

"A few. Some of the native students. But I'm not here for them." She pointed to one side of the field of gravestones. "That's where I nearly died. The blight was eating a path toward me when a STAND busted through the unpowered exit door. He burned back the blight while my friends and I fled to safety. He saved my life.

"After I joined the Peacekeepers, I tried to locate the STAND who rescued me. I wanted to thank him, to let him know he'd made a difference." She smiled sadly. "And then I found out he was already dead. He was one of the seven who died, not long after he saved me, before they were ordered to pull back. He went into Cushwa Dome to save a group of Lunarian students cut off from escape, exactly the way he'd come for me. Those students made it out ... but he didn't. His name was Malcolm Bryce, and none of these graves are for him."

Isaac gazed across the gravesite but didn't say anything.

"But one should be." She let out a slow sigh. "Thanks, Isaac. I'm glad I could come here."

"Anytime."

The guidance arrow led them two levels below Meshel Dome to the dark basement of the building. Frosted glass walls on either side provided glimpses of racks upon racks of humming, blinking, clicking infosystem nodes, and the air overhead shimmered from waste heat.

The arrow stopped at an unmarked door and faded away.

"Is this his office?" Isaac asked.

"That's what the map says."

"Hmm." He palmed the door buzzer.

"Oh!" came a bright, eager voice from the other side. "Coming! Just a moment!"

The door split open, and an elderly man peered through. He wore a dark blue jumpsuit with flared bell bottoms and the golden BU of Byrgius University stuck on the chest. An unruly curtain of white hair fell behind a narrow, sunken face, and his body appeared somewhat stretched by life in low gravity, which seemed odd considering what Susan had told him about the Admin-sanctioned enhancements used to fortify every citizen against low-grav deterioration. An abstract sigil floated above the back of his left hand, showing two connected chain links, one of ivory and the other of jade.

The man's bright eyes flicked across the two newcomers and lit up with gleeful attentiveness.

"May I help you?" he asked with a wide, friendly smile.

"We're looking for Ethan Tunstall," Isaac said.

"Speaking. Are you the investigator I was told to expect?"

"That's right. I'm"—Isaac paused ever so slightly, not yet comfortable with the title—"*Investigator* Cho. And this is my deputy, Agent Cantrell."

"A pleasure to meet you both. We get so few Peacekeepers down here nowadays." He shrugged. "Or ever, really."

"That's normally a good thing," Susan commented.

"Oh, quite right you are, ma'am. Quite right." Tunstall backed up and beckoned them inside. "Please, come in. Make yourselves at home."

"Thank you."

His office was bigger than Isaac had expected, given the forgotten, dead-end quality of the path leading to it. It might have been a storage room at some point in the past, but it was now furnished with an automated kitchen, two sofas, and a massive desk. A pair of large industrial printers took up most of one wall. A combination of abstract and physical portraits took up another, and a third "wall" provided a virtual view of rolling hills as a strong wind rustled through the tall grass. Smaller windows floated over Tunstall's desk.

Do those sofas convert into beds? Isaac wondered to himself. *Does he live down here?*

"Can I get you anything in the way of refreshments?" Tunstall hurried over to the smaller sofa and began dragging it to the front of his desk.

"No, thank you." Isaac reached up to remove his cap, but when he tugged on it, he discovered the inner band was stuck to his head. He frowned and tried to wiggle the bill, but the hat wouldn't let go. Finally, he grabbed the bill with both hands and pushed up but only succeeded it straining his skin. The hat refused to release its death grip.

"Susan?" he whispered, glad Tunstall had his back turned.

"Yeah?"

"I can't get my hat off."

She glanced to Tunstall, saw him adjusting the position of the sofa, then reached over and tried to plunk the cap off Isaac's head. It wouldn't budge.

"See?" he whispered urgently.

"Did you release the headband?"

"The *what*?"

Tunstall busied himself with fluffing the pillows on the sofa.

"You need to release the dynamic friction band on the inside," Susan whispered, tapping the side of her own cap. "There's a hardwired switch underneath the bill."

Isaac ran his thumb across the underside of the bill, found a dimple, and pressed it. The hat released its grip, and he yanked it off and smoothed out his hair.

"What's a hat need a friction band for, anyway?"

"To keep it from coming off in zero gee, of course," she said as if it were the most normal thing in the worlds.

Back at the sofa, Tunstall had moved on to adjusting the positions of individual pillows in an effort to . . . arrange them symmetrically? Isaac wasn't sure.

"That's quite all right, Mister Tunstall." He urged the man away from the sofa.

"Are you sure? It still looks a bit janky to me. You two are guests here, and I want you to feel comfortable."

"We're fine, I promise you."

"You sure I can't get you something? Maybe some coffee or a light snack? I have some excellent sugar cookie patterns stored in the food printer."

"Again, no thank you," Isaac stressed. "We're here for information."

"What we need are the *Weltall* qualifier records," Susan added.

"We have"—Isaac grimaced as he presented the copy-and-paste document—"a search warrant."

"Ah, yes!" Tunstall's eyes gleamed. "The tournament! What a treat that was! I just finished rewatching the final matches, in fact. So glad we could host it here at Byrgius. Maybe it'll help inject some life back into the campus." He shook his head sadly. "I hate to admit it, but the place never truly bounced back from the attack. It's a shame, really, because we have plenty of room for more students, but applicant numbers are way down, even a decade later. No one wants to earn their degree from 'Blight U.'" He shuddered. "Such a repulsive nickname. Wish people would stop using it."

"Can you grant us access to the event records?" Isaac asked.

"Oh, certainly. Any specific part you're after, or do you want it all?"

"All of it, if possible, but we're most interested in the records for a player named Elena Sako."

"Elly?" Tunstall's brow narrowed with concern. "Why the interest in her? I thought she was over in SysGov for the finals? Is she back already?"

"No, she's still over there," Susan said. "The tournament hasn't finished yet."

"Oh, of course, I understand." Tunstall paused and then frowned. "Wait a moment. You *know* the tournament isn't over."

"That's right," Susan said. "Sako was doing quite well, last we saw her. She's one of only two players left."

"Oh!" His eyes lit up again. "Then, you were there? In SysGov, I mean? You saw her in action?"

"We did." Susan nodded.

"Oh, isn't she just *wonderful*? And so humble, too. Here, take a look."

Tunstall turned around, and his back lit up with golden abstract signatures.

"I think Elly's is near the right shoulder blade."

"She . . . signed your back?" Isaac asked.

"Oh yes! I managed to collect signatures from most of the players, but some declined to sign, and a few more were charging *horrendous* prices. But not Elly! Didn't charge me so much as a centi-E, bless her sweet soul. Even gave me a little peck on the cheek." He tapped the chain link sigil on the back of his left hand. "Don't tell the missus, okay?"

"Your secret is safe with us," Isaac said dryly.

"Wish she was one of our alumni, but it's been so hard for us to attract talent for our sports program." He turned back around. "Maybe that'll change, though. The chief executor's outreach has brought so much renewed interest in Luna. I voted for him, you know. Knew he was the right man for the job. I had a good feeling about Christopher First from the start. Even liked his campaign slogan. 'Your best choice is the *First* choice.' Ha ha. So catchy."

Isaac cleared his throat in a polite effort to swing the man back on track.

"I'll have you know I'm one of the Admin's biggest proponents here at Byrgius. I don't see eye-to-eye with the rest of the faculty, I'm afraid. I think that's why they moved me down here." He indicated the room they stood in. "But the joke's on them, because now I have a bigger office!"

"Mister Tunstall," Isaac cut in before he blabbered anymore. "The records of the qualifier?"

"Ah, yes. Right!" He placed a hand on his desk. Several windows opened in front of the landscape view. "There. All records for the *Weltall* qualifier unlocked for your inspection. Unfortunately, they're not sorted properly. I haven't finished cataloging them, you see."

"Thank you. We'll manage."

Isaac opened a comm window.

"Yeah?" Cephalie answered.

"Come meet us in Meshel Dome. We've got a job for you."

✧   ✧   ✧

"My word!" Tunstall exclaimed, staring over Cephalie's shoulder in disbelief as she rocketed through the maze of data. "It was going to take me *hours* to properly tag, categorize, and annotate all those files, but you, my dear, have done the job in *minutes*! I've met some skilled archivists in my time, but never one quite so swift." He selected a file at random and expanded the header. "And so thorough, too! It's like you know my filing system better than I do!"

"Thanks." Cephalie winked at him. "I've always had a knack for data. You could even say I was born to it."

Isaac cleared his throat.

"What?" Cephalie shrugged at him. "It's all true."

"That's beside the point," he warned.

"What did you say your name was?" Tunstall placed a hand on her shoulder and leaned closer to her.

"You can call me Cephalie."

"'Cephalie,'" he repeated, sounding out the name. "Is that short for something?"

"It is."

Tunstall waited for her to fill in the rest, and when she didn't, he grimaced before continuing.

"Well, if you're ever interested in joining the fast-moving field of data archiving, please don't hesitate to look me up. Here, let me give you my connection string..."

"Sorry, but I'm spoken for."

"Ah, well," he sighed. "The good ones always are."

Susan leaned over to Isaac's ear. "Should we tell him she's not human?"

He shook his head emphatically no.

"Aha!" Cephalie exclaimed.

"Find something?" Isaac asked.

"I did, but let me go over what I *didn't* find first. I started by working through Sako's records during the tournament, but nothing unusual came up. Lots of match statistics. Lots of other miscellaneous files, too, like meal and lodging invoices. Nothing I wouldn't expect to see for someone in her position. However, that changes when we take a look at her transportation record after the tournament ended, but before the Admin feel-good tour started. Or should I say *records*."

She expanded two files until they filled the space in front of Tunstall's desk.

"There are two of them," Isaac noted.

"Exactly. Both show her leaving within an hour of each other. *This one* tells us she bought a train ticket from Byrgius University and her final stop was Tycho Crater City. The invoice lists the reason for the trip as visiting her parents in Tycho's Block D2. However, the *second* departure has her renting a surface shuttle."

"Where did the shuttle go?" Isaac asked.

"Don't know. There's no invoice listed for it, so if she actually was on that flight, she didn't charge the Admin for it. Even so, the shuttle should have logged a flight plan with the university, but I don't have access to those."

"Allow me." Tunstall leaned over Cephalie's shoulder, and in the process managed to drape an arm around her. He splayed his fingers against the desk, and additional archives unlocked. "There. You can now access the port's outbound flight plans."

"Thanks, kiddo."

"Kiddo?" Tunstall frowned in confusion.

"Hmm, what have we here?" Cephalie trawled through the data and pulled up the shuttle's flight plan. "Looks like it also took her to Tycho Crater City, but to Block F9 instead of D2."

"Block F9," Isaac murmured, and looked over at Susan.

"The Niner Slums."

CHAPTER TWENTY-FOUR

THE OLDEST PARTS OF TYCHO CRATER CITY RESEMBLED BYRGIUS University from the sky with various-sized domes joined by connecting tunnels that showed little evidence of long-term planning. Its *newer* parts were rather different, as the old "downtown" gave way to an expansive, organized grid of monolithic towers to form the city's "uptown" blocks where the running lights of civilian craft flitted through the airless sky.

"*Zhu hǎo yùn,*" Nina said over the intercom from the chronoport's bridge.

"Thanks," Isaac replied, now seated beside Susan at the front of the Cutlass transport. "You too. We'll catch up as soon as we can."

"Detaching." Susan toggled a control on the abstract interface, and the docking clamp released with a loud *clank*. The Cutlass dropped away from its berth below *Defender-Prime*'s wing, and she angled down toward Block D2 while the chronoport continued on to Block F9. A virtual blue outline pulsed around their destination tower, and she locked in their automated approach.

"Block D2?" Isaac asked.

"That's right." She leaned back. "Isaac?"

"Mmm?"

"I didn't want to bring this up back on the ship, but wouldn't it be best if we all headed for the Niner Slums? Why the detour to talk to Sako's parents?"

"You know you're free to speak up whenever you feel the need. You didn't have to wait for us to be alone."

"I know. And I would have if I'd been concerned, but you seemed to have a plan in mind, and I didn't want to undermine you. I'm more curious than anything else."

"We're heading to D2 for two reasons. First, Cephalie and Nina are going to need time to figure out where this mysterious second Elly went, if they can pick up the trail at all, and that's time we can use to check out the other lead."

"And the second reason?"

"They're her parents. If Sako has been radicalized, there's a good chance they've noticed."

"Okay. Makes sense." She nodded to him.

The Cutlass dipped toward the highlighted tower, which rose from the gray landscape as a white cylinder, its surface unblemished by physical windows. Abstract signs dotted the exterior, marking locations like the "One-Twenties-Ville," the "D2 Oasis," and the "Thirty-Industrials."

"Where do her parents live?" Isaac asked.

"Level 126. Right there." A small cutaway near the top of the tower blinked. "Pretty high up, too."

"Is that significant?"

"Maybe. Real estate tends to be more desirable near the top."

The Cutlass curved over the tower, then slowed until it stopped to hover above one of several hexagonal indentations in the roof. The vectored nozzles eased the craft down into the dock, and it settled with feathery lightness.

The roof irised closed, and the sealed dock jostled then began a brief descent into the tower. The chamber filled with air, shuddered again, shifted sideways, and locked in place. Above them, an empty dock slotted into position.

Isaac and Susan released their harnesses and exited out the back of the transport. Susan took care of their docking fee at an automated terminal, and they left the dock through a malmetal door.

"Haven't had to use that number in a while," she commented with a wry grin.

"You're not paying for this out of your own pocket, are you?"

"Oh, no," she assured him. "It's a work account."

The docking atrium was a white-walled, hexagonal space. Walkways lined each of its eight levels, connecting with the dynamically docked chambers or leading to the tower's pedestrian paths, internal trains, and elevators. Thin, pedestrian bridges cut across the levels, and advertisements for food, games, and shows floated down the center.

Isaac followed Susan through the dense crowds. He thought they might have to work around some of the denser pockets, but the crowds shifted out of their way as soon as people caught sight of their uniforms. Whether that was out of fear or respect for the Peacekeepers—or perhaps a combination of both—Isaac wasn't sure.

Susan led them to the public elevators on the far side of the atrium and entered the level 126 destination code. It was a short trip, and when the door slid open, the stark whiteness of the elevator gave way to friendly, pale blue walls and virtual windows that provided glimpses of the Lunar landscape. Or the sides of other towers, as was more often the case. More pedestrian paths branched off the elevator station, and a floating sign declared this area was part of ONE-TWENTY-VILLE.

"Which way?" Isaac asked.

"Umm." Susan brought up a map. "Their apartment is part of One-Twenty-Six dash Three Residential. Down this way."

The elevator station opened into a small grassy park bisected by a trickling stream meandering through a few apple trees, and a picturesque blue sky portrayed on the ceiling three stories up. Apartments lined the park on all sides, interrupted with the occasional restaurant or store. The two detectives took a stone path around the park and followed it to the back of the residential area.

"Here we are," Susan declared. "One-Twenty-Six dash Three dash One-Eighteen. Home of the Sakos."

"Mmhmm."

The sign above the door read: THE SAKO HOUSE. The words bobbed on a cheerful cloud with a rainbow arching overhead.

Isaac palmed the buzzer, and they waited.

And waited.

And waited.

He palmed it again.

A virtual image of a warmly lit interior replaced the door, its details obscured by a privacy filter.

"Yes?" asked the blurry woman standing behind the door, her voice tinged with worry.

"Good day, ma'am." Isaac pinged the woman with his DTI

badge. "I'm Investigator Cho and this is Agent Cantrell. We're looking for Kana and Emile Sako. Are they in?"

"They are. I'm Kana." She placed her hand on an interface by the door. The virtual image vanished, and the door split open.

Elly Sako took after her mother, who shared many of the same facial features, though the gray strands mixed through her dark hair and the more prominent cheek bones differentiated the two at a glance.

"My husband is in the shower. He'll be out shortly. What's this about?"

"We're working on a case involving your daughter, and we'd like to ask you and your husband a few questions. May we come in?"

"I— Well, yes, of course." She backed away from the door. "But what's going on? Is Elly in trouble? Is she all right?"

"Your daughter was in good health last we saw her. And she was doing quite well in the tournament. However, she and another player have received threatening messages, which is what brings us here today."

"You were over in SysGov?"

"That's correct."

"What sort of messages are we talking about?"

"Death threats, I'm afraid."

Kana gasped and put a hand to her mouth.

"I assure you, we take this matter *very* seriously. We wouldn't be here otherwise."

"But what are you over here for? Shouldn't you be in SysGov making sure she's safe?"

"That's a task for her security detail. Again, may we come in and ask you a few questions?"

"What's going on here?" barked a man stomping toward the door. "Who the hell is pestering us at this—"

He stopped in his tracks, his damp chest bare and a black and white checkered towel wrapped around his waist. He took in the two Peacekeeper uniforms, and his anger slunk away.

"Emile," Kana began, "they're here about Elly, and—"

"Elly?!" he blurted, his face twisting with new worry. "Is she all right? What's going on? Why are you here?"

"Mister Sako," Isaac said patiently. "Please allow me to explain the situation."

✧   ✧   ✧

"Would you please state your name for the record?" Isaac said.

Kana sat on a couch opposite Isaac in the living room with an abstract view of the park outside. Susan was sitting down with Emile in another room for a similar interview. Isaac would have preferred both family members to be data isolated, but he lacked the means to ensure they weren't passing digital notes to each other. They'd have to settle for conducting simultaneous interviews.

"Kana Sako."

"What is your relation to Elly Sako?"

"I'm her mother." She smiled. "She's an only child. Emile and I have talked about having a second kid, but you know how it is. Life gets in the way sometimes, and the next thing you know your kid is all grown up and you're wondering if you still have the energy for another. I do regret her not growing up with a brother or sister, sometimes."

"What do you do for a living?"

"I'm a data analyst in the Department of Energy. People think that means I work in the basement reactor, but in all honesty, I hardly ever venture below the seventies."

"You're referring to this block's level numbers?"

"Yes, sir. That's right. I'm currently studying power usage trends aggregated by both time and tower area, which my management will then use to plan infrastructure upgrades. Hopefully, we can keep ahead of any demand spikes." She chuckled. "I've always had an affinity for math. I know the work might seem dry to most people—and it is to a certain degree—but I enjoy it. Between the two of us, Emile has the more interesting job."

"What would that be?"

"Oh, he's a programmer for SunSoft!" she said with pride. "He even worked on the original version of *Legions of Patriots*, specifically the game's combat mechanics." Her eyes twinkled. "He still receives royalties from that one. I think his career is one of the reasons Elly took to being a gamer so well. She was always a bit of a daddy's girl."

"Why did she go into teaching initially?"

"Well, Elly always had a soft spot for those less fortunate than us, and she thought teaching in a poorer block would be a good way to make a difference. That's what she wanted most after graduating college. To make her mark upon the worlds in a positive way." Kana shook her head. "Which landed her in that godawful slum job."

"You're referring to the teaching position in Block F9?"

"Yeah." She sighed. "Should have taken any number of nicer posts. Even had an offer from the D2 Oasis. But the slum was the one she wanted."

"Why that one?"

"Because it was in the worst area. To her, that meant she could do the most good by working there. That was her logic, anyway."

"Did you and your husband approve of her career path?"

"No. We were lukewarm at best about the teaching career, and we *definitely* weren't happy about her taking a post in the Niner Slums. We argued about it quite a bit, but she didn't back down. It worked out in the end, though. Sometimes children have to learn their lessons the hard way."

"How did the job pan out for her?"

"It didn't. The area was horrible. The students were horrible. The other teachers were horrible. The experience beat a lot of the optimism out of her, for better or worse. About the only bright spot in all of it was the principal. Her name was Debra something. Began with an H, I think."

"Debra Heller?"

"Yes, that's the one! Elly would always have something nice to say about Debra during our calls. I could tell the woman had her back. They became very good friends, but one friendship wasn't enough to make *that* job any less of a soul sucker. I think Emile and I celebrated with a whole bottle of wine when she finally left."

"Did your daughter seem happier as a professional gamer?"

"Oh, yes! And she's so *good* at it, too! I'm not much of a gamer myself, but Emile *loves* to point out all the unusual tricks she pulls. He makes her matches a treat to watch. And besides, she's made so much money doing this! The two of us do all right for ourselves, but she blew right past us!"

"Did she keep in touch with Debra Heller after leaving F9?"

"If she did, she never mentioned it."

"Anyone else she might have stayed in contact with from her teacher days?"

"I doubt it. She didn't get along with most of them, and she was ambivalent toward the rest. Heller was her only true friend down there."

"Did your daughter ever talk about any connections the school might have had to Free Luna?"

"No," she shook her head with a confused expression. "I don't recall anything of the sort."

"What about connections Debra Heller may have had to Free Luna?"

"Sorry, but I don't remember her ever mentioning Free Luna at all. Except maybe once or twice when they were in the news."

"How would she characterize the group when she did discuss them?"

"I honestly couldn't tell you. Whatever she said, it didn't strike me as noteworthy."

"Are you aware of your daughter's charity donations?"

"Yes. We've talked about it a few times. The amounts seem a bit"—she smiled sadly—"excessive to us. We've cautioned her about spending too much, but she's quick to point out how much money she makes nowadays. Honestly, as long as she's keeping an eye on her financial future, she won't hear any complaints from us. Maybe a note or two of caution, but that's all. Besides, I also think it's healthy for her to donate this way."

"How so?"

"She wanted to help people in those slums and went about it the hard way for two whole years, but all that bought her was a lot of grief and stress. That was a tough lesson for her to soak in, and her self-esteem took a shot from it, but with her new career, she's found a different way to meet those same goals. I guess you could say it's a case of her working smarter, not harder."

"Then you haven't noticed anything unusual regarding your daughter's finances?"

"No, sir. Not at all."

"Do you still speak with her regularly?"

"Sure. She calls about once or twice a week."

"Anything else of note? Any atypical actions or statements from her recently?"

"No, not that I can think of. Lately it's been the 'Weltall Channel' when talking to her, if you get my meaning. It grows a bit tiresome at times, but I listen to her all the same."

"Moving on." Isaac brought up a calendar and removed the privacy filter. "There's one specific event I'd like to ask you about. According to records at the *Weltall* qualifier, she took a train here after she qualified for the finals. Do you recall the visit?"

"Oh, yes! I remember!" Kana smiled brightly. "She was so excited. She even took us out to Lox's to celebrate."

"Lox's?"

"Only the best restaurant in the Oasis. *Very* high end. Can you believe they don't print out a single item on their whole menu? Not a one! Everything they serve is prepared by hand."

"Did your daughter talk about the finals during dinner?"

"Are you kidding? She hardly talked about anything else! She was practically bouncing off the walls with excitement. I can't remember the last time I'd seen her that happy."

"I see." Isaac closed his notes. "Thank you for your time, Missus Sako. I believe that's all we need for now."

✧   ✧   ✧

"Their stories match," Susan said after she and Isaac finished comparing notes. "Dead end?"

"Looks like it." Isaac rested an elbow on the Cutlass's main console. "Sako was with her parents that night, which begs the obvious question of who went to the Niner Slums. Let's head that way. Cephalie and Nina might have something for us by the time we arrive."

✧   ✧   ✧

The Cutlass swooped in toward Block F9, and Isaac could already see how the notorious block stood out from the other monolithic high-rises. It still possessed the clean white of the neighboring towers, but its uniformity had been marred by a patchwork of additional, off-color plating at a few points along its exterior.

Defender-Prime sat in a large alcove atop the roof, and Susan took the Cutlass in to join it.

"Was all of that done during the Niner Riots?" Isaac asked.

"Most of it," she explained.

"'Riot' doesn't normally include venting a building to vacuum."

"It does if the rioters use big enough explosives."

"Is it safe? Structurally, I mean."

"It should be. The riots ended seven years ago. There are a few areas they never repressurized, but everything else should be fine."

"What caused the riots?"

"That." Susan pointed to the tall, skeletal frame of a building near the edge of Tycho Crater City.

"What's it going to be?"

"The correct question is what *was* it. It used to be a DTI

suppression tower. The first ever built on Luna. Protests against its construction were the bloody seeds that led to the Niner Riots of 2973."

"Then the rioters won? You never finished the tower?"

"Oh, no. They lost. In more ways than one, you could say. A lot of people's homes were destroyed, and we built the tower anyway."

"Then why's it look the way it does?"

"Because we repurposed its antenna. We've done that with a few other towers, too, pulling out the hardware to build our *Portcullis*-class mobile suppressors instead of constructing all new antennae.

"The locals, often sensitive to any Peacekeeper overreach—perceived or otherwise—protested the tower's construction. But those protests intensified over time until they finally spiraled out of control. The result was a complete breakdown of law and order in the tower, leading to rampant looting, arson, open attacks on local police and Peacekeepers, violent gang warfare. You name it."

"Big explosions?"

"Yes, a few of those, too."

"Were you involved?"

"In the counter-riot ops? No. The DTI kept to the construction site while other departments handled the rioters. There *was* one direct attack on the construction site, but it didn't get far." She frowned and turned to him. "And then the Admin pushed back. Hard."

"Casualties?"

"Yes."

"Many?"

"Yes." She shook her head. "It was...not our finest hour. And it all ended up being for nothing. On both sides. *Everyone* lost."

Susan brought the Cutlass down into one of the smaller hexagonal docks. The roof sealed, and the dock dropped into the underlying logistics of the roof port before locking into place. The port itself was the same tall, hexagonal space he'd seen in D2 but with maybe a tenth the people passing through. Only two advertisements floated in the air, and a combination of anti-Admin slurs and what looked like gang tags dotted the walls. A few vagrants slumped against the walls. One glanced over at them with glazed eyes.

"The locals shouldn't give us trouble this high up," Susan said, "but stay alert, just in case."

"Understood."

Isaac followed her across the level to the elevators, which they took up to the chronoport's dock.

"The unemployment rate in this tower is north of sixty percent," Susan added. "And that number goes higher the farther down we are. People here don't have much to do beside drugs, abstract isolation, and finding new ways to hate on the Admin."

"Lovely."

They entered a private room off the side of the chronoport's dock and found Cephalie, Nina, Noxon, and two Wolverines waiting for them next to a virtual view of the ship. Susan locked the door behind them.

"Isaac!" Cephalie quipped with a wide grin and spread arms. "You bring me to the nicest places!"

"How were her parents?" Nina asked, standing next to her forensics backpack.

"No surprises, and no new information," Isaac summarized. "You two?"

"We have the second Elly's destination," Cephalie announced. "Once she arrived, she placed a call to a man named Kurtis Slater, who lives down in level 31. After that, she took an elevator down to the same level."

"You sure the information's solid?"

"As sure as I can be. From the looks of it, the infostructure here's been screwed over so many times by so many people, it's more porous than a sponge."

"Then it sounds like we should pay Mister Slater a visit."

"Before you go, you'll be interested in this." Nina opened a virtual file over her palm. "Noxon was able to pull Slater's criminal record. He's in the Peacekeeper database with an arrest record for providing material support to a Free Luna cell. Most of it in the form of unregistered vehicles."

"Slater..." Susan mumbled.

"Something on your mind?" Isaac asked.

"Yeah. I think Pérez and I might have brought him in. We busted a lot of Free Luna cells over the years, and the name sounds familiar."

"You're right," Nina confirmed. "Pérez was listed as the one who made the arrest."

"Looks like we're heading down to level 31," Isaac said. "Cephalie, Nina, it's probably best if you both stay on the chronoport. Susan and I will head down and—"

"I'll come, too," Noxon cut in, "along with the drones."

"Do you think that's necessary?"

"I don't think it's *enough*, but it's what we have," he growled. "If I'd known we were heading into this accursed tower, I would have brought more drones." He placed a hand on his slung assault rifle. "And bigger guns."

✧   ✧   ✧

The elevator stopped a third of a meter above the target level, and the door shuddered open. Isaac frowned first at the misalignment, then at the flickering lights in the cramped, circular elevator station, and finally at the food wrappers and dirty clothes strewn about the stained carpet. He was about to step out when the smell hit him. It was a fetid mixture of sweat, urine, feces, motor oil, and coffee, which made him suspect the stains were the results of public defecation.

"That's..." He coughed into his fist. "Unpleasant."

"Let's make this quick," Noxon warned, climbing down. "Before these idiots realize we're here and decide to try their luck." The two Wolverines followed him out.

"Right," Isaac agreed, his eyes watering at the stench.

"You okay?" Susan asked.

"All part of the job."

Noxon and the Wolverines led the way down a cramped corridor filled with stagnant water from a leaking water main. The corridor opened into a two-story park, smaller but similar in layout to the one where the Sakos lived, but this "park" was a barren stretch of dead grass and dirt. Its lone tree had wilted long ago, and someone had painted a crude Peacekeeper on its bark and had, apparently, been using the tree for throwing knife target practice.

A few barefoot kids played in the dirt, and an elderly couple watched them from a nearby balcony. A group of six young men perked up as the Peacekeepers passed through. Most of them wore red jackets slashed with black stripes, which screamed "gang colors" to Isaac's senses.

They entered another utility tunnel and cut through to the next area.

"We're being followed," Susan told the others.

"I saw them," Noxon confirmed. "Did you see any weapons?"

"Knives and a club. No guns. You?"

"Same."

The next residential area resembled the first, except a nearby leak had turned its dirt park into a pool of stinking, trash-strewn mud. A vagrant sat at the edge, naked from the waist down with his bare feet in the mud as he stared up at nothingness, though whether from a drug haze or uninhibited abstraction was hard to tell.

Drugs, probably, Isaac surmised, *given his lack of pants.*

They stopped at an unmarked door.

"Map says this is the place." Susan glanced back the way they came. The six gang members lurked along the far wall. "It seems we still have our audience."

"Drones, establish a perimeter centered on this door," Noxon ordered. "Twenty-meter exclusion, five-meter warning buffer. Ignore anyone inside the apartment."

The two Wolverines spaced themselves out on either side of the door, and a pair of concentric rings—one yellow and one red with scrolling messages in bold letters—appeared in everyone's shared vision.

"What will happen if they violate the perimeter?" Isaac asked.

"The Wolverines will open fire," Susan said.

"Is that necessary?"

"With a *taser* first," Susan added hastily. "If that fails to subdue the target, then they'll switch ammo types and shoot to kill."

"Let's hope it doesn't come to that." Isaac ran his hand over the buzzer. Nothing happened, so he tried again. Then a third time. "Does anything work properly down here?"

"Allow me." Noxon placed a hand on Isaac's shoulder and urged him aside. "I believe I know how to fix it." He raised a fist and pounded on the door so hard the malmetal plates segmented down the middle to form a thin crack. "Open up, Slater!"

"Fix it, huh?" Isaac asked.

Noxon shrugged without apology.

The door shuddered apart, and a man with long, matted hair looked them over with a bored expression on his pale face. One arm and a leg were in medical casts, and he hunched forward on a metal cane. The man's face matched the one in Slater's file, though the years had not been kind to him, it seemed.

"Kurtis Slater, I presume?" Isaac asked.

"Took you people long enough. Well, come on in." Slater shook his head and walked back into a dingy apartment that stank of alcohol and vomit. He swept food wrappers and empty drink cans off the cushions of a stained sofa and plopped down into it with a pained gasp. "Have a seat. My house is your house, such as it is."

Isaac eyeballed the room. He didn't see anywhere else to sit except on the sofa next to Slater, and that cushion looked wet.

"I'll stand, thank you."

"Suit yourself." Slater picked up an open can from a tray next to the sofa and took a swig.

"Mister Slater, I have a few questions I'd like you to—"

"She was a beautiful young thing." He set the can down.

"I beg your pardon?"

"Looked as sweet and wholesome as an angel. Bright eyes, soft skin, silken hair. Breasts out to here." He gestured with both hands in front of his chest. "Is that who you're here about?"

"Would this be the woman you're describing?" Isaac summoned a picture of Elly Sako.

"Yeah, that's her." His face curled up into a snarl. "That's the bitch who beat the living shit out of me."

"She assaulted you?"

"Of course, she did! You think I broke my own bones for the hell of it? She fuckin' worked me over! She even broke my leg *after* I gave her what she wanted! Said it was for giving her a hard time!" He shook his head. "Bitch! I'm lucky one of my neighbors helped me reach the free clinic up on fifty-five."

"Perhaps it would be best if you started at the beginning," Isaac suggested.

"Look, it's really simple. That bitch came down here about a month ago asking after my old Free Luna contacts, and I didn't give them to her."

"You're still in contact with Free Luna?"

"Yeah, but it's not like I do any *work* for them, so don't get all excited. I already served my time, thank you very much." He paused to thump his chest, then belched. "I chat them up to see if they can send a few Escudos my way. Since helping them out the last time went *so fucking well* for me. And occasionally they do. You know, for old time's sake. I think they feel sorry for me. Can't imagine why."

"The woman was after your contacts?"

"Shit, you catch on quick for an Admin stooge."

"Which contact?"

"How the hell should I know? She asked for *all* of them. Almost like *she* didn't know which one she needed. And when I didn't give them to her, she fucked me up!"

"Did she say what she needed the contacts for?" Isaac asked.

"Nope. Just asked for them, then beat me up, then demanded them." He blew out a breath. "Then broke my fucking leg."

"We'll need that list of contacts," Isaac said. "I can provide a search warrant, if you need to see one."

"Oh, save yourself the trouble. Here!" A list of connection strings appeared in the space between them. "Go find that bitch and beat the shit out of *her*." He sank into the cushions and grabbed his drink. "It's what you clowns are good at, after all."

"Thank you." Isaac copied the strings. "Is there anything else—"

"You have entered an exclusionary zone," warned one of the Wolverines outside. "Move back or I will be forced to subdue you."

Susan and Noxon both spun to face the door, hands reaching for their weapons.

"Sounds like you've got problems of your own," Slater cackled.

Isaac accessed the apartment's virtual window, and the wall vanished, revealing a cluster of six gangsters encroaching on the perimeter. The youngest one edged up to the red circle and chucked a rock at the closest Wolverine. The drone sidestepped the projectile and returned fire with a pair of taser bolts to the gangster's chest. He convulsed and dropped onto his back with a sloppy splash.

"Fuck!" shouted the gangster with the pipe club.

Noxon strode out, holding his rifle in one hand, but keeping it aimed at the ceiling.

"Disperse now," he ordered in a soft yet commanding tone. "Or else."

"Or else what, tin man?"

"Drones!" Noxon commanded. "Switch to lethal ammo!"

Mechanisms whirred inside the Wolverines' heads.

"Oh, shit!" The gangster dropped his club. He turned and ran while the others scattered, leaving their tased comrade alone on the ground.

"Not how I would have handled it," Isaac commented as he stepped out of the apartment, "but it seems to have worked."

"For now," Noxon said. "Let's get out of here before more show up."

CHAPTER TWENTY-FIVE

"UHH!" NINA RAN BOTH HANDS BACK THROUGH HER HAIR. "THIS list of names is almost worthless!"

"It's all we have to work with," Isaac said, walking into *Defender-Prime*'s conference room. He and Susan sat down across from Nina and Cephalie.

"What seems to be the problem?" Susan asked.

"First, all these names are pseudonyms." Cephalie gestured down the floating list. "Some more obvious than others. Unless 'Blood Salt' is a common name in the Admin."

"It's not," Susan said matter-of-factly.

"What about the connection strings?" Isaac asked.

"I put together a simple, automated call," Cephalie said, "just to test if anyone would answer. No one did."

"Not one?"

"Nope. My guess is someone on this list let the others know the Peacekeepers might come snooping. If they're smart, they've all switched to new strings by now."

"Which leaves us with a list of fake names and dead connection strings," Nina groaned.

"Hold on," Susan said. "What was that about the list being *almost* worthless?"

"There *is* one outlier," Cephalie explained, "though I'm not sure how helpful it'll be." She highlighted one of the names. "Meet Sebastian Jende, aka 'Moon Pony.'"

"His alias is 'Moon Pony'?" Susan snorted out a quick laugh. "Lame."

"What's special about him?" Isaac asked.

"His connection string is invalid—not unresponsive, invalid— and the reason is obvious when we consider this string *is* listed officially, unlike the others. Jende was arrested two years ago on charges of data smuggling, weapon pattern theft, and conspiracy to commit murder. Crimes like that led to his connectome being forcibly extracted and his body recycled. He's currently serving out a life sentence in an Admin prison domain."

"It seems strange that Slater would still have this guy's old string, though," Nina said.

"He didn't strike me as the organized type," Isaac commented dryly.

"Where does this leave us?" Susan asked.

"Not sure," Isaac said. "The two big questions on my mind are who's the Sako look-alike and which name on the list was she after? If we knew the goal of her visit to the Niner Slums, then maybe we can figure out what she was planning."

"And who she's working with," Susan added.

"Right." Isaac stared at the list, then let out a long exhale. "There seems to be only one place to try next."

"You mean the prison domain?" Susan suggested.

"Would it be possible for us to interview Jende?" Isaac asked.

"Sure. The domain will be managed by one of the Department of Incarceration's server towers. All we have to do is pay the warden a visit and get permission to abstract into the domain. All standard stuff."

"Then where do we need to head? Cephalie?"

"Jende's being kept in prison domain number 303. The server tower's not far from here."

"Then that's our destination."

The blue obelisk of the Admin server tower loomed over a barren gray plain in the middle of nowhere with no evidence of either roads or sealed tunnels leading to it. Drones as large as the Cutlass circled the tower in slow, methodical patrols, and turreted weapons glinted around the top like a thorned crown of metal.

A hangar opened on the side of the tower, and the chronoport slid inside before it dropped into the docking cradle. A group of security synthoids and Wolverines greeted them at the gate while their identities were verified. The process took longer than usual due to Isaac's "junior provisional" status, but Noxon had already forwarded all the necessary documentation to DTI HQ, which the DOI personnel could access as part of the verification process.

Isaac and Susan were permitted inside after only a short delay and a few questions. They rode one of the elevators to a few floors below the top of the tower.

"Investigators, hello!" Warden Edgar Dressel greeted the two of them with firm handshakes as they exited the elevator. His yellow eyes gleamed with energy as Isaac's hand nearly disappeared within his gray-skinned palm. "A pleasure to meet the both of you."

"Likewise, though actually, sir," Susan corrected, "I'm not an investigator. I'm merely a special agent within the DTI."

"Oh, my apologies." He smiled broadly at her. "I hope I didn't offend you."

"Of course not, sir."

"By the way, I see you're using one of our newer synthoids." Dressel knuckled her on the shoulder. "Been toying with the idea of swapping to something more modern myself. How's it working out for you?"

"Quite well," Susan replied. "This model allows me to interface with both Admin and SysGov infostructures, which comes in handy with my current assignment."

"I can imagine! And you." He gestured to Isaac with an open hand. "You're *from* SysGov, if I read your file correctly."

"That's right."

"*And* you're a DTI Investigator?"

"So I've been told."

"Fascinating." Dressel put his hands on his hips. "Sorry about the delay letting you in. They like to check with me whenever someone unusual shows up. No offense, mind you, but the two of you qualify there!"

"I suppose we do at that."

"Shall we step into my office so we can discuss what brought you out here?"

"Yes, please."

Dressel led them down the hall to a modest-sized room dominated by a heavy slab of moon rock set atop two boulders.

He sat down behind his "desk," and abstract screens lit up above the slab.

"So." He leaned back in a chair that also appeared to have been carved from moon rock. "How can I help the two of you?"

"We'd like to interview one of your prisoners as part of an ongoing investigation." Isaac presented the warden with Jende's file.

"Let me see that." Dressel drew the file over to his hand and his eyes skimmed over it. "Jende, huh." He summoned a second file and ran a finger down the list. "Yes, I see him now. Domain 303. It's one of our minimum supervision domains. We transferred him there after his first year."

"Does that mean he's a troublemaker?" Isaac asked.

"Quite the opposite, actually. We use 303 as a reward for good behavior, which his record shows he demonstrated consistently during his first year of incarceration. If he keeps this up, he may even become eligible for parole in a few decades."

"What'll happen then?" Isaac asked, more out of professional curiosity than anything else. "I mean, since he doesn't have a body."

"We'll print a civilian synthoid for him and set him free, of course." Dressel's brow furrowed. "Why do you ask? Is that different from what you do in SysGov?"

"The question doesn't often come up, since we don't abstract criminals against their will."

"Huh. Interesting." Dressel shrugged. "To each their own, I suppose. Seems like a liability having dangerous criminals running around with their physical bodies. Best to strip them down to their thoughts. They're more manageable that way. Can't hurt themselves or others if they're just data. Not in any permanent way, at least."

"I guess you do have a point there," Isaac conceded, though he couldn't move past the forced-abstraction part of the Admin prison system. Despite whatever reasoning the Peacekeepers might have, the act of forcibly removing someone's mind from their body represented a heinous violation of the sanctity of one's own connectome, at least from a SysGov perspective.

"So, what's your interest in Jende?" Dressel asked.

"He's a former member of Free Luna, and his name came up in a list we obtained recently, so we believe he may have information vital to our current case. Three separate crimes have been committed during the ongoing Weltall Tournament in SysGov, and there are some indicators Free Luna may—"

"*Weltall!*" Dressel's eyes widened with delight. "Well, how about that! I was just wondering about the tournament, and here you show up. How're the matches going? Are our players doing well?"

"Some better than others," Isaac said. "Masuda and Lacan have been eliminated, for various reasons, but Sako is still in the fight."

"Elly? I knew it!" He flashed a toothy grin and slapped his desk. "I just *knew* she had it in her!"

"You've heard of her?" Isaac asked.

"*Heard* of her? I've done more than that." Dressel walked over to the wall. He pressed a hand against an interface, and several shelves extended out. "I'm one of the first people to sign up for her fan club. Membership number 99. Ha! Just managed to slip in before all the double digits were taken. I could tell she had potential from the first time I saw her play. Ah! Here it is!"

He pushed the top shelf back in to reveal the next shelf down, which held a silver long-barreled pistol resting atop a red pillow. He slipped fingers from both hands underneath the weapon and then, with the utmost care, presented it to Isaac. Someone had etched a line of black script down the flat side of the barrel casing.

"She . . . signed your gun?" Isaac asked.

Dressel nodded, an almost childish grin on his face.

"And she was *so* nice about it, too. Didn't even charge me for it. Even talked to me afterward, though I tried not to take too much of her time. There were other people in line, after all."

"I see."

"Though, to be clear, it's not *my* gun." He placed the weapon back on the pillow and slid the shelf closed. "It's my grandfather's, may his soul rest in peace. He was a professional gamer before joining the Peacekeepers. *And* became one again after he retired, though his reflexes weren't what they used to be by that time. The Lightning Edge they called him."

"Oh!" Susan perked up in her seat. "Was his name also Edgar Dressel?"

"Why, yes. Yes, it was."

"I think I might have heard of him." Susan beamed at Isaac. "My old *Legions* coach liked to share inspiration quotes from famous gamers, and the Lightning Edge was one of them. Stuff like 'winners make their own luck.' That sort of thing."

"I think we're getting sidetracked here," Isaac pointed out.

"I—" Susan paused, and the smile melted off her face. "Yes, of course, you're right."

"Anyway, Warden," Isaac said. "That's the situation. May we speak with the prisoner, or is there something else you need from us?"

"No, just sating my own nosy habits. Let me get things sorted out for you." He opened a comm window.

"Yes, Warden?" replied a female Peacekeeper.

"Charlotte, I've got two guests from the DTI who need abstraction into 303. Get things set up on your end, would you?"

"Right away, sir."

Isaac materialized on the edge of a field of corn stalks taller than he was. He squinted up at a blue sky shot with wisps of high clouds, and the bright, midday sun warmed his face. Susan popped into the virtual world next to him.

Isaac turned around in a circle. They stood on a dirt road between the corn field and a freshly plowed one. A horse tied to a wooden cart neighed at them. He could see a pair of windmills turning in the distance near what might have been a grain silo.

But no people.

"Isn't Jende supposed to be nearby?" he asked.

"I thought that's what she said."

A giant black arrow materialized over the cornfield.

"Ah. There we are." Isaac headed into the cornfield and began picking his way through the stalks.

"Hey, Sebastian!" exclaimed an unseen woman from up ahead. "You've got a big pointer over your head!"

"Does it say anything?"

"Nah. It's just a big, dumb arrow. What's it mean?"

"No idea. They should label these things better, if you ask me."

"Think someone's looking for you?"

"If so, they won't have to look hard."

Isaac pushed through the corn and stepped into an open patch where either the corn had failed to grow or had sprouted into stunted, sickly stalks that only came up to his waist. A man and woman stood in the clearing, backpacks on the ground stuffed with corncobs.

The man's round face and generous belly matched Jende's file, but his ears extended back into prominent points and his long hair shimmered in the sunlight with an ethereal quality.

The woman turned to them with orange, glowing eyes. She possessed red skin, black hair, and a pair of horns that formed a crooked V on her forehead.

"Oh!" The woman smiled and waved at them. "Hi!"

"What are you supposed to be?" Isaac asked her. "A demon?"

"I'm a *tiefling*." She stressed the word, her red tail whipping behind her. "I've earned enough domain points to make cosmetic changes to my avatar." She smiled and batted her eyes at him. "I've been such a good girl, I can even cast simple spells now."

"Congratulations?" Isaac said.

"I'm still working on my avatar, as you can see." The man smacked his belly, which undulated in rolling waves. "Going for the fey look. I started with the hair and ears, but I've got a long way to go, unfortunately. Need to keep earning those domain points."

"Speaking of which, would you two like some corn?" The tiefling offered them a cob. "It's *delicious!*"

"We'll pass."

"You sure? I could even run to the farmhouse. Boil them up and slather them with butter. It may be simple, but a little butter on these babies really brings out the flavor."

"No, *thank you*. We're looking for Sebastian Jende."

"That's me." The plump man gave them a halfhearted wave. "Though, I imagine you already knew that, what with the big arrow over my head." He placed an ear of corn into his bag and stood back up. "What can I do for you?"

"We have a list of names and connection strings for you to look at," Isaac said. "We believe an unknown person has contacted at least one of them, and we'd like your input on who it might be and what this individual might be after."

"Okay," Jende said doubtfully. "I'll do my best. You're asking for a lot of guesswork, though. These Free Luna names?"

"We believe so. Your name was also on the list."

"Got it." He nodded. "That might make this easier, then."

"And the fact that they're former colleagues of yours?"

"That's their problem. The way I see it, I'll be spending the rest of my life in here. This"—he gestured to the cornfield around them—"is my reality until I'm paroled or decide to self-delete. Best make the most of it."

"That's the spirit!" The tiefling clapped him on the shoulder.

"By the way, am I being paid for this?" He rubbed his hands together. "Not to sound greedy or anything. Just want to know where we stand."

"I don't know about pay," Isaac said, "but I've been authorized to award you with up to ten domain points for your assistance."

"*Ten?!*" His eyes widened.

"Yes, that's right."

The tiefling whistled. "Damn, Sebastian! That's enough to edit out your gut!"

"I know! Holy shit! Umm." Jende held out his trembling hands. "Can I see the list, please?"

"Here you go." Isaac summoned the list over his palm and presented it to Jende.

"Hmm." Jende took the list into his hands and expanded it. "Yes, yes. Looks a bit out of date, even for when I was still active, but I can work with this. I recognize most of the aliases and a few of the strings. A lot of these are *very* minor players, though. The kind of people who play at the cause and talk a good talk but would never put their skin in the game. You're not after those sorts, I take it?"

"Most likely not."

"Yeah, thought so. Oh, what's this?" He highlighted one of the names near the bottom. "Now *this* one is more interesting. The Unmaker, otherwise known as Victor Massi. One of the most dangerous people I've ever met. We called him the Unmaker for a reason. Our aliases weren't supposed to tie into our duties, like Blood Salt or Green Voice."

"Or Moon Pony?" Susan asked with a raised eyebrow.

"Yeah, just so," he continued without a hint of embarrassment. "But everyone called Victor the Unmaker. Or Mister Unmaker, if we were being polite, which the smart ones among us tended to be. He's a wizard with explosives. And not only the bombs themselves, but finding ways to hide them. That's what really makes him scary. Anyone can run a search and find the plans for a bomb, but it takes someone with true talent to keep it hidden." Jende tapped through the list of names. "If you're asking me who the scariest piece of work on this list is, I'd have to say Victor in a heartbeat. The rest of these names are chumps compared to him."

"A bomb maker," Isaac murmured, all manner of dark scenarios playing out in his mind. Could someone have smuggled a bomb aboard *Defender-Prime* and brought it to the Crimson Flower?

Of course they could, he thought gravely, *if the bomb was hidden well enough. No security system is flawless.*

"We need to warn the others," Susan said.

"You're absolutely right," Isaac said. "Thank you, Jende. You've been very helpful."

He opened a menu and selected the exit option.

"Be sure to tell the warden I helped!" Jende shouted as they faded into nothing.

CHAPTER TWENTY-SIX

"*DEFENDER-PRIME* SHOULD BE BACK WITHIN THE HOUR." SUSAN joined Isaac at a round table in the server tower's executive food court. "They need to cross about halfway over to SysGov. At that distance, *Pathfinder-Prime* can receive their telegraph. They'll message Pérez, let him know about the bomb threat, then come back here."

"Sounds good," Isaac said, nodding.

"You sure we shouldn't all head back to SysGov?"

"Not yet," Isaac said. "We may still learn who brought the bomb over, assuming our theory is correct. We can leave the bomb search to Pérez, but we have our own job to do here."

"Okay. Makes sense."

Isaac's stomach growled audibly.

"Want me to grab you something?" Susan asked.

"Yes, please. Any recommendations?"

"Well." Susan twisted around in her seat and scanned the room. A long row of food printers took up one whole wall, but the lines were short. Abstract signs blinked over the printers at the far end, and one of the signs read TURBO!!

"Most of the printers are generics, but they've got a Turbo franchise."

"Turbo?"

"Technically it's *Turbo!!*" She spoke the name with enthusiasm. "They put two exclamation points at the end."

"Any good?"

"I think so. It's the Admin equivalent of the Meal Spigot. Fast and scrumptious."

Isaac's eyes perked up.

"How about I pick out something for you?" Susan said, rising.

"Sure."

"All right. Be back in a few."

The line for Turbo!! was the longest but moved with rapid efficiency due to the speed of the franchise's printers. She transmitted her order while waiting in line and grabbed her food-laden tray less than a minute later.

"I'm not sure I'm *this* hungry," Isaac said when she set the tray down between them.

"It's not all for you." She served him his plate. "Here. The gyro platter is yours. The chocolate chip milkshake and chocolate fudge ice cream are for me."

"Isn't that a lot of food for you?" he asked, eyeing the supersized desserts. "Not that it has any effect on you, but you normally just peck during meals."

"It's been that sort of case." She tilted the milkshake toward him. "Want some? I printed an extra straw."

"Let me try the gyro first. Thanks, though."

"Sure thing." She sucked on her straw, then stopped and frowned when nothing came out.

"Something wrong?" Isaac asked, the gyro almost to his mouth.

"A chip got stuck in the straw." She sighed and drank from the edge of the milkshake. It left a frothy mustache over her lips. "What's next for us? Head after Victor Massi?"

"Ideally, yes. Though I'm not sure how we go about that. The trail's a month old and very cold. We'd struggle to follow it under the best of circumstances, but if Cephalie's right—and I'm inclined to agree with her—then Massi has gone into hiding, along with everyone else on Slater's list." He took a bite from his gyro. "Wow. This is good. Is this tzatziki sauce?"

"Tzatziki Turbo. It's their own special recipe." Susan took another sip from her milkshake, expanding her froth mustache.

"Susan? You might want to . . ." He mimed wiping under his nose.

"What? Oh!" She cleaned her mouth with a napkin. "That just means it's a good milkshake."

"I'll bet." He took another bite of his gyro, chewed, and swallowed. "Let's assume for the moment everything we learned from Jende is true."

"Which seems likely."

"Agreed. Having Pérez search for the bomb is a solid step in the right direction, but we're dealing with people who know how to hide these things. Any additional information we can learn could prove critical to finding it. That's what we need to accomplish over here, but I'm not sure how to get it done."

"Why don't we grab the fake Sako?"

"Susan." Isaac sighed at her. "If it was that easy, we'd already be doing it."

"No, I'm not talking now. I mean back when she met Slater."

"But she's not with Slater anymore."

"Yeah, but she was a month ago."

"She—" Isaac paused and blinked. "Wait a second. Are you suggesting what I think you're suggesting?"

"You mean go back in time and snag ourselves a copy of the perp for interrogation?"

"But ... can we?"

"Sure. We know exactly where Fake-Sako's going to be. Or was, I should say." She smiled at Isaac. "Verb tenses and time travel still give me fits. Anyway, we can pick a spot along her route to Slater's hobo hole, set up an ambush, and nab her. Simple. I spent years of my life doing similar ops for DTI Suppression."

"Yes," Isaac agreed, clearly struggling with her train of thought. "But *can* we?"

"Look at it this way. You're a DTI investigator, at least temporarily, and we already have the chronoport. We can finish a leisurely meal, and when the ship returns, we share the plan with the others and head into the past. Negative-one month transit is nothing for a *Pioneer*-class. We can cross that in half a minute, absolute."

"You say this like it's such an ordinary thing."

"In the DTI, it is. Gordian Division may have clamped down on all unnecessary time travel, but over here we do things differently. Time travel has been a routine part of our investigations for well over a decade. I mean, they even put it in the name. Department of *Temporal* Investigation."

"I suppose you do have a point there."

"What do you say, then? Shall we give it a try?"

"Hmm." Isaac stared off to the side, then he looked back to her and smiled. "Sure. Why not?"

Defender-Prime phased out at negative-one month back from the True Present. It hovered high above Tycho Crater City's Block F9, its belly an indistinct blob of wavering darkness, shrouded by the photonic mimicry of its variskin armor.

"Phase out complete," the ship's temporal navigator reported.

"Position confirmed," the realspace navigator added. "Variskin active, and altitude stable."

Nina leaned over to Isaac in the next seat.

"Is this really the past?" she whispered to him.

"So they say. Why?"

"Because it looks the same as the present." She gestured to the external camera view of Block F9.

"We're only one month back."

"I know, but shouldn't it be different somehow? Shouldn't it look different? Shouldn't it *feel* different?"

"Let's not get carried away." He released his harness and headed down the central corridor back to the ship's maintenance bay.

An armored Noxon sat in a jump seat next to Susan, while Susan's combat frame stood beside her. The combat frame was a sleek humanoid machine covered in weapons and maneuvering boosters with its variskin set to Peacekeeper blue with white racing stripes.

"Which one are you in, Susan?" Isaac asked.

"Over here." The combat frame raised a hand then tapped her lifelike synthoid on the head. "It's empty now."

"I see now why you suggested this plan."

"What do you mean?"

"You just wanted to get back in that thing."

"It *is* one of the perks of this idea."

Susan-the-combat-frame finished harnessing her inert synthoid to the jump seat.

"You ready for this?" Isaac asked.

"Of course." She gave him a thumbs-up. "All I have to do is apprehend one young woman. How hard could it be?"

"What's the rifle for?" He pointed to the heavy rail-rifle attached to her arm.

"Just in case."

"And the shoulder-mounted grenade launcher?"

"Just in *extra* case."

"Uh huh."

"I'm leaving the incinerator behind," she said, as if it were a huge concession.

"That's..." He let out a slow sigh. "That's good. It's healthy to show restraint."

"You know I like to be prepared. Besides, if I blow up the perp accidentally"—she shrugged—"or on purpose, we can perform a microjump and try again."

"It's one of the benefits of time travel," Noxon added. "We can always make another attempt, because the past will still be there, right where we left it."

"Any risk of something bad happening to the timeline?" Isaac asked.

"About as close to zero as it gets," Noxon said. "The True Present is the most stable point in a universe's timeline, and the DTI has performed hundreds of similar operations without ever branching the timeline. This one will be no different."

"We'll take care of things, Isaac. Agent Noxon and I are professionals."

"I know. Just thought I'd ask." He glanced over Noxon's body armor. "You don't plan to join her in your own frame?"

"I would," Noxon said with a frown, "but it's back in SysGov."

"See?" Susan said. "This is why I insist on taking it everywhere. You never know when it'll come in handy."

"Hard to argue with you now. Be safe out there."

"I will."

"Shall we, sir?" Susan asked Noxon.

"Let's." He sealed his helmet in place, then led the way over and down into the Cutlass. The craft was empty except for the pair of Wolverines in their charging alcoves. Susan sealed the top hatch and depressurized the cabin. The vacuum wouldn't bother her combat frame. It *could* damage Noxon's cosmetic layer, which was one reason for him to wear the armor.

"The target should arrive in a few minutes," Noxon said over her abstract hearing.

"I'll be ready." She split open the rear hatch and stared down upon Tycho Crater City. The blocks were an organized grid of white pillars beneath her. She switched on her variskin and walked off the edge.

She plummeted through the vacuum, soundlessly, airlessly, the towers below rushing toward her. She fired a short burst of thrust from her shoulder and feet boosters, adjusting her course to align with the edge of Block F9's roof.

Lunar gravity might be roughly one sixth as strong as Earth's, but a long, frictionless descent piled on the meters per second, and she fired her boosters again, this time in a sustained burn that decelerated her until her feet touched down with delicate lightness.

She switched her boosters off and crouched on the roof, an indistinct blur against the white surface.

"In position."

"Target shuttle inbound," Noxon reported over the encoded radio channel. "Tagging now."

A circular reticle appeared over a glinting shape in the distance that rapidly resolved into a boxy, fat-fronted outline of a craft never meant for use in an atmosphere. It slowed to a hover above one of the many open docks and began its descent.

Susan hurried to the dock and slipped over the edge as the craft touched down. She dropped to a low crouch, her systems and weapons ready for anything. The ceiling irised closed, and the dock shuddered loose from the roof while atmosphere poured in. The dock traveled down and then sideways until it connected with the port atrium, and the abstract outline over the door switched from red to green.

A side hatch on the shuttle swung up, and Elly Sako—or someone who looked just like her—paced toward the exit. She swept her gaze back and forth over the dock.

Susan knew variskin had its limits, which was why she stayed perfectly still. The technology didn't allow photons to flow around her like the more advanced metamaterials used by SysGov. Instead, the variskin produced an active camouflage image designed to mimic her surroundings, but it was far from perfect, especially on a system as small and geometrically complex as her combat frame. Still, she could only be seen from one angle, and that allowed the system to operate at peak effectiveness.

It *should* have been enough to keep her hidden.

Sako's gaze passed over Susan's position, and a flicker of recognition widened her eyes. She spun on her heel and kicked off the ground, flying back toward the shuttle.

Shit! Susan thought. She fired her shoulder boosters, her variskin struggling to keep up. She grabbed the lip of the shuttle hatch with one arm to bring her to a halt, and blocked off Sako's retreat with her body.

"Elly Sako, you are under—"

Sako twirled in the air. She slammed the combat frame's torso with a roundhouse kick, and Susan knew instantly she wasn't fighting an organic woman or even a civilian synthoid. The force of the impact warped malmetal plates out of alignment and lit up yellow warning indicators in her mind. Her fingers sparked, stripping paint and metal off the shuttle hatch.

Fake-Sako touched the ground and leapt past the off-balance combat frame.

"Oh no you don't!" Susan grabbed Fake-Sako's foot. She yanked her back out with the intent of tossing her into the open, but Fake-Sako thumped Susan's head with another powerful kick. Her optics blurred, and she fell onto her side, the woman's ankle still in her grasp.

The impact crashed her variskin execution, and her skin reverted to blue with white racing stripes.

"A STAND!" Fake-Sako exclaimed.

A third kick pounded into Susan's neck, bringing with it enough force for Fake-Sako to pull free, even while Susan's fingers cut through cloth. Strips of synthoid cosmetic flesh tore loose, revealing the gray artificial musculature underneath.

Susan anchored one foot with the dynamic friction pad on the sole and fired her shoulder boosters, levering herself up into a standing position. She cut off her thrust and used the momentum to throw herself forward, arms spread to tackle the synthoid, but Fake-Sako twisted out of the way, dropping to a crouch and swinging into Susan with an uppercut.

The punch sent a shock rippling through Susan's artificial body, and more warnings flared in her mind. She swung her rail-rifle around and aimed it at the synthoid's head.

"Freeze!" she commanded. "Don't make me shoot you!"

Fake-Sako grabbed the end of the barrel with one hand and shoved Susan's aim aside. The two grappled with each other, locked at close range. Fake-Sako headbutted Susan, blurring her optics again, but Susan headbutted the synthoid back, tearing loose a flap of cosmetic skin over one eye.

"My head's harder!" Susan growled.

Fake-Sako snarled at her then shoved her into the side of the shuttle, denting the thin paneling.

"What the fuck is going on out there!" The shuttle pilot peeked his head out.

"Keep your head down!" Susan snapped, lighting her shoulder boosters but not firing them at full power. Hot air scorched the pilot's face, and he scrambled back toward the cockpit, which was exactly what Susan wanted him to do.

She switched to full thrust and forced Fake-Sako back toward the dock wall, but the synthoid twisted in her grip again and grabbed the base of one of her shoulder nozzles. She forced the ball joint out of alignment, and the exhaust propelled Susan into the floor face-first. Sparks flew as she slid across the ground, losing her grip on the synthoid.

Fake-Sako scrambled to her feet and hurried toward the dock exit.

"Stop right there!" Susan raised her rifle from her prone position.

Fake-Sako palmed the door open.

Susan fired a warning shot that struck above the door. The pilot squealed in fear, but Fake-Sako ignored the discharge and disappeared through the opening.

"Shit!" Susan rose to her feet. "Target on the move! Pursuing!"

"Do you require assistance?"

"No!" Susan fired her boosters and shot into the atrium, scanning above and below her. She spotted Fake-Sako midair two levels down. The synthoid landed with a brief stumble, then righted herself and sprinted across a connecting bridge on her way to the elevators.

They were the only two people in the atrium.

Good, Susan thought with icy calm.

She locked onto one end of the bridge with her grenade launcher and fired while Fake-Sako was only halfway across. The projectile detonated half a meter over the bridge in a bright ball of fire that stripped the bridge's sheet metal flooring.

Fake-Sako leaped over the gap and passed through the expanding fireball. Shrapnel cut across her, tearing away more cloth and skin, baring more of the synthoid underneath. She landed on the far end, kicked off the floor, and rushed toward the elevators.

Susan leaped down, fired her boosters to quicken her descent, and landed with a thump, only to see Fake-Sako disappear behind a closing elevator door.

"Like that'll stop me."

Susan reached the doors and forced her fingers into the seam, then ripped the doors open and leaped into the dark shaft. She fired her boosters, lighting the shaft and accelerating her descent until she slammed into the top of the elevator car, knocking it partially out of alignment. Emergency brakes engaged, and the car ground to a halt.

Susan peeled a ceiling panel back and pointed her rifle at the synthoid.

"You've got nowhere to run. Surrender, or I'll be forced to—"

Fake-Sako leaped up through the hole and tackled Susan. The two of them smacked into the side of the shaft, and Susan kicked off. She tried to steady herself, but her foot slipped on the loosened ceiling panels, and they both fell into the elevator car. Fake-Sako used the opportunity to roll over and straddle the combat frame. She put both of her fists together, raised them over her head, and brought them crashing down onto the combat frame's chest armor.

Armor bowed.

She struck a second time, but Susan caught the third blow and clenched down on the rogue synthoid's fist. She forced the Fake-Sako's arm back, squeezing down on her digits like a vice. Fake-Sako bared her teeth and tried to pull free, but Susan's grip was too firm. She crushed down even more, contorting the hand into an unnatural shape until—with a sudden jerk—she ripped the synthoid's ruined hand off.

Susan grabbed Fake-Sako's neck and threw her back. The synthoid crunched against the wall, undeterred, defiance burning in her eyes. She pushed off the wall and charged Susan, swinging with her good arm.

Susan caught that blow as well, then grabbed the synthoid's bicep with her free hand and began to tear the two pieces apart. The cloth sleeve ripped, and cosmetic flesh split open.

Fake-Sako kicked her, denting her shin armor, but Susan wouldn't let go. Fake-Sako smashed the shattered wrist of her damaged arm into the combat frame, but Susan twisted the two halves of the arm she held, then tore the arm apart.

Strands of artificial muscle whipped through the air, and Susan tossed the severed forearm aside. Fake-Sako tried to throw another kick, but Susan grabbed her by the throat first, lifting her up before she slammed her foot into the synthoid's flailing leg. The force of the blow crumpled the synthoid's knee mechanisms, folding the lower leg in the wrong direction.

Susan tossed the synthoid onto the ground and loomed over her.

"Had enough yet?"

Fake-Sako used her one good leg to put her back to the wall, then pushed off the floor to stand again. She raised her arms into a fighting stance, though the form lacked some of its menace given the missing ends of her arms.

Susan pointed her rifle at the synthoid's center of mass.

"Put your hands—" She paused and reconsidered her words. "Put your *arms* up."

The synthoid didn't move, only glared at Susan with hate in her eyes.

Susan didn't know whose connectome was in this body, but their fight had revealed much to her. Fake-Sako had recognized her hidden combat frame, even through the variskin illusion, and she'd done so almost instantly. Whoever this was had experience with variskin, either working with it or trying to detect enemies through it. Perhaps both.

Fake-Sako hadn't known she was up against a combat frame at first. Perhaps she'd guessed the hidden Peacekeeper was a flesh-and-blood operator in variskin armor, and if she'd been right she would have won, likely killing whoever tried to bring her in.

On top of that, she was both a skilled combatant *and* familiar with STAND combat frames. Knowledgeable enough to know she could redirect one of Susan's booster nozzles with her hands and enough force.

Finally, Susan knew it was only the advantages of her hardware that had allowed her to prevail. She would have lost if they'd been on equal footing.

She raised her rifle meaningfully.

"I'm not going to ask again."

The synthoid spat at her.

"Suit yourself."

She fired four shots in rapid succession, one into the base of each limb.

The synthoid collapsed to the ground.

Susan reached down and grabbed it by a headful of hair from its tattered scalp.

"Target subdued," she radioed to *Defender-Prime.* "Heading back."

She fired her boosters and rocketed up the shaft.

CHAPTER TWENTY-SEVEN

SUSAN, STILL IN HER COMBAT FRAME, TOSSED THE BROKEN SYNTHOID into a chair in one of *Defender-Prime*'s storage rooms. The room had been cleared of spare-parts containers and the reinforced malmetal door allowed it to double as a brig when needed.

Fake-Sako's broken limbs twitched, and she began to slide off the chair.

Susan grabbed her by the shoulders and readjusted her so she wouldn't fall out of the seat. She sealed the door behind them, then faced the prisoner. The tiny malmetal plates across her armor had worked out all the dents, and her combat frame was once again visible in its base colors.

"Have anything to say for yourself, Felly?"

The synthoid raised an eyebrow. Her *only* eyebrow, since the cosmetics had been stripped from half her face.

"Felly?" she asked.

"Yeah. Fake-Elly. Felly. I figure I have to call you something. Unless you'd like to tell me your name."

"I'm not inclined to do so."

"It'd make this process easier. We'll get the information out of you, one way or the other."

"Oh, I know that. Better than you realize." The prisoner smirked at her, lips only covering half her jaw. "Agent Cantrell."

"Now this is a surprise." Susan put her hands on her hips. "You know who I am."

"It wasn't hard. I recognize your voice," the prisoner said. "On top of that, you're one of the few people to use the new Type-99 combat frames."

"You seem pretty knowledgeable about us Peacekeepers."

"As anyone who opposes you should be."

"I get the feeling we've met before."

"We have."

"Thought so. I've brought in a lot of terrorists over the years. Care to refresh my memory? Maybe give me a hint. I bet if you give me a small hint I can guess which one you are."

"I'll pass, if it's all the same to you."

"Oh, come on. It's not like you have anything better to do. I already kicked your butt."

"Maybe so," the prisoner conceded, "but I'm going to guess we're not in the True Present, and that means I'm not the current version of me."

"Who knows? You might be."

"No, I think not. How else could you have known when and where to pick me up? No, this has the DTI's fingerprints all over it. Besides, you brought me back to a *chronoport*. How much more obvious could you get?"

"Sure. Fine." Susan shrugged. "You're a past version of you. Which means we might have already caught your True Present version."

"I don't think so."

"Why not?"

"If you had caught the current version of me, then we wouldn't be having this conversation. There'd be no point."

"Why's that?"

The prisoner smirked at her again.

"Come on." Susan leaned against the wall and crossed her arms. "Talking is so much more pleasant than the alternatives. Why not give it a shot?"

"On one condition."

"You're not really in a position to make demands, but I'll hear it."

"How far back in the past are we? A few days? A few weeks? More than that?"

"Why do you care?"

"Because I'm a copy and I want to know. Does there have to be anything more to it than that?"

"All right. If I tell where we plucked you out from the time-line, what do I get in return?"

"My name," the prisoner said. "My *real* name. I'm sure you've realized it's not Elly Sako."

"Yeah, that seems pretty obvious."

"My name should make for a suitable bargaining chip, don't you think?"

"You first."

"Oh, I don't think so." The prisoner shook her head. "I'm not about to give up what few bargaining chips I have for free."

"Fine. Give me a sec."

<Well?> she asked silently over a private channel.

<Go ahead,> Isaac sent back. <Let's see where this leads.>

<You've got it.>

"We pulled you out at negative-one month," Susan said aloud.

"A month, huh?" The prisoner nodded slowly. "That makes sense. Yes, that makes perfect sense. Thank you, Agent Cantrell. Seems there's nothing to be gained by sticking around. I'll see you soon. Or rather, another version of me will."

The prisoner's eyes rolled back into her head, and her jaw gaped wide. Her torso bulged as if she were taking in a quick exaggerated breath, and smoke poured out of her mouth.

Susan poked the synthoid in the chest, and it slumped life-lessly in the seat.

"Well, shit," she sighed.

✧   ✧   ✧

"What do you have for us?" Isaac asked, pacing around the partially disassembled synthoid on the table. He joined Susan, once again in her standard body, along with Nina and Cephalie.

"Quite a bit," Nina began. "First, this isn't an Admin synthoid. It's SysGov, and heavily modified, too."

"Yeah, I got that impression," Susan said.

"No, I don't mean the performance level." Nina flopped the synthetic corpse onto its back. "Here, take a look at this. See the vertical slot in the spine? Look familiar to anyone?"

"That resembles the slot you have in your back, Susan," Isaac said.

"Yeah, it does," she agreed.

"A SysGov synthoid modified to accept an Admin connectome case?" Isaac asked. "Is that what we're dealing with?"

"That's *exactly* what we're dealing with. And not just any synthoid, as Susan found out. This is a high-performance security model. Not as good as what SysPol issues, but pretty darn close. It's right on the edge of what a civilian could buy with the right permits."

"Do we have any clue whose connectome was loaded?" Isaac asked.

"We have this." Nina held up a charred cartridge about the size of her palm.

"An Admin connectome case," Susan noted.

"Right you are. And one with all the surface identifiers removed. It's clean of prints or DNA. The suicide charge fried the memory, too. I can't see anything inside. I *might* be able to perform a partial recovery once we get back home and I can use my drones, but that's still a dicey option."

"Why's that?" Susan asked.

"Identifying connectome fragments is tricky on the best of days," Cephalie explained. "Normally, we'd need an inert copy of a person's mental save-state from their mindbank as a point of reference, and even then, it's *just* a reference point. Connectomes change over time, sometimes drastically. It's not like our minds are static programs, after all. Even artificial ones like mine."

"Right. This thing"—Nina waved the cartridge in the air—"is in bad shape. I'll only be able to pull out a fraction of the connectome, even with a deep analysis. Let's call it ten to fifteen percent, just as a guestimate. That's hardly enough to find a match if I had a *full* save-state as a reference point.

"On top of that, what am I supposed to compare it to? Does the Admin keep connectome save-states of its prisoners?"

"No," Susan answered. "Copying connectomes is strictly outlawed."

"Then the *only* thing I could build a match off of is the original connectome." Nina threw up her hands. "Which kind of defeats the purpose of the deep dive, don't you think?"

"Right," Isaac conceded with a grimace. "What *does* this synthoid tell us?"

"The fact that it has an Admin-style connectome case tells us a little," Susan said. "There are only two kinds of people in the Admin who have these. STANDs and former prisoners who were abstracted."

"Then this fake could be a terrorist you brought in," Isaac speculated. "She—or he—recognized you and was familiar with how the DTI operates. A Free Luna operative could fit that description."

"Could be," Susan agreed. "Also, this synthoid all but confirms the presence of a conspiracy between at least two people. One from the Admin and one from SysGov."

"And who do we know came over here with a synthoid sex harem?" Cephalie asked with a crooked smile.

"Kohlberg," Susan said. "You think he's our man?"

"This body just catapulted him to Suspect Number One," Isaac declared.

"We can't prove he corrupted the *Weltall* program," Nina said.

"We couldn't *disprove* it either," Isaac pointed out. "He received the program from Ergon, and he loaded it into the pods. We may not know how the program was changed, but we know Kohlberg had more and better opportunities than anyone else."

"We might be able to prove his guilt with this body," Susan said. "Remember how one of the synthoids looked like Sako?"

"But with a darker skin tone and a few other differences." Isaac nodded. "Yeah, I remember."

"What if at one point that synthoid matched her perfectly?"

"And then was altered to hide the evidence?" Isaac nodded. "Good catch. We'll need to check into that when we return."

"That's the SysGov side of the conspiracy," Nina said. "But what about the Admin side? Do you still think Sako's involved?"

"Hard to say, but I'm leaning away from it." Isaac crossed his arms. "We don't have any solid connections between her and the crimes, and neither Kohlberg nor Sako could have been in this synthoid, given they're both still organic. If she *is* involved, then we're dealing with at least three people."

"Which still leaves us with an Admin coconspirator to find," Susan said.

"Yes, that's a problem." Isaac rubbed his chin and stared down at the husk.

"Susan?" Nina asked. "Any ideas there? You're the one the synthoid recognized."

"No. Not a clue."

"It might help for you to look over your old mission records with the DTI," Isaac suggested. "Maybe something in those files will help jog your memory. Perhaps even shine a light on a connection we've missed."

"Good idea. I'll get in touch with DTI HQ and request the file copies."

"Anything else to add?" Isaac asked Nina.

She gestured to Cephalie with an open hand.

"I did find one more interesting tidbit." Cephalie patted the synthoid husk. "Managed to pull it out of the infosystem. The memory was fried by the suicide charge, but I was still able to extract a few files. Most are things like shuttle tickets and Slater's connection string." She waved her hand indifferently. "Information we already knew. But one of them is new and kind of weird. Here."

She summoned the wireframe outline of an oversized teardrop. A half-sphere base about the size of her palm extended upward into a cone that ended in a rounded point.

"What is it?" Isaac asked.

"A very simple schematic. See the dimensions on the side? I'm showing it in one-to-one scale. Whatever this represents, it's meant to fill a very specific shape."

"This could be related to the bomb," Susan theorized. "If the fake meant to pass this schematic on to Massi, then the shape might tell us the space the bomb needed to fit in."

"Which we can use to find it before it goes off!" Nina finished.

"Yes, but what *is* it?" Isaac took hold of the teardrop, spun it onto its side with both his hands, then inverted it. He tilted his head. "I feel like I've seen this before. Anyone else find the shape vaguely familiar?"

Susan shook her head.

"Hmm," Isaac sighed, staring at the suspended shape. "Regardless, we have enough evidence to bring Kohlberg in, especially if this synthoid turns out to match one of his, *and* we have an important clue that may lead us to the bomb."

"If we head back now," Susan said, "we can send word ahead to Pérez in half an hour."

"Which would place us on-site in one hour." Isaac glanced over each of their faces. "Anyone see a reason for us to stay?"

Nina and Cephalie shook their heads.

"We'll need to secure the body for transit first," Susan said.

"Yay," Nina groaned. "More time in zero gee."

"I'll get in touch with DTI HQ and grab copies of my old

mission files." Susan stepped out into the central corridor and headed for the bridge.

✧   ✧   ✧

Susan sat next to Isaac on the bridge, both of them strapped in as the chronoport flew through the transverse on its way back to SysGov. Her old mission files floated in front of her. She scanned over the latest entry, found the list of captured or killed terrorists, and skimmed through their bios.

She'd captured a *lot* of terrorists over her ten years of service. Blown up a lot of them, too, but none of the names struck her as likely matches.

What traits am I looking for? she thought as a means to focus her mind. *Skilled close-quarters combatant. Experienced fighting STAND combat frames. Knowledgeable in DTI tactics and operational procedures. Knows me personally. Was once abstracted for time in a prison domain.*

Who could that be?

She swiped to the next entry and began reading, but then stopped and leaned back in her seat with a frustrated grunt.

"No luck so far?" Isaac asked her.

"No. How about you two?"

"Still not sure where the bomb might be?" Isaac said, the teardrop shape hovering in his hands. "With a bit of luck, Pérez's team may have already found the bomb."

"We'll know soon enough." Susan checked the time. "Eight minutes until we can contact him." She blew out a weary breath. "Eight more minutes of *this.*"

"Keep at it. Kohlberg may tell us who he's working with, but then again he may not."

"I will." She shifted in her seat and began reading again.

She swiped through one report.

Then another.

And another.

The minutes ticked by, and none of the terrorists she read about were even close to a match. Never mind that most of them were dead or still in prison!

Maybe I'm going about this the wrong way, she thought to herself. *The person needs to be dangerous enough to have ended up in prison but been there long enough to have been paroled.*

The thought made her furrow her brow.

Wait a second. I've only been at the DTI for ten years. Anyone I brought in that dangerous should still be in prison. They wouldn't be eligible for parole until twenty-five years into their sentence. Which means...

Wait a second.

Wait one damn *second.*

She ran a search through each of the case files. Every prisoner she'd brought in who'd been abstracted was still in prison. Every last one.

Which meant the person inside Fake-Sako wasn't one of these terrorists.

But if he/she wasn't a name from the past, then who?

Skilled combatant. Knows combat frames. Knows the DTI. Knows me. Not organic anymore.

She pondered those attributes, rolled them around in her mind until finally a dark realization struck her. She sat up in her seat, and her eyes snapped wide.

Oh no!

"Captain," said the bridge telegraph operator. "We're now close enough to communicate with *Pathfinder-Prime.*"

"Excellent. Spool the investigator's message and—"

"Stop!" Susan shouted. "Don't send that telegraph!"

CHAPTER TWENTY-EIGHT

IT HAD BEEN A LONG ROAD FOR ELLY SAKO, AND THE ODDS HAD been stacked against her, but her moment had finally arrived. She'd fought through the qualifiers, clawing her way past all the opposition to become one of only three Admin finalists. She'd endured threats to her life, seen another player rattled by the same, and even been treated like a criminal by that SysPol detective, but finally—*finally*—it would all be worth it.

She sat in the isolation pod for what would be the last time and watched as the All-Predators she'd seeded across the map swarmed toward Wong Fei's lonely star system. Her own forces lurked nearby in the void between stars while her scouts sent back a constant stream of data and visuals.

Wave after wave of All-Predators crashed against Wong Fei's formidable defenses. His focus on a defensive, turtling posture had granted him both a massive economic lead and a stalwart defense, built up as concentric spheres of integrated defensive platforms spread in a sphere 0.01 light-years across. His industry suckled on the star, transforming the raw matter into massive warships equipped with endgame weaponry, even as the All-Predators ate through outer layers of his defenses.

She couldn't tell which would win, and she *needed* to be sure. That meant it was time to get her hands dirty.

She permitted herself a cold grin.

"Wouldn't have it any other way."

She commanded her meager fleet closer to the apocalyptic conflict around Wong Fei's star. The ships under her command weren't much—she'd spent far too many resources climbing the tech tree and seeding All-Predators to have constructed a sizable armada—and worse, she'd need to keep her avatar core close to maximize their effectiveness. One wrong move, and either the All-Predators or Wong Fei's own forces would squash her like a bug.

About the *only* things she'd invested in outside her primary strategy were the stealth systems on her ships. Wong Fei had yet to show any sign he knew she was so dangerously close, and a surgical strike from her fleet in the right spot at the right time could make all the difference.

It was a risky, almost suicidal move, but that held true for her entire plan, and like the rest of the strategy, she decided to roll with it. So many gamers across so many games and tournaments chose to play it safe. They studied the probabilities of this matchup or that tactic, picking only the options with the highest statistical probability for victory.

Weltall was still in prerelease, but its mechanics had already been scrutinized, both by nonsentient programs on the Admin side and, in all likelihood, full-fledged AIs on the SysGov side. Those efforts had defined a "standard" game of *Weltall*, if only in theory, and many players flocked to the safety of "what the math says will win me games."

But those player types expected to encounter similar cultivated approaches from their opponents. Hit them with the unknown, strike at them from a dark corner, force them out of their comfort zone, and even the most experienced players would fall.

That said, she knew not to underestimate Wong Fei. She understood she was the underdog in this matchup, but she also knew the moment called for bold action. She'd spent so much of the tournament slinking around in the void, plotting against the other players like a cloaked assassin. It would have been easy—even comfortable—to stick to the same approach.

But that sort of timidity would not lead her to victory, which was what she wanted more than almost anything else in this moment, and so she edged her fleet closer, as close as she dared, and then watched and waited for the prime moment to strike.

Her scouts pinpointed the location of Wong Fei's avatar core, deep within the densest thicket of megastructures near the star. A star he'd supped at so greedily it was now half its original mass.

All-Predators swarmed the system by the billions, and every juggernaut they defeated—every megastructure they destroyed—only fed into their voracious, necromantic cycle.

The omnivorous machines breached Wong Fei's outermost defenses, devouring them, spawning copies of themselves that in turn assaulted the last and final layer outside the star. She could see the cracks in his armor, perhaps not wide enough for her fleet to wedge open, but if she waited long enough...

Yet even now, even in his last desperate stand, he was *still* adding more factories, and the dual tides of production and destruction started to swing back in his favor. His star was down to a *third* its original mass, but the All-Predators were nearly exhausted as well. Nearby systems had been stripped bare, the tide of approaching vessels thinning into the millions. Soon, only the All-Predators already in-system would remain.

"Time to end this."

Sako studied the flow of battle and picked a spot where the All-Predators had thinned, prompting Wong Fei to shift units elsewhere, shoring up more beleaguered points along his perimeter.

"There!"

She brought her fleet up to full power, abandoning all pretenses of stealth, and charged in at full speed, her avatar core shielded by a dense escort of her toughest ships. All-Predators and static defenses tore at her fleet from all angles, but the sudden injection of fresh forces caught both by surprise, and she burst through with most of her fleet intact.

She angled down toward the star, straight toward the cluster of factory megastructures around Wong Fei's avatar core. She threw her ships forward with reckless abandon, pushing their drive systems to self-damaging levels. A blizzard of missiles and lasers shot up toward her, eating away her forces, but she rushed in, returning fire, her largest and toughest ships on a collision course with her opponent's core.

Wong Fei's forces swarmed in from all directions, and the All-Predators swept in behind those. Her tiny fleet was an insignificant speck in the wider, grander battle. But it was in the right place, at the right time!

And that's all that matters! she told herself viciously.

Her fleet was sealed in, trapped with no hope of escape, but escape was an alien concept to her mind now. All she wanted—all she *needed*—was to destroy one last construct. One little, tiny target in a violent maelstrom of ships and ordnance and energy and death. She rushed forward, fearlessly, suicidally, unwilling to relent until she'd claimed victory for herself.

The first wave of her ships crashed into the final layer of megastructures, consuming them in violent cataclysms of kinetic energy. Wong Fei's avatar core lay bare before her. She only had to reach it!

Her last few ships screamed in for one final assault. Just a little bit—

—the game interface faded away, and the view zoomed out, switching to spectator mode.

"But..."

Her own core dispersed into a cloud of expanding plasma. The abstraction faded to black, and match statistics scrolled down her field of vision.

Wong Fei had won.

She stuck her elbow on the side of the pod and rested her cheek on her fist.

"Damn it. So close!"

✧   ✧   ✧

The isolation pod opened and Wong Fei climbed out to stand victorious atop the stage. The crowd greeted him with a thunderous ovation.

Whew! he thought to himself. *That was close!*

He tugged his shirt down, straightening it, and walked over to Elly as she exited from her own pod. She wore a forced smile, and he could see the disappointment behind her eyes. A part of him felt sorry and a little guilty, but they had both agreed beforehand to throw everything they had into the competition, to be honest with each other and to fight at their absolute best.

Any lasting relationship required a foundation of honesty, and perhaps this game had served as their first true test. If so, they'd both passed. They were professionals, after all. It would have been unseemly for one or the other to take a dive just because...

Well...

Wong Fei gave Elly's hand a firm shake, and Kohlberg guided her off the stage where Pérez took over and escorted her through one of the staff exits leading to the understage. He wasn't sure why only one bodyguard tailed her today or why the head of the DTI security detail had taken it upon himself to assume the duty. Perhaps they'd received complaints from the Crimson Flower and had decided to tone down the visible portion of her protective detail? If so, were there other agents lurking nearby? Perhaps scattered throughout the crowd in plain clothes?

That didn't seem to fit with the Admin's modus operandi, but admittedly he still knew so little about Elly's people. Even after deciding to...

Well...

Kohlberg returned with the frosted glass trophy in hand, ActionStream's meteor resting against his chest. He was about to scale the stage when Wong Fei shook his head and waved him off.

"What's wrong?" Kohlberg asked, his voice coming through crystal clear despite the raucous crowd.

"I'd like to give a speech."

"That's not on the schedule. Can it wait?"

"This is important. Please?"

"All right." Kohlberg frowned and backed away from the stage. "But try to keep the length manageable, okay?"

"I'll do what I can."

Wong Fei took his place at the very center of the stage and swept his gaze over the packed stadium.

"Ladies and gentlemen and abstracts!" He spread his arms to the crowd, and the clapping and cheering died down. "I know the award ceremony is supposed to follow right after the match, but there are a few things I'd like to say before we continue. I've asked permission to give a little speech, and our hosts have graciously given me permission to do so.

"But before that, I'd like to express my gratitude to our wonderful hosts from ActionStream." He dipped his head toward Kohlberg. "They've run a stellar tournament under what I believe we can all agree have been less than ideal circumstances. Would you please join me in a round of applause for Sven Kohlberg and the rest of the ActionStream team?"

Wong Fei began clapping, and the crowd joined in. Kohlberg shifted the trophy to one arm and waved with the other.

The applause died down, all eyes turning to Wong Fei. He clasped his hands behind his back and took a deep breath before continuing.

"One of the reasons I fought so hard throughout the competition was so I could give this speech." He flashed a disarming smile. "Of course, I *also* wanted to win. That comes with being a professional in this line of work. If victory wasn't important, I wouldn't last long, now would I? But, beyond claiming victory in this first of what I hope will be a series of joint tournaments, I also wanted to make use of the unique platform victory could grant me.

"And so, we come to the topic I wish to speak to you about. There are a great many subjects worthy of discussion in our societies, but the one I wish to focus on today is relationships."

Murmurs of surprise—and perhaps confusion—echoed through the stadium.

"That's right. Relationships. Big ones, small ones, in-between ones. Let's take a few moments to talk about all of them." He cleared his throat. "When you think about it, isn't our society nothing more than a complex, interlocking web of relationships? And, if you extrapolate that further, aren't our *two* societies now in a unique relationship of their own?

"I of course speak of the Admin and SysGov. Two very different societies, so used to being alone in their own corners of the multiverse. *Comfortably so*, one might argue. But now thrust together, each forced to deal with a neighbor they don't understand. And because of that lack of understanding, one they struggle to trust.

"Trust is the key to all of this, you see. Because no relationship can survive for long in the absence of trust. Without it, doubt worms its way into people's minds, polluting how they view the actions of others. Worse, trust can't be given." He paused and shrugged. "Well, it can, but not *meaningfully*. Trust—true trust, lasting trust—is *built*. Built by deeds. Built and maintained by even more deeds, because trust can be powerful and lasting and yet so terrifyingly fragile at the same time.

"So we must build a foundation of trust in order to guide this unique relationship into a prosperous future." He spread his arms again. "But isn't that what we've been doing here? Yes, this tournament is an unimportant competition for an unimportant game involving a handful of people. But at the same time, it would not have been possible if we didn't trust each other at least a little. Enough to take the chance and see if that trust could mature into something stronger, more long-lived. And I hold to you that we—despite some bumps along the way—have achieved that goal!"

The crowd cheered, some rising from their seats. Kohlberg began to scale the stage once more, but Wong Fei waved him off urgently, and Kohlberg took a step back with growing disdain on his face.

"Relationships," he continued, and the crowd died down once more. "Big. And small. It's a small one I wish to talk about next. Small when compared to the epic scale of transdimensional politics. But at the same time so much larger to me."

He began to pace back and forth across the stage, talking and walking.

"I think a lot of us reach a point in our lives where we're no longer surprised by relationships, whether they be with organic youths, the venerable synthetic, or the post-physical abstract. Whether *we* be organic or synthetic or abstract. Certainly, as someone who transitioned to the synthetic some time ago, *I* didn't think a relationship could surprise me.

"But then one did. I met someone about a month ago, and it's that relationship I wish to speak with you about." He gave the crowd a cautious smile. "She didn't know I was going to do this, but I hope she understands everything I'm about to say comes from my heart. I wouldn't share it so publicly if it wasn't.

"I met someone, you see. A young woman with a *very* different background from mine. At a glance, you might think the two of us have almost nothing in common beyond a passion for the same profession. And you'd be right. We haven't known each other very long, but in that time I've grown to trust her. And through that trust, my feelings have blossomed into something more profound.

"The match you just witnessed is yet another reason I trust her. We both promised each other we'd give this competition our all, that we wouldn't go easy on each other or let our feelings get in the way. This may seem like a small gesture to you, and perhaps it is, but it's one that builds upon layers of existing trust and respect. Think of it as one event stacked atop many others, all ending the same way. Ending with honesty and respect and mutual trust that pays off. Eventually that trust builds high enough and strong enough that you become willing to take greater risks. A leap of faith, if you will.

"Love is . . . a strange thing to quantify. You know it when you feel it. You might not know *why* you feel it, but there it is. However, in this instance, I *do* know why I feel this way. Despite our vast differences, I've met someone who complements me so well, who is almost like the second half I didn't know I was missing.

"Until I found it."

Kohlberg began a rambunctious round of clapping, and some of the audience took the cue and joined in. He put his foot up on the stage, but Wong Fei shot a stern look his way and waved him off. Kohlberg held out the trophy, but Wong Fei shook his head and gave him a quick shooing gesture.

"Not yet," he hissed.

Kohlberg sighed and relented once more.

Wong Fei smoothed the front of his shirt and turned back to the crowd. The errant clapping died down.

"I know it's bad form to have the runner-up on stage. It's uncomfortable because all attention is focused on the victor, but I believe this is one case where an exception is warranted. Would you please all put your hands together and welcome Elly Sako back onto the stage!"

Elly peeked her head out through the understage exit, and Wong Fei gestured for her to join him up on the stage. She stepped out, slowly, and made her way tentatively to his side.

"What are you doing?" she hissed through clenched teeth, her face etched with a volatile combination of worry, anxiety, anger, and joy.

"Exactly what my heart tells me I should," he answered, taking gentle hold of her hands, then projected his next words across the stadium's shared hearing. "Elly Sako. I was alone, but then I found my soul mate. I came across the woman I wish to spend the rest of my life with."

He dropped to one knee before her, her hands still held in his.

"You're doing this *now*?" she whispered, eyes moistening. "In front of everyone?"

He nodded solemnly to her.

"I thought long and hard about what I should offer you today. Picking the appropriate tradition is . . . a murky process for the two of us. Would a ring be the right call? Maybe an abstract sigil? In the end, neither struck me as fitting. What then could I offer to you?

"And then I hit upon the perfect choice. Something both of us wanted. Something valuable—not in a material sense—but because of the effort required to earn it. Something that, at least for this moment in time, is absolutely unique."

He bowed his head and gestured with one arm to the trophy in Kohlberg's hands.

"I offer you my victory in this tournament, and the symbol of that victory, in exchange for your hand in marriage."

"You big dummy." Elly sniffled and wiped at her tears.

Wong Fei looked up into her glistening eyes, his arm still extended to the side. He made a quick "come here" motion with his fingers, and Kohlberg—sensing his moment had finally arrived—mounted the stage and hurried over.

"What is your answer?" Wong Fei asked.

Elly smiled down at him.

"You already know. It's—"

One spot on the domed ceiling exploded into a thousand glittering shards.

✧   ✧   ✧

Susan's combat frame crashed through the stadium's ceiling, her boosters firing at full power. She rocketed down toward the stage in an indistinct blur of motion, her variskin struggling to keep up with the screaming descent.

Kohlberg was the first to see her. His mouth opened into a wide O of surprise, and he jerked backward, the trophy slipping out of his fingers. She fired one last burst from her boosters to adjust her course, aiming for the narrow window between Kohlberg and the two players, then cut off her thrust.

The trophy fell lazily through the air, and she grabbed it in the brief moment before she thumped into the stage. The impact quaked the surface. Elly screamed. Wong Fei took her into his arms to shield her, and Kohlberg fell onto his butt before scrambling off the stage on his hands and knees.

Susan crossed the stage in an inelegant bounding roll, the trophy in her hands, even as beads of glass rained gently, harmlessly onto the stage and audience. She stripped the malmetal armor from her torso and arms to form a protective cocoon around the trophy, the layers growing thicker by the second. She rolled to a stop, slammed the cocoon into the stage, and then threw her body on top. She didn't know how strong the explosive was, but—

The trophy detonated, and the armored cocoon breached with enough force to hurl her high into the air. She crashed next to the smoking crater with another thump, red alarms flaring in her mind's eye across her chest and left arm. Shrapnel had stripped the grenade launcher from her shoulder and had transformed her torso into a metal porcupine. Another piece had embedded itself in her rail-rifle, and the firing capacitors were faulted and off-line.

If that had hit the crowd…

She struggled to her feet. Pieces of shrapnel had penetrated deep enough to cut into some of her artificial muscles.

"Sven Kohlberg!" she declared, her voice booming over the stadium's shared hearing. "You are under arrest for…"

She trailed off, because he wasn't in sight anymore.

Kohlberg hurried through the understage tunnels, eyes wide as he pushed past confused and worried staff.

What the fuck is going on? his mind raced. *Did the trophy explode? It wasn't supposed to do that! Did he do that? But I was right there when it went off! Someone could have been killed! I could have been killed!*

Is that what he wanted? Me and the winner blown to smithereens, and the crowd cut to ribbons by shrapnel?

Oh, this was a bad idea! This was such a bad idea! Why the fuck did I go through with this?

What if they think it was me?

Oh, shit! I need to get out of here!

I NEED TO GET OUT OF HERE!

He sprinted into the open grav tube and commanded it to take him to Pistil Plaza. He needed to get out of the Crimson Flower. And then, he'd— He'd—

He didn't know!

He had no fucking plan for this! What the fuck was he supposed to do *now*?

Gravitons propelled him down through the tube and brought him out onto the wide expanse of Pistil Plaza. He was about to break into a run, but his legs turned to jelly and he stumbled forward onto his knees.

Seven of SysPol's eyeball drones formed an arch in front of him. An abstract image of Detective Cho appeared between him and the drones.

"Hello, Kohlberg." The detective flashed a cool smile. "We've been expecting you."

"I can explain!" Kohlberg pleaded. "Really, I can!"

"I'm all ears."

"You see..." His eyes darted across his surroundings, and then he kicked off the ground. The soles of his shoes squeaked on the polished stone, and he dashed back toward the open grav tube. He'd almost reached it when one of the eyeball drones smacked into his back and bound his limbs in prog-steel.

He teetered forward and cringed at the approaching floor. His face would have smacked against the stones if not for the drone's care.

"What a *fascinating* explanation that was," Cho commented. "I do believe I'd like to hear more of it. Would the local station be an acceptable spot for us to sit down and have a chat?"

Kohlberg hung his head as his entire body fell limp in defeat.

✧　　✧　　✧

Emergency strobes winked in Susan's abstract vision, and guidance lines pulsed toward the stadium exits, leading the audience to safety. Despite the sudden explosion, the SysGov citizens were filing out in a calm and orderly manner. Either they all possessed nerves of steel or—

"Is this part of the show?" someone asked.

"I don't know, but that explosion was *awesome*! I felt my spine vibrate!"

Ah, Susan thought. *That would explain it. Sometimes ignorance is bliss.*

"Was that a bomb?" Wong Fei rose and helped Sako to her feet.

"Could someone *please* explain what's going on?!" Sako asked while Wong Fei helped her up.

"Stay down!" Susan commanded, sweeping her gaze left and right. "This isn't over!" She pointed to the stage's new crater. "Hunker down in there!"

"But—" Sako began.

"Questions later! *Move it!*"

Wong Fei nodded. He took Sako's arm, and together they climbed into the crater and crouched under the ragged lip. Susan stood nearby, rail-rifle raised even if she knew it was busted. She tried commanding her armor to seal the hole in her chest, but the plates stuttered against the shards of shrapnel.

She checked the two understage exits, one on either side of the stage. Both represented low-elevation approaches because of the ramps, which meant an assailant emerging from them wouldn't have a clean shot at the players unless he scaled the stadium steps or reached the stage itself. That would buy her some time, but without a functioning weapon, her options were limited.

"That you, Susan?" Pérez called out, stepping into view near the base of a ramp, his rifle raised and aimed straight at her.

"Stop right there!" Susan aimed her own rifle at him and placed herself between Pérez and the players. The audience had almost finished filing out, leaving the two players as the only remaining targets.

"Step aside, Susan. I don't want to shoot you. I only need to finish what I started."

"You know I won't do that."

"No. I suppose not."

"Pérez?" Sako asked, her head dangerously close to being blown off. "What's he—"

"Stay *down!*" Susan shoved her head back into the crater.

"If I have one regret," Pérez said, pacing up the ramp, weapon raised, "it's that you had to get wrapped up in this mess."

"*One* regret?"

"Maybe a few others." He tilted his head. "Why haven't you shot me already?"

"Why haven't *you* shot *me?*" she deflected, unsure if he realized her weapon wouldn't fire.

"Because I don't want to kill you, Susan. You're an innocent in all this. You don't have to die."

"Kill me? I'm in my combat frame!" she bluffed. "What chance do you think you have?"

"A good one. You look awfully banged up. That explosion took a lot out of you. More than you're letting on. A few shots in the right spot, and I bet I could shatter your case."

"Then why don't you try?"

Pérez didn't answer, merely adjusted the grip on his rifle. The two STANDs stood across from each other, weapons aimed, but neither moving nor shooting. No other agents arrived, which troubled Susan.

There should be at least one more agent nearby, she thought. *Pérez must have changed the coverage plan.*

"I'm sorry about this, Susan," he said at last.

"It's a little late for 'sorry,' don't you think?"

"I know you don't understand what I'm doing. Or how important it is."

"Then why don't you make me understand?" Susan asked, playing for time, which was the only move she had left.

"I wanted to. I really did. I almost told you when you first arrived at the Flower, but I knew I couldn't risk it. That idiot Kohlberg was already a huge liability. I couldn't afford any more variables." He lowered the rifle ever so slightly. "In the end, this is a path I needed to walk alone. Even Kohlberg didn't know the full truth."

"That path ends here, Miguel. Give it up."

"No. You stopped the bomb, but you haven't stopped me. I can still reach those two and finish the job. Maybe you'll kill me and maybe I'll kill you, but those two are already dead."

"Then why haven't you tried it yet?"

Pérez didn't say anything. The barrel of his rifle inched down a little more.

"No one has to die today," Susan said.

"If they don't die today, others will die tomorrow. Don't you see? I haven't lost sight of what it means to be a STAND. I'm doing this *because* I'm one!"

"You idiot!" she snapped. "We became STANDs to protect the weak! Not butcher them!"

"I'm no butcher."

"Doesn't look that way to me!"

"This isn't slaughter; it's surgery. A few small, insignificant deaths to prevent a greater tragedy." He shook his head and raised the rifle, drawing a bead on her once more. "Enough. This is your last chance. Step aside."

"I will not," she said with finality.

"Then you leave me no choi—"

A heavy rail-rifle barked from high above, firing through the hole in the stadium's dome. Noxon's first shot cracked Pérez's weapon in half. His second shot shattered the synthoid's left shoulder, and the third blew the upper half of his head clean off.

Pérez took a blind step, slipped and flopped forward onto the ground. Susan boostered over, landed next to his splayed body, and planted a firm foot on his back.

"You were stalling for time." He laughed over her virtual hearing. His tongue lolled out over the lower half of his jaw, oily fluid leaking from the base of his skull. "I see now. You *would* have shot me if your weapon still worked. You weren't trying to talk me down at all."

"That's right," she said.

"Well played, Susan. Well played."

"You of all people should know I don't hesitate when there are innocents behind me and evil in front," she said with absolute conviction.

"No, I suppose not." He laughed again and shook the lower half of his head. "But in my defense, I'm new to the whole villainy thing."

CHAPTER TWENTY-NINE

ISAAC CHECKED ON KOHLBERG THROUGH THE VIRTUAL WINDOW in front of the door. The interrogation room was one of five in the CFPD's first and only precinct building. Kohlberg sat with a hunched head, frowning at the table and wringing his hands excessively.

"Ready?" he asked Susan, who'd returned to her standard body once more.

"Of course."

Isaac palmed the door open and stepped in. Kohlberg's gaze snapped up, and he bit into his lower lip while Isaac and Susan took their seats. The LENS floated around to behind Kohlberg's back, ready in case the prisoner became... recalcitrant.

"Sven Kohlberg." Isaac opened his notes and shifted them to the side. "We know most of your actions in support of Pérez's conspiracy, but there are a few areas we'd like to clari—"

"I'll cooperate!" he blurted.

"That's good. Strictly speaking, we don't need your cooperation, but—"

"Will I get a reduced sentence if I do?"

"Please allow me to finish."

"Yes, sorry." Kohlberg hunched his head and slouched in the chair.

"What I was about to say is I will take your level of cooperation—and how accurate and *complete* it proves—into consideration. I will then take the information you provide into consideration when I pass on a sentencing recommendation. Fortunately, in your case, you seemed to be after very different ends than your coconspirator, and I will take that into account in my recommendation as well. The decision, however, will be up to the prosecutor assigned to your case. Is all of that information clear?"

"Crystal clear." Kohlberg nodded his head with gusto.

"Very good. Then let's start with a point of particular interest. Your motive."

"Ah." Kohlberg let out a long exhale, slouching even more to the point where he resembled a deflating balloon. "That."

"Your actions seem to run counter to the prosperity of Action-Stream, and through them, your own good fortune."

"Actually, that's not how I thought this would play out."

"What did you think, then?"

"ActionStream already had a distribution contract locked in with the Admin's Department of Software. So you see, it didn't matter how the tournament went. It could have been a complete failure. The tournament could have literally blown up in our faces and it wouldn't have mattered. Actually, now that I think about it, it almost *did* blow up in our faces."

He chuckled at the thought, but his mirth turned sour when Isaac and Susan failed to join him, and he cleared his throat before continuing.

"Anyway, that contractual framework would remain in place. We were on the path to profit from business with the Admin independent of the tournament. It was our *competitors* I was hoping to sabotage."

"How so?"

"A number of them were in the process of negotiating distribution rights with the DOS, and according to my information, Titan Omni and Checksum Error were only a few weeks away from signing distribution deals. We were the ones who trailblazed through a maze of legal hurdles. We *earned* our contract, but then our competitors waltz in at the eleventh hour and proceed to skate right up to the finish line!"

"Threatening your profits by intruding on this new market?" Isaac asked.

"Exactly! So, this one day I'm over in the Admin on business. I think it was about two months ago." He shrugged. "Not sure. Anyway, I'm in the DOS tower, and the crew of *Defender-Prime* is there, too, since they didn't have any other passenger jobs. Pérez comes up to me, and we start talking. We hit it off, and next thing I know, I'm ranting up a storm about these other companies and how they're taking advantage of all my hard work!

"He didn't say a whole lot that day. Just listened, except for an encouraging word here or there to keep me talking. It wasn't until a week later when we talked again, and he mentioned a hypothetical. What if something were to happen that made these other companies get cold feet? Wouldn't that be great for Action-Stream! It started as a theoretical exercise, at least in my mind.

"We talked some more, and eventually the conversation settled on a big scare during the Weltall Tournament. That's what Pérez suggested. Something that would show our competitors that tensions were still too high between SysGov and the Admin. Something severe enough to frighten them off, or at least delay them until our own products gained a foothold on the market.

"That's when Pérez hit me with it. What if we actually *did* it?"

"What was your response?" Isaac asked.

"I asked him if he was serious. He shrugged it off, but in a kind of nod-nod wink-wink sort of way. Like he was only *saying* he was all talk. But I didn't buy that attitude from a STAND. They're people of action, not words." He gestured to Susan. "You know what I mean, right?"

"These conversations eventually led to a conspiracy to 'scare' your competitors?" Isaac asked.

"Yeah." Kohlberg lowered his head. "Yeah, that's right."

"Did Pérez suggest something specific for the 'big scare?'"

"He did. He wanted a shocking message delivered during the award ceremony. Something like an explosion of bloodlike smart-paint that spelled out a threat. Like the whole 'leave or die' thing I came up with."

"How did you react to his recommendation?"

"I thought it wouldn't be enough." Kohlberg frowned. "He seemed oddly focused on that one event. I told myself at the time it was a lack of imagination on his part. Or maybe a lack of perspective. He didn't understand the industry like I did. Those companies weren't going to be scared off by one splashy event. There needed to be more. Something to put a real chill on the Million Handshake Initiative. It needed to be a sustained *series* of bad incidents. One biggie wouldn't cut it."

"Did you ask Pérez about his motives?"

"Yeah, I wondered about that, and I did ask him. He gave me a line about hating ACs and not wanting any more 'dirty AI companies' in the Admin, but I didn't buy it. I assumed he wanted to keep the real reason to himself, but I was fine with that. I guess I settled on the judgment he was a convenient idiot I could use."

Isaac raised an eyebrow at the man.

"Yeah." Kohlberg slumped his shoulders. "I *know.*"

"What followed after your initial agreement?"

"We put a plan together for the big scare, which would involve the trophy erupting into blood paint. That's when things got . . . a little strange."

"How so?"

"Pérez told me he needed a synthoid. One that looked like an Admin citizen. He said he needed the body to procure the payload for our trophy in secret. I told him I could handle the payload on my end. I mean, seriously, I could walk outside, chat up a member of the League, and borrow a few paint grenades. Easy, right? But he insisted we use a payload made in the Admin."

"What reason did he give?" Isaac asked.

"League grenades would be recognized as SysGov tech, and he wanted the big anti-AC message to be from the Admin. I suppose that part of his reasoning made sense, so I went along with it. Plus, his approach came with a big advantage for me."

"Which was?"

"It would make it harder to trace an Admin payload back to me. In the end, I went along with that part of his plan and helped him with the synthoid. He provided biometric data on a few of the players, enough to produce a passable cosmetic layer. Initially, he gave me a bunch of guys, though." Kohlberg rolled his eyes. "I *explained* to him I only collect *female* synthoids, and I wasn't about to buy a male one just for him. I sent him away, and he came back with a few female selections, including Elly. Ah, Elly." He let out a dreamy sigh. "How was I going to say no to *that* one? I mean, *damn*! Am I right?"

Isaac and Susan remained straight-faced.

"Uhh, anyhow. He also wanted the synthoid to have some punch, so I bought him a used security synthoid. Got a great deal on a nice one, too. I had it modified to look like Elly and installed with an Admin case port in the spine. He provided the pattern for that last bit, which was compatible with SysGov printers. The mod shop didn't have any issues completing my custom order."

"He had a pattern for part of an Admin synthoid?" Isaac asked. "That was adapted for SysGov printers?"

"That's right."

"I have similar files, if you recall," Susan said. "My superiors provided me with SysGov-compatible patterns for all my spare parts. They may have done the same for other synthoids who spend a lot of time over here."

"Ah. Yes, that would make sense." Isaac turned back to Kohlberg. "What then?"

"Pérez went and got what I suppose ended up being an explosive. We snuck it into the trophy while we had the award over at Byrgius, and I took possession of the Elly synthoid. I even made some minor configuration changes to the cosmetic layer to prevent it from looking *too* much like her. As far as *Pérez* was concerned, that was the end of our preparations. But *I* had other plans."

"Go on."

"The big scare during the award ceremony was all fine and good, and it would have handled the Admin side of things, but I felt there needed to be some SysGov-sourced animosity. That way, *both* sides would be hesitant to continue negotiations."

"Which led to the severed head in Elly Sako's room."

"Right. I used the same data that went into the Elly-synthoid's cosmetics to develop a food parody of her head. Even came up with the 'leave or die' message myself. Simple, yet effective. As for the prankware, I'm sure you know how easy it is to get hold of these days. That only left one problem."

"How to load the prankware onto the food printer."

"Exactly. I *could* have done it personally. I had enough access to the players to pay Elly a visit with the right excuse, but I didn't want to turn myself into a suspect, so I convinced Pérez to do it for me."

"Wait a second," Isaac said. "You tricked your coconspirator into loading the prankware himself, and in so doing, inadvertently sabotaged his own plans to detonate a bomb at the tournament?"

"Hell, yeah!" Kohlberg gave him a toothy grin. "See? I'm not the only one who's an idiot here! In a strange way, I saved a ton of lives today."

"That's . . ." Isaac sighed and shook his head. "Never mind."

"How did you convince him to do that?" Susan asked.

"I told him the prankware was for a peeping program so I could watch Elly through the printer's camera." He giggled. "Can you believe he bought that? What an idiot!"

Isaac and Susan glanced to each other wordlessly, then turned back to the prisoner.

"I initially thought you'd finger Wong Fei, given his criminal record," Kohlberg continued.

"Which is why you asked me about the case the first time we met," Isaac observed. "What about the 'leave or die' message in the game?"

"Ah, yes! You *almost* had me there, but I was one step ahead of you!"

"We checked the entry chain of file transfers. From your desk, to your pendant, to the pods, and we found no discrepancies to explain the message."

"I'm sure you did, and I'm sure whoever looked over the infosystems did a thorough job. But you missed one key piece of evidence."

"Which was?"

"This is actually kind of funny." He laughed and shook his head. "You were *this* close!" He held up his thumb and forefinger.

"And this mystery piece of evidence is what, exactly?" Isaac pressed.

"Remember when I handed you my corporate pendant? I had three of them around my neck."

"I do."

"I gave you the wrong one. I actually loaded *two* of them with the UAM. The second one had an additional script on it I used to perform the edits locally, on the pendant itself."

"Which is where your programming background comes into play," Isaac noted.

"The script wasn't anything fancy. Just enough to embed my message into the UAM. I was terrified you'd ask me for all three. If you had, you would have found me out, I'm sure. But I outsmarted you that time!"

"Perhaps," Isaac conceded, "but would you like to know one of the secrets of detective work? You had to outsmart us for the entire duration of this case." He flashed a thin smile. "*We* only had to outsmart you once."

"Huh." Kohlberg frowned and chewed on the inside of his cheek. "Didn't think of it like that."

"Maybe you should consider that while you await your sentencing."

"Maybe so." He exhaled.

"Your testimony explains two of the three crimes before the finale," Isaac said, continuing on. "What about the third one?"

"The League protesters?"

"Did you send them the keycode?"

"Yes, that was me. I sent them two messages. One to hopefully get them cooking up a plan so their break-in would be more organized, and another to deliver the keycode itself." He shrugged. "I thought it'd be more dramatic that way. I made sure to send them a copy of the *Admin* keycode, again to deflect suspicion from me."

"I see." Isaac closed his virtual screen. "That'll be all for now. Your cooperation will be noted in my report."

"Still can't believe it," he muttered.

"What's that?"

"The whole bomb thing that idiot tried to pull off." Kohlberg shook his head. "I mean, seriously. A bomb in the trophy? Good grief! Someone could have been *killed!*"

"Yes," Isaac said dryly. "I believe that was the point."

Isaac checked the virtual window of the next room over. LSP had confiscated Pérez's original synthoid and replaced it with a standard prisoner model. The scrawny, carrot-hued machine possessed a plain, oval face and barely enough muscles to stand and walk under its own power. LSP technicians had added a backpack to this one, which included an Admin-style connectome interface tied to the synthoid's systems via a cable connected at the base of the neck.

He glanced to Susan, who stared through the same window intently. Her face was a stoic mask of professionalism, but through it he could detect troubled undercurrents.

"I can handle this one alone, if you like," he offered.

"No." She shook her head, and her eyes met his. "I'm seeing this through."

"Of course." He gave her a quick nod, then palmed the door open.

He and Susan may not have seen eye to eye all the time. They might have had their minor disagreements, born from the differences in their backgrounds and approaches to problem-solving, but she'd never *disappointed* him. Not once, and that streak continued as she filed into the room, ready to look her former friend and mentor in the eyes.

"I know how this will end," Pérez declared, head held high, face calm and composed, eyes locked on Isaac.

"How will it end?" Isaac prompted, taking his seat. Susan sat down beside him, and the LENS floated over to Pérez's side.

"My government will request my extradition if they haven't already, and your government will grant the request. I'll stand trial in an Admin court, be found guilty on all charges, and then be sentenced to life in a prison domain. Afterward, I will request the right to self-deletion, which I will execute immediately after it is granted."

"You're giving up, then?" Isaac asked.

"It's not a question of giving up. It's the fact that I have no hope of parole and also have no desire to live the rest of my 'life' in a digital fiction."

"You seem to have thought this through."

"I tend to be that way," he replied neutrally. "You have questions, I take it?"

"We do."

Pérez nodded. "I'll answer them."

"Just like that?" Isaac asked with a sweep of his hand. "No request for leniency? No bargaining at all?

"No."

"Why not?"

"It's simple. There's still some small chance explanation will have a positive impact, and because of that, I'll see this nasty business through to its end. You can have all the answers you want."

"Very well, then." Isaac doubted *any* explanation would justify his crimes, but he wasn't going to complain about an effortless interrogation. He opened his notes and spread them out to his side. "Why don't you begin at the beginning?"

"The beginning." Pérez's eyes flicked down, then back up. "I suppose you could say it started with the Dynasty Crisis. The calamity that destroyed an entire universe. I was there, serving on *Hammerhead-Prime* while it and the rest of the fleet battled the time machines of the Dynasty, and their time fortress, the *Tesseract*.

"There wasn't a full complement of STANDs in the fleet. The chances of a boarding action were low but not zero, and our numbers reflected that situation. I saw no action that day, but I did watch the battle unfold. Watched as we deployed chronoton bombs that ripped time and space apart. Watched as the Earth was consumed by a hole in the very fabric of the universe.

"Not our Earth or your Earth, of course, but *an* Earth with a history and culture all its own. Now reduced to nothingness. As if all those lives had never existed. Do you know what started the Dynasty Crisis?"

"What?"

"Utter stupidity and obscene arrogance. The stupidity and arrogance of people telling themselves they possess mastery over the laws of the multiverse, when in fact they are mewling babes not fit to leave the cradle. Perhaps one day our societies will have matured enough for us to venture out from the cradles of our own universes to explore the grandness of the multiverse with wisdom and care." He sneered at them. "But that day is a long way off. The Dynasty Crisis made *that* truth abundantly clear to me."

"Which led you to take matters into your own hands," Isaac added. "To do something about the unfitness of our societies."

"Correct." Pérez gave him a firm nod. "Take the Million Handshake Initiative as the latest example of our collective brainlessness. Our two societies are not fit to maintain our *current* levels of transdimensional travel, and yet we're looking to *expand* them? For what? A little bit of extra commerce? What utter nonsense! Only a few people have absorbed the correct lesson from the Dynasty Crisis. One of the rare examples is your League, despite all its flaws.

"I struggled with my own thoughts and feelings for a time, and eventually decided to do whatever I could to harm the relationship between the Admin and SysGov. *Any* decrease in cooperation would be beneficial, and so I began to look for a way to realize my goal."

"When did you decide on the Weltall Tournament?" Isaac asked.

"After I met Kohlberg and put up with his infantile rant about how unfair it was for other companies to take advantage of the groundwork he and ActionStream had laid. I approached him, cautiously at first, and eventually succeeded in recruiting his aid, even though I struggled at times to maintain the fiction concealing my true goals.

"Kohlberg was a useful idiot and nothing more. He provided me with an easy way to get the bomb where it could do the most political damage, which was right in the heart of the stadium. I wanted the explosion to have as much impact as possible, and I decided a detonation during the award ceremony would fit that goal. A powerful enough explosive would not only kill the winner—and Kohlberg, conveniently—but also maim or kill audience members in the closest rows. It would transform the emotional high of victory into a devastating, blood-soaked tragedy. *That's* what I sought to achieve. It also didn't hurt that Wong Fei, a SysGov player, was the predicted winner. Having an Admin explosive take out a famous SysGov citizen would only make the attack more impactful."

Susan bristled at his words, jaw clenched, fists tight on the table, but she said nothing, and Pérez didn't bother to look her way.

"Is that when you worked with Kohlberg to obtain the bomb?" Isaac asked.

"It is. I couldn't rely on Kohlberg to provide the explosive, otherwise the trophy would have burst into a harmless shower of fake blood." Pérez rolled his eyes. "Stealing ordnance from the DTI was equally untenable. Too many risks. Too high a chance of detection. After looking at my options, I eventually decided some of the terrorists I'd hunted over the years could provide the solution I needed, which was an undetectable, untraceable explosive that could be placed in the trophy.

"From there, I set out to contact a Free Luna demolitions specialist. I didn't have enough information to reach one directly, but I did know a former Free Luna loser named Kurtis Slater, whom I'd personally arrested some time ago. Kohlberg provided me with a synthoid look-alike of Elly Sako, and I used it along with copies of her PIN registration to move about Luna relatively undetected. I visited the Niner Slums and met Slater."

"Who refused to hand over his contacts."

"His mistake," Pérez said coldly. "I beat the information out of him and then worked my way through the list until I eventually found a terrorist named Victor Massi who, after some convincing, provided the explosive. He delivered it to an agreed dead-drop location, I picked it up, and Kohlberg installed it in the trophy. After that, all the pieces I needed were in place."

"What went wrong?"

"*Everything*," Pérez growled. "My empty-headed partner decided one scare wasn't good enough for him. We'd already moved the bomb into position undetected. No one had any reason to suspect us, let alone predict a bomb plot, but then *he* decided to cook up this ludicrous parade of attention grabbers!"

"Which started with the severed head in Sako's hotel room," Isaac said.

"I blame myself for that one," Pérez said. "Kohlberg asked me to load a program into Sako's hotel printer, and I didn't ask enough questions. I decided to humor him to keep him happy, at least until I no longer needed him, but after the severed head showed up, I had to think fast. I delayed LSP for as long as possible and used the time to plant evidence on Lacan's wearable."

"Why Lacan?"

"Because he was one of the few people who could have loaded it. And, unlike Wong Fei, for example, his heated argument with Sako made him a more believable suspect. I already had the prankware program in my possession, so making it look like the program came from him was easy."

"After that, we entered the picture."

"Which complicated matters greatly," Pérez said. "Your presence made any overt action difficult, and so I stuck to my assigned role. I did my best to act normally during your investigation, biding my time until I could detonate the bomb during the award ceremony. I was careful to maintain a veneer of cooperation and openness, such as when I told you *I* could have been one of the people to corrupt the printer."

"Which proved effective," Isaac admitted. "After all, who would expect the culprit to willingly list himself as a suspect?"

"My framing of Lacan also worked out, at least initially. In fact, I thought I'd won within the first few hours when you arrested him."

"But then Kohlberg struck again."

"That he did," Pérez seethed. "And this time he didn't need help from me. He used his own expertise with SysGov UAMs to target Masuda with a second message. It was infuriating! I'd just finished cleaning up his first mess, and he goes and makes *another!*"

"Which is why you were so...strangely uncomposed after Masuda was threatened," Isaac noted.

"I'll admit I lost my cool there. I wanted more than anything to chew Kohlberg out, but you two were right there, and I did my best to deflect attention from my outburst."

"I should have suspected you right then and there," Susan said. "The man I knew would never have lost his temper like that. Not for such a small setback."

Pérez said nothing and kept his eyes on Isaac.

"Your outburst makes a lot more sense in hindsight," Isaac said. "Kohlberg had just reopened our investigation, which put your plot at risk once more. How did you handle that?"

"I made one more attempt to redirect your investigation," Pérez said. "It was a subtle one, but my options were limited. I was the one who brought the behavior of the League protesters to Noxon's attention, who then brought it to *your* attention."

"Which diverted us to the League branch," Isaac said.

"I considered that a small victory. Any time you spent away from the real trail brought me that much closer to my goal. And then you left for the Admin. At that point, I thought I'd won. Noxon even placed me in charge of security once more, removing any remaining barriers between me and my goal."

"How did you react to our telegraph about the bomb threat?" Isaac asked.

"I wasn't sure what to make of it. I had no idea how you came about that information, but you were still over in the Admin. You knew there *might* be a bomb, but that was all you knew. You didn't know I was involved, otherwise why warn me about the bomb? I set the other agents to work searching for it, confident they would fail to find the bomb in time. There was a chance they'd find it, of course, but any other action would have looked suspicious, and the risk was low. The trophy had already passed multiple inspections, and I made sure the bulk of the agents were focused on the wrong locations.

"I used a similar technique as the tournament drew to a close, even turned your message about the bomb to my advantage. I faked a bomb threat to the hangar and set every agent to work searching for it while I took over guard duty for Sako. That left me as the only DTI agent nearby, just in case the bomb failed to do its job."

"Which it did," Isaac noted.

"Now that's something I'm curious about," Pérez said. "How did you know the bomb was in the trophy? Did Kohlberg mess up again?"

"Not this time," Isaac said. "I figured out the bomb was in the trophy."

"How?"

"Your other synthoid," Isaac explained. "Or rather, the schematic it held."

"But that synthoid is still in Kohlberg's apartment. How did you . . ." Pérez trailed off and stared down at the table. "Wait a second. You must have learned the bomb was in the trophy while you were still in the Admin. But that means . . ." His eyes widened. "Oh, I see now. You recovered the schematic from the synthoid, but the only place and time you could have done so is in the past." He looked up. "I didn't expect that."

"Neither did I," Isaac admitted, "until Agent Cantrell applied her experience in the DTI to this case and suggested that course of action."

"But how did you learn the bomb was in the trophy?"

"I puzzled that out on our way back, based on the shape and the assumption a bomb on stage was a likely scenario. I then made the connection between the schematic's teardrop shape and the ActionStream logo's falling meteor. Meanwhile, Agent Cantrell deduced it was your connectome inside Kohlberg's harem synthoid.

"Once we had those pieces, Agent Cantrell proposed a . . . rather daring course of action. We couldn't risk sending a telegraph to *Pathfinder-Prime*, because we couldn't guarantee who would receive it. If you did, what would prevent you from detonating the bomb remotely right then and there? We needed to neutralize the explosive first, and Agent Cantrell volunteered herself for the task."

"I see." Pérez turned to her for the first time since she'd entered the room. "You couldn't have known you'd survive the blast."

"Do you think that would have made me hesitate?"

"No." He shook his head. "I suppose not."

"My combat frame is a tough piece of work. The odds were in my favor, and it allowed me to reach the bomb as quickly as possible. I'm more surprised you didn't shoot me. Or shoot up the stadium while the audience was still filing out."

"I'm not a monster."

"You could have fooled me."

"Originally, I was going to detonate it as soon as Kohlberg handed the trophy to the victor, which I had hoped would be Wong Fei, but I would have settled for Sako if she'd won. Kohlberg was standing close enough to Wong Fei for me to take them both out, but then Wong Fei started his speech. I was standing next to Sako in the understage at the time, and that gave me a hint as to where this was going. I thought I had time to see how it would it all play out.

"Taking out the winner was one thing, but killing both of them in the middle of the first marriage proposal between our peoples was on a whole different scale. That's why I waited."

"Only you waited too long," Susan said stiffly.

"You're right, of course. I triggered the bomb shortly after you arrived, but you managed to contain it. Both Sako and Wong Fei were still alive, and I needed to finish the job. Sure, I could have fired at the audience, but what would that have gained me?"

"A body count?" Isaac suggested.

"To what end?" Pérez countered. "The players had transformed themselves into a symbol of unity through their actions, and I needed to destroy that symbol. No, it was the players or nothing."

"Then why didn't you shoot me?" Susan asked.

"I . . ." Pérez lowered his head. "I couldn't. Call it hesitation. Call it losing my nerve. Call it whatever you want. I'd had *time* to accept the idea of killing the players, along with Kohlberg and the bunch of nobodies in the audience. Time I needed to convince myself I was doing the right thing. But I couldn't process all that in the short moments we stood across from each other."

"Which allowed Agent Noxon to get into position," Isaac added.

Pérez nodded. "And now . . . you fools have made matters worse."

"I don't see it that way," Isaac said.

"Of course not. But look at what happened. An agent of the DTI just came crashing through the ceiling to prevent a bomb from going off during a major streaming event. That's going to bring our two peoples *closer*, not push them apart!"

"You should realize something by now," Susan said stiffly.

"What's that?"

"You're a relic of the Admin's past. Of militarism and xenophobia and resistance to change." She plucked at the DTI emblem on her breast. "Maybe I'm a part of that past, too. But Elly and Wong Fei are different."

"How so?"

"They're our *future*."

Isaac paced down the corridor in the CFPD alongside Susan.

"That about wraps up our work today," he said. "How are you holding up?"

"Okay," she sighed.

"Just okay?" he asked, looking over to her.

"Yeah. It's a lot to process, though. I used to look up to the man. I learned how to be a STAND from him, but now I find myself remembering our time together, wondering if my own feelings and convictions could become twisted like his. If I could someday convince myself that wrong is right and evil is good."

"Evil resides in every heart," Isaac said with a shrug, "yours and mine included. We all struggle to deal with it, and most of us triumph more often than we don't. It's a private war in every person, but we don't wage it alone. We have laws and morals and the society we're a part of to aid us in distinguishing right from wrong, good from evil. We have friends and family and coworkers, too. Each contributing in their own way to help us recognize evil. Sometimes they fail, of course. Sometimes the 'wisdom' we're listening to isn't wisdom at all, and it leads us down the wrong path."

"Sorry to say it, Isaac, but you're not helping."

"What I mean to say is, taking all that into account, *I'm* not worried about you turning into Pérez. Not tomorrow, not ever. Not in the slightest."

"Why's that?"

"It's simple." He smiled at her. "Because *you're* worried you might. And those worries mean you're working hard to keep yourself in check."

Susan smiled back at him.

"Also," he added with a shrug, "because I have some of those same worries myself."

"Nah." She gave him a doubtful look. "You?"

"Not in a set-off-explosives way. But I do fear I'll someday commit an abuse of power. A lot of responsibility comes with being a detective. Over the past few years, I've seen others in SysPol bend the rules, even break them. But the fear I harbor is a good thing. It's healthy to have it, because it means I'm keeping an eye on myself." He gave her a quick pat on the arm. "So take comfort in your fear. It means you're a good person."

"Thanks." She sighed. "Though that has got to be the weirdest way you could have phrased it."

"Sorry. I'm not used to giving pep talks."

"Also, what does this tell us about your pastimes?"

"What do you mean?"

"Well..." She gave him a crooked grin. "You seem to always gravitate toward the evil characters and factions in whatever game we play. Like building your deck around Excrucion in MechMaster or roleplaying the evil characters in *Solar Descent*."

"*Lawful* evil. We've had this discussion before."

"Yes, yes. Lawful evil." She chuckled. "I'm sure that makes all the difference." They turned down a corridor and headed for the entrance. "On a different topic, what about Kohlberg?"

"What about him?"

"Any thoughts on what his sentence will be?"

"Five to ten years, I'd guess. Which might be the best thing for him since he broke up with his IC. He was clearly not as far gone as Pérez. Give the Panoptes counselors enough time, and who knows? They might turn him back into a well-adjusted, law-abiding citizen."

"You really think so? After what we saw in his apartment?"

"Hope springs eternal," Isaac replied in way of a nonanswer.

They reached the station lobby and were about to head out into the plaza when Elly Sako and Wong Fei stood up from a bench near the exit, flanked by a pair of DTI agents. Sako hurried in front of Isaac's path.

"Miss Sako," he greeted her, stopping.

"Here!" She bowed her head and extended both hands. An abstract sigil appeared before him. She then sidestepped in front of Susan and presented an identical sigil. They each resembled the ActionStream meteor logo, but the tail was elongated, looping around to form a circle.

"This is..." Isaac drew the sigil to his palm, and additional text filled the interior. His wetware took a moment to translate the Admin version of English. "This is a wedding invitation?"

"That's right!" Sako said brightly.

"We would be honored if you two could attend," Wong Fei said, joining them. He slipped his arm around Sako's waist and she leaned her head against his shoulder.

"Congratulations," Susan said.

"Thanks!" Sako replied.

Isaac frowned at the invite.

"Is something wrong?" Sako asked.

"No, I'm just thinking about the job. We're usually not this far in-system, so attending might prove difficult depending on our caseload."

Susan raised a meaningful eyebrow at him.

"But I'm sure we can arrange something with our superiors," he finished, catching her look. "Also, Miss Sako, I feel I owe you an apology, in light of our last talk."

"Oh, don't bother." She waved the notion aside. "I may have overreacted a tad myself, and it all worked out in the end."

"We know it was a challenging case," Wong Fei added. "We're just glad you were able to figure it out in time."

"Yeah, otherwise we'd be *dead*!"

"We did cut this one pretty close," Susan admitted.

"By the way," Sako said. "What about Lacan? What'll happen to him?"

"He's already been cleared of all charges and released. I also had a discussion with ActionStream management to arrange a small token of apology for him. They've agreed to provide him with a complimentary invite to their next Weltall tournament, in recognition of how he was unfairly excluded from this one."

"Aww." Sako frowned, eyes twinkling with mischief. "You sure you couldn't have kept him in his cell a *little* bit longer? You know, maybe until right before we leave? Or maybe even longer than that?"

"I'm sorry, but no." He shot a quick look over to Susan, his eyes laughing. "That would be an abuse of my authority."

CHAPTER THIRTY

A DAY LATER, SUSAN WALKED ACROSS A LUNAR BEACH FOR THE first time. She adjusted the shoulder strap of her black bikini and enjoyed the sensation of sand oozing through her toes with each step. The sand wasn't the beige or caramel common to Earth beaches, but rather a pale, ghostly Lunar sand, warmed by the sun and wetted by the ebb and flow of the sea.

The uniform granules under her bare feet didn't possess the chaotic coarseness of natural erosion, because *this* was a manu-factured beach, built for an artificial ecosystem by a society that *had changed the angular rotation of a moon because they wanted shorter days.*

That part still boggled her mind.

She wondered what it would look like if she reached down, drew a random handful of sand, then examined them under a microscope. How similar would each of the grains appear? Surely, the random clunking of grains together had marred the original, manufactured perfection at least a little.

It's still a beautiful sight, she thought to herself, a content smile gracing her lips. Massive waves crashed down in what appeared to be slow motion to her Earth-raised perceptions, their size fueled by a combination of Luna's low gravity and Earth's impressive tidal pull.

She strolled at a leisurely pace across the sands, heading

for a cluster of foldout chairs and beach towels under a wide, translucent umbrella. The sun was high and hot in the sky, but the crowds were still manageable enough for the SysPol team to enjoy a quiet corner to themselves.

Isaac lounged in one of the beach chairs, hands behind his head and a wide-brimmed hat over his face. Even Cephalie had gotten in on the relaxation. She lay on a tiny, virtual blanket by Isaac's head, clad in a striped one-piece swimsuit. Susan walked up beside them, and Isaac pushed the brim of his hat up with a finger and opened an eye.

"Is it everything you'd hoped for?" he asked.

"Everything and more," she replied with a satisfied grin. "Where's Nina?"

"Surfing," Cephalie pointed. Susan followed her finger to a pair of swimmers on hoverboards riding an inbound wave. Nina was laughing with a young man in a swimsuit so tiny and tight it left almost nothing to the imagination.

"She rented a spare board if you want to try," Isaac said, nudging a flame-decorated board by his feet.

"Maybe later," Susan said. "Aren't you going to take a dip, too?"

"That's what I'm in the middle of."

As if on cue, a wave crashed down, frothing in slow motion up the beach. The water moistened the tips of Isaac's toes before retreating.

"I'm not sure that counts," Susan pointed out.

"Close enough for me." He adjusted his hat to see her better.

"He's taking a lazy day," Cephalie whispered as if this were a dark secret.

"You better believe I am. After a case like that, I think we can all use a little downtime." He sat up in the chair. "By the way, I know a Lunar beach was at the top of your list, but there are other sights we can see before we head back to Saturn."

"Oh?" Susan replied, her interest piqued. "Like what?"

"Well, there are the big ones. Like the Armstrong Monument and the Armstrong Memorial Space Elevator. No trip to Luna is complete without a stop there. Also, the space elevator has the Apollo Capsule Café at its base, which is one of the most famous coffee shops in all of Luna."

"Armstrong Memorial..." Susan considered the name. "Who's it named after?"

"Neil Armstrong."

"Who?"

"What do you mean 'who'? It's Neil Armstrong. Haven't you heard of him?"

Susan shook her head.

"First organic to set foot on Luna?"

"Still doesn't sound familiar."

"Surely there's *something* named after the guy in the Admin. Or at least, I don't know, a memorial plaque where the original moon landings took place."

Cephalie climbed onto Isaac's shoulder and glared at him with her hands on her hips.

"Yes?" Isaac asked. "Can I help you?"

Cephalie held up a sign that read: REMEMBER YOUR HISTORY CLASSES!

"Not this again." Isaac rolled his eyes. "And I *am* remembering my history correctly, thank you very much."

"Maybe," Susan said softly, "but perhaps that's not what she means."

Cephalie stomped toward his head and shook the sign in his face. Isaac sighed with a grimace, but then a spark of doubt crept onto his face, and he paused in thought.

"Wait a second," he said after a lengthy silence. "Did the first moonwalk happen before or after World War II?"

Cephalie swapped her original sign for one that read: AFTER.

"Are you sure?" he asked incredulously.

"I think she's right," Susan said. "That's how it played out in my history, and since our timelines diverged in 1940..." She shrugged.

"I could have sworn the landings were before."

The text on Cephalie's sign turned bold red.

"Fine," Isaac relented with a sigh. "I'll take your word for it. But in my defense, the twentieth century is a *dense* part of history. And it all happened a millennia ago, so excuse me if I don't remember the sequence right. I work in Themis, not Gordian, after all."

"My point"—Cephalie's sign vanished, and she planted her hands on her hips—"is you have a deputy from the Admin, which means it would benefit you to be more cognizant of the historical differences than most people."

"Uh huh," Isaac replied, unimpressed. "I think you're making a bigger deal of this than it needs to be. It's not like I offended anyone by not knowing the twentieth century by heart. Susan, did I offend you?"

"No, of course not."

"There you have it." Isaac laid back and covered his face with his hat once more.

Cephalie teleported to Susan's shoulder and held up a sign that read: I'LL STRAIGHTEN HIM OUT. DON'T YOU WORRY.

"It's okay."

HE REALLY DOES APPRECIATE YOU, the next sign read. I SWEAR.

Susan smiled and waved her off.

She'd noticed similar comments from Cephalie in the past and she thought she understood what the AI was trying to encourage, but the truth was she was already in a relationship with Isaac. A *professional* relationship, and it was abundantly clear to her that's all it would amount to, regardless of any inclination she might (or might not) have in other directions.

Certainly, Isaac was an attractive young man, and not just physically, though there was that. He'd earned her respect with both his tireless work ethic and dogged pursuit of the truth, no matter what obstacles were thrown in his path. A case might frustrate or confound him, but he seemed incapable of giving up. It was as if the thought of dismissing a case as unsolvable couldn't find its way into his mind, and she admired that relentless aspect of him.

But it was clear to her he was laser-focused on his career, to the exclusion of all else. That was a personal choice of his she both understood and appreciated since it resembled her own path to becoming a STAND, and as his colleague, she had no desire to complicate both their lives. She respected him too much to do otherwise.

It would never work out, anyway, she told herself.

"Hey, everyone!" Nina walked over, a mischievous grin on her lips and a hoverboard under one arm. She tossed the hoverboard onto their blankets then put her hand on the shoulder of the strapping young man next to her. "Everyone, this is Gerald. He's a student from Venus. He's studying to become an environmental engineer."

"Hey." Gerald extended a hand to Susan. "Such a pleasure to

meet you! I read all about how you brought in that criminal. I subscribed to the *Nectaris Daily* while I'm here, and they had a big, front page feature on the Weltall Tournament."

"Why, thank you." Susan shook his hand.

Isaac pushed the brim of his hat up and eyed the young man suspiciously.

"The *Nectaris Daily*, you say?"

"Yeah, man. Big splash on their front page with pictures of these two." He pointed to Nina and Susan. "I'm not one for the news, but it was so interesting, I read the whole thing! And then, what do you know, but I run into *both* these lovely ladies on the beach! How lucky can I get?"

"Oh, I have a feeling your luck hasn't run out." Nina gave him a playful pat on the butt, and his face turned a fierce shade of red.

"Anyone else listed as helping to solve the case?" Isaac asked, his voice coming across like he was in detective-mode.

"What?" Gerald's voice squeaked.

"In the article. Were other people listed as contributors?"

"Oh, sure." Gerald nodded. "There was this Noxon guy. You know, from the Admin. He shot the criminal. Then there was this other guy named Lotz. He was in there, too. I think he's a state trooper or something. Not much was written about him. Maybe a sentence or two. The article didn't even include his picture."

"Anyone else?"

"Umm...nah, man. No one comes to mind."

"You say you read the entire article."

"The whole thing, man. The whole thing."

"I *see*," Isaac said. "But no one else was listed?"

"Don't think so."

"You sure? Maybe someone else? Someone in SysPol. The person who figured out the bomb was in the trophy, perhaps?"

"Oh yeah!" Gerald's face lit up. "You're right, man!"

Isaac raised his eyebrows in anticipation.

"Yeah, yeah!" Gerald pointed to Nina with both hands. "The article said *you* figured out where the bomb was!"

"Oh, *pfft*!" she dismissed. "They're always exaggerating things about me. Ever since I cracked the Apple Cypher case."

"That was *you*?" Gerald's eyes widened in hero-worshiping amazement. "The one where some crazy guy made all those food printers spit out nothing but apples? You solved that one?"

"Yup!"

"Wow! Amazing!"

"I don't believe this." Isaac pulled his hat down to cover his entire face.

"Umm." Gerald looked down at Isaac, then glanced to Nina. "Did I say something wrong?"

"Nah," Nina said. "He's just sore because his name hardly ever appears in the news."

"Oh, wait. Is he in SysPol, too?"

"Yeah, but you wouldn't know it from the news. He thinks it's a big deal."

"I do *not* think it's a big deal," Isaac stated, his voice muffled by his hat.

"Then why do you sound so upset?" Nina teased.

"I'm *not* upset."

"Come on, Gerald." Nina wrapped her arm around his. "How about you and I have a few drinks and chat some more? You can tell me *all* about Luna's water cycle."

"Sure, Miss Cho! I'd love to!"

"Oh, please! Call me Nina!"

The two sauntered off to an open-air bar further up the beach.

Isaac let out a long, guttural groan into his hat.

Susan knelt by his side. "Are you really upset?"

"Maybe a little?" He took his hat off and sat up. "Is it really so hard for reporters to, I don't know, *report* the correct facts?"

"Yes," Cephalie said firmly from her perch on his shoulder. "It *is*."

"Look at it this way," Susan said. "I had to fly through a roof and take a bomb to the chest before people around here started respecting me."

"I guess you have a point there." Isaac blinked. "Wait a second. Have you been getting good press since the tournament?"

"A few articles here and there."

"Of course," he sighed.

"You know," she gave him a crooked smile, "all you need to do is abstract. Then we can stuff you in a combat frame and shoot you through the roof on our next case."

"I think I'll pass."

"It'll get you noticed," she teased.

"Maybe, but crashing through the roof to save the day is

more your thing." He let his own smile slip. "I wouldn't want to steal your thunder."

"Oh, speaking of which," she began, "I received a message from Director Shigeki."

"Which one?"

"The younger one. Head of DTI Foreign Affairs. He asked me to check with you and see if it would be all right to switch your investigator status to inactive."

"Sure, they can do that whenever they like. The position came in handy, but I think that's all behind us. There's nothing left to do on this case except fill out reports."

"You sure?"

"Why wouldn't I be?"

"I don't know," Susan said. "A status like that could prove useful in the future."

"Susan." He gave her a doubtful look and stood up. "What are the odds we'll get assigned another Admin case anytime soon?"

"Could happen."

"But it's not likely. What with us stationed out at Saturn and most interactions between the two universes happening around Earth. Which is fine by me. Dealing with one legal system is hard enough."

"I suppose you're right."

"But we can talk about that some other time." He took off his hat and tossed it on his beach chair. "For now, what do you say we try out the waters?"

"Sounds great to me," Susan replied eagerly.

Over three hundred eighty thousand kilometers away in Earth orbit, Jonas Shigeki was in a good mood. Dahvid Kloss, who sat across from him in the Argus Station conference room, was decidedly *not* in a good mood.

Smile, Kloss, Jonas thought wryly. *This is a great day!*

He had many reasons to be in a good mood, but perhaps the most obvious was the progress everyone had made on the Providence negotiations. The leaders of both the Gordian Division and the DTI had come to an agreement regarding the construction of Providence Station, and Jonas was confident the agreement would be ratified by both their governments. That meant the Admin would not only get its hands on SysGov counter-grav technology, but they would also reap the benefits from both the construction *and* the research performed by the future station.

Kloss had *other* matters on his mind as he drummed the table with his fingers, a deep scowl on his face.

"It was worth it," Jonas declared.

"I beg to differ."

"Oh, don't be such a whiner. You can hardly call that a chewing out."

"You were only there for the start."

"So?"

"It went on for a while."

"Come on. It couldn't have been *that* bad," Jonas protested, leaning back in his seat. "After all, Dad talked to me, too."

"He chewed *you* out?" Kloss asked incredulously.

"*Talked* to me," he stressed. "Hardly any chewing."

"How'd he find out you were involved?"

"No idea."

"*I* didn't tell him."

"I know that." Jonas shrugged. "Doesn't matter how. Dad's perceptive like that sometimes. Saw right through both of us."

"That he did."

"Still worth it, though. I even chatted with him afterward, showed him how useful the investigator position proved. We could have easily had a much larger mess on our hands."

"That much is true," Kloss agreed.

"And he agrees with me. Though, it would have been even better if Espionage hadn't slipped up."

"What do you mean?"

"I'm talking about Pérez, of course. How exactly did your people miss a loose cannon like him?"

"We're not mind readers," Kloss bristled. "Pérez was clean across every one of his evaluations, including the most recent round we performed after the Dynasty Crisis. The systems are in place to detect problematic individuals like him."

"But those same systems failed to catch him before he almost blew up a goodwill tournament."

"Don't you think I know that? Rest assured, we'll be taking a hard look at our processes with an eye for where to make improvements. Is that what you wanted to talk to me about? How I and the rest of Espionage failed everyone?"

"No, I just like messing with you."

Kloss let out a weary sigh. "Then what *are* we here to discuss?"

"Your newest junior provisional investigator."

"The first and the *last*," Kloss stressed. "What about him?"

"Here. Take a look at this."

Jonas placed his hand on the table, and a proposal materialized in front of Kloss. It was something Jonas had whipped up in his free time over the last day, after Cho and Cantrell had cracked the *Weltall* case. In hindsight, it seemed so obvious to him, and with Cho now a DTI investigator (who could be reactivated with little effort), the groundwork was firmly in place.

After all, why limit the pair to rotations in *SysGov*? Why not bring them both over to the Admin for a chance to serve under Kloss in DTI Espionage?

Kloss read through the proposal, his face growing darker with every sentence until he began to let out a pained, drawn-out exhale. The exhale turned into a groan, and Kloss grimaced at the document as if he were struggling with a bad case of indigestion. His voice wheezed out at the end, his lungs empty. He sucked in a sharp breath and looked up across the table, eyes like swords.

"I didn't hear a 'no' in all that drama!" Jonas observed.